The Sin of Obedience

by

Kenan Heise

authorHOUSE™

1663 LIBERTY DRIVE, SUITE 200
BLOOMINGTON, INDIANA 47403
(800) 839-8640
WWW.AUTHORHOUSE.COM

This book is a work of fiction.

First published by AuthorHouse 09/21/04

ISBN: 1-4184-1926-5 (e)
ISBN: 1-4184-1925-7 (sc)
ISBN: 1-4184-9009-1 (dj)

Library of Congress Control Number: 2004094462

Printed in the United States of America
Bloomington, Indiana

This book is printed on acid-free paper.

Cover photo: Richard Cahan

Cover Design: Danielgraphics

Dedicated

to those who have sought the absolute

Chapter 1

This is about me.

I feel as a ghost as I tell you who I have been.

My name is Michael Jordan, Michael Richard Jordan, not the great basketball player, a winner. I have been a drunk, a loser.

My life is over and at the same time it is beginning.

Each turn in the road has been signaled by a name change and so it is now.

Once, I was chosen of God and select among men. I have lost the role, the cloth and the anointing, which awarded me such honors and so lofty a place in the universe.

I was all but certain of heaven, being a man with a special mission.

Now, I must start over, learn to speak, think and feel.

It happens to others, convicts when they leave prison, newly divorced people and young children when they lose their parents.

We are who we have been.

Now, I must be who I will be.

I tell you this because a voice has asked it of me to do so. It is my dead father's. In my dreams, he spoke to me from the middle of a garden of roses, urging me to "Smell them, Michael. Smell the roses." Then, he whispered to my dreaming heart, "Tell your story.

Do it." Such was a personal, painful challenge I could not imagine carrying out.

His words and meaning reek of personal freedom and responsibility, frighten me almost out of existence. These were not the terms on which I lived my life, which has been one focused on holy obedience.

Still, I am determined to listen to the voice and unlock for all this jumbled mystery, my life.

A note:

The writer has used "I" in the preceding paragraphs. For reasons that are powerfully personal, this has proven to be exquisitely painful. To minimize this to a tolerable level of distress, the following account of the life and journey of Michael Richard Jordan will be written in the third rather than the first person.

Chapter 2

Mikey had a mission, a seemingly magnificent and mysterious destiny. It would entail a white charger on which he would gallop heroically down the days of his years. He would ride high above his fellow man, headed out on a journey that would prove resplendent and rewarding beyond his imagination.

He believed this because his mother did.

The young boy first sat upon this heroic-sized, metaphoric horse when he was yet a young child, lost in its proportions and purpose. Later, he would sit astride it with far more ease, making horse and rider, mission and man, seem one both to himself and to others. But, even in his tender years, when he was yet only five years old, a week short of entering the first grade at St. Mary's Catholic Grade School, he was aware of it. Certain he was even then that he was traveling this path and going upon a mythical, magical mission.

Up until then, Mikey had still been a self-pleasing, self-contained little boy who owned his own world.

The 1930s Depression—like stale, forever-unchanged air—hung over the nation and his streetcar-served neighborhood on the North Side of Detroit in particular. This little, blue-eyed boy with dishwater blond hair was living there with his father and mother on a street of inexpensive, tiny homes.

Richard Jordan, his father, was out of work. Both he and Mikey's mother, Anne, protected this seemingly chosen child through their own personal sacrifices, warding off the painful arrows of poverty. The couple often regularly denied themselves even the smallest pleasures in order that he might not know want of any kind.

Mikey's mother stayed up late night after night, sewing "new" clothes for him out of scraps of cloth acquired by ingenious means. His favorite was a sailor suit she had made out of what had once been a woman's dress. His father, rather than take the streetcar when he went to look for a job, usually walked so he could stop to bring home a treat for his son.

Was the child Jesus, Mikey would later wonder, ever more sweetly coddled by his parent?

In the 1930's, Detroit and much of the rest of the world were drab. They wore hues of black, gray and brown; colors that could best absorb or at least hide dirt. Homes and fences had not been touched up in years, commercial signs painted during the prosperity of the 1920's had long since given up their brightness and color to years of soot-filled air. Clothes, with the notable exceptions of a dress or a suit for going to church or in which to be buried, were now washed out, thread-bare or mended with stitching that sometimes did not match the previous attempt.

Children had little or no sense of any of this unless they momentarily caught it in a parental argument or tear.

For adults, it was different. Everything around them seemed to bespeak the times, the name for which was no different than that for the emotion which gripped their psyche and soul.

Not participating in the seeming Depression era conspiracy against them was Dame Nature, especially in her spring and fall colors. Her dresses were gloriously green and the hair of her trees was freshly tinted in the way no woman on this block or any other nearby could afford. And, after the first snowfall, whiteness for a short, grand moment was not a color exclusively reserved for the rich but rather bedecked every house and yard of the poorest resident of the neighborhood.

And each home had a patch of well-tended flowers, contrasting with the drabness of the days and promising better ones. In the backyards were more, mixed in with the ever-practical, but not-always successful, vegetable plot.

To Mikey, as a little child, color and aroma were something personal, especially on the profusion of roses that adorned the ice-cream-cone shaped trellis on the side of his house. The rich hues and nose-tickling odors told him life was swell and its pleasures were there just for him.

Later, as his days came and went, he would note with nostalgic great disappointment that roses were losing the sweet smells he recalled them exuding in these days. The loss would be symbolic and co-mingle with an awareness of his own childhood, which was slipping away or already had.

Throughout his growing years and early adulthood, he would seek to find a way back to the simplicity of this age. As a man, he would yearn for the same, but would eventually give up searching for it, forsaking it rather for self-denial and that great journey on which he had been sent. He would focus then on goals rather than roses, on what he saw as his purpose and his mission, rather than on life and its flavoring. Such purposefulness would seem enough, all the reward he dared ask

His father, with conscious intent, let his little son be or else found ways to join him in his play. The greatest joy he could imagine was carrying his son on his back across the lawn, romping as horses might in the wilds of the West.

His mother, on the other hand, imaged their son riding a steed in the crusades or crossing the mountains as a missionary. She would at such times be urgently serious toward her "little Mikey" and make a small request of him as though she saw him in training.

Their friends and neighbors called the Jordan boy "bright" or "as sharp as a tack." When they said such things, the compliments brought neither a smile nor a "thank you" from Mikey. He knew they spoke the truth. Each time, his mother would put her hand on his back and remind him, "You have a God-given responsibility to use that smartness of yours for the greater honor and glory of God. You have a mission."

The word "mission," he knew, was fully intended to be life directing. Once, he asked his mother what it meant.

"Being on a mission," she told him, "means that you have been chosen, that have been sent on it by someone far more important than you are. This tells you that you are very, very special."

These words helped Mikey feel good about himself, really special; but they were also scary, especially after she had explained it was God Almighty who had chosen him and whose finger would be directing him.

Some day, going on a mission would be what he would do, he figured out. It would be in the future. It would be exciting. He had heard of airplane pilots being on missions. That would be great. That is what he would choose.

Any sense that he would in fact have a choice, however, ended with an incident that happened on a sweltering day in August when he had just turned five years old.

His mother remained unaware that he had wandered off by himself to the candy store on Woodward Avenue, a full two blocks away from his home or even that he had done it before. A neighborhood such as his was not suffering at the time from fear of its children being taken or molested. Starting six years before, with the kidnapping of the small son of Charles and Anne Lindbergh, a fear had been created among the rich and famous that their progeny could be taken for ransom. In Mikey's and other poorer neighborhoods, parents could not easily imagine the idea of their children being abducted for any reason. Still, even many of the most impoverished mothers, like ducks looking after their broods, tried their best to keep their offspring always in sight.

This is not to say the young did not sometimes meander off or that there was no danger once they got out of view. There was, and the five-year-old boy found himself that day entrapped and frightened by it.

Mikey, this day, had no penny for a treat at the candy store so he amused himself first by looking over the tempting selections there and then running up and down the two flights of stairs behind the

6

shop. It was beneath them that he noticed an old trunk with inviting travel pictures pasted on its sides. No longer needed by its owner, the box awaited being thrown out.

Memories of his father's stories of pirates and their treasures jumped up and down in his head as he approached the ornate wooden box. He opened it, but there was nothing in the trunk, not a thing. He turned and started to walk away when he realized it was just the right size in which to hide. And so he did just this, escaping the world by pulling the top shut on himself.

Even before the lid was completely closed, the small boy started to sense a numbing regret. The all-surrounding darkness that followed the sound of a click confirmed his worst fear.

Pushing with his small hands, Mikey instinctively tried to force the lid open. It did not give. The trunk was becoming stuffy and really, really scary. He hit at it again and again, using his fists, striking at the wood above him and at his sides. Still, it did not give.

His bent little body tightened with an all-over ache, which he had never before experienced. His breathing changed and his eyes delivered tears to his tiny, flushed cheeks. His lungs filled and helped produce the loud cry of a terrified young animal, trapped in a life-threatening cage. It stopped suddenly, ending in a whimper and a sniffle. A moment's hesitation was followed by a swallow and then the distinct scream of a human child.

"Mama," he cried, as though she were but a room away listening to a soap opera on the radio instead of paying heed to him.

"Mama," he called again, his squeaky voice reaching for an even higher note.

"Mama" once more came from his throat, but it was mixed with a simpering cry that more gurgled than shouted it.

No voice responded. No one came. His young muscles went limp. His spirit joined them, passively surrendering to the great sense of being in the jaws of a hopeless fate.

Mikey, without a thought of what he might do, was aware he was trapped. For once, being a bright, smart little boy brought him no aid or answer. He was captured, he fantasized, by a great and dark monster, one that seemed to know how to send a pain right into the middle of his chest. His sobbing competed with his sniffing for new and fresh air.

Dimly, he knew that this had been his own fault. He had done something, maybe several things that would have displeased his mother.

And she, or perhaps somebody else, maybe God, was punishing him.

"I will be good," he promised, sobbing.

Then he heard, or rather thought he did, a voice.

"Stand up," it told him.

And, even though the roof of the trunk should have stopped him from rising to his feet, he did try to stand up. And, as he did, his tiny back surprisingly broke through the rotted wood of the lid. Half in the trunk and half out of it, he once again was breathing fresh air.

He looked at the container in which he had almost smothered to death and again started to sob. He would live. His mother as a result would not be mad at him for dying.

Life did not end at that moment. Rather it changed. Rather it cracked out through its shell like a duckling and looked for something or someone on whom to imprint. A boy who at a deep, personal level had never been touched by fear now had been.

This was not the first time in his very short existence that Mikey had come close to death. His mother, just days before, had once again recounted the story about how when he had been a baby he almost died but had been saved by what could only be called a miracle.

She had told the story often and he strangely believed he remembered it happening.

"Mikey," she told him, "when you were only eight months old, you were a very sickly and underweight baby. I was scared you were going to die. I was sure of it."

She then pulled out a worn photograph of herself with him as a small child in her arms.

"I thought I was going to lose my little Mikey," she said "So I had the lady next door take this picture so I would have something by which to remember you."

The little baby boy in the picture had an impetigo rash across his face. He also had, his mother added in her telling of it, a double hernia and very little desire to eat.

"You were my little skin and bones," she told him. "People just kept asking me, 'Is he going to make it? He doesn't look very good.'"

"They had pretty much convinced me you weren't," she added. "Even the doctor we took you to wasn't so hopeful himself."

After her next-door neighbor had taken the picture on the front walk and headed back home, Mrs. Jordan put Mikey in the baby buggy and smoothed the blanket covering him. A woman in her fifties, twice her age, approached them.

"Ma'am," the stranger said, "I hear you have a sick baby here. I live over by John R. I have the power of healing."

His mother pulled the carriage closer to herself.

"Oh, I'm sorry," she apologized. "We're Catholics here and we don't believe in that," she asserted.

"That's O.K.," the woman said, supporting her words with an acknowledging smile.

Mikey's mother relaxed her vigilance as her eyes scanned the stranger standing in front of her. John R, that street with the strange name, was only a couple of blocks away and nothing about her appearance, not her dress nor the darkness beneath her eyes, showed her to be anything but one more poor neighborhood woman. A slight rip in the woman's sleeve, mended by a safety pin, made his mother conscious of this fact. Mrs. Jordan, on her part, because of having had the picture taken, was wearing her Sunday church dress.

The visitor, after gently stroking the baby's small, ashen cheek, closed her eyes for a second as though concentrating on something and then opened them and smiled.

"Well, I'll be going," she said, adding, "He'll be all right." She then left in the direction of the street on which she had said she lived.

As Mikey's mother later told it time and again over the years, the small boy by the end of the next week had gained two pounds and his impetigo rash and hernia were gone.

"And what an appetite my little boy then developed!" she told her close friends and later Mikey himself. "It may have been a miracle, who knows? She did stroke him, but that was the only thing she did. He got all better real fast. Things like that happen. It could have been a coincidence too, but even Father Kelly says, 'God works in strange and mysterious ways.'"

Mikey had liked the story whenever she told it. He was the center of its unfolding details. The narration seemed to say he was the object of what his mother believed to be a miracle. It also said that God would not easily let him die.

As he grew older, in his confused moments, he told himself that these two events--the woman using her "gift of healing" and the voice telling him to stand up in the trunk--represented proof he was special. They reinforced the conviction that his life had been spared through a mysterious, if not miraculous, intervention, not once but twice.

His escape from the trunk changed him. He had promised in that hopeless situation to be good and had made the pledge at a crucial time. He did not know exactly what this should mean, but all indications told him that it had a lot to do with being obedient, doing what he was told. He belonged not to himself, but to somebody else. That, he decided, was the way it was supposed to be.

Even though he was only five years old, he reasoned instinctively that finding the voice he had heard and obeying it was his destiny. He knew it. Especially when other kids picked on him and after times when he had embarrassed himself, he remembered this. During those moments in which he didn't feel good or was afraid, he still understood that he was a person with a mission. Sometimes, he took chances, toyed with fate, used a bad word or acted out of spite or anger.

Chapter 3

The early grammar school years, for Mikey, proved easy. They were often a downhill ride on a High Flier sled. As his classmates in the first grade struggled with sentences such as "Dick See Dick run." and "Spot. See Spot run." he was taking books out of the library and reading them all by himself.

His class had 40 kids, the youngest was little Mikey Jordan. The teacher conveniently made use of him as her personal assistant, a role which would continue as school progressed. It was a status that helped promote his image among the nuns of St. Mary's as smart and as good a boy as any whom they had ever had. His quickness and easy grasp of material enabled him to assist other children and ward off for some the deep resentment they felt toward him as the "teacher's pet."

Mikey was not as perfect a little boy as he thought himself to be and nowhere near as much as he wanted others to perceive him as.

Sometimes he fibbed, and he almost always got away with it. He had three reasons for telling lies. First, it was a game. He won. Others did not. Secondly, he shaved the truth to protect and exaggerate the image of his goodness. Finally, his mother and teachers inevitably accepted his brazen attempts to recoup and cover himself. Only his father gave him an occasional look that said he saw through whatever Mikey was selling as the truth.

He also cheated. Yes, he did. Several times he kept a penny of the change when his mother sent him to buy eggs from "the Egg Man" or items from the grocery store. He was smart enough to pocket only one cent at a time and not to brag to anyone about it, even though he wanted very much to do just that.

Successfully stealing from one's parents during the depth of the Depression, when every penny was counted, took some doing. Mikey was not the only first grader at St. Mary's to tell a lie or to try to cheat, but he truly believed the others were always getting caught and he never was. He reminded himself of that often.

Sometimes, he wished he had brothers and sisters, especially brothers, but then he would recall a ditty he had heard kids recite. It ended, "I told Ma. Ma told Pa. Johnny got a lickin'. Ha. Ha. Ha." The first grader took those words seriously. He figured that a sibling would always be telling Ma and he would constantly be getting lickin's. No brothers and no sisters. No squealers and no competition.

The idea of a lickin' terrified Mikey, not because he was afraid of the pain. He was not. No, it was the act of disapproval that he could not stand. Furthermore, whoever it had been who had sent him on his mission might see and record it and could cause him to lose his favored status. That thought terrified him.

Slowly, but certainly, he found himself telling fewer lies and only rarely stealing a penny when he was sent to the store. He knew he could do it. That was enough. Occasionally he was still tempted, but it was only every great once in a while that he succumbed. He was perceived by older people as an extraordinarily good little boy. Himself, he secretly saw as being both bad and good. He felt, however, that he was in control. The way he saw it he was as good as he wanted to be and also as bad.

Mikey was still in the first grade. Not all was perfect by any means. Occasionally, he wet the bed, a matter of deep personal embarrassment to him, even if his mother simply changed the sheets afterwards and never spoke of it. One other thing he often did would bring a flush of regret to his face. He would say things that sounded grown-up to him, but which did not to adults or even older kids. He slowly learned to cover better and to use his cute little boyishness to get away with any seeming pretentiousness.

It was in the second grade, however, that six-year-old Mikey Jordan hit his stride. His mother told him that his teachers had discussed having him skip the second grade, but she decided not to do so for two reasons. First, he was already the youngest child in his class and secondly, he would miss being part of the first communion training and ceremony with his class. Much of the second grade curriculum in religion was devoted to it and he would have to be taken out of his third grade classroom to go to the lessons and the practices.

No, Mikey Jordan would not miss the second grade. Ultimately, he was glad. It would turn out to be among the best years of his life, one in which he found a direction.

Everything would start to come together for him in the study of a single subject. He was clearly the best student in his class, but he prided himself most over his knowledge of catechism. It would have not been a defeat for him to get an arithmetic or geography answer wrong—which he didn't—but catechetical instruction was different. The answers in that subject were absolute, integral to his being and, most of all, the key to his highly-focused purpose and mission.

He had been told the story of King Arthur and the search for the Holy Grail. He not only believed it, but also saw it as a model of his own quest.

When he was walking home or playing during recess, a catechism question and answer would often flow through his thoughts.

"Who made me?"

"God made me."

"Why did he make me?"

"He made us to know, love and serve him in this world and to be happy with him in heaven."

Mikey cherished the answers, especially that one. Through it, *The New Baltimore Catechism* was telling him in what he considered God's own voice where he was coming from and where he was going to and why. Here, he was only six years old and he had this answer in his head and could recite it whenever he was asked or even thought about it.

Even more importantly, that catechetical response told him who he was. "God made me" were magic words. Focused as he was on himself and his world, he did not see that it meant God made everybody. He concentrated on the "me" in the question and answer as though it were all about him.

And the answer was right. It was God's truth. This amazed him. The church, the catechism, sister and his pastor, all confirmed it. So did his mother.

"Everybody knows it," he assured himself.

But even that wasn't enough for him. If those answers were right, then the whole catechism was, absolutely so. It had to be. Like the Bible, it was—to him—God's word. That was true even for answers he did not fully understand such as the one to the question, "What is a sacrament?" His quick and accurate reply was "An outward signed instituted by Christ to give grace."

He especially liked questions that offered lists of things for answers such as the corporal and spiritual works of mercy, the cardinal sins and the conditions for a mortal or a venial sin. The one that impressed people most was his reciting of the "fruits of the Holy Ghost."

"Tell them the twelve fruits of the Holy Ghost," his mother would request when company was at the house.

The six-year-old would reply, "Charity, joy, peace, patience, benignity, goodness, long-suffering, mildness, faith, modesty, constancy and chastity."

Guests, who aware that their children and they themselves had trouble remembering all ten commandments, would usually give an awkward response such as: "Long-suffering, that's what I'm best at."

His father would wince and hope that his wife would not ask the child for the seven gifts of the Holy Ghost, seven sacraments or eight beatitudes. No matter what, he would—directly or indirectly— not attempt to match his wife's controlling directions for the boy.

14

He sought no performances from their son. The personal freedom, which he held so dear, would be violated.

He loved Mikey more than he loved himself, more even than his wife. But, how to reach him? What to say if ever he did?

Richard Jordan was shy, perhaps deliberately so. He held back. He had a great affection for words; but they did not seem to work, at least in direct human relationships. If his son were in danger from a car heading toward him, he would as easily jump in front of the vehicle as attempt to save him by ordering him to run.

He would rather show an emotion than express it verbally. His constant kindnesses toward his family he felt far more sincerely than his telling them that he loved them. This way of being himself seemed to work with his wife. With his son, he questioned whether or not it did.

Mikey was polite and too obedient. He found the phrase, "I love you, Daddy," easy to say.

The boy did not understand was who his father was and what his message was for him. It was far more complex than what his mother and his son's simple catechism textbook offered.

His son was beginning to walk through life begging to give up his nascent sense of freedom for what he was being told was a higher good.

To what extent was the cause of all this that Mikey was a child only beginning to mature emotionally? Or how much was it the result of the plan that others were determinedly fashioning for him?

His father was concerned the first case scenario was melting into the second beyond any going back, that his son was in the street and a vehicle of highly-motivated purposefulness was heading toward him. It was being driven by the child's mother and schooling. Richard Jordan had neither words nor a confident plan to save his child from being run over by it.

He could try. He could say something, show Mikey what he thought and felt; but he knew in his heart it would alienate rather than help.

The only plan he could conceive or hold to was to spend as much time as possible with his son and continue his effort endlessly on into the future.

With a somber foreboding, he deeply feared that he might not get all the time he expected to have. Yet, nothing—even this fear—interfered with the abiding hope that that was the wellspring of his life. Despite the world situation, Depression and his lack of being able to reach his son, the future would be good and things would work out. Deep-down optimist that he was, he believed that life for his son would turn out well.

How to convince him of that, however?

He looked for a metaphor, a symbol, with which to represent the ideas he wanted to communicate.

All that kept coming into his head was, "Stop and smell the flowers," but what he wanted to say was far more than that. Then again, it was not about what he wanted to say. That was irrelevant. It was rather what he wanted his dear little Mikey to hear: what was tuning out the five radio stations and delivering the message of but one.

The ideas would not form into words. Rather, it was as though he heard notes and strains of music that he wanted his son's ears to pick up; he willed him to observe the colors of a tree in the midst of its fall change; to share the flood of unanswered questions that could help lead him to independent discovery and truth.

Oh, it was so much to wish for a six-year-old; but he envisioned his son's potential and wanted such a future for him.

Oblivious of such notions, however, Mikey rode forward on his mother's quest. Even though so tender of age, he steadfastly held himself back from a natural curiosity about the mundane, often nonsensical aspects of childhood. His attention dealt with God, with the absolute, things religious and therefore, to him, far above the interests of a child.

His classmates had to learn catechetical answers in order to make their first communion. For them, this memorizing was an interruption in the flow of their lives, rather than the core of it. If Mikey were sitting close to one of them, he would impulsively help by whispering or mouthing the answers. Sister Frances just let him do it. She had 40 students to get through the process.

Catechism was about God, the church and something called the Mystical Body. To Mikey, it was ultimately about himself. Even if it weren't, he still would have excelled in it, simply because it was about memorizing, something he did very well. The only time he seemed to stumble was when he had to reason something out for himself.

In his grade school catechism, the answers were clear and certain. In giving them, one was either right or wrong. And Mikey and his responses were correct. This, they always were.

He liked his parents very much and loved to please them, but sometimes his father seemed to try to make it difficult by asking him questions with answers which he had to figure out rather than remember.

Whenever his father started with the words, "What do you think…?" Mikey knew one of them was coming.

One day he answered, "Daddy, I don't want to think. I just want to be right."

In words that confused the six-year-old boy, his father replied, "That may be the wrong answer."

As smart as he was, Mikey prayed to be even smarter.

Every night as part of his prayers, he recited:

Let us pray.
O God, who did'st instruct the hearts of the faithful by the
light of the Holy Spirit, grant us in the same Spirit to be truly
wise and ever to rejoice in His consolation. Through Christ
Our Lord. Amen.

And that prayer was working. Even by his own measure, he seemed to be getting smarter. And, because his mother had so impressed the idea on his mind, he accepted his intelligence as a special gift from God, from "the light of the Holy Spirit," one that told him and the world that he was special.

Chapter 4

Sister Grace, the school principal, had prayed over the matter before making a decision. Mikey, she would allow to skip the third grade even though he would be only seven years old as he entered the fourth.

His classmates, who had endured his help when they were studying for their first communions, were glad to see him leave. He was simply too much for them. It was not only that he was too smart, but also that he was so good that the teachers, the principal and their parents continually held him up as a model. A few other kids were able to accept or at least ignore Mikey, but even these also had to contend with his reputation as someone above everybody else.

It mattered little anymore. They were rid of him as they entered the third grade; and he, the fourth. Their school year opened for them without him in the class.

His new classmates were the ones now confused by this boy smaller and younger, but smarter than they. They reacted to the annoyance by persistently teasing him. They nicknamed Mikey, "The Twerp," and generally ignored him as an outsider who all but did not exist among them.

He dealt with them by becoming quiet and withdrawn. Mikey quickly learned to cover for not knowing things he might have learned in the third grade. His penmanship, though, suffered from his writing having not received the attention it would have had if he gone through the third grade. The difficulty people had in reading what he had written was obvious, especially to Sister Martin Rose, his new teacher, who made critical notes about readability on his papers.

Mikey began a painful effort to improve his handwriting. As the results started to show, his teacher quit deducting grade points because she had found his papers "unreadable." As a consequence, the A's began reappearing on his report cards.

As his confidence returned, he once again saw himself on a hill in life, one from which he imagined he could see as far as he wanted.

His father began to take him to a ball field to watch semi-pro baseball teams play. Except for one time when they saw a game in which the teams actually played on donkeys, Mikey would sit and read a book he had brought along. Soon, his father switched tactics and began regular trips with him to the local public library.

Most deliberately of all, his father took him on a bus down to Belle Isle, a large public park on an island in the middle of the Detroit River. Fishing, which his father enjoyed, proved much too sedentary and boring for the little boy. He would become antsy, pacing back and forth and yell at the fish to bite. Still, wanting to please his parent, Mikey refused to complain or admit he did not want to go.

His father's hope was to deepen the bonds between himself and his son, but it did not seem to be happening, and he knew it. Still, he did not want to push his son in any way and so he chose a different tack, going for long walks there together. The island-park was several miles in length and full of trees, woods and trails.

"If I had my life to start over again," he told his son, "I would learn the names of all these trees and make them my friends."

That idea set well with Mikey. He had no friends. This island had tens of thousands of trees that were each just waiting, according to what his father was saying, to become someone's friend.

"Daddy," he asked, "which ones do you know?"

His father introduced him to oaks, maples, pines and ashes.

"I know their genus, but not their individual species," his father said. "I can tell you that we get syrup from maples, build furniture out of oak and make baseball bats from ash. All the furniture in our home is pine. At least, I think it is."

Mikey nodded.

"Friends!" he said to himself.

Their next trip was to the local branch of the Detroit Public Library.

"I just want to wander around a little by myself, Daddy," Mikey said. "All right?"

"Sure," his father encouraged.

The young boy, sensing only vaguely what different worlds the two were in, did not want his father to realize that he was about to attempt to carry out what his parent had merely dreamed of doing. He would learn the names of the trees and, then, he would be able to make them his friends.

Going to the nature section of the library, his hands picked through the shelves until they came across a book by Charles Herbert Otis titled *Michigan Trees.*

Mikey fell in love with the book. It was full of detailed black and white illustrations of leaves, buds, fruits and flowers. The small, leather-bound volume had in it all the trees that could be found in the state. Many of their names, he could not even pronounce. Others such as oak, ash, cherry, maple and poplar he easily recognized.

Best of all, the book contained difficult, almost unbelievable words in it. He grinned to see them there. They were listed at the end in what was called a "glossary."

He picked out a few of these special words and memorized them as well as their definitions, stumbling over the pronunciations, but getting the spellings correct:

Apiculate. Ending in a short-pointed tip.
Calyx. The outer part of a perianth, usually green in color.
Obovoid. An ovate solid with the broadest part toward the apex.
Pistil. The seed-bearing organ of a flower, normally consisting of an ovary, style and stigma.
Rugose. Wrinkled.
Scurfy. Covered with small bran-like scales
Spagnous. Resembling or allied to the genus, *Spagnum,* a moss.

21

Boy, what words! And there were lots more like them. They did not make sense to Mikey, but this did not matter. They were part of a different language, one that he could master. Learning these terms and making them a part of his relationship with the trees on Belle Isle afforded him a treat beyond anything he could ever hope to imagine.

All this newly acquired information became part of his mission. He felt this, but he knew it for certain after reading a poem by Joyce Kilmer that ended with the telling words, "But only God can make a tree."

This book was like being able to learn to read all over again. He had always been a little disappointed he could not remember the initial experience. It seemed to him as though he had been able to recognize printed words as long as he could remember. Now, he had a new chance to let whatever was going on in his head explode and so illuminate something that was now darkness. What could be more exciting than that?

He paged quickly through the book to find words and descriptions that he could not understand whatsoever. Each of these sat there as an opportunity and challenge set out, it seemed, for Mikey Jordan to understand and master in the future.

The young boy would tell no one else. They would not understand. This volume would be a secret between him and his friends, the trees. He would come back here on Saturday mornings and memorize as much as his brain could comprehend in a visit.

Father and son would take the bus down to Belle Isle on Sunday afternoons whenever they were free to do so. Mikey would fish patiently with his father, even sometimes catching a few. The two would then go for extensive hikes through the woods.

As Mikey stopped to inspect bark, leaves, buds and flowers, his father quickly developed a good notion of what was going on. He said nothing about it. He knew this was his son's secret and best for him to respect it. He would have loved to learn with his son or even from him, but the small boy did not offer.

On more than one occasion, the subject of Mikey caused words between his parents, as his mother constantly fawned over her son, driving him like a lamb up and down the hills that appeared before them.

"My God," his father said. "You never challenge the boy's thinking!"

"Don't use God's name in vain," his wife chided. "No, you're right. I do not challenge my son. I do not need to. He does enough of that. If you talked with Sister Martin Rose, you would know how very well he is doing in school."

"I know he gets near-perfect marks in school, even after skipping the third grade," his father said. "But, is he learning to think or even to feel for himself?"

"John, the boy is only seven years old, going on eight," his wife protested in a way that he recognized was meant to end the discussion.

"Yes, but is he allowed to be just that, a little boy?" his father asked. "I fear for him, for his future."

"His future is certain," his mother answered with fierce determination. "God has chosen him for something very special."

"Wrong answer," her husband thought, but once again said nothing.

If in the fourth grade Mikey were not doing the kind of thinking his father wanted him to, that did not mean he was not drawing conclusions.

One day he was half paging through his catechism textbook and half day dreaming about what he would accomplish some day when he began to make a series of discoveries that would mark his life.

"God is a he, just like I am," he said to himself. "He's a man, not a girl, not a woman. When he was little, he was a boy like me. He's not like Sister or those silly girls in my class or my mom either. This is great!"

That everyone considered God to be a male was to be the first of four realizations he uncovered about his own reality, ones that would satisfy him deeply and help him define for himself who he was.

The second came fast upon the first. At a Fourth of July celebration in front of the local post office, he came to realize the next part that—as an American—he was at the top of another human pyramid.

"We are Americans and we need to learn to be proud of that fact," the speaker was saying, "It was our American soldiers and our American know-how that won the Great War. I say if people are not happy with this country, let them leave it. If you are not proud to be an American, then I say there is something wrong with you. But, if you are proud of being an American, then I say, 'God bless you.'"

Mikey was stunned. It was clear that speaker must be talking about him. The third grader had waved his small American flag as the parade went by, but he had done nothing else. He had not even said something to show he was proud to be American. He did not wish to have to leave the country and he most certainly did want God to bless him.

He immediately did the only thing he could—he daydreamed about giving a speech in which he told the speaker and everybody else in town that even though he might be only seven, going on eight years old, there was no one more proud to be an American than he was.

"I am very, very proud I am an American," he later boasted to his mother, "just like that man today said I should be."

"You should be," she answered. "That man was the member of the Detroit City Council. But it is even better that you be proud to be a Catholic, because that is what God wants."

"Then, I am proud to be a Catholic, a boy and an American," he said.

That night, Mikey fell asleep with a smile on his face and fullness in his chest as he thought about who he was.

Several months later he discovered what he felt was more about who he was. His father had a good friend from work, named Charles. His mother described the man as "a Negro" and said, "Negroes are God's children too. We should always remember that." It was almost the exact same expression Sister Martin Rose had used at school in talking about the people in Africa and there was a connection. Both, unlike him, were black.

Mikey thought about it and was glad to realize he was "one of God's children" and he did not have to put a "too" at the end of that description. He liked being a member of God's immediate family and having the color of his skin as a clear reminder of it.

His being white thus joined three other proud facts about himself of being male, Catholic and American. Together, these formed the foundation of his ego and self-image.

His mother had said being Catholic was the most important. He thought so too, but he was not quite as certain about that as he was about his catechetical answers. Maybe being a boy was better. He liked being white and an American too. As with his mission, each one of these characteristics helped mark him as being chosen by God to be someone special.

Mikey once blurted it out to his father, "I am so very happy to be whom God has made me: a Catholic, a boy, white and an American."

His father reacted with a sad, stunned look.

"What are you saying, Mikey?" his father asked. There was a rare criticism in his tone.

"Nothing. Daddy," he quickly backtracked. He realized that his father did not understand and therefore had disapproved.

"I don't really believe that." Mikey stammered. "I was only kidding. I heard somebody at school say it and I wanted to know what you thought about his words."

"I think that saying those words reflects on the child and his family," his father said. "I am very glad to hear that you do not believe any such thing."

"It was like when you get caught bragging about something," Mikey thought. "You have to pretend you didn't mean what you said. I'm never going to be heard saying that again, especially not around him."

"Daddy just doesn't understand God," he concluded to himself. "It's because he is a convert."

His mother had earlier responded to the same words with a smile, pat on the head and a hug.

Chapter 5

Mikey had learned to read script while still in the second grade. It led to one of the mysteries of his life, the words contained on a frayed piece of notepaper he discovered between the cushions of the clean, but sagging couch that dominated the living room of his small, family home.

The script was arranged in a strange form somewhat like the *Dick and Jane First Grade Reader*. The pattern was also similar to that he has encountered in a volume of poetry, but the final words did not rhyme as they did in that book.

The handwriting was his father's. That, he knew.

Some of the words and phrases that appeared there did not make complete sense, but then neither did the whole piece.

It read:

Whence,
whither,
why?
As we move around
the oval track of life,
I think I hear
someone laughing.
I wonder.
Is there a grandstand?

Mikey struggled to memorize both the words and the pattern before slipping the piece of paper back where he had found it. Committing things to memory was something he ordinarily did with ease and speed. This effort proved more difficult because he could not grasp either the sense of what was on the paper or the form in which it was written.

And, he had questions, difficult ones.

Had his father composed this or copied it from someplace else?

How did it fit in with his own view of truth as based on *The New Baltimore Catechism*?

What was the oval track of life? He knew the phrase meant that life was somehow circular to the person who had written it, but religion taught him that it was journey that went in a straight line.

And, furthermore, if there were a grandstand, who besides God was in it?

More confusing than any of these questions was: Why ask, "Whence, whither and why?" and not give the answers? This was farther from his grasp than were the sun, the moon and the stars.

The catechism, the church, the priests, the nuns and his parents were there to give complete and correct answers.

Mikey did not inquire. He never asked his father or anyone else, ever.

But, then neither did he ever wonder how there could be three persons in one God or how Christ could be the head of the Mystical Body or what it meant to be "conceived without sin." He did not even ask what it meant to be conceived.

Mikey wanted to know everything, but mysteries were not included. They were out of bounds and he accepted this the way he assented to the fact that two and two are four and that the absolute exists but the relative either does not or does not matter.

These thoughts in the same handwriting would not be the last ones he would ever discover or prove how confused his poor father was.

Chapter 6

When he reached the sixth grade, Mikey acquired two buddies, if not friends, Nicky Koenig and Paulie McGuire. It was not an equal relationship. Two years their junior and much smaller, he was more tolerated than liked by them. The rest of his class could now choose between two new nicknames for him, "Smarty-pants" and "Goody-goody Two Shoes."

Nicky and Paulie, however, realized he could be useful. He was resourceful and quick-witted. For one thing, he supplied them with names to throw at a group of seventh grade bullies whose taunts confused and made them mad. Nicky and Paulie could never think of comebacks. Mikey, they realized, could. His tongue was sharp and he came up with insults no one understood. He was also useful to help the two of them with their homework and any projects they had to put together.

In order ever to find Nicky and Paulie, however, Mikey had to go looking for them. When they needed a favor, of course, they came to him. On the other hand, the fact that they tolerated him was a buffer from his own loneliness and contempt shown toward him by others of his classmates, including the girls.

"Don't let it bother you," his mother urged, when he grudgingly mentioned it to her. "They're jealous of how smart God made you. That's too bad for them."

His father, on the other hand, would say, "Come here." He would then hold his son a hug, but Mikey would break loose because he felt his father should have an answer for him, a suggested way with which he could put down and confuse those who picked on him.

He preferred to take solace from his mother's inference that his enemies were actually God's.

Mikey spent most of his time by himself. While he was not athletically talented, he devoted himself with such intensity to any activity in which he was engaged that the results were often surprising. He could not hit a baseball out of the infield, but he learned how to bunt. He always ran to first base even when it seemed certain that he would be thrown out. He knew there was a possibility the first baseman would drop the throw, which in fact happened surprisingly often. In trying to catch or stop a ball thrown or hit to him, Mikey would get in front of it. If he could not field it with his glove, he made his body block it, willingly enduring pain or discomfort as a result.

After watching his son play one day, his father told him, "Michael, you do quite well." Mikey expected him to add, "for someone your size" or "for someone who can't." While his father didn't add such a comment, his son was convinced that was what he was thinking.

Even though his mother once said that his father had been an excellent athlete in his high school days, Mikey never heard him speak of it. He could still hit and throw a ball as well as any individual in the neighborhood and could kick a football, his son knew, farther than anyone expected.

Mikey grew content to be alone. He loved to daydream about himself as a hero getting recognition over and over. Otherwise, he spent his free time reading and watching the trains go by on the Grand Trunk Railroad. His evenings were spent tuned into his favorite radio shows *The Shadow, The Green Hornet* and *Captain Midnight*. He also listened to some of the adult programs, including

First Nighter, Fibber McGee & Molly and *Amos 'n Andy*. Nothing matched dialing up his boy-hero show, *Jack Armstrong, the All-American Boy*.

He also had a hobby, which concealed a deep, deep secret. He collected matchbooks, ones with various local advertising on them. At first his mother raised the fear he might use the matches left in one of them to start a fire, but she quickly realized her little son was too responsible and carefully behaved to do anything such as that.

His secret involved a different kind of smoldering.

For Mikey, who loved to roam the neighborhood, matchbooks were easy items to come by whenever he went searching for them. He would look down on the sidewalk almost anywhere and there would be one or sometimes, several. These had been given out free by perhaps a bar, hat store, grocery, car repair garage, insurance agency or even funeral home. Usually, when he found one, he already had a half of a dozen identical covers, but you never knew when he would pick up one that was completely new, even from a different part of the city or another state.

Some covers had lengthy advertisements on them, while others offered one or two-line jokes along with a firm's name. Any number of these were about farmers and their daughters. As smart as he was, he rarely understood the humor, although he surmised that they were about sinful sex, which had to do with the sixth and ninth commandments. He was not sure why they were supposed to be funny, but they were something forbidden and that made them exciting in a secret way.

Nobody, he was sure, could suspect that anyone as good as he would be interested in the sex stuff or the scantily-clad women he found on the most desirable of them.

The bigger part of his collection he kept in five cigar boxes under his bed. They were the last things he looked at before kneeling down to say his night prayers. The really titillating ones he hid in an old paper bag under a floorboard in the attic. These had women clothed in unbelievably short dresses, pieces of underwear or skimpy swimming suits. They almost always advertised a bar, car repair shop or bowling alley. He didn't look at them often for fear of being caught. It was not really necessary. Their images, in full color, had become imbedded in his memory.

Many of the matchbook covers had phrases on them such as "American Beauty" or "Wouldn't you like to see more of her?" Almost half depicted women in bathing suits or shorts. His favorite, for some reason, was of a waitress. She reminded him of a woman who worked at a restaurant across the street from his school, although that woman was actually much heavier.

Each item in his secret collection was precious, almost a sin in itself, a little piece of what it meant to be bad. To the young boy, these matchbook covers were somehow a key to understanding what sex was about and the meaning of a curious phrase he had read, "wanton desires." The illustrations were in some way—and he didn't know how—a part of the other Mikey, the one he never let anyone else ever see.

He was tempted to show Nicky and Paulie. He was sure they knew things about sex that he did not. This collection would prove to them that he was just as smart about it as they were. Telling them, however, would be really dangerous. What if they squealed? He couldn't just lie to get out of it. The collection could be found and used against him and he was much too clever ever to let that happen.

And then there was God. He knew, but did He? Mikey was not even willing to tell about the collection in confession. If he didn't confess it, then perhaps God wouldn't know. Maybe that's how God worked and that's why He wanted you to confess your sins. Mikey knew that was not actually true because the catechism made it clear that God is "all knowing." What the young would-be saint, willing-to-be sinner really feared was that the priest to whom he told his sins would order him to get rid of the matchbooks and he did not want that. No, instead, he continued to confess sins of pride about how smart he was and that he had uncharitable thoughts about the kids who had picked on him.

Could he catch something such as a sin-caused illness from the covers? That was another question. His mother had warned him about unnecessarily touching his body "down there" or picking up things on the street when he didn't know what they were or where they had come from. He told himself that he knew where the matchbooks had come from. They said so on the covers. She had warned, "Don't pick up things off the sidewalk or street. You might catch something, become sick." This helped add one more challenge to the secret side of her little boy. He was simply too smart to allow that to happen. He would know if he saw the "things" about which she was talking.

These were not days Mikey could ever call happy. He wandered away from home a lot, but he always returned by the time that he said he would. Mostly, he looked to the future and the belief that something special awaited him there. That conviction made the aloneness he felt as well as the annoyances provoked by his classmates endurable.

Learning alone seemed to satisfy him. Geography, for example, helped him find out about new countries and how to be able to spell such exotic places as Czechoslovakia and he could tell you that *Firenzi* was the Italian name for Florence, Italy.

Math was almost as certain as catechism and he liked that. While his classmates were learning their arithmetic tables, he was working algebraic problems.

History also talked to him. Even though there were wars and revolutions, the good guys in the end almost always seemed to win or at least most of the books he ever read said so. At first, he would start to see something bad happening and then a hero would come along and make things better. Lots of times these men would die in the end, but then they would become martyrs, which was a good thing for it was a good way to please God and even get canonized as a saint.

Learning about the history of the Catholic church filled him with excitement the way playing with a puppy could for other children. That really was the ultimate story of good guys versus bad guys. Even the bad people in the church, like sinful popes, probably repented in the end and went to heaven. He liked to think so.

If he were going to die because someone was going to kill him for his faith, he fantasized that he would try to convert that person as he was dying. But what would he do about his matchbook collection? If they found that after he died, he would never get canonized. He read about one guy, whom they wanted to canonize, but didn't because they found his body turned over in the casket. They figured out he must have been buried alive. He had clawed at the lid of the coffin so they decided he had possibly committed the sin of despair and so the Church did not canonize him and never would.

Mikey would solve the problem about his sin-tainted collection somehow. If he thought there were any chance in the immediate future of him being martyred, he would take the matchbooks out from under the rafter and burn them. He determined to do it before he started on his mission, but until then, he didn't have to do it.

"Until then," he told himself, "I should think about getting rid of it."

One fall day, Nicky and Paulie came to his door looking for him. They had actually come to his house and asked for him. The pair told him they wanted him to go for a walk with them. He agreed. Only after they got a block from his house did they explain what they had in mind.

"You know Sally Reuther," Nicky asked.

"Of course," Mikey said, thinking it a stupid question. She was in their class and generally acknowledged to be the cutest girl in the sixth grade at St. Mary's School.

"Well, we know something about her," Paulie said.

"Oh," Mikey said, trying to act nonchalant.

"Yah," Nicky said, "we seen her without her clothes on."

Mikey couldn't believe what his classmate had just said.

"That's what you say," Mikey challenged.

"You can see her naked, too," Paulie added, nudging him. "We can fix it up for you."

"What do you mean?" Mikey asked, his blood rushing all over his body and making him warm.

"Here's the deal," Paulie explained. "Every Wednesday after school she takes dance lessons. When she comes home, she takes a bath and changes her clothes. You can see her do it cuz there's no curtains on her window."

"Are you kidding?" Mikey whispered.

"No, we ain't," Nicky said. "You can see for yourself in just a few more minutes. What you do is get in this box in the lot next to her house. We cut a hole in it and you can watch her window and no one can see you."

"Wow!" Mikey said. "Wow!'

Just then he turned and saw Nicky wink at Paulie. It reminded him of the first time he had heard sounds over the crystal set he had built. A message came through loud and clear and Mikey was quick to understand what was happening.

"It's a trap," he told himself. "And they are not going to get me."

"That's great you guys, really great," he said. "You know what, I got a pair of binoculars at home that will help me see even better. I am going to run there and get them. You guys wait here. I'll be right back."

"Good," Paulie said. "Real good. Be right back though because she's going to do it in just a few more minutes."

"Don't worry," Mikey said. "Now, you guys wait here. All right."

"Sure, Mikey, we'll be here," Nicky assured. "You can trust us."

As he walked quickly away, he thought he could hear them giggling. He went home, got his toy binoculars and went down to watch the trains go by on the Grand Trunk Railroad.

The next day when asked him why he had not come back to hide in the box, he told them that his mother had said he had to stay home and do his homework.

"How about next week?" he asked.

"Yah," Paulie said; but by then everyone had forgotten about it and Nicky suspected that maybe Mikey was tricking them rather than the other way around. They had already invited several other kids to hide and catch Mikey watching Sally's window from a box. Now they had to get out of it by saying that they had changed their minds.

"Two and a half more years and I'll be out of grade school with these morons," he told himself.

In the meantime, he learned to serve at mass, answering the prayers in Latin. To the priest's, *"Introibo ad altarem Dei,"* which meant, "I will go unto the altar of God," he responded, *"Deus, qui laetificat juventutem meum,"* which his teacher translated as, "God, who gives joy to my youth."

Serving mass was something truly special. For one thing, the girls in his class could not serve mass. The pope had made up that rule and it excluded even nuns, although they would sometimes answer the prayers, but that was all.

"This is great," Mikey said to himself as he started memorizing the Latin prayers. He worked on it for just part of the afternoon and evening and, by then, had memorized the priest's words as well as the server's responses. Sister Ruth, who had taught boys how to serve mass and perform what she called "the rubrics," knew he was an extraordinarily smart little boy. She was nevertheless amazed at how intensely he had studied and how quickly he learned what she taught. Sister never commented, of course, on the fact that she herself could never get it down it so perfectly.

Up to this point, he had been uncomfortable sitting in church, working hard not to let anyone realize how boring he found it except for those times when he really concentrated on the ceremony. Now, Mikey began to feel attending mass was worth it because he was being let in on a little part of something magical, an exclusive secret mystery of which he was now a part.

"I wonder how many kids there are in school," he asked himself, "I'll bet there's at least 300, but only about eight or ten of us ever get to serve mass."

Every morning, he went to the sacristy in the hope that one of the boys assigned to serve mass had forgotten or couldn't make it. As a result he sometimes got an extra opportunity to be a server.

"Pop," he asked his father one day, "did you serve mass when you were a kid?"

"No, I never have," he said. "When I was a boy, I was not Catholic. I converted just before I met your mother."

Mikey was always shocked to be reminded of this. His father was a convert. He had not gotten the training in catechism that he himself was receiving in school. A convert! That's almost like not being a Catholic at all.

"After all," he thought to himself. "It was not my father's fault he was born a Protestant."

"But," he decided, "I will never ever tell anyone that my father wasn't always a Catholic."

Still he thought a lot about it and finally asked his father, "Pop, what was it like to be a Protestant?"

"It was all right," his father. "In many ways one religion is as good as another."

Mikey was all of ten years old when his father said that to him, but he was certain that in all those years no one else had said anything more heretical in his presence. It was as though his father were operating a steam shovel against him and he were a tree. His dad's words seemed to lift him up out of the ground, roots and all. His father was in open denial of the supremacy of the one, holy, catholic and apostolic church. It was like the Gospel account in the Garden of Gethsemene when St. Peter denied that he even knew Christ. What his father had said was the kind of response that the enemies of God tried to force the martyrs to agree to or else be killed.

Starting that night he began saying a silent prayer that God would forgive this sin. He feared greatly that such an attitude would keep his father out of heaven and that the family would get there without him. He prayed as hard as he could that God would understand that his daddy really didn't mean it.

Chapter 7

To Mikey, learning to serve mass represented a signpost on the path into his future, a promise that the long-anticipated mission would someday, somehow be announced to him. He would be selected for that special role, he knew, just as naturally as he had been chosen to be an altar boy.

One morning as he was standing up at the altar with a priest, an idea that had long been amorphous became clear to him, that of someday going into the seminary. It built on a desire that had germinated unimpeded within his heart. The intent now took on a growth of its own, filling his head and then, more and more, the whole of him. Focusing on the sweet simplicity of the notion, he began to recognize it as a grand hope and insulation against the loneliness and rejection he was feeling from his classmates. It would be the perfect revenge. He would become a priest and rise up above them all.

More than anything else, he was conscious that his becoming a seminarian and eventually a priest would please his mother, someone for whom he loved doing things such as opening doors, cleaning the basement without being asked and writing short, rhyming poems. Mikey in spring and summer would hunt for flowers in nearby lots. He would pick them, hold them behind his back and then ring his mother's doorbell. She would come to the door, smile and ask him, "Yes?" as though he were one of the myriad of door-to-door salesmen who peopled those Depression years. Looking serious, he would wait a moment and then yell, "Surprise," and bring out the flowers.

The actual ceremony of announcing his intention to enter the seminary would have to be timed just right, he thought. He would need to tell his mother in a way that would startle her and simultaneously give her the unmistakable message that he was doing it, in great part, for her. He imagined casually mentioning it in his night prayers while she was hovering over him. What a surprise that would be! He thought of whispering it to her at mass, perhaps on a Saturday morning, while they sat together in an almost empty church. He daydreamed about her reaction, seeing her swoon and reach toward heaven in joy and ecstasy. He expected her to say, "Thank you, my little Mikey." It was the name she used for him when she was demonstratively pleased with something he had done.

In the meantime, he waited for the perfect opportunity.

Serving mass came to foreshadow another, darker part of his future. One day, right after mass, the assistant pastor smiled and told him to empty out the water and wine cruets and then rinse them. The priest gave him a little knowing nudge and added, "Go ahead. I used to do it when I served mass as a kid." The young priest then left the sacristy without glancing back.

Mikey could not understand why the assistant pastor had talked and nudged him the way he did. But, as he was preparing to empty the small amount of wine left in the glass cruet, he realized that the priest might have been encouraging him to do something other than pour it out. No, that could not possibly be what he meant. But, yes, it was the only answer.

The young altar boy decided not to do it. He thought he might eventually, but he would bide his time. He had learned it was safer to hesitate before going along with plans and schemes proposed by others, especially if they entailed something that could put him in harm's way. He was willing to take an occasional chance, but consistently chose to do so on his own terms. He could remember several instances when this approach had kept him out of trouble and saved him from being embarrassed. If he were ever concerned that drinking the wine left over from mass was sinful, he now knew to which priest it was to be confessed.

Another opportunity to taste the mass wine came within a week. An older priest visiting the parish saw him standing at the door of the sacristy and asked him to serve for his mass. He gladly accepted. The visitor rapidly mumbled his way through the beginning parts of the mass. Mikey kept up with him easily because he didn't need the priest's prayers as cues for his responses. He knew the server's own lines too well to become confused. The elderly man, obviously physically ill, finally cut the ceremony short and left the church quickly. The sister who usually served as the sacristan was not there, but the cruet was and still had in it most of the amber wine.

The small altar boy took off his surplice and then the cassock, which was dragging on the floor. Picking up the water cruet, he poured its contents down the sink. He was about to do the same with the wine, when he looked around and saw that he was totally alone. Still, he hesitated, but finally raised the small container with its strange-colored liquid to his lips and let several drops drip onto them. The taste was not as sweet as he had expected but rather tart and a little strange. Then, with his tongue, he retouched the particles of wine left on the outside of his mouth and relished the thought that what he was doing was savoring an apple from the Garden of Eden.

Mikey quickly poured the rest of the remaining wine down the drain. He had done it. He had tasted the forbidden fruit. He had not been struck dead by the wrath of God, nor been cast out of the garden. He breathed deeply, and made himself act normal as possible.

It was a Saturday morning. As he walked home, he felt older. He abruptly decided it was time to change his name. From that moment on, he decided it would no longer be Mikey, but rather Michael. When he reached home, he walked up to his mother and told her in a demeanor as serious as he could muster, "Mother, I do not like the name people call me. From now on, I want to be 'Michael.'"

"Mikey, is something wrong?" she asked, frowning under the thought that her little boy might be growing up faster than she wanted.

"No, Mother, nothing's wrong," he responded. "Just don't call me Mikey anymore. I don't want anyone to do that."

"O.K.," she said and patted his head. "Can't I even call you 'My little Mikey?"

"No, my name is Michael," he said.

"I was just teasing you," she said, but both of them knew she was not. It would not be easy for her to change. She knew she would slip and call him "Mikey," and then have to say she was sorry.

To his father, from then on, he would for always and for at all times be "Michael."

And Michael, it was to Father Carl Coggins. The priest friend of his father's had invited him to serve his mass on Sundays at his storefront mission church in a segregated neighborhood of Detroit.

Father Carl was as unique an individual as he had ever encountered. Unlike the pastor and the assistant at St. Mary's, he was neither authoritative nor like another big kid. His father called him "as friendly as all outdoors." The priest, who had an accent acquired growing up in Louisville, talked like no one Michael had ever heard before.

"Father Carl," his father told people, "could charm the fuzz off a peach or get fish to jump out of the water to take his bait."

Michael thought his father was exaggerating but everybody did like to stand and listen to the priest no matter what he was talking about.

His father liked Father Carl and so did Michael. The people who came to his church on Sunday were also happy with him because he was kindly and seemed interested in them.

"There is no colored question," Father Carl often said. "In God's eyes, we're all colored, even those of us from the South."

"He does have an ability to save souls," Michael's mother told everyone, repeating it often to her son and to her friends.

Michael saw her statement as a key to his own life. What he felt he had to learn was how you "save" a soul.

The priest's style was flamboyant and imposed throughout the church right down to his young server. There were posters on the mission's walls rather than paintings and the background behind the altar had a big picture of Christ with a very dark face. Michael's "duds," as Father Carl called them, were not the simple black and white cassock and surplice he wore serving mass at St. Mary's. Rather, the cassock was bright red and the short, blouse-like surplice over it was fluffy and billowy white with intricate lace edgings.

His father, who went along with Michael one Sunday, said on the way home, "Father Carl, you put on quite a show. It's more like some Protestant church than a Catholic one."

"I wish you wouldn't say that," Michael chided, remembering his father's earlier statement about one religion being pretty much the same as another. But privately he knew that the description was at least partially right this time.

Whatever quality it was Father Carl possessed, it represented the very magic the young grade school student most seemed to lack. The priest was "winning," everybody said. Michael himself, he well knew, was not. Yes, he was special. While all his smartness was something others might be in awe of, it also helped keep them at a distance. Until now, the approval of his mother and attention from his teachers had been enough.

This man, this priest of God, had an attraction and a power over other people that earned him their admiration and their smiles. Michael wanted to be this way, but he was not.

Father Carl, Michael's mother explained, was a missionary. His church, located in a well-worn storefront, was not really a parish, but rather was called a "mission." She said that it was a "part of the apostolate to the colored." He did not quote to her the priest's explanation that in God's eyes everybody was colored, even the white people in the South.

Those two words, "mission" and "missionary," kept Michael awake that night thinking about them. His destiny, he believed with anxious intensity, was "to be on a mission." Therefore, he too would be a "missionary." But, what was his mission to be? It was about time that he learned? He was sure that going to the seminary would be a big move in that direction. Becoming a priest and being popular and winning souls for God as Father Carl did, was that it? Or was it even bigger? After all, had not God for good reason made him as smart as he was?

Father Carl's popularity with the congregation after mass allowed Michael to be alone as he put away the vestments and acted as sacristan. In this role, he actually got to touch the chalice, something no other kid he knew was permitted to do. In catechism, Sister Miriam had explained that the laity could never touch the chalice, the monstrance or any other sacred vessel used to hold the Blessed Sacrament. As a server, he was allowed to hold the paten under the chin of those receiving communion, lest the host fall toward the floor. Michael deeply treasured his new role, telling no one about it lest someone find a reason to object.

The position he held also gave him the task of disposing of the unused wine left after mass. Michael found himself not only sipping and tasting it drop by drop, but routinely finishing it off. He felt a little charge from it, but dismissed the possibility of getting drunk from wine the way he saw happen in movies and heard about on radio programs. But, the thought that it somehow held a magic power to do that to a person who got careless with it excited him. That far, he told himself, he would never go.

One day, he blurted out to Father Carl his intention of going to the seminary. He also told him that it was "a secret for now."

"That's good," Father Carl said matter-of-factly. "If you need a reference, I'll be glad to give you one."

Michael was stunned. The priest had been paying little attention to him and he thought his announcement might change that. It did not seem to phase him even a little.

"I guess the souls that need to be saved are more important to him," he told himself. "I won't mention it again."

More and more, he was coming to grips with the fact that before he announced his intention of going to the seminary to anyone else, he would have to throw away the secret part of his matchbook collection. He could not risk being caught or exposed. People would not understand and he probably could not lie his way out of it. He did not want to give up the collection that had become such a repeated little pleasure to him, but he knew now he had to do so. Bigger things awaited him.

How to dispose of it? A person as clever as he would not just dump it in the garbage lest it could be traced back to him. Michael thought for a short time of sticking it in either Nicky's or Paulie's desk, but he had no appetite for such vengeance. He liked to think how many ways he could get back at those who did things to him or called him names, but such plotting was purely mental exercise rather than a scheme to act with intent. He disliked being vicious or hurting anyone, but he most certainly did take pleasure in contemplating it.

He walked home from school on a back street looking for places to dump the matchbooks. Most people burned their garbage and sometimes their trash in small, cement catch-alls for that purpose in the alley behind their homes. If it couldn't be consumed by fire, it could be put in a box or whatever container they had in front of their houses. Everyone, including your neighbors, or at least their kids, was then expected to go through it to see what they might salvage.

Some kids, like Peter Jones, who lived down the block, were especially good trash pickers. Michael was not above it either, but he didn't come from a family with seven kids like good old Peter did. The latter and the rest of the Jones household could use almost everything he could find. And that instinct for reclaiming unwanted stuff was exactly what he feared. People watched other people's trash and someone could spot him dumping his collection and then come looking.

Three days went by and still he did not find a safe place to get rid of it. Finally, he came up with a very good idea, the trash bin behind the tavern that gave away matchbooks. No one would question them being there.

He decided to rid himself of them in the morning on the way to school. There would be no one around the bar and few people on the street.

He knew his plan was not perfect, but it had reached a very high standard of planning and cleverness. He took an additional day, however, to make certain there was not something he might have overlooked.

The next morning when he heard his mother going down the basement stairs to start the laundry, he arose and tiptoed up to the attic. He took a sweater with him to wrap the paper sack containing the matchbook covers. He carefully removed the floorboard. As it was still fairly dark, he was not surprised that he did not immediately see it. As he reached back into the six-inch high space between the floorboard and the ceiling below it, his heart seemed to disconnect. The bag, he was certain, was there; it had to be. It was not.

Michael went quickly to his room. He immediately returned to the attic to check again. Somehow he must have looked in a different space than where it should be. He had not. There was only one place. It was not there.

"Figure this out," he told himself, but he trembled as he said it. He considered telling his mother he was sick and staying home to think, but it would mean ending his perfect attendance record and bring about all kinds of havoc and concern. His mother would be extraordinarily suspicious

Who could have discovered it? His older second cousin had been over a couple of weeks earlier. Let's see. Had he looked at his matchbook covers since then? He wasn't sure. He could always remember. What was this? What was happening? Was everything unraveling? He honestly didn't know, but his heart was pounding in a way it never had before this.

Michael ordered himself to concentrate, but he was not certain on what. Who had done this? And why had that person not confronted him yet? This was perplexing. If the matchbooks had been taken in the last few days, he might have avoided the whole problem by getting rid of them earlier. Oh, if only he had done that. Stupid! No, he was not that. He most certainly was not.

He returned to the attic one last time to look for clues. He found none and his ever self-assured reasoning was not filling in the gaps. It was so painful, so frightening. The boom would drop on him. He knew it. Maybe it wouldn't. Yes, it would, it surely would.

Was there something he could do? Could he make up a story? Should he? Could he ask his mother some indirect questions and see what she knew?

Michael went to school that day, but sat through his classes without his usual sharpness and aggressiveness. For once the hand that was always raised didn't go up.

No one said anything and several days passed slowly. He scarcely could think about telling his mother he wanted to go to the seminary. He might hear her respond, "You, who collected matchbooks of girls with hardly any clothes, you want to be a priest? Oh, the shame!"

As more days passed, he began to suspect that his mother did not know.

"She is not good at hiding anything," he told himself.

Did his father find it? Wouldn't he have told her? His father was a puzzle to him, one he didn't spend much time trying to figure out. It could have been him, but Michael had no way of knowing. Whatever had happened, there was now someone out there who knew what he had done, who had seen his innermost secret. That person could expose him and his kingdom would come tumbling down.

"Damn," he said and it was the first time he ever used that word, "I would prefer that they would confront me with it. This, I can't take."

The truth was that he was glad no one had brought it out into the open. If he could only figure out who had found it and why that person said nothing.

Chapter 8

The flow of life, as it starts to seem predictable, sometimes rushes away from the shore just as it is expected to break upon it. Something quirky happens in the middle of a person concentrating on determining what is going to happen next.

Two groups of people—gamblers and geniuses—tend to be most affected by this shift of fate. What they have in common is that few, if any people regularly foresee the future as inaccurately as they do. Stubborn, defective memories alone help them forget how often their past hunches and predictions failed miserably.

Mikey was not a gambler, he trusted not in odds but rather in his own intense focus. The discovery by someone of his matchbook cover collection provided just such an opportunity. He concluded with certainty that this person was going to confront him. It would then be his task, his challenge to make up a lie such that no one could prove he was doing just that.

First, he would say, "Oh that. Is that still there? That was from when I was a real little kid. I found it but I couldn't figure out what to do with it, so I hid it somewhere. Where did you find it?"

He could attempt to implicate certain unnamed classmates who had put it in his desk to trap him. He would argue that he was horrified with the pictures and put them away where no one would ever see them again.

It also crossed his mind was to say, "I prefer not to say anything more. A classmate, who was ashamed at having collected them, asked me to dispose of them because he knew I was not interested in them. I promised him I would never tell on him and I intend to keep that promise."

Mikey had not decided which story to present, but was confident any of the three would be effective.

No one confronted him. No one gave the least hint of having removed them.

He began an incessant search for his collection, in case someone moved rather than disposed of it. As a result, he discovered not his matchbook covers but someone else's secret. It was a cigar box full of poetry in his father's handwriting. He found it in a compartment of an old trunk in a corner of the attic.

He was not enthused about reading the verses and started to put them back unread. His curiosity was too strong to resist. Mikey memorized carefully how the box had been set in the trunk and the arrangement of the pieces of paper before taking up the top one to read it. He wanted to leave no trace of it having been disturbed.

Mikey hoped to find something in them of which he could approve: a poem that was really a prayer, one that confirmed the truth of the catechism or a laudatory verse about himself. Most of all, he hoped to read one that acknowledged doubt about his father's semi-heretical views, if not an out-and-out recanting of them. He wanted so much for his father to be with him and his mother on the true, certain path to heaven.

What he looked for was not there and that which was at best proved confusing.

Their words did not rhyme and he wondered whether or not his father were smart enough to do that.

The subject matter was all over the place

The first poem was about Helen Keller, a girl whom his father had spoken of with admiration. She could not see, hear or speak; but she somehow managed to communicate. He imagined himself like that and concluded that because he was smart he would find a way to break through the barriers she had, probably more easily than she had.

His father could have written a swell poem about him if he had. It would have told how God's grace had enabled him to grasp the existence of a personal God and understand things despite any limitations.

Alas for Mikey, the poem seemed to go in a very different direction. He read it twice to see if maybe such a message were somehow there.

His father's verse read:

Helen Keller
couldn't see them
but she could touch the stars,
reaching them
on beams
of fierce personal freedom,
common sense perspective
and unshakable tolerance,
materials often invisible
to the human eye.

Mikey imagined his teacher reading the poem to the class and asking what was wrong with it.

His hand would shoot up and he would answer: "Besides not rhyming and not being very good poetry, it fails to show the hand God or his grace operating in Helen Keller."

To the next very short poem, he had no such objection, although it was not real poetry either. But he did like the thought, the feeling of it:

It was titled, "Trains."

Trains.
Have you ever noticed
they go away
but their magic doesn't.

The next one might have been about him, but only when he was younger and said a lot of dumb things.

It had the title: "The Darndest Things."

Kids say
the most awful things
and the most wonderful,
sometimes
at the same time.
And we adults
who think we always know the difference
turn into monitors and censors!
What a mistake!

Mikey didn't like the image of an adult as a monitor, who was a student who stood in the hallway and kept other kids in line. Still, the poem showed that his father realized at least some of the time that what his son said was wonderful.

The last of the poems that Mikey read showed how far away his father was from the spirit of the catechism.

The title was strangely written: "Responsibility, as in Personal."

It read:

When the word,
"personal,"
is put in front of
"responsibility,"
a good strong,
healthy
word, it becomes pregnant,
the bearer of our meaning,
of our purpose.

Again, the young boy could see his hand go up in the classroom to refute his father's writing.

"He shouldn't use that word about having a baby," he would say. "Also, the author, who would have you believe he is a poet, misses entirely the point of what our meaning and purpose are. I guess him to be a convert, one who never studied *The New Baltimore Catechism*."

Mikey thought his father should hide such writings as much as he had needed to conceal his own matchbook cover collection.

What kind of lies would his father make up, he wondered, to defend himself if his secret were discovered?

"They could never be as good as mine," he told himself.

Chapter 9

When enough time had passed since the disappearance of his matchbook collection, Michael returned to plotting how he would announce his intention to go into the seminary.

He took one last look at the hiding place. Nothing was there.

The impact was immediate. The young boy was no longer the same unabashed kid in his pride and self-confidence.

Michael was ready to graduate from the eighth grade but he would not turn 12 years old until the middle of the summer. Now, even his classmates had started to show some off-handed, but grudging respect. He was only a little kid to them, but a very determined one. To those with whom he would graduate, he was "Goody-goody Two Shoes," albeit with a very slight twist. Even though he was still only 11, they changed his nickname without even realizing it. They started to call him "Mister Goody-goody Two Shoes."

The differences between them had never seemed greater. They were already in puberty or heading toward it. He was not. It was one of the few words they understood better than he did. The girls would have considered his collection of matchbooks ridiculous; the boys would have found them interesting for a few moments; but hardly as important as he had thought the covers to be. To his mind, however, everyone would have recognized it as shamefully sinful.

Willy-nilly, he, Michael Richard Jordan, was not concerned over his classmate's opinions of him, puberty or anything involved in it. Unlike them, he did not want to impress his peers, attract members of the opposite sex, or start growing up and some day marry. Rather, his focus was on pleasing his mother as well as all others in authority. He would go to the seminary. It would set him apart and prepare him for the mantle he was to wear. It was right.

He told his parents, both of them, at supper one evening. His thoughts ahead of time had been far more about his collection and the trouble he still might be in over it. He watched both parents for any reaction that would let him know if either were holding back something.

"I want to go to the seminary," he said. It was that simple. No flourish. No dramatic timing. His voice was quiet.

His mother smiled, walked over to her son and kissed his head.

His father just nodded several times as though saying, "All right, son."

Neither of them gave any indication that he or she knew anything about his impure matchbooks.

His mother immediately began telling her small network of friends and relatives: "My little Mikey's going to the seminary, you know."

The first person she notified was her sister in the convent. She wrote the letter that night and walked to the post office to mail it the next morning. When she had finished notifying the rest of those people whom she felt "ought to know," she started telling still others. They included, among others, the butcher, the Egg Man and several of the door-to-door sales people who came to her door. Positive responses by listeners led to her purchasing their products. Almost all of this was done away from his presence, but she seemed most proud when she was able to put her hand on his head and inform someone.

His father made only one comment about it and that was a few days later when he told his son, "We will miss you, Michael. I will miss you."

When his mother mentioned about his going to the seminary, it seemed as though everyone had a story about a relative or a boy from their hometowns who had studied for the priesthood. In the majority of cases, the individual had quit the seminary.

"The Egg Man," his mother complained to her husband, "was the worst. He told us he once had a cousin who went to the seminary but got some girl pregnant while he was home on vacation. That man told that story right in front of our little Mikey. Can you imagine that?"

His father simply shook his head and then added, "What is this world coming to?"

Quitting the seminary some day or having to leave it because he got into trouble were not concerns of Michael. He knew that nothing could or would get in the way of his becoming a priest. It was his destiny to be ordained and no detour could stop that from happening, most of all no woman, not even one as alluring and as those pictured on the matchbook covers.

He actually took satisfaction in hearing about kids who had quit the seminary, so certain he was that he wouldn't.

Sister Grace, who was Michael's eighth grade teacher and the school's principal, was almost as proud as his mother was. He was her class valedictorian and won all the scholarly honors that could be had, although another boy tied with him in writing and a girl got first in art. She announced at the graduation ceremony in church that "our own" Michael Richard Jordan would be going to the seminary in the fall.

What she did not say was still a secret between her and her special pupil. Not even his parents knew yet. With Sister Grace's help, Michael had sent off a letter of application not to the seminary for the Archdiocese of Detroit but rather to one in another state, where boys prepared for life in a religious order as well as for the priesthood.

All was not certain, however. The pastor could be a problem, a big one, in giving any boy a required recommendation.

It was Michael's father who arranged the meeting with him. Trying to get this priest's permission was like asking a girl's father across ethnic lines for her hand in marriage. Only it had to be done. You could not elope into a seminary. You had to have a formal letter of recommendation from your pastor to get in.

His father and mother both attended the meeting and so did Sister Grace. It took place on a Saturday evening at the rectory after Michael's father had come home from work and the pastor had finished hearing confessions.

The pastor had a reputation for being immovable and formidable. Sister Grace knew that no boy had ever received a letter of recommendation from him. She did not tell Michael or his parents,.

If Michael felt fortified by having his parents and principal with him, the pastor had countered by insisting his assistant be at his side. As personally dominant as the older priest was, that is how intimidated and sheepish the assistant, Father Lewis, could be. The latter spent most evenings in his room making model airplanes. It kept him from suffering what he called, "the wrath of the boss."

Finished with the informalities--in which the pastor had addressed both parents by their first names—he quickly got down to the business of the meeting, the grilling of a boy who dared to want to enter one of the most exclusive clubs in the world, the Catholic priesthood.

He chose to make the first question sound innocent and friendly.

"Why, my boy," he asked, "do you want to become a priest?"

After sending the question like a shot across the tiny ship's bow, the white-haired, red-faced pastor sat sternly back in his heavily-upholstered chair and waited for not only the right answer but also the proper tone. And if the small boy sailed past this danger signal, others would be put in front of him. The priest's responsibility, as he saw it, was to winnow out the weak and the misdirected and in all righteousness refuse to write a letter to the seminary authorities. It was no less, he felt, than God demanded.

Sister Grace had briefed the pastor in as few words as possible as to what she thought of her little prodigy. She intended to let the pastor discover Michael's talents and goodness rather than make Michael meet her strong endorsement. The priest therefore had no warning that he was facing a child who could weave in and out of the catechism and Catholic teaching. If it were a right answer the pastor was seeking, this boy knew it.

To the why of going to the seminary, Michael answered, "I want to serve God."

The hint of a smile crossed Sister Grace's face. She always avoided taking on this man. Any battles she fought with him were waged below the surface and only after careful strategizing. This time she had an extremely young but competent stand-in. She understood the challenge here. The first thrust and the responding parry had augured well.

The pastor, however, was still the master. Rigid, he moved back ever so slightly in his chair, put his hand to his chin and waited a moment before delivering his next question. It was a tough one.

"Do you feel worthy to be a priest of God, my son?" he asked.

"I feel called by God," the boy answered. "If I am not worthy may God make me so. If I am, may He keep me so." It was an answer he had read in the life of a saint.

The pastor recognized it as just that, but he also had to acknowledge to himself that it was the right answer. He was not without a follow-up question.

"How do you know you are called?" the priest asked quietly. "Are you sure it is not simply that you want to be ordained for your own personal reasons?"

Sister Grace was surprised by the last part of the question. She herself enjoyed playing chess and felt the pastor was moving out and away from the fortification of his king row and doing so early in the exchange. It was recognition on his part that the boy also knew how to play the game.

"A vocation to the priesthood represents a calling by God," the boy answered. "I will know if I have been chosen to be a priest if I meet the requirements for Holy Orders, that is, if I am of excellent

59

character, possess the sufficient requirements of learning, have the intention of devoting myself to the sacred ministry, be of good health; but, most of all, if the seminary authorities approve me and the bishop calls me."

"Well said," the assistant pastor blurted out to the consternation of the pastor, who was conducting this session to avoid seeing any more young men, such as this assistant, be ordained.

"Father," the older priest chided. "This is my responsibility, not yours."

"Give me real answers, boy, not ones from the book," the pastor added, speaking directly at the diminutive eighth grader in front of him. "Show me that you can do that. Tell why you think you are worthy to be a priest of God."

A hesitation, an almost painful pause, ensued.

Then, a strange thing happened. Michael's father stood up.

"If I may be allowed to interrupt for just a moment," he said. "Michael answered that question the other day when I asked him and I'd like to tell you what he said."

"You would?" the pastor queried with smothered consternation.

"Yes," Mr. Jordan continued. "He said that he believes that Jesus wants him to be a priest and that he wishes to go to the seminary to find out if that is true."

Michael nodded in agreement.

The pastor stood up. Although he towered over Mr. Jordan, he bent down enough to look the other man straight in the eye. The expression on the layman's face, however, was as intense and direct as his own.

"Checkmate," Sister Grace mouthed to her young pupil.

"It was the perfect answer," she later told him. "I believe the pastor was so flustered that somehow he thought you and not your father had just given it."

"I will write the letter," the pastor said as he abruptly left the room.

Indeed, it was the best possible answer, except that it was a complete fabrication, an outright lie. Michael had never said anything like that to his father and was in a panic searching for an answer from his memory when his father had intervened.

Michael had never considered his father capable of doing what he had done, especially since the matter pertained to him and religion.

Recalling the matchbook covers, the young boy took a quick breath and then let it slowly out.

"Son," his father said. "The way I see it we gave that priest our best one-two punch."

"That is disrespectful," his mother said with a vehemence that bordered on wrath. "Michael did no such thing. He respects his pastor and the church he represents." When she added the latter words, her eyes shut and her head bobbed.

Michael nodded toward his mother as though she were right.

Sister Grace gently smiled at his father.

For reasons he could not comprehend, his father's comments indicated to him that it had been he who had discovered his collection, disposed of it and said nothing. In that moment, he became certain of it.

"We will have to buy you a suit," his mother was saying, making it clear that the road to the seminary was truly open and she was prepared to make all those sacrifices necessary for him to march down it.

When they got home, he would tell them his secret, that he had applied to a different seminary, one for the Dominican order, which was located out of state.

They went instead to an ice cream parlor and his father made an announcement that was even more stunning and consequential than his own.

After they had sat down in a booth and Mikey was allowed to order the banana split supreme, his father starting talking.

"Son, I'm happy for you today," he said. "It looks like you are going to be able to do what you have chosen for yourself in life. When I was your age, I wanted to go to college but I did not get to do that. I've tried to be a successful inventor. That has not happened either. It is most important to me that my son, my only child, gets to do what he wants and to be happy."

This was not his father talking. Something was wrong. He didn't usually say this much about himself.

"Daddy," he started to voice his questions, but then didn't.

"Michael," his father said, almost crying, "I also have news today about my future. I have already told your mother. Now, I am telling you. In some ways, it is a lot like yours."

Michael held his breath until his father, who was trying to make light of it, finished. This news was not going to be good.

"I too have been called in a way," he continued. "I have been drafted. I am going to go to the war. They have started calling up fathers now and I will have to report next week."

Michael wanted to cry, but he couldn't. He was too scared. Two months earlier he had gone to the funeral service for a young man down the street who had been killed in Italy.

He went over and hugged his father and finally the tears, tiny ones on a small boy's face, came profusely.

Chapter 10

It was the quickest summer of his life, but one which he would think back on in the future during good times and bad.

The response from the Dominicans was highly personal, but also somewhat hesitant. In it, Father Kilian Harder O.P., the seminary rector, picked up on every sentence in Michael's inquiry as well as in Sister Grace's resounding endorsement of her apt pupil. His comments were friendly and flattering toward the young applicant. Only the last paragraph indicated any hesitation or doubt.

Your age poses a problem. We hesitate to accept anyone who is only 13 years old unless he will turn 14 shortly after arriving at the seminary. I understand you are just now about to celebrate your 12th birthday. Sister Grace has written that you are mature and intelligent beyond your years. My first thought is for you to complete a year at a local Catholic high school before joining us. I will, however, be in your area in three weeks and would like to meet you, your parents and your principal at that point and we can then better decide what is best for you.

Upon first reading the letter, Michael was horrified. The idea of going to any high school other than the seminary for even a day, much less a year, was terrifying to him. He would be heading into an oven worse than the fiery furnace, Sidrach, Misach and Abdenago faced. The three men in the Book of Daniel in the Old Testament had escaped unscathed. He would not. The people and the environment would be miserable, intolerable.

Michael reread the letter over and over. With each perusal he found additional encouragement for his hopes of entering the Dominican seminary in the fall. All of them put together, though, did not completely remove the fear that he would not be able to go.

It was not a good time for him. He was worried about his father. In June, the Allies had invaded France on the beaches of Normandy and the casualties were extraordinarily heavy. The papers did not say how many, but he could read between the lines and he was frightened. The Germans had not surrendered, as some had predicted they would on D-Day. His father had 17 days from his announcement in the ice cream parlor until the day he had to leave for basic training or "boot camp." He worked at his job until the day before he left.

"We need the money," Michael heard his father explain to friends who had come over to say good-bye.

On the Sunday before he left, his father borrowed a car and took his wife and son to Belle Isle. He had a surprise for Michael. It was a fishing rod and reel, with lures and a tackle box. They spent much of the afternoon fishing first in the river and later in the lagoons. They snagged nothing but an old tire, about which they laughed hard and long.

"This fishing pole will catch its share of fish before it's worn out," his father promised.

Michael gripped it tightly as they went for their last long stroll in the woods. His mother, meanwhile, sat on the running board of the car and watched the freighters pass on the Detroit River. Traffic was unusually heavy because of the fighting and the fact that the city was shipping out war materiel.

"If anything happens to me," his father said, "I don't have much in the way of worldly goods to leave you. But I have always considered this island mine, even more so since you and I have shared it. I now bequeath it to you."

"Oh Daddy," Michael moaned, using the name he had called his father since he could first speak.

There was nothing more to say, even though he tried to find something.

The next day Michael and his mother and son saw their soldier husband and father off at the large, huge bustling Michigan Central Depot train station. Other men had come there to go off to war. Many families waved good-bye as a few were able to hold back their tears at least until the train had pulled out.

Standing on a bench, Michael gave his father a tight, urgent hug and whispered into his father's ear, "Come back, Daddy. Please come back."

"I will if I can, son," his father said while holding him in a tight hug. "Think of me, Michael. If you do that, I will be there for you."

And then he was gone.

The next several days passed slowly and then one afternoon, Michael answered the door and there stood a tall, heavy-set priest accompanied by Sister Grace.

"Michael, this is Father Kilian," the nun said.

Mrs. Jordan came up behind her son at the moment.

"Father," Sister Grace continued, "this is Michael and his mother, Mrs. Jordan."

"Hi, Mike, Mrs. Jordan," the slightly graying priest said. Until that moment, the young boy had never liked the name, "Mike," but the priest said it in a way that fit him fine.

"I understand Mr. Jordan has just gone off to the army," the Dominican continued, "I hope he's all right and that you are well."

"Oh yes, Father," Michael's mother replied. "We're all fine. My husband is too. He's in basic training and he says it's tough on someone his age, but he's doing well. We were expecting you tomorrow. Pardon the house, I..."

"Please, Mrs. Jordan, you don't have to apologize," the priest replied. "My plans got changed at the last minute. I tried to call, but apparently you do not have a phone."

"We are getting one," she answered, embarassed. "It was the first thing my husband did when he found out he had been drafted, order a phone, but there's a long wait with the war on. I'm sure we will be getting one fairly soon."

"That's good," the visitor replied. "May we come in? I hope this is not inconveniencing you too much."

"Oh I'm sorry, of course," she replied. "Here, over here. This was my husband's chair. It is very comfortable. I'm sorry it's a little worn. I was going to a find a doily to cover the spot. I just didn't get a chance."

"Please," the priest said. "I feel very comfortable in your home. You remind me of my mother and how she acted under similar circumstances."

"Mikey," she said. "I mean Michael. Would you get his hat?"

"Of course," he said.

"How could she call me that in front of him?" Michael asked himself, hiding his irritation behind an accommodating smile.

Michael returned from the next room and sat down on the chair he had brought in for himself. The priest waited for him to sit down and noted how far his legs hung above the floor once he was seated.

"Mike," the older man said. "I've had a chance to talk to Sister Grace today and she has said some very good things about you. She spoke well both of your character and your intellect. She said you are deeply interested in anything connected to the church."

"Yes, Father, I am," he said. "And thank you, Sister, for saying nice things about me." Inwardly, however, he felt relief. This moment had come and no one knew of his character flaws. The one connected to his matchbook collection was safe, known only by a family member who was occupied taking basic training in another state.

"Mike," the priest continued, "I want to ask you something. At the seminary, all the boys in your class would be older and bigger than you are. To be honest with you, I think you may find at times they would tease you about this. Do you foresee a problem with that?"

Michael quickly sized up the question. He decided the priest was more open to his going to the seminary than his letter had indicated. Apparently, Sister Grace and he had had a long talk. The fact that she too was a Dominican probably helped. Still, he couldn't be certain.

"No, Father, I don't," he answered. "I know that younger kids get picked on, but I can hold my own. I actually find it easier to be with older boys than those my own age. I get along with everyone. That's the truth."

If he had said, "That's the truth!" after his statement about getting along better with older boys, Michael would have been telling a lie. It was not exactly one when he said it after his comment, "I get along with everybody."

"Tell me again why you want to become a Dominican," the priest asked. "I know you said it in your letter, but I would like to hear it from you."

"Well," Michael began. He then hesitated for a second, because he had learned the power of a well-placed pause. The answer was immediately at his beck and call, but a hesitation gave the impression he was reflecting while he was talking. It also tended to catch the other person's attention better.

"As Sister Grace told you," he continued, "I am very interested in everything about the church. It is God's means for saving the world. The Dominican order has played a big part in helping people to understand God and his church and to protect them against heresy."

"That, young man, is better than I could have put it," the priest said.

"I can't say that I know a lot about what St. Thomas Aquinas wrote," the 12-year-old continued, "but I certainly want to do so. He was a wonderful member of the Dominican order and he gave the church its theology."

"Well, Mike, that is true and not true, but this is not a theology exam," the priest. "Thomas clarified and organized theology, but the church did have it before he was born."

"I did not mean to imply they didn't," Michael backtracked.

"You know, young man," the priest continued. "I can't help but think that my suggestion that you take a year of Catholic high school before coming to the seminary would be a prudent one. Sister Grace has argued strenuously with me that it would not be necessary, but we cannot be too careful in such matters and we would lose nothing."

Michael and Sister Grace had played chess together. She knew he was capable of strategizing in ingenious ways but not even she could have ever guessed what Michael's next move would be.

"You know, Father, I respect what you are saying," he responded. "I read your letter on the point and I have thought about it. I don't particularly want to attend a Catholic high school and probably shouldn't if I feel I have a vocation. I think maybe a better idea might be for me to go to the diocesan seminary for that year."

The priest's face became pale. He was out recruiting for the seminary that he headed, pure and simple. He saw himself as a religious version of the college coaches visiting the homes of athletic prospects and talking to them about joining their sports programs. Father Kilian's role was not a great deal different, although the boys he was interviewing were much younger and the positions he was ultimately trying to fill were on the altar rather than the playing field. It was one thing to put a candidate off for the year and another to let him attend the competition's school. And this kid was an extraordinary prospect.

Sister Grace looked at Michael. She knew his move was a feign, but this priest didn't.

"Maybe I can do something, Mike," he said. "We at the seminary need to consult about this. I have to ask God for divine enlightenment and so do you. Pray that God will make this clear to all of us."

"I have some tea I started when I saw you coming to the door," Mrs. Jordan said. "I hope you will have some."

"Yes, of course," the priest responded. "That would be kind. Mike, do you follow the Detroit Tigers? How they going to do this year?"

"Yes, I do, Father, they're going to be great, but so are the St. Louis Browns," the boy answered. "The Browns have never won a pennant before. I'm afraid this might be their year to do it."

That same day, the priest left town to return to the seminary. The next day, when he got back to his office, he dropped Michael a note asked the young boy to fill out all the required documents "just in case."

"This could be my greatest recruitment ever," he told himself. "He could be my all star."

Michael did pray about it as suggested and within two weeks his prayers were answered with an unqualified acceptance letter.

He then began to attend to other urgent matters in his life, finding ways to make money. He already had a paper route, but the family needed more income than that from him.

Even though he was only going on 12 years old, Michael found there were actually a number of jobs open for him. With the war, came a tremendous manpower shortage. He could have worked at the supermarket, where his mother had taken a job, but he would have had to lie. He would have had to say he was 14. He wouldn't do that. He tried to apply to become a theater usher, but again the same problem arose. Several of his classmates had found work, but they were two years older than he was.

His paper route, that he rode his bike on in the mornings, did not make him much. In fact, his earnings came out to less than $1 a day. He needed more. Because of his family's poverty, they would not have to pay tuition or room and board at the seminary. Those who could not afford it didn't have to come up with the money. But other expenses such as clothes, school supplies and busfare to get there and back posed real problems. He did not want to be as burden on his mother.

Michael finally found work. It was caddying. He could make $1.25 for a "loop," carrying a player's clubs for 18 holes. The caddy master was reluctant to give the small boy a chance, but the war had depleted all his regulars and many of their substitutes.

The first day Michael caddied, he was exhausted by the time he got to the ninth hole. Like the 18th, it was near the clubhouse. Michael hoped the golfer would quit there, as he had heard some occasionally did. The member and the rest of his foursome went to the tenth tee and drove off for that hole. By the time, they got to the long hill on the 15th hole, the golfer picked up first the bag and then his 11-year-old caddy and carried both up it.

The incident was the talk of the golf course, members and other caddies alike. The next day, however, Michael was again sitting on the caddy bench waiting for another loop. The caddy master passed him by for three days, but on Saturday tried him again. The member later took time out to tell one and all that the little kid was great. He had an eagle eye for following and finding a golf ball no matter how deep in the rough or woods it went. Also, he seemed to know all the rules for caddying.

Within weeks, Michael was making as much as $4 to $5 a day, taking on two loops a day and getting good tips. He was also phenomenal at finding lost golf balls and could get as much as $1.25 when he found and sold a pre-war one he occasionally found.

Once again, his peers were hard on him. They saw he blushed if they used foul language or told raunchy jokes. They loaded on him with details of their sexual exploits, real and imagined, and called him every foul name they could think of. His naiveté left him. The blushing stopped. So did the fun they got out of riding him.

From their comments, he learned or thought he did, but it was a very fractured picture and he knew it. More disturbing, they raised questions in his mind, but these were often bizarre. When he did get answers, these went nowhere, perplexed him and made him even more aware that there were pieces of the puzzle, big ones, missing. Of such matters, he knew little and understood less.

In acquiring knowledge, if not always understanding, his instinct was to choose the right door, knock on it until it opened and then grasp reality from whichever facts and pieces of information were available to him. It worked in math, geometry, chess, mechanics and of course religion. Even in sports it helped. But sex wasn't proving to work out the same way. For one thing, he had no one he could dare ask. What hurt was that other people did seem "to get it."

Michael got hold of a pamphlet, "Boys and Purity," by Father Charles McGuire. It started off with some promise, telling about how confused boys could feel about girls and sex, but then the booklet itself started saying things and not saying them at the same time. He threw it away in frustration and disgust.

Finally, he gave up on the subject and decided to forget about it.

"Later," he told himself.

It was near the end of July and a wonderful thing was happening. His father was coming home on a furlough because his basic training was over. He had called on their new phone and told them he hoped to be assigned to what he called "The States," because the rumor was they were not sending soldiers who had children overseas. But then he got his assignment. He was heading for Europe. He couldn't say that exactly because it was classified information, but the soldiers knew what different designations meant.

When his father arrived home, he didn't want to talk about the army at all. He told his wife and son that another soldier had taught him a Spanish saying, *Que sera, sera,* "Whatever will be, will be."

Michael didn't like that expression and he was not happy about the army or the war.

His mother had asked him to pray every night that his father would not have to go overseas. He had begged God, had made promises and had asked the Blessed Mother to intervene on his father's behalf. Neither God nor Mary heard his prayers and he did not know why. When he asked the priest in confession, the confessor answered, "God works in strange and mysterious ways. He has a reason for what he does. We just do not always know what it is."

His father's spirit perked up the last few days he was home. He took Michael fishing twice and they caught fish both times.

"See, I promised you this pole would catch fish," his father said.

Then, his father left on the train and was gone.

Michael tried not to think about him and what might happen. He put the fishing pole away in the attic and started getting his things together to go to the seminary.

Chapter 11

Michael's mother had an expression from her childhood that encapsulated his anticipation of going away to the seminary: "Waiting for your ship to come in."

As a child, she had believed that there was a ship, that it would come in and that all would be better. She commingled it with another, more sacred expression that she spoke of very seldom and with whispered awe, "the second coming of Christ."

Her son's expectations were more deeply rooted in this world. They were about seminary life and all he anticipated it would mean to him. Everything bad that ever happened in his day to day life would be corrected. Instead, he would be given the opportunity to experience all that he had ever hoped for and more.

He let himself have and build on these feelings of anticipation, ones that often are more rewarding than the realities that follow could ever be. His only pain came from the fact that it had not yet come to be.

Also, Michael anticipated that, in the coming days, he himself would be bigger, more mature and even smarter.

As he had watched his grade school classmates growing up, he suffered the frustration that these life changes were not happening to him in the least. He was certain that, by the time he returned from a year at the seminary, he would be much taller. His arms and muscles would be heavier and his face would have lost that "little boy" look that plagued him and encouraged people to say he was cute. He probably would be better even at playing baseball and certainly at basketball, although he was not completely confident he would ever improve all that much.

The young boy sensed instinctively that his much-regretted tendency to say or do awkward things would melt away at the seminary as the pressures he faced lessened. Michael was almost there, but as much as he worked at it, he still embarrassed himself. For example, he tried to impress people with big words and was flatly awkward when anyone ever tried to compliment him.

"My teacher estimates that my IQ is nearly 200," he twice boasted to other people. Twice was two times too many, he came to realize. Their comments such as "Oh that's nice" did not mean they were impressed but rather that, if they believed him, they didn't care.

It was only after someone wrote the number "200" on a piece of paper and stuck it on his desk that he realized how grandiose his boasting must have appeared to others; but, even worse, that it could be used against him.

As a result, he resolved to tell others little about himself, but at the same time to accomplish everything he could. He would speak with actions rather than words. He would do all he could to excel at his studies, at which he would be more than apt.

Michael wanted to know Latin and maybe even possibly be able to speak it before arriving at the seminary. He had already started studying a first year Latin book that someone had given him. He was more than half way through it two weeks after he first opened the textbook. He was not always certain how to pronounce some words yet, especially the ones with the letters "a" or "c" in them, such as the Latin pronunciation of Caesar. Was the "c" at the beginning of it hard or soft and what exactly did that mean?

Going to the seminary was not principally about him changing, but rather the ways in which his world around him would. It was not so much that he would grow up, but that others would recognize that he had developed and matured and would care that he had done so. He would sense it from the reactions of Father Kilian. The Dominicans would like him and realize his mission and his love of all things connected with the Catholic church.

His brilliance and determination to be good—characteristics for which other kids had made fun of him—would be respected at the seminary. There, others were striving for the same thing. He would be challenged rather than put down. He would be appreciated. Of this, Michael was certain.

To adjust better and be fully responsive to the exciting world that he would encounter in the seminary, he had already decided to make a change, a big one: his name.

Father Kilian had called him, "Mike." That suited him fine. "Mike," he would become. "Michael" would be left behind at his house and at his grade school, as "Mikey" earlier had been.

Although he had seen photos of the seminary buildings and grounds, he could not quite picture what they would look like. The vision he had lacked a central focus. He was surprised to realize that he had never pictured how the chapel might appear. He saw pieces, but not an image of the whole. That was all right. He would simply wait.

The day came.

If his anticipation had been as high as the sky, the reality was to prove better. He got off the bus and was picked up in an old Ford and brought to the buildings that housed the seminary. Upon first seeing them, he opened his eyes as a professional photographer might a lens, hoping to capture every detail and bit of light.

Father Bart, the seminary's disciplinarian, accompanied by an older student, met him at the door. The priest immediately recognized his newest charge as obviously his youngest.

"Welcome to your new home, Mike," he said. "I am Father Bartholomew, the disciplinarian here at the seminary. Father Kilian has told us good things about you."

As he abruptly turned to leave, he added, "Supper will be in an hour. In the meantime, Jeremy here will show you around. He is a second-year student."

Mike stood transfixed. The priest was wearing his religious habit. Although he had seen pictures, he had never actually encountered a Dominican priest or brother wearing one before.

The religious habit worn by the members of the Order of Friar Preachers, as they were historically known, was dramatic and even beautiful.

Mike's skin tingled with excited awe as he saw for the first time the Dominican habit he anticipated some day wearing.

The priest before him was dressed in a fulsome tunic made of white wool with a floor length foot-and-a-half-wide scapular covering his front and back. In addition he wore a dramatic cape with a hood, called by the Dominicans, a *"capuche."*

Father Bart, as he was known to the students, was girdled with a wide, black leather belt, from which hung a 15-decade or 170-bead rosary with a large crucifix dangling at the end.

No Paris designer could have created a more striking effect or stunning habit for a religious figure.

In addition to white, Mike would learn, the Dominicans also at times donned a black *capuche* and the *cappa magna*. The latter is a black cape worn from November 1 through the Easter Vigil. It is used at mass, at the major hours of prayer and when a member of the order is preaching.

The black hood and cape gave the Dominicans their historic nickname, "Blackfriars."

Mike formed at that moment an impression and a conclusion that he would never get over. These were the clothes for him.

The second-year student, Jeremy Wilson, introduced himself, took his bag and showed him "the place." This included the dormitory, his locker, the study hall and the many areas used for sports and recreation. The library was enormous and friendly. The school had an outdoor swimming pool and even a two-lane bowling alley.

The central building was set on a small hill. It served as the chapel. Behind it was his new home, a yellow brick structure from the 1920's. It stood three stories high and had two wings. The rooms were quite expansive, especially compared to the small, two-bedroom house in which he had been born and lived.

The chapel was another revelation. It was more attractive than any of the churches he had visited in Detroit. Its walls and ceiling were covered with frescoes that depicted the life of St. Dominic and pictured the prominent Dominican saints. The altar was by far the most beautiful one he had ever seen. The statues of the Blessed Virgin and St. Thomas Aquinas, which appeared as the highest form of art Mike could imagine, flanked it.

By way of contrast, his parish church seemed little better than the Veterans of Foreign Wars assembly hall on John R street. Services for St. Mary's were in a basement, while the pastor and congregation waited for the parish's coffers to fill up and the war to be over so that the supplies needed to build the desired church could become available.

Surrounding the buildings were almost one hundred acres of land, mainly grass, which the young seminarians would keep cut with a fleet of hand lawnmowers. The seminary's gentle rolling hills and large, open campus areas for playing baseball and football captivated the city boy.

And then, there were the woods on the property. Mike felt as though he had brought his friends with him and being given a chance to make new ones. Many of the trees here were quite different from those on Belle Isle, a low, wetland, almost marshy environment. Here, several hundred miles farther south, the rolling hills and sandy soil supported vegetation that was quite distinct. His *Michigan Trees* book would not help much here.

He noticed that some species of birds were different also and he wanted to be able to identify these.

All of these seminary features brought him a sense of delight and pleasure. It was as though he had moved from the cold to the Caribbean, from a slum to the other side of the tracks and from a shack to a mansion.

He had arrived at the foyer of heaven.

Mike did not see it as a lush summer camp or getaway, but rather as a shrine to the intellect and to the holiness of God's church. It seemed a peaceful place where serious studying and striving for religious goals were supported and rewarded. He had reached the Promised Land with the pledge of yet an even greater life.

He wished his parents could have come with him to see this place. They would have been happy for their son.

Mike wrote both of them letters that day. To his mother, he described the chapel and the kindness of the priests he had met. His other weekly letter went to an APO box. He did not know when or where his father would receive it, but he wrote that he was happy in his new life. He half wanted to ask about the war and whether or not his father had seen combat yet, but was afraid lest the answer be "Yes."

He started meeting the other seminarians at dinner. Out of 112 students in the school, 54 were freshmen. This reflected the fact that the numbers in a class were whittled down every year as some members quit or were asked to leave. The number of seniors was 17, less than a third as many as there were in his first year class.

His classmates came from around the country. Several were from the South and had never seen snow. Two others were from Detroit. He was indeed the youngest and smallest in the school. As such, he stood out in the crowd or got lost in it, depending on what was happening.

As days turned into weeks, the other students proved friendly, although several told him they had thought at first he was some seminarian's younger visiting brother. When they had choose-up games in sports, he was the last player selected. He was kidded by his fellow students and even by several faculty members. His unofficial nicknames were "Mike, the Midget" and "Mike, the Mascot."

In class, it was another world. He shone with a brightness even more spectacular than he had demonstrated in grade school. The competition here was tougher. Several of his classmates knew full well how to pull down "A's." This meant 93% or higher. The grading system at the seminary, however, used numerals rather than letters. His papers were regularly returned to him with 100's or 99's on them. One professor, who didn't like giving out 100's, would never mark a test as a result higher than 99.

He seemed not to make mistakes and kept ahead of his class in every textbook. If there were a point of disagreement of fact between him and a teacher, he was the one to bet on as being right. Occasionally, he was wrong, but few people ever realized it because he first tested the waters before offering an opinion or stating a fact.

Holiness became a somewhat more complex issue than it had been in grade school. There, he had operated under a veneer of doing what appeared right or, more often, simply what he was told to do by his mother or teachers.

The seminary had rules. These were in writing and they governed matters such as talking in study hall, running in the corridors, addressing priests as "Father" and being on time for each and every function. They had little to do with sanctity, but he observed the letter of every one of them.

In his striving to be a saint, he assiduously read the book, *The Imitation of Christ*. For centuries, this volume had guided seminarians, nuns and priests and even the laity in their attempts to follow piously in the footsteps of Christ. It espoused submission to God, reflection, humility and self-deprecation. It focused on the perfection of Christ as the ideal model and attempted to show the reader what He wanted and expected from each person in the most specific details of their lives.

Mike saw the book's precepts as an extension of what he had read in the catechism. The latter was more instructive and authoritative than *The Imitation of Christ*, which was more intense and introspective in its attempt to draw the individual to a spiritual melding with Christ as a person's model.

The young prodigy could not content himself with the small volume's reputation for being an aid to meditation, so he attempted to focus on its core message. It was a mountain at which he kept chipping. The more he whittled it down, the greater became his certainty that it was the Church that mattered and obedience that counted.

Certain phrases kept going over and over in his mind. They were:

"Christ, as the head of the Mystical Body, is the head of the church."

and

"We must submit to the church as we would to Christ."

All this represented easy spirituality for the young prodigy. It focused on authority and submission. He felt that he needed to synthesize and thus to embrace the utter simplicity of it.

"To obey," he wrote down on a piece of paper he kept in his desk, "is to love."

He felt so strongly about it that he looked for opportunities in which to practice the virtue of obedience. He was less ostentatious in his submission to authority than he had been in grade school. He didn't speak about it but he saw obeying church laws and seminary authorities as the clear and only way to heaven and to holiness.

Other boys began to see certain aspects of "Mike, the Midget" as rather formidable. Students who were used to being first in their class in grade school found themselves a distant second behind him. A few, who chafed at some of the rules and the rigidity with which they were sometimes enforced, began to treat him as part of the established structure rather than one of them. Even his youth and smallness began to be resented rather than turned into a matter for teasing.

Mike, ebullient and happy, was painfully slow to grasp the undercurrents working against him. The first few waves of it he did pick up on but he dismissed them as a mere continuation of the affectionate teasing he had encountered in his early weeks at the seminary.

He had become helpful to a couple of other seminarians, assisting them with their homework and seeking their companionship, but he soon found himself swimming upstream even in these relationships.

The first report card day changed his status at the seminary. During an evening assembly, every six weeks, each student's name and grades were read off as all sat expectantly and listened in study hall. For many it was an indication whether or not they were meeting the scholastic standards required for them to continue in the seminary. The order in which they were called out by the rector was that of class rankings. The freshmen were first.

Father Kilian, after a short speech explaining the seminary tradition, took in his hand the first report card. He read the name: Michael Richard Jordan and announced: Algebra, 100; English, 99; history, 100; religion, 100; Introductory Science, 100; music, 99;

conduct, 100. A buzz went through the stunned study hall. It was loudest at the back of the hall, where the seniors sat. No one in the room had ever heard any grades, the likes of which the rector had just called out.

Mike Jordan, stiff and disoriented from the student body's reaction, got up from his desk to go the front of the study hall and receive his report card from the rector.

Something then happened. The president of the senior class, Eddie Golf, who sat in the center of the last row, stood up. He raised his head and chin in a gesture of pride and started clapping. Others around him picked up on it. The noise they created waved to the front of the room and first-year seminarians, who had just that morning said how tired they were of "The Midget." They now found themselves joining in the applause.

He was everything they had said he was, but somehow he had just transcended all the complaints, standards and even traditions of the seminary. They were irritated by and proud of him at the same time. This, however, was his moment and, led by the school's student leader, they willingly acknowledged it for him.

Mike felt in awe of this response to his grades. He did not understand what it meant, but he liked it. He cast his eyes down as he walked forward. Father Kilian, standing on the stage, normally had to bend down slightly to hand a student his report card. The rector too added a gentle clapping to the students' applause. The top first-year scholar, however, was so short that the priest had to come down off the stage in order to have their hands exchange the grade sheet. The students, seeing the awkwardness of the situation, broke out in an affectionate laugh almost as loud as their clapping. Mike smiled, made a small, embarrassed wave and sat down.

Only then did Mike realize that his grades had not only been extraordinarily high, but also truly historic. For the first time he saw that brilliance could be not only an asset, but also a burden. He loved the applause, but it was putting him on pedestal. If someone wanted to take a shot at him, it couldn't be with some petty, jealous little arrow. He was too respected on his dais for them to do damage. However, just as the rector could not reach him and still be on the stage, so no one could be a simple, close friend. It afforded a loneliness that would be with him all his days.

That day changed Mike as much as it did his classmates' attitude toward him. He found himself less and less the outgoing, always trying-to-please little kid. Now, he was becoming more serious, more reserved. He knew he would forever be a riddle to others.

Mike walked frequently on the seminary grounds, often by himself. In addition to his fondness for the trees, he taught himself the names, habits and classifications of butterflies, birds and even insects.

He usually carried a book with him. He would sit under a tree and read about ancient history and dabble in mental puzzles.

The word went around that he was a "child prodigy," although no one said it to his face. They did write home about it to their parents. Someone left a book out about child prodigies for him to read. He saw it and ignored it.

Mike occasionally entertained the idea of answering some questions wrong on exams to deflate the viewpoint circulating about him. He did not want to be first forever, but neither would he ever find satisfaction in backing off from his brilliance. He could not and never did.

His brains were God-given, as his mother had often pointed out to him. He had no right to misuse or deny their power to understand or to ask and answer questions.

His destiny was still there and his brilliance would lead him to it, but he was aware more than ever that the journey was going to be a lonely one.

There was a lake on the seminary property stocked with fish. He decided that when he returned from Christmas vacation he would bring his fishing pole back with him. He would catch them and let them go as his father had taught him. It would remind him of the one person who for even just a few seconds had separated him from his great loneliness.

Each week he wrote his mother and father two letters and received two from her. They told her he was doing well in his studies, reading *The Imitation of Christ* and enjoying walks outside. Mike told humorous stories about his classmates as though they had happened to him. He also said Father Kilian had asked to be remembered to her although this was not true.

Chapter 12

In the future, whenever he pondered what had gone ill with his life, Mike's thoughts would return to that Sunday morning, December 3, 1944. Each detail, every minute of his time, all the words spoken were etched in his memory: waiting for one more review that somehow might change them or let him slip back to the time of his childhood that had died there and then.

On Sunday mornings, the seminarians attended two masses. The first at which they took communion was said at 8 a.m. There followed the same routines as the rest of the week. They then had breakfast and a half-hour morning recreation period.

At 10 a.m., wearing their suit coats when at this one set time each week it was obligatory, they attended a second mass, a solemn high one during which various parts of it were chanted, incense was used and three priests were on the altar. Two of these performed the roles of deacon and sub-deacon. A senior seminarian was master of ceremonies, two younger classmen served as acolytes or altar boys and a fourth student was the thurible or incense pot bearer and kept it swinging to keep its small coals burning.

The audience for the Sunday solemn high mass usually included a few lay people, often a couple of visitors as well as several seminary employees. The nuns, who cooked and did the laundry for the seminarians, also attended this ceremony. They had their own chapel, where every other day one of the priests said daily mass for them at 5:30 a.m.

Looking out into the audience this Sunday morning, Mike was stunned. He saw someone who looked very much like his mother even to the headscarf she wore over her head. He stared and focused on the figure half-hidden by a pillar and his heart began to pump in a way he thought others around him could hear.

"Please, dear God, help me," he prayed, deliberately trying not to think about the only reason that might have brought his mother here, if it indeed were her.

As mass ended, he knew that denial would not work. Father Kilian stood next to the small seminarian put his hand on the boy's shoulder. Tears appeared in Mike's eyes and started to roll down his cheeks. He knew and understood everything, but still hoped it might not be as completely as bad as his imagination told him it was.

"Your mother is here," Father Kilian told him. "She would like you to stay in chapel so she can talk with you. She's a wonderful woman, Mike."

The other seminarians filed out of the chapel and looked at him. Many of them either knew or had figured out what was going on and tears started to well up in their eyes also.

Michael sat next to his mother in the pew and held her hand. Neither spoke. She saw he understood.

"How?" he asked. The tears had stopped, but his small face remained wet.

"They didn't tell me exactly," she said. "I just got a telegram and it said he was killed in action."

That was it. His worst fear. No reprieve. Nothing would ever take it back. It was not a dream, not a nightmare. His father was dead, dead forever.

No more tears came. There was no shout, no screaming out, "No, God, no." There couldn't be. He was in chapel. If he had yelled that or anything else here it would have been blasphemous. His mother and the rector had foreseen this.

He thought of the words that the priest had once said to him in confession, "God works in strange and mysterious ways."

The woman next to him was his mother, who needed her little boy to care for her now more than ever. He was now all she had. He took her two hands and squeezed them in his.

"Oh Mother, it must be so hard for you," he said. An emotional let up followed as he focused on her and off his father and himself.

"What do you know about it?" he asked.

"I just got the telegram and then a letter," she said, her own emotions seemly having dried up and been replaced by calculated words.

He stopped for a second. Any letter would not have come at the same time as a telegram, but well after it.

"When?" he asked.

"This week," she replied.

"No, the telegram?" he inquired.

"That was last week," she said.

"But why, why didn't you come sooner or call?" he asked.

"I just wanted to make sure," she said. "They make mistakes, you know. Mikey, I did not want to tell you and then find out it was not true. Besides I had your letter in my hand. You were doing so well. You were so happy and you had several exams coming up. Did you do well on them?"

"Mother," he said, "Daddy is dead." He caught himself and withheld his criticism of her for bringing up about his exams. And he ignored an even more severe one he wanted to make for her not telling him, for treating him like a baby. No, he would not chastise her, especially now.

"I have to go to the bathroom," he said and got up and walked out of the chapel. He went to the one in the infirmary, where he knew no one would be or could hear him. Once there, he expected the tears to gush, as they never had in his life. He first whispered the "No" he could not say in the chapel. Then, in a complete surprise, he threw up his entire breakfast.

He quickly began to clean up his mess, carefully wrapping it in paper towels and flushing them down the toilet. He wanted to make certain no trace or indication was left. He began to worry that someone might interpret it as a sign of his immaturity. Then, suddenly, the reality of his father's death once again fell upon him like a smothering blanket.

As he looked around the infirmary, he wished that he were sick. Then maybe the news he had just received would be some form of feverish delusion rather than reality. He could concentrate on getting well instead of figuring out how to come to grips with what he had been told as true.

Mike began to pace and the monotony of his steps started to give him respite when he suddenly recalled his mother sitting alone in the pew in chapel. He knew he must return there. He must help her.

He passed two fellow students on his way back and they looked him square in the face and then diverted their glances downward. They knew; they all did. That made it the more real. And it let him realize that he would not be able to tell anyone, certainly not in his own way and time.

His mother had moved from sitting in the pew to kneeling. Her rosary was in her hands and the beads were moving fast through her fingers. It was what she did and how she did it when she was most nervous.

She had grown older than he remembered her. Her hair sticking out the sides of her babushka, seemed grayer even if it were not; her back more arched against the front of the pew, her face more worn. She glanced at him and then back at her beads.

They didn't talk much more. She shook her head when he asked if there were anything he could do or say. Time passed and he could hear the other students filing down the main corridor toward the refectory, where they would have lunch.

Father Kilian stopped in the chapel and asked whether either were hungry. They both shook their heads and then went out into the lobby with him.

The priest spoke in an intimate, supportive way that he seemed not to be able to do in the chapel.

"Mike," he said, choking as he found the word, "I'm so sorry. You too, Mrs. Jordan. I speak for the rest of the faculty. You have our prayers, as does your husband and father. The high mass was said for his soul and we will each say one for him this week."

Mike did what otherwise would have been too embarrassing for him. He gave the priest a hug.

"Mike," the priest continued. "I want you go home with your mother. Christmas break will start in two weeks. You go home and come back after the holidays. You are up on your studies. You will miss little."

It is not what Mike would have wished. In some ways, it might have been easier for him to stay at the seminary, where he had been so happy; but that was not a real alternative either. He would have been miserable there also. At least in going home, he could help his mother and that thought alone seemed to give him any relief.

The two left that afternoon by bus for Detroit. The 300 miles home took them not only back to a life he had gladly left, but also to a climate that was colder. As he watched out the window, he saw some small patches of snow on the north sides of embankments and hills. Gradually, it became more than just splotches. Then he saw some on flat ground and even a little on the side of hills that faced the sun. By the time the bus arrived at its destination, he was looking at several inches of snow on the ground.

Mike wondered what the weather was like where his father had died and was buried. He struggled with two images of him, one from when he was alive and the other was of him lying in the cold foreign ground.

His mother showed him the letter. It was written by his commanding officer and addressed to his mother. The address correctly listed her first name as Anne, but did so without the "e" on the end. It was a spelling she considered "non-Catholic."

It read:

Dear Mrs. Jordan,

By now you will have received official notification from the army that your husband, Cpl. Richard M. Jordan, has died defending his country. As his commanding officer, let me express my own sympathy for your great loss. He had just joined my company so I did not know him well, but please let me tell you the men admired him. He died valiantly fighting on the front lines against a well-

entrenched force and his death was quick. His death and those of the others who have sacrificed their lives to defend our country will not be in vain. They will not only win the war against the forces of National Socialism but also help bring about the peace.
    Capt. Robert R. Holbrook

Michael needed to learn the facts. How had he died? What had happened? Had it been a bomb, a machine gun, a bayonet? Without knowing any of this, he felt there could never be real images. His father deserved for his only son to know.

Later, Mike would do extensive research about his father's death. He would find out little. Seemingly, his death was not important enough for the army to record any of the circumstances. Capt. Holbrook, who had written the letter, was killed a week later, he would subsequently learn.

What he did come to realize was not a happy conclusion. His father died fighting in the Hurtgen Forest, between Belgium and Germany. The battle seemed to Mike quite unnecessary. As in the Civil War Battle of the Wilderness, the generals had their men fighting trees as well as soldiers. Some historians would later compare the Hurtgen Forest to Gettysburg and would point out that the Allies' generals poured more troops into that forest than General Meade had at his disposal at Gettysburg. The number of casualties was similar. Yet, few Americans would remember the tragedy of Hurtgen Forest. It would be overshadowed by the Battle of the Bulge several weeks later.

Mike later would believe there was a conspiracy to obliterate the memory of the Hurtgen Forest and the men who died there. It was an embarrassment that could and should be laid at the feet of incompetence on the part of the American military leaders.

His father, as best he could determine, died the first night he was on the front line. How, the records did not tell.

Mike never buried his father. There was a mass at St. Mary's. All the school children attended it. Father Kilian came for it. The World War I members of the Veterans of Foreign Wars were there, many in uniform. A flag was ceremonially folded and presented to his mother.

But none of this buried his father. He needed him now. He had never realized that in the past. Now, he did but it was too late. His father was somebody to whom he could have talked about his feelings and his problems. He would have listened. Mike knew that now.

At home, his mother and he spent a lot of time sitting together in the living room, but they spoke little. She would glance up at him and give him a short, sad look and he would return one. Occasionally, she would begin asking him about the seminary and his studies and expect him to give cheerful accounts of his accomplishments as though nothing had happened. He accommodated her, often answering the same questions she had asked two hours earlier about grades that he had received or compliments he had been given.

"You are happy, aren't you?" she would ask.

"Yes, Mother, very happy," he would answer, only half-aware of the irony of the question and answer himself.

For Christmas she gave him a sweater and a book about the life of the Blessed Virgin Mary. He gave her a new headscarf, at least partially because her old one reminded him so painfully of seeing her in the chapel that day and remembering what her presence there had meant.

Finally, the day to return to the seminary arrived. With it came relief at again being able to leave. He feared that each of the priests and his fellow seminarians would come up to him and remind him all over again of his loss. It did not happen.

His mother sat in her rocking chair the night before he left. Her fingers were moving as though there were rosary beads in them even though there were not.

"Michael," she said. "There is something we need to talk about. It pains me, but it is necessary."

The young boy always tried during such an introduction to a conversation to figure out what it was all about. He prided himself at being consistently able to surmise. This time he was confused. Did it have something to do with going back or not being able to go back? Was it some secret about his father? He squirmed in his seat, unable to guess.

His mother took a deep breath, but did not continue. This was a bad sign, a frightening one.

"Michael," she repeated herself word by word. "There is something we need to talk about. It pains me, but it is necessary."

"Yes, Mother, please tell me what it is," he begged.

"It is something I discovered and have waited a long time to tell you," his mother said. She then waited for him to guess everything so she did not have to say it.

And he did, almost completely. It was his matchbook collection. She had been the one who had found it. He should have known. Somehow, after all that had happened, it no longer seemed as important as it once did.

"You found it, Mother," he asked, "In the rafters."

"Yes," she said. "I was so ashamed for you."

He had no apologies to make, no lies to concoct. It was sad. That's all it was.

"I'm sorry," he said, but he meant only to cover any pain that she had felt.

"You can't do things like that and become a priest," she said. "It's a sin and you know it. Your father, when I told him, did not want me to throw them away. He said they were yours, but he did not understand the way a person who grew up Catholic does. I do. I knew you wanted to be a priest and you would have to give up things like girls and any impurity."

Michael wanted to leave the room, but he could not get up. He intended to say nothing, but he did.

"Mother," he said looking into her stern eyes, "I'm sorry I collected those. You were right to throw them away. I will never do anything like that again. I do want to be a priest and it was a sin."

She still sat there. His act of contrition and firm purpose of amendment were not enough to remove the disappointed look on her face.

"I confessed it to a priest and God has forgiven me the sin I committed," he lied.

And then as he watched, his mother's body relaxed in her chair and she smiled at him.

For her, all had become well with the world, at least as far as her son was concerned. God had forgiven his sin.

Chapter 13

He had been home several days when his mother handed him an envelope addressed to him in his father's handwriting.

"This was in his effects," she said matter-of-factly.

She did not speak her husband's name or even refer to him as "your father." Mike understood this mannerism that might seem strange to someone else. It was much easier to avoid direct reference to the man who had been such an enigma probably to both of them and now was past that.

He thanked his mother for the envelope, and put it on his lap. It was still sealed and he wondered whether she might have steamed it open and decided she had not.

Mike did not open the envelope or even think about doing so. His feelings were too painful and, he knew at a level he could not acknowledge, still too negative toward his father to do so.

He left it at home. He did not even want to take the missive back with him when he returned. Nor did he not bring his fishing pole to the seminary after Christmas, even though he had promised to do so in a letter that his father probably never got to read. He was angry with the man whom he had asked to come back from the war and who had not, but who had died instead.

His father had been killed. Had he been careful enough? Perhaps he might have exposed himself to gunfire needlessly. The young seminarian had read that GIs who were smart and aware of the dangers they faced lived longer. Could his dad have avoided going to war? A Catholic could be a conscientious objector. Why had he not? So what if he were in prison instead? He'd be alive today. Also, another thought...If he had gone to college, he might have been able to become an officer. Didn't they survive longer?

Was there something Mike could have done? Could he have talked his father out of going, made him go AWOL? Could he have warned him, told him to be more careful?

He did, you know. That's what he meant when he asked him to come back.

But all that was over now. Whatever had happened to cause his death, however avoidable it might have been, his father would not return. Mike and his mother would not be going to the train station to meet him. His dad would never be coming to see him at the seminary. He would not be at his ordination or first mass.

To Mike, without his writing his father twice a week, the seminary was not the same. Those letters, and his thinking about them ahead of time, had started to become the most meaningful moments he had spent in his time there. During them, he had begun to discover a different part of himself, a reflective one in which questions were more important than answers. When something happened such as the whole school applauding his report card, it took on some reality only after he had written a few lines asking his father what he thought it meant. He had not bragged, but shared his confusion and wondered what it would represent for the rest of his life.

That person was dead. He was in heaven, or, if he had not died in the state of grace, in hell. This was confusing. Such a possibility, no matter how remote, was terrifying and unbearable.

Almost any other boy, under the circumstances, would have presumed his father to be in heaven. It was the easy consoling thing to believe. His mother said his father was with God. She was certain of it. He had been a good man, a kind one. He was not, however, a true believer as Mike and his mother were. Scripture and prayer book passages identified faith with salvation. And how strong had his father's been? What if, in the trenches and at the last minute, he had ranted against God, had disavowed his belief, his faith? Mike did not think his father had, but he was haunted by the possibility it could have happened.

His father was dead. It was over. He had been judged.

God's judgment was the most final of all things.

Mike lived in the future. His mission was there as had been going away to the seminary. Now the religious life as a Dominican and the priesthood were. Heaven awaited him, a reward for dedicating his life to God and church.

His father had no future. His past was everything and each of his deeds, including his comment that one religion is as good as another, had been put on the scale. Mike could pray for him, but supplications in his father's behalf were relevant only if he were in purgatory and Mike was trying to deal with the fact that he might not have made it that far.

He prayed for his father anyhow, but did not get to sleep easily at night.

Things had changed in many ways after he returned to school.

Mike himself had. Some of his clothes no longer fit. He could see space between his pants cuffs and his shoes. His suit could no longer be buttoned. He was growing.

Still, he was the smallest kid in the school by far. A classmate of his had been almost as short as he but he was among the four boys who did not come back after Christmas. Two had not being doing well in their studies. The other two were complete surprises to him.

Mike could not comprehend why a student who could make it would give up trying. All right, so some seminarian or other might have become interested in girls. That made some sense, especially if he were lured into it. But why quit otherwise, when the seminary was so great and the priesthood such a treasure in so many ways?

Had not God called them also?

Another seminarian, a second-year student, left in the middle of January. It was Jeremy Wilson, who had taken Mike around on the first day. He had been kicked out for having repeated an off-color joke. The classmate to whom he told it had reported him and the friendly sophomore was simply gone the next day. Mike later learned the joke that other students were afraid to quote lest they suffer the same fate. The dismissed student had jokingly described a girl's bathing suit as "Two bottle caps and a cork."

Several months later, Mike found a fellow classmate hiding in the cloakroom, where the students hung their suit coats until they needed them for Sunday mass or a special occasion. The kid was crying almost uncontrollably. Trying to console him didn't help.

"What do you know about it?" the kid screamed at Mike. "You're too little to understand."

Mike left. He realized the boy had become homesick and was getting it out of his system. He did not leave the seminary and the two of them never again spoke of the incident.

Winter was changing his habit of walking around the grounds and communicating with nature. An oak tree that ruled the southwest corner of the property was a particularly good friend. He still did visit it, but not as often. Mike attempted to get interested in basketball, but he didn't take shots because it was a rare occasion when he could hit the basket, much less sink one in it. He did, however, become skilled at dribbling the ball and aggressively stealing it from opposing players.

Some of his grades dropped a little because he did not feel like working quite as hard as he had. For him it meant receiving a 96 in history. His conduct, Latin and English grades never went below 100. No one applauded his report card, but he did determine to keep up his own standards and ignore theirs, no matter who they were.

His letters to his mother were ritualistic. What he wrote about had little to do with his day-to-day existence. He quoted from spiritual books he was reading, talked about the priests and asked about her. She responded by telling him about novenas she was making, extra masses she was attending on Sundays and what the pastor said in his sermons. They were letters from two lonely persons each trapped in their own shells.

The other students left him alone in his sadness and he was relieved and thankful for it. One would occasionally start to tease him and then stop in the middle and give him a sympathetic look.

His hand was not the first to go up in class. It was the last and then only when no one else knew the answer.

His school job, performed on Wednesdays and Saturdays, was cleaning the guest parlors. It was a task that was usually assigned to an upperclassman, but he was given it and made the most of it, cleaning the rooms until they were spotless. As he did so, he would sometimes wonder how different it might have been if he had been told about his father's death here instead of in chapel.

He was blending into the seminary not in the sense that the other students saw him as one of them but rather because he was accepted as the school brain, a rarity, almost a treasure.

The other students never seemed to get over regarding him as someone who had lost his father suddenly, tragically and in the war.

In weekly touch football games, teams had six players on a side. It was understood that because he was extra small and could not really block anyone the team with him on it was allowed to have seven players. No one complained about it.

Mike became comfortable with being taken for granted. He watched as other students sat in study hall during recreation and copied the disciplinary rules five or ten times for various infractions. He once had to do it when the whole class was punished because several kids were talking during a speech from a visiting missionary. There were no exceptions, but he most certainly had not been one of the miscreants.

What was hard for him was the lack of excitement as the months passed. He needed jolts in his life. One came weekly from the anticipation that built up on Saturday nights. Every two weeks and sometimes oftener, the seminary showed a full-length movie on a large screen in the study hall. It was always one that had been given an A-rating by the Legion of Decency, usually a film at least one or two years old. *The Song of Bernadette* was one such title. It was the story of the young girl who experienced a vision of the Blessed Virgin at Lourdes in southern France. The movie was a very popular one in theaters throughout the country and had won several Academy Awards. The seminarians got to see it even though it was less than a year old. Other movies were usually either Westerns or comedies.

He was especially fond of films that featured the comedian Joe E. Brown. The broad smile and friendly humor of the comic brought laughs that helped him temporarily put aside his sad bag of memories.

Rumors circulated among the students that there would be one at 7 p.m. this Saturday. These, as much as the films themselves, helped to break the monotony as the school year dragged on. Certain students had channels to find out earlier than the rest. Others checked with them about the latest possibility. Someone would say that such and such a seminarian had seen the large round metal cans in which the films were shipped. He may have been able to read one or two words such as "The story of..." or "Red..."

Mike treasured the possibilities as much as anyone did. The movies themselves were not always great. The expectation, however, was. He desperately needed little things to which to look forward. They were distractions, not only from remembering his father's death and tragedy, but also the loneliness that gnawed at him.

He looked for other little things. He played Monopoly, chess, cards, sports and crossword puzzles. He had to stand on a chair to do it, but he also played pool rather well. His interests ranged from the deeply spiritual to the ancient world. The librarian found him checking out a new book every day or two. The number of books he read was phenomenal, whereas many students considered two or three a year worth mentioning.

The newness of the seminary along with its scholastic challenges filled his veins at first and created the highs upon which he came to rely. He pushed himself hard physically, running and playing to his very limits. Intellectually, he did the same with his mind. None of it was ever enough. He started drinking coffee, several cups at a time, and this too along with a high sugar intake helped for a while.

All this tied in with not only his father, but also his mother. His father was out there, pushed away from his thoughts, but still meshed in the knots of his psyche and memory. His letters to her meanwhile started growing longer and more fanciful. She loved them. He invented stories to tell her and then had to be careful after she wrote back, asking for more details.

Father Kilian censored the mail before it was sent out. It had to be handed into him without being sealed. He knew he would probably get a call by the rector. It never happened, although on two different occasions the priest made references in conversation with Mike to something that had been in letters he had written home to his mother. Still, the big confrontation which he was inviting did not occur.

Then along came the state tests.

In high schools throughout the state, students took tests in several major subjects, including English, math and Latin. The seminary had not deigned to participate in the competition in the past. This year, the faculty decided to try, some students believed, because of their young prodigy, Mike Jordan. Only the freshmen and sophomores would compete.

There was no fanfare preceding the tests. On the day before they were administered, students were told about them. The first class or freshmen took them in Latin, English and algebra. The sophomores had geometry instead of algebra. These would then be graded and the test results used to determine which student in each subject would represent the school in a statewide competition.

At supper one evening, the top three scorers in each category were announced. To no one's surprise, Mike came out as the top freshmen on all three tests. No scores were given. After the third announcement and the student body had clapped appropriately, Eddie Golf stood up with a water glass in his hand and said, "I propose a toast to Mike, not our midget anymore, but Mike, our marvel."

Mike blushed, a reaction he did not have even when the same, senior class president had initiated the clapping after the grades were announced on his first report card.

The names of those who finished second and third were then read out. As a student could represent the school in the competition for only one subject these runners up had to wait until the faculty decided for which subject Mike would be selected before finding out which of them would be chosen to go to the "finals."

Mike was given Latin.

He took the challenge. The small, brilliant seminarian did it by borrowing books of second and third year Latin texts as well as several books written in the language. He read them as others did novels.

Mike stoked his competitiveness for the occasion. It was the kind of adrenaline surge for which he had been looking. It temporarily dispelled the morose cloud under which he had walked since learning of his father's death. He was always with a Latin book of some kind in his hand. At the same time, his other subjects did not suffer as he consistently pulled down 100's or, at worst, 99's.

Father Bart drove the six young competitors to the regional competition site 40 miles away. The tests were multiple choice with the correct answers to be marked in with a lead pencil so the tests could be graded electronically. Mike found himself on a campus of a local college. It was non-sectarian and a bit baffling to the young seminarian. The coeds seemed unusually pretty and often dressed in ways with which his mother would have strenuously disagreed if she had an opportunity to do so.

He had a good chance to notice them well because he walked out a little after half way through the allotted time.

Another student followed him out and commented, "I just went blank too. That was hard."

Mike shrugged his shoulders and said, "Yah, I guess so."

The other student would have been amazed to know that Mike had not only completed the test, but also felt he had scored the supposedly-impossible 100 on it.

Sending Mike off to the scholastic wars bearing the school colors and reputation was a matter of pride for students and faculty alike. His Dominican seminary had as a motto over the gym, "*Mens sana in corpore sano.*" The phrase translates, "A healthy mind in a healthy body." The school, following the Dominican tradition, plowed far more resources into its development of the mind than it did the body. It did not, for example, participate in inter-scholastic sports, although its students did play a series of two games in basketball and baseball against the local diocesan seminary.

Michael Jordan's results did not disappoint: he took first in the state. Father Bart heard from an official of the college where the test was taken that the young prodigy had scored a 100, but it was not confirmed.

For Mike, the announcement of his achievement was overshadowed by what else happened that day. Germany surrendered. Everyone was celebrating. He went to the coatroom and cried. The end of the war in Europe meant the GIs would be coming home. His father would not be among them.

Chapter 14

It was the last day of his freshmen year at the seminary, a beautiful, warm Sunday in June. He and all the other students were already packed and ready to leave to go home for the summer. All that remained was the final solemn high mass, lunch and then the graduation ceremony for the senior class. He would not see the place again until he returned late in August for his sophomore year.

As for the graduates, they would be going on to the novitiate in early August. There on August 15, they would be invested in their religious habits as members of the Dominican order. Life would become dramatically different for them as of that day and not the least of the changes would be their names. They would assume new first names and become known as "brothers."

The members of the senior class were still, for the most part, blurs to Mike. The seminary was both a family and caste system. The students were friendly, knew one another's names and even were aware where they came from. They had some sense of regard for individuals but the different class members rarely mingled.

The seniors were not one but three steps above him. They were different and this started with experience. They had lived through seminary years in which they had not only matured, but also survived a system in which more than half of their classmates had dropped out or been asked to leave. From this, they had learned not to become too close to anyone else lest they be hurt if or when that happened to either party. Individually, each had found out that what best helped a seminarian avoid such a cut, whether voluntary or not, was a focus on one's goal. Still, there always awaited the possibility of something unforeseeable, a capricious twist in the selection process.

Mike looked at the graduating group in wonder. He sensed they knew a reality he was just beginning to learn. Put simply, it was the enormous distinction between the religious life and "the world." This dichotomy came up repeatedly in sermons, in various instructions, in confession, in spiritual guidance and even in conversation. The more the students identified with the milieu of the seminary as well as the priesthood for which they were preparing, the more they assented to the differences between those two realms.

His calling was a personal one from God himself and was defined in sermons and guidance books as no less than "seeking perfection." His vocation to be a religious and priest put him on a high road upon which a lay person did not, could not walk.

"The world," as defined for the seminary authorities and the "spiritual directors" they provided, was not in itself evil, he was told. In fact, it was presented as being just short of such in so far as it was not something good and holy as was the calling from God to be a priest or a religious.

As a result of the dichotomy, the world was the realm of the laity, members of a different and lesser club. It was one to which you could not belong and still be on your route to the perfection that the Almighty demanded of those in the religious life and the priesthood. This path alone was the royal high road for the select of God.

The world, on the other hand, was easy to join. It was where Mike would have ended up if he had fallen from the exalted path he had chosen in going to the seminary. He never had any idea how difficult this road could be until he saw other people dropping off it. Certain seminarians whom he had never expected to see leave and simply go out into the world did so. And, once these had, they did not come back.

Mike did not realize that he was getting a mere introduction to the distinctions between the clergy and the laity of the church. The intense, focused particulars of the differences would not come until after he had entered the novitiate and even more when he had joined the priesthood. Then, it would be as though the 13 years he would spend in the seminary were a period of digging a deep and wide trench between himself and the lay Catholic or even more those who were not of his faith.

For now, what he had to give up to get a place on the high road were the freedom to leave the grounds, the right to exercise his own will in broad areas of his life, the use of money in the sense of having any in his pockets and all or anything to do with having a personal relationship with a girl.

These would be just for starters. In entering the one-year novitiate, he would give up his family for the most part, change his first name and avoid almost all contact with the outside world. After completing this intense introductory formation period, he would be required to take vows to obey his religious superiors, not to possess "worldly goods," and to refrain from marriage and sex.

A growing awareness of these realities was what most separated the fourth-year students from the freshmen. To the average senior, lower classmen were not only naive, but also still bore the scent of the world. The millstone of seminary training had still to grind them into finer flour.

All of this made it the more surprising that on this Sunday morning before the graduation ceremony Eddie Golf, a senior, took Mike for a walk.

"You have been extraordinarily nice to me," the younger boy said. He wanted to ask "Why?' but he didn't.

"That's what I wanted to talk with you about," the graduating senior said. "I want to apologize."

"Apologize?" Mike asked.

"Yes," Eddie said. "The minute I saw you I felt you didn't belong here. The seminary faculty makes more than its share of mistakes. To me, you were obviously one of them. We all come here too young, but you more so than any other student I had ever met."

Mike was stunned and could not talk. This older student had been his hero all year, an inspiration.

"I will tell you how much I resented it," Eddie said. "I am the one who gave you the nickname, 'Michael, the Midget.' I even told Father Bart that I thought they were making a mistake and had accepted you at too young of an age. He told me it had not been his decision."

At this point, Mike looked down and started to turn away.

"Then," Eddie continued, "the rector read off your grades. I realized at that moment that you were something, really something."

Mike wanted to say, "Thank you," but no words came. This senior had also just said that he did not belong here.

"It was the same with the state tests," Eddie continued. "I thought the rest of us needed to acknowledge that you are gifted. It is something right and good to take pleasure in the accomplishments of our brothers rather than to be jealous of them in any way."

"You are kind to me," Mike said.

"We all have to sweat at studying and learning as well as at doing what is right," the older student said. "You don't even seem to have to work at being good. It's phenomenal."

"The latter is not entirely true," Mike corrected. "It has something to do with my mother. She is a very good person."

"I'm not sure that is always true, Mike," Eddie responded. "I may be out of order in telling you this, but I saw what she did when your father died."

"What do you mean?" Mike asked, frightened by the direction in which the conversation was going.

"I saw that you were told about it in chapel," Eddie said. "The other students did too. We all said that is the last place we would want to hear that kind of news. Under those circumstances, you couldn't scream, if you had needed to."

Mike was horrified by the idea of publicly showing rage under those or any other conditions. It was the very kind of thing that he feared might have sent his father's soul to hell.

Eddie saw that he had lost contact with the young freshman. His underlying purpose had been to reach out to him and make a connection. He himself had been lonely and lost in his first year and he wanted to do for Mike what no one had done for him, but he knew he had gone too far.

"You miss your father, don't you?" Eddie said, changing the subject.

"An awful lot," Mike replied.

"I've always been afraid of losing my parents," Eddie confessed. "Whenever I heard the phone in the lobby ring, I thought it was someone calling to say that one of them had died."

"I don't think it was so bad that they told me in chapel about my father dying," Mike defended weakly. "My mother..."

"That's all right, Mike," Eddie interrupted. "I shouldn't have said that."

"It's O.K.," Mike returned. "You made me feel really good when you clapped about my grades. I thought all the kids would resent me for them."

There had been so much more that Eddie had wanted to tell his little protégé, but alas the channels were clogged. Somehow, this much younger boy with whom he was walking would need to be encouraged to develop not only his intellectual and spiritual sides but also his humanity and love of himself. Unfortunately, both of these seemed to burn with such a low flame.

Eddie dropped trying to use words. Instead he took the little hand of the other in his much bigger one and squeezed it hard. He then gently punched him in the shoulder in the way in which young men do to tell each other that they are friends and are all right. Mike punched him back although having fully stretched his arm and he only managed to land his fist into Eddie's wrist.

Eddie wished there were someone like himself with whom he could talk and share doubts about his vocation and choice in life.

"I'm afraid," he might have said to such a person, "that I would have left long ago, but it could have meant coming to terms with a world that I had been taught to fear and look down on." If he shared that with this first year student, maybe Mike would understand about being human and having clay feet, something he seemed incapable of grasping. Prodigy that he was, the young seminarian could not begin to understand such facts of life.

He and Mike returned to the building in time for lunch. The graduation program followed it at noon so the students could get off and make their trains or buses and parents driving their sons home could get on the road.

The ceremony took place in study hall, which also served as the school auditorium. The graduating class had only 15 students in it. Benediction, a short ceremony with trappings similar to those of a solemn high mass, would then be held in chapel.

After the rector and Father Provincial had addressed the graduates, senior class president Edward Golf was introduced as the valedictorian.

Mike had not known that Eddie would be class valedictorian or, for that matter, that there would even be one. He had not been much interested in the upcoming ceremony because it so little involved him. Now, it did.

"At other graduations," the senior began, "valedictorians speak of their classes splitting up and individuals going into the work world or on to college. It is an end and a beginning to them. To us here today, it is neither. We are on a journey in an effort to seek perfection. We have not attained it, although some among us have more than others. I am not one who has, as my Greek professor will gladly testify."

The students laughed.

"Of course," he said. "No one ever attained perfection in Greek, at least since Aristotle and Plato. We'll have to see what will happen, however, when our school's young marvel starts taking that ancient language. I went for a walk with him this morning and encouraged him to study real hard. Only kidding, you guys."

Loving the attention, Mike joined heartily in the laughter, even though in a more sensitive mood he could have felt it aimed at him.

"We are told to avoid the world," Eddie continued. "But we are not asked to ignore it. There is a great world war being waged in the Pacific Ocean. Many young men our age or just a little older are fighting and dying there. Every day at mass we are encouraged to pray for them. That is good, but we need to remember them in other ways, and not just the Americans. Some young men of our generation will not live to see the next. We cannot forget them. We need to remember that we are no better, no more special than they."

"Also, it behooves us today to remember those who started with us, but who have left the seminary and, as a result, are not on this platform. They were our classmates, our friends. Again, we miss the point if we feel as a result of our being here we are any better or more special than they."

The student body and faculty both started to stir. This was not the usual seminary valedictorian speech. It was about the outside world and it was one of their own forcing the audience to think, jarring even those whose minds had wandered during the earlier speeches and had gone on to thinking about what they would do in the summer.

Not all the faculty members liked what this student was saying, as their uncomfortable body language had begun to show. Chaos was the result when one did not follow the script and this young man was not. Seminary training like that being given in East Coast prep or other select schools was based on the opposite of what he was saying. The core idea of such education was that its highly-select group of students are special to start with and all others are less so. The purpose of the institution is to afford them educational advantages that will make them more so.

The disagreement with the speaker's jarring views ranged from mild to strenuous. He had said that those who had left the seminary--especially the ones who had been told to leave—were not the flotsam of the voyage.

Unspoken, but never to be contradicted, was the concept that the seminary represented survival of the holiest and smartest. No one was ever to look back as he had dared to do.

Father Bart, the school disciplinarian, was not one of the faculty members who held to this thinking. He started an applause that was met with hand clapping by many of the students. But others of the priests and even a sizeable number of the students grasped the implications of his words and did not join in..

Pleased to see the student who had given him unexpected applause at the beginning of the year was receiving the same, Mike joined in enthusiastically.

"I want to thank the faculty and my classmates for the last four years," Eddie continued. "This is a good class, a good school, a good seminary and a wonderful religious community to which we belong. I speak for my whole class when I say that."

These comments met with a more wide-spread applause.

"Having said that this is a good seminary, a very good one in which God must be pleased with the efforts of all," the valedictorian continued, "I add a note, a question of my own. We all here know of Blessed Martin DePorres, a lay brother from Latin America, and a member of our own Dominican order. In the church, he has attained the rank of blessed, just one step short of sainthood. Someday, we can be certain, he will be canonized as a saint. Brother Martin, as we know, was a Negro. Yet, as we look today at ourselves at our seminary and our province, we fail to see any members of his race as part of our community. I say this not in criticism but as a challenge to us all."

The crowd hushed and the eyes of several faculty members rolled to the ceiling in obvious displeasure.

"And finally," he said with a slight bow of his head, "I want to thank God and his Blessed Mother for being so benevolent and kind to me, to members of this graduating class and to all of us. In addition, while I know we are all in a hurry to get out of here, I want to extend this thanks to the faculty and to the entire student body."

Then, in an extraordinary gesture, Eddie Golf named from memory every faculty member, followed by each student in the school. Each of their names he expressed in an intimate, personal tone as though he were speaking to them as he might a friend or a brother.

When he finished, he turned and walked off the stage. No one, realizing his speech was over, applauded at first. Then, those who did see him as a brother and friend started, slowly and then louder and louder, until they began picking up and banging down the backs of their seats to make even louder noise.

The rector, sensing that many faculty members were not pleased with the boisterousness of the response, finally ordered every one to chapel for Benediction.

Mike saluted Eddie when he passed his desk, as he would have his own father.

Chapter 15

In coming home for the summer, Mike was like a competitive swimmer climbing out of the pool. He could still feel the water on him, but the draw of gravity upon returning to land was awkwardly removing him from his far more comfortable environment.

His house presented a special shock. The rooms in which he had lived the first 12 years of his life seemed so tiny that their limited proportions gave him a sense of walls closing in on him. His living space was no longer the casual and expansive freedom of the large areas in the seminary buildings. It was instead a small, five-room cottage with an attic and half basement that encompassed him.

Once he had settled in at home, his mother became almost as omnipresent as God. Except during the day, when she worked at the grocery store and he was at the golf course caddying, Mrs. Jordan was always there, in the same room or the next one.

More than a presence, she was an overwhelming reality. Together, they did shopping, went to the park, and attended daily and Sunday mass as well as Tuesday evening novenas. Occasionally, in each other's company, they went to see movies such as "How Green Was My Valley" or "It's a Wonderful Life."

Though overwhelmed by things his mother did and said, her son never outwardly demonstrated impatience or rebellion. It was as though he were still her infant and they continued to be connected by an invisible, life-sustaining cord. On her part, lest he disappear out of her life as her husband had, she intended to keep him in sight as much as possible. Mike, feeling a continuing responsibility to care for her, was thereby kept subservient. He would have considered it a sin to offend or in any way deliberately irritate her. The commandment that demanded, "Honor Thy Father and Thy Mother," was core to his thinking. Now the sole parent, she more than ever did not hesitate to take advantage of getting her way in even the most trivial of matters.

Mrs. Jordan used the memory of her late husband, stating her wishes or demands in such expressions such "Your father would have wanted you to..." or "I know your father would have told you to..." Each time he knew it was a way she had of enforcing her own will and still it worked. Other than in these expressions, neither of them ever spoke or reminisced about husband or father. It would have been too painful.

All these things were etched in the little book of life rules that he believed had to be obeyed. Since he was a baby, such instructions and regulations represented an additional list of God-ordained commandments. They were only corollaries of the Fourth Commandment, to honor thy father and thy mother, especially the latter. No matter what these represented they shared the same, great obligation for him as the Moses-given commandment itself. Now that he was older his sense of obligation had become even sharper. He had no thought or strategy to change his mother or to counter her demands. It would have been easier for the 12-year-old Mike to get into Briggs Stadium and hit a home run off Detroit's star pitcher, Hal Newhauser, than for him to say the simple word "No" to her.

In addition to his new awareness of the yanking around he got on his mother's puppet strings, another factor helped torpedo any possible closeness or intimacy between them. He now feared that his mother was capable of knowing his most personal thoughts and feelings. Had not she discovered his matchbook collection even though it had been hidden perfectly? Had not she then judged him on it, without warning or consultation? Finally, had she not destroyed it without a qualm?

In his mind, he could never challenge her right to penetrate his privacy whenever she deemed it necessary. He was surprised that his father had even dared question her authority, as when he did so about the matchbook covers.

While he had been at school, he had a way to hold her at bay. By fictionalizing in his letters the realities she sought, he had faked the required obsequiousness. Now, under her eye, that was no longer possible. Getting caught at it in any way would have been inconceivable.

His only time that was truly private was when he was caddying or in transit to and from the golf club. To get there, he took the streetcar to Royal Oak, a northern suburb, and then walked to the course. Occasionally, unknown to his mother, he would hitchhike at the entrance to the golf club, trying to get a ride from a club member who might be driving into Detroit. When he succeeded, he could spend the saved carfare on a comic book, one that he would then read and discard before arriving home.

His mother and the seminary officials had spoken despairingly of all comic books "and their culture." He acknowledged to himself that they were "stupid," "beneath me" and "my addiction." Once, he had purchased a science fiction magazine with a scantily clothed woman on the front cover. In the illustration, she was being harassed by aliens. After buying it, he stopped in an alley, glanced at the pictures and read the story titles. Then, certain he would be seen, he threw it in a trash can, brown sack and all.

Mike listened with perked up ears, as he had the summer before, to other caddies discussing girls and what all they claimed to have experienced with them. He understood about kissing and he didn't. Even though he had continued to acquire many seemingly relevant facts about the subject of sex since last summer, few if any of them made sense.

Without passion or deep interest, he continued to follow the war, now being waged in the Pacific. The fight for the island of Okinawa was finally over, with the Japanese losing almost 100,000 men in the battle. He wondered for brief moments whether there were boys in Japan now missing their fathers as he did, but he also felt the patriotic impulses that came from the hurrah of the news that resulted from GIs killing a lot of the enemy.

Dick Roiles, an 18 year old with a bad limp, ran the caddy shack at the golf course and told him enthusiastically about an army private on Okinawa being responsible for killing 58 Japs.

"Roiles," as the guy wanted to be called, liked to engage the young caddy and just about anyone else in conversation.

In a spurt of rare openness, Mike told him, "My father was killed in Europe. It took the fun out of the war for me." Then he added, "Please don't tell anyone about my dad."

"I won't," his new confidant promised. "I got my own story that I don't wanna tell people. I volunteered for the army when I was 16, went to basic training and then broke my foot, real bad. I was discharged, but my older brother and my best buddies in training were sent to Europe. Their ship was sunk and they both drowned. I would have been with them. I only tell ya that cuz yer Dad died and I know how ya must feel."

Mike gave him a nod of recognition, although he was not certain whether or not to believe the story. He hoped he would not find that Roiles was lying. If his account were true, then at least someone he knew out there had that same empty feeling inside him as he did.

One day, Roiles asked him, "Do you know about those Schuyler Scholarships? You're a smart kid, a real smart one, and your father was killed in the war. You could get one of them."

"What are you talking about?" Mike asked.

"This club member, Mr. Schuyler, has been making a lot of money off the war. I mean big bucks. So now he gives out this scholarship every year for some deserving caddy to go to college. I bet you could win something like that. I just thought I'd tell ya."

The idea of a scholarship hit Mike like a gust of wind coming from an unexpected direction. It was scary and caught him off guard. His education was supposed to come from the Dominicans and from the church. It was inconceivable that it could ever be from anywhere else. And yet, a scholarship! He was not tempted to change course, but it was the first time he had even had a notion there was a different one, an option.

"Thanks, but no thanks," he said quickly.

"Just thought I would tell you," his companion responded.

"I ain't that smart," Mike lied.

He never told Roiles or anyone else personal things about himself, such as the fact that he was Catholic, that he was in the seminary or even where he lived. Most certainly he never spoke of his grades. At the golf course, he was somebody else, and he liked that. His identity, he once bragged to himself, was as secret as that of Clark Kent. On the Saturday following that thought in which he compared himself to the alter ego of Superman, he admitted to a sin of pride in the confessional.

His caddying let him forget about many of the pressures on him as a result of his being a seminarian and chosen for a mission. Here, it was day to day. No goals. No high standards to meet. He liked that, even though it afforded the opportunity of becoming extremely bored .

He hardly looked at the calendar. Life was in slow motion for him. Returning to the seminary was off in the future, along with everything else about him.

Then, came the atomic bomb and the surrender of the Japanese.

The war had climaxed and then it was over. Just like that!

Even though his mother faithfully kept up with the news on the hour over radio station WCAR, she uttered only a single comment to him about the earth-shattering world events, "We have to remember to thank God in our prayers for his ending the war. Your father would also want us to do that."

Mike did not know what to make of the atomic bomb or how to feel about the war ending. Often over the months, he had walked out of the room and stood on the porch while his mother listened to the hourly Cunningham News Ace news on the radio. The war had stopped being an absorbing curiosity and drama for him the day he learned his father had been killed. Until then, it had been about winning and was a compelling thing. Now, it was personal, a strange anomaly that caught him up and squeezed innocence out of him. It had gone from being understandable, to complicated and perplexing beyond his capacity to comprehend.

The now 13-year-old knew too much about some matters to feel he grasped them with any certainty. When he looked at the optional ways of viewing matters such as war and peace, life and death, good and evil, and other dualities, he became confused, then stultified, painfully so. He envied everyone else. They did not seem to be afflicted with his problem. They went from "a" and "b" to "c," while his logic got lost somewhere in the end part of the alphabet.

As a younger child, he had made lead soldiers, melting the metal before pouring it with a small ladle into a variety of molds. At the start of the war, the people who had died on both sides-- even the young man he knew down the block--were more like these leaden figures than real people. That was before his father's death. Eventually, he threw out the lead and the objects he had made with it, painfully mindful as he did so of St. Paul's commentary about putting aside the things of a child.

All of this went on the inside of the young seminarian. He spoke of it to no one. It was a matter of a dialogue between himself and an inner voice, not something to be shared. He knew that if he talked of it, his words and sentences would be different than were his thoughts.

This inner struggle between two sides of himself presented irreconcilable views of reality. It was, he did not doubt, the underlying cause of what happened the day the war ended.

It was August 15, 1945, the feast of the Assumption of the Blessed Virgin Mary, a "holy day of obligation," in the Catholic church. He had gone to a high mass at the parish before caddying. There were very few golfers this day. He thought at first it was because of the holy day, but quickly realized it had to do with the announcement that the war had ended.

He and Roiles stood next to the caddy shack and pitched pennies. He was not good at it until he started losing and the pressure began mounting for a comeback. The caddy shack manager was the opposite. He had a natural talent for tossing the coins, but easily lost his concentration.

Roiles, who had been not only distracted but also nervously excited, took the two pennies Mike had just won and put them into the young caddy's shirt pocket.

"I have a surprise for ya," he said. "I think you're going to like it."

The truth was that Mike did not usually enjoy surprises. They represented individuals trying to force him to do something he did not want to. The word, "surprise," was a cover for an attempt to trick or cheat him out of his lunch money or some other possession. Or, even more typically, it was to show him a dirty picture or the figure of a naked woman on a comb or the bone part of a jackknife. They wanted his reaction in order to embarrass, outsmart and then laugh at him.

The only person he could imagine trusting to show him a surprise was Roiles. He had not betrayed his trust yet and he had had opportunities.

The older boy took Mike behind the caddy shack and had in his hand a brown sack. In it was a bottle. He pulled just the neck free of the opening at the top.

"Here," he offered. "It's real expensive stuff."

"What is it?" Mike asked.

"It's snappes whiskey," Roiles answered. "The best. I got it from my uncle. I been saving it. I figured with the end of the war and all, you know. This is the best way to celebrate it. We'll drink to yer father, you know. He'd want that."

Mike was surprised that Roiles was starting to sound a little like his mother.

"And to your brother," Mike said.

"What?" Roiles said. "Oh yah, to my brother."

"And to the guys you were in basic training with," Mike added.

"Yah, to them too," his companion said, raising the bottle above his head.

Mike was shocked that he had so quickly agreed to share the whiskey with this older kid. He had said he was going to do it. Now, he had to. There would be consequences. This could be worse than the matchbook collection. Maybe, he didn't, though. Perhaps, he could still back out.

"Maybe, we ought not do this," Mike offered.

"Mike," Roiles yelled at him. "My God, yer father died fighting this fucking war and ya can't even take a drink in his honor and in honor of the other guys what died. Who the fuck are ya? A fucking sissy?"

The language that Roiles used immediately told Mike that the back door he had hoped to use in order to escape was not available to him. If he really did not want to put some of the snappes down his throat he would prove himself as hard as Roiles was. He would have to go nose to nose or risk losing his incipient friendship.

"Well," he said, hesitating for a second to find the best path for himself.

In a flash, he knew what he would do. Simply put, he wanted to take a drink of Roiles' liquor. He wanted so to drown, if only for a moment, the war and his father's death with it. He wanted pleasure rather than pain, forgetfulness instead of the unending, ever-present responsibility and sense of duty. He even grabbed the bottle in order to swig it down more quickly.

"That's my man," Roiles said, congratulating him.

Mike kept hold of the bottle and took a second drink.

His companion's face broke into a smile and his hand patted Mike solidly on the back.

Roiles took the bottle and swilled down a large gulp.

Mike reached for it back and had one last slurp. Some liquor poured from his lips and on to the floor.

The back of the caddy shack started to undulate and his legs to grow weak. His insides warmed. He wanted to say something, but his mouth talked funny.

"Come here a minute," Roiles said. He then took the bottle and poured some of the whiskey on Mike's shirt.

"Why did you do that?" the younger boy slurred. "Shit. Now, my mom's going to know for sure."

It was the first time in all of his 13 years that he had ever said "shit" in the presence of another person. It warned him that he was not himself and in trouble. What his buddy has just done by pouring liquor on him clinched it.

"No, don't ya worry about it, little Mike," Roiles said. "Look, you're a little woozy, but that will wear off. The stink won't. You

116

fucking tell your mom that a member had a bottle in his golf bag and spelled some on ya. Ya ask her to wash your shirt very first thing ya get in the house. She'll believe ya and feel sorry that ya smell of whiskey even after you're taken the shirt off for her."

"Jimminee!" Mike exclaimed. He had done something terrible, but if he were clever enough he would not have to suffer the consequences.

Chapter 16

Mike's second year in the seminary started off not well and got worse. As he moved on and upward toward his goal and mission, the mountains he had to climb this year loomed hazardous and high.

The first cataclysm came two weeks into the year. He learned of it by overhearing the conversation of two priests.

"He left, that's all I know," Father Brian, a newly ordained member of the faculty, said while talking to the disciplinarian.

"Too bad, Brian," Father Bart responded. "He was one I really liked. The other students around here respected him. What was his order name again? Wasn't it Brennan?"

This did not make sense. Who was this Brennan whom "The other students around here respected?" Mike must have misunderstood the name. It was not the kind of error he often made.

A week later the matter became sadly clear. On the bulletin board covered over by several announcements, he found a list of the seniors from the June graduating class along with the new name each had received when he was invested with the Dominican habit. After that of Eddie Golf was "Brother Brennan."

He now knew Eddie was the individual about whom the two members of the faculty had been talking. He had left the novitiate, the Dominican order and his studies for the priesthood.

That was all Mike knew.

"Why?" he asked himself

The answer was not there. Eddie had either left or been cut out of the religious community to which Mike was aspiring, gone as absolutely and finally—it seemed—as his own father had from his family. The short-term novice, the senior who had had such a personal impact on him, would not be part of his future, not even a little bit of it. He had returned to the world.

How could Mike understand what Eddie had done in leaving? He had no facts, no background, no resources and not a shred of information, just as he had no answer about his father's death.

Eddie Golf, "Brother Brennan," had quit or been asked to go after spending less than one month in the novitiate.

Mike asked Father Bart as well as two other faculty members and several seniors whether they knew anything about Eddie's leaving. Each of them either shrugged his shoulders or answered, "We haven't heard anything."

It was rare for even the grapevine to pick up anything about someone leaving, and he understood this. A departed seminarian left behind memories, an empty desk or choir stall and that was about it. This happened despite the fact that the day before the individual seemed as close to the rest as though they were members of one family. If someone did chance to know more, a confidant or closest friend, that individual was usually pledged to secrecy.

Still, Eddie was more than just another seminarian who had left. He was a legend at the seminary, an extraordinary leader, and a role model of near mythic proportions.

For Mike, he was still more. He was the only big brother who had ever come into his life and the only person other than his father who had truly tried to penetrate his barriers, his fortress.

Yet, Eddie was gone from the Dominicans abruptly and without an explanation for those left behind, those who had taken to heart his counsel and the startling, personal words of his valedictory speech.

The valedictorian had said each of them was on a journey in their search for the perfection that the religious life offered. Not all of them were anymore. Not Eddie. The way which he had presented was more real than those that which others had offered. His words had toned down the impossible idea of self-perfection. Yet, now, ironically, Eddie was no longer on that pathway himself.

Had Eddie simply gotten in his skiff and sailed out beyond the placid waters of the seminary's harbor? He had gone back into the world. For one as committed as he seemed this was inconceivable.

If Eddie could not make it in the novitiate, guided as he was by a singular gyroscope of reason and maturity, how could anyone else hope to sail through the turbulent waters ahead in seminary life?

Unanswered questions, all these and more.

"Would it have helped if I had heard the news of his leaving more directly or simply been told that Eddie had left?" Mike wondered. "Probably not, but why can't the order be more straightforward?"

Mike was so startled and upset that he discovered himself actually questioning the ways of seminary authorities.

The truth was that Mike found himself missing somebody whom he would not have seen or spoken to for another four years, until he was a member of the Dominican order and a first-year philosophy student and his friend, three years his senior. Somehow, the young boy had assumed the older one a for-certain part of his own future, someone who might be teaching along side him some day at a university or serving together as missionaries in the Far East.

Mike knew he had to forget Eddie, because that is what the system told him he had to do.

He did not do it that way. In an extraordinary act for him, he wrote a short letter addressed "Bro. Brennan Golf" c/o the novitiate. A note on the envelope said, "Please forward." He tore up the envelope and readdressed it, "Edward Golf," c/o the novitiate.

Kenan Heise

It read:

Dear Eddie,

I have been informed that you left the novitiate, but I was not told the reason. I am writing mainly to wish you well, but also to thank you for the great kindness you showed to me.
God bless you, Eddie, and let us pray for one another.

Your friend,
Mike, the Midget

Mike handed in the letter unsealed, as he was required to do with all his mail.

He decided he would include Eddie in his prayers at mass every day.

In the meantime, he did not receive a reply and could not be certain whether his letter was forwarded.

His father had told him when he left that if Mike kept him in his thoughts, he would always be there for him. The young seminarian often recalled that promise and now it extended to Eddie Golf as well as his father.

Even before hearing about Eddie, the 13-year-old, second-year student sensed that he would have to plan ahead if he wanted to survive in the seminary. He realized it would be vital to have things to anticipate. These included rewards, stimuli and even jolts that could help stop him from being overwhelmed by loneliness and boredom. His freshman year, except for his father dying, had not been a bad one. It had gone fast, but it had tended to slow down as the year worked its way along.

What these little extras were to be he already had started plan.

He had a classmate who spoke Polish and another who knew a little German. If he would spend the first half this year learning German and the second half, Polish, he would at least keep himself busy in a way his studies alone might fail to help him do.

Mike asked the school librarian for any books that could help him learn these languages. None were available, but the priest in charge promised to try to borrow or purchase them, if he could.

Time passed by and the librarian told him the procurator, the priest in charge of the seminary's purse strings, had not yet acted on his request. In the meantime, Mike relied on his classmate's memory of German words and expressions.

He started a journal, but quit when he realized there was a constant conflict between his inner thoughts and those he was willing to put down on paper. Something did come of it. After a while, he had started writing down some of his ideas in code, one he made up as he went along. Afterwards, he continued his interest in playing with ciphers and actually found a book on the subject in the library. He created elaborate ones, but never made a record of these, preferring to keep them in his head instead.

It was in mid-November that the young seminarian ran into a situation worse than any he had ever found himself in before. The problem, he did not see coming and, after it was past, he was not certain exactly what happened.

The first signs of it had to do with geometry and serving mass.

He especially loved geometry. It was a matter of memorizing an almost infinite number of intricate theorems and axioms and then placing them in a framework of strict, mathematical logic. Intellectually, it was as though he were in a baseball game with the power to throw strikes and hit home runs at will. It took Mike little effort to grasp the subject and he soon found himself working nearer the end of the book than the beginning.

In the course of doing this, he ran into a classic, insoluble problem: how to trisect a given angle, any one, by using the tools of geometry. Mike had been assured it was impossible, but quickly discovered there were hundreds of ways to attempt it. He was determined to try each of them and, if necessary, invent more of his own.

He was determined he was going to do it. If one had looked in on the area of study hall where the second-year students sat, that individual would have seen many of them mouthing the words of theorems and corollaries as they tried to memorize them. The smallest member of the class, on the other hand, could have been viewed racing through page after page of geometric patterns created with his compass and ruler.

As a sophomore, he had started being allowed to serve mass. Whenever he did, he found he had been selected out by the handsome young priest, Father Tom, who was also his geometry teacher. The latter could be detected from some distance by the smell of his Old Spice cologne. He treated the young seminarian as though he were special not only as a student--which he already knew he was--but also as a person. For him, the priest and teacher had a ready smile, a friendly pat and an intimate, kindly tone.

After Father Tom's mass, which always started and finished five to ten minutes after those said by the other priests, Mike found the sacristan had already left. Father Tom's vestments needed to be put away and the water and wine cruets had to be emptied and rinsed.

Mike was able to indulge himself with a little wine. He could not believe such an opportunity fell so consistently into his lap. He was aware he was not the only server ever to have done it. The assistant pastor of his parish had said in effect he that had sipped it when he was young and another seminarian once mentioned that he too had. There must have been others.

At the seminary, other than after serving for Father Tom, the occasion rarely offered itself since a priest or the sacristan was usually around. And, even given the chance, there seldom was much wine left over in the cruet. The fact that Father Tom said mass later than the others and apparently did not much like mass wine gave Mike unprecedented opportunities to develop a taste for it and the small jolts he obtained from drinking it.

In the classroom, Father Tom virtually ignored Mike, rarely even glancing at him; but outside it he found occasions to work closely or at last be with him. He always asked how his pursuit of trisecting an angle was coming and encouraged him to discuss his latest efforts. When the young seminarian was demonstrating his work, the priest always seemed to take the opportunity to stand or sit physically close to the boy.

Mike felt the two were becoming good friends as the older man more and more confided in him, even sharing with Mike critical comments about the rector and other members of the faculty. Father Tom often had a piece of chocolate in his pocket to share and never forgot to add a compliment about Mike's special talents and what a nice young man he was. On several occasions, he brought along a section of the newspaper and left it out for him to peruse. The students were not usually allowed to read the paper.

The more frequently such things occurred, the more confused Mike became. He sensed he was beginning to have some strange power over this man and he began to be afraid of it.

Mike, furthermore, did not like breaking rules as much as Father Tom seemed to think he did. Still, he didn't want to tell the priest this. He felt as though he had a friend and he did not want to offend him. He occasionally did test the waters and ask the older man for things, such as a sports page article about the World Series between Mike's Detroit Tigers and the Chicago Cubs. Whatever he requested he got and usually a piece of chocolate to go with it.

As pleased as Mike was with having the relationship, he sometimes avoided Father Tom or would fail to meet him at an agreed upon time and place.

Then, one day, the priest said he had a special plan just for the two of them. He had gone to some trouble to acquire the sports section of the Detroit Times newspaper from the day after the Tigers won the World Series. He wanted to let Mike read it, but it would have to be done in private. He proposed that Mike excuse himself from attending the Benediction service by saying he was sick. They would then meet in a visiting parlor and Father Tom would bring the paper with him.

The young seminarian knew the priest had more in mind than showing him the sports section of the newspaper, but he did not know what. He was eager to go and strangely reluctant at the same time. For a moment, he pictured the priest for some reason or the other showing up with several matchbook covers with scantily-dressed females or a picture of woman with no clothes. He didn't know why he thought this because Father Tom had never done anything like that. He chastised himself for imagining such an idea. Still, there was something about the man that aroused unusual physical feelings in Mike.

Mike showed up in the parlor and the priest was waiting there for him. The latter had cookies and a Coke rather than any pictures. He did have the newspaper. They drank the soda pop from the same bottle and ate the cookies, with the younger one getting the majority of them. It was a decisively forbidden repast in a time and place that added to their flaunting the rules together.

Father Tom raised the bottle of Coke and proposed a toast, "Here's to us." Mike then took the soda, raised it in agreement and sipped it.

The priest then slipped his arm around him and pressed their bodies together. The stirrings Mike had felt earlier now became more pronounced. His breathing became confused and he grew aware that the same was happening to the priest. The older man looked him straight in the face and smiled. Mike attempted to return the pleasured look.

"Are you enjoying this?" he whispered to Mike.

The young boy had become aware of the older man's full body and was electrified and paralyzed by the feelings it engendered

In terms of his goal in courting this boy, the priest—in uttering that question—had made a mistake.

The young seminarian was stunned. In his confusion, he had completely lost sight of the fact that he had a choice in the matter. This priest's words had unwittingly reminded him of it. In this situation, Father Tom was not a "seminarian authority," not part of the power establishment that would determine whether he could continue on his studies. He was rather someone to whom he could and had to say, "No." From Mike's vantage point, that is exactly what the question called for.

"No, I don't think so," the boy answered and then awkwardly pulled himself away.

The priest was startled. He had not meant to ask a question to which "No" could be the answer. This episode, he had intended to go considerably farther than it had. He had carefully planned and schemed to get here. Now, he knew instinctively he would neither conquer nor climax. This boy now was his enemy, a dangerous one who could ruin everything by reporting him. He could only hope that he had planted enough self-destructive land mines by getting this kid to break enough rules and to feel so involved in this clandestine meeting that he would never do that. Mike clearly read in his face the fact that the priest now feared and hated him.

Mike turned and walked out of the room with a sickening sense of personal shame and a loathing for the man. Whatever had just happened, was not out of a friendship that Father Tom had seemingly been extending to him. He did not know exactly what it was and did not want to. He never established a proof for how to trisect a given angle. On his next report card, Mike received a 95% in geometry, the lowest grade he had gotten in high school aside from gym. He missed two trick questions in material that had never been covered.

It took Mike three months to get up the courage to report the incident to Father Bart. Even then, it was only because he witnessed a young freshman being slowly and similarly lured by Father Tom into his private club. And he said nothing about the chocolates or the newspapers, much less the mass wine.

Father Tom never taught that subject or any others to young boys in the minor seminary again. After Mike had reported him, the priest was transferred to the Dominican priory that served as a motherhouse.

The young seminarian, on his part, had been thrown into a briar patch and there was no one to offer him any salve for his wounds or understanding to replace his confusion.

Chapter 17

Mike's third year at the seminary was, in many ways, his easiest. It was not so for his classmates.

The difference was Greek. Studying the ancient version of it was a required course for third and fourth year seminary students. It started with learning pronunciation and then its 2,500 year-old alphabet. This was a somewhat interesting part for many students. The language, however, also included verb tenses and noun endings, which proved complex beyond many students' comprehension or willingness to learn.

Fortunately, for both Mike and his classmates, the seminary had appointed an elderly scholar to teach Greek. He was Father John De Deo, a man with a vivid imagination and a few tricks up his sleeves.

He started with rote learning and focused on each student grasping the fundamentals. He stayed with this tactic during the first 20 pages of the text, a period that seemed to go on forever, but which actually lasted only until the majority of the students had some capacity to remember a number of Greek words. Then he picked up speed and covered the subject from *alpha* to *omega*, slowing down whenever the class started to stumble or grow weary and confused.

Father John De Deo often spoke Greek in the classroom. His favorite expression was *Eisceinou*, which translates "Shame on you," though he said it more like a tease than a criticism. Soon, the students started saying it to one another for him. The priest entertained the class by translating popular songs and Christmas carols into Greek and getting the students to sing them.

Despite all their best efforts, the majority of students continued to find Greek an unusually complex and tedious subject. They all would pass it, but that result seemed more a result of the generosity of the teacher than the ability of the students.

Mike was torn. Which is the better way to teach a course? This way or one that favored the strong students over the weak? Does a teacher cut out the bells and entertainment or strive for intellectual mastery? He, for example, would have personally liked to be reading some of the philosophical texts in the original Greek.

Father John De Deo was a master of caring not so much for the best student as for the average one.

Mike's class now had 21 members in it out of the original 54 who had started as freshmen a little more than two years earlier. Gone were all the slowest students, the offbeat individuals, those who had personality quirks and whose health had come into question. A few of the best and brightest were gone but not many. Students who had been average or below in their grades, no matter what nice guys they seemed to be, no longer remained a part of his class.

The weak students had run into four years of Latin, two years of Greek and demanding educational standards as demanding as that of any Eastern prep school.

A large percentage of would-be priests had been weeded out before any applicants were admitted to the seminary. It was clear that God did not call to ordination in the Catholic church any who could not meet the standards of a school that required four years of Latin, two years of Greek and a curriculum worthy of the prep schools that routinely supplied the Ivy League schools with college freshmen.

The catechism had taught them that a sign of vocation was that the candidate "have the prescribed learning." Now, they were realizing what this could mean.

Mike did not resent this. Rather, he appreciated it. He was getting an education as commensurate with his brilliance as he could hope for. The students with whom he was being trained were select and the classroom in which he studied was thereby enhanced to his great scholastic benefit.

The words "chosen," "select" and "elite" were melded together in the defining principles of this system geared to raise its students above the rest of society, as they were at the schools for the nation's upper class and its highest military leaders.

It was only slowly that Mike understood this. The more he did so, the prouder he grew of it. Similar stratified programs had built the infrastructure of the ruling societies in ancient Greece, Europe during the Middle Ages and Britain when it ruled an empire. Classrooms in those times and places eschewed the slow and the weak. They did not admit female students and they had a purpose that disdained the benefits of a democratic education and culture.

Mike felt a connection with the students of Aristotle, the great universities of the 13th and 14th centuries and Cambridge and Oxford since then. He understood the principles of education that governed both them and Catholic seminary training in the United States. The fundamental idea for schools in all these systems was to select an elite body of students and give it the best steps toward privilege that tradition and money could provide.

Two courses ran like a rope connecting the best schools in the world. They were Latin and Greek. The absorption by students of these languages had worked only when it was buttressed by a support system unavailable to the average student in the United States or elsewhere in the Western Hemisphere. High school kids in 1945 in many cities in the United States were introduced to Latin and a few even to Greek. Theirs was but a shadow of the kind of education in these subjects taught in any prep school or seminary.

Mike was caught by the conflicts that made the elite quality of his education possible. He was not comfortable with the great drop off of students that had taken his class from 54 to 21. He did not approve of the fact that those students who could not master Latin were told they did not have a vocation. Although he wanted to and sometimes did help other students having difficulty in Greek, he appreciated it was offered to him and he mastered it. The reality that such standards might do injury to others in their pursuit of the priesthood, he found an acceptable aspect of the system.

When someone asked him what the seminary was like, he proudly compared it with English or Eastern prep school.

Up close, the process could seem discriminatory and prejudicial, he acknowledged, but in the end it gave the Catholic church priests and especially the ranks of bishops an opportunity to stand on the same intellectual platform with lawyers, doctors, university professors and military leaders.

Furthermore, such a selective process and seminary training were necessary to create and maintain the hierarchical structure of the church. It was through these means that the clergy and the bishops were developed. The church in the Dark Ages and even now in some Third World countries has suffered from the problems that can arise from a poorly trained and educated clergy.

He resolved the conflict with the off-quoted Gospel phrase, "Many are called, but few are chosen." It put God's stamp of approval on the process through which he was rising as cream in the church. In his prayers he acknowledged the kindness of God in selecting him and he attempted to show his appreciation.

More and more, Mike was understanding the relationship and how factors fit together in creating and maintaining the church to which he belonged. He saw his part in it and knew it was one that would grow.

He always chuckled to himself when a professor started a course with a lame excuse why the seminarians needed to study any subject, be it algebra, physics, Greek or civics. The subject was a required part of the plan. That was enough. Each of the students were being developed and trained to play an interesting and significant role in operating the church. They needed a broad education to perform well. It was not to be challenged or changed anymore than the idea that the church was able to be truly catholic and universal because its clergy and leaders had a common language, Latin. He thought seminary training ingenious and a proof of the validity of his church.

In his junior year at the seminary, Mike took quite a different subject, one that was more challenging to him than any he had ever taken. It was called "third year religion" but it proved to be a lot more. Courses he had taken with that name before were effortless for him. This one was not.

His religion course, for once, was not one in which he could simply fall back on his thorough comprehension of *The New Baltimore Catechism*. The reason was that this time it included what approximated a sex education.

Somehow, the brilliant young seminarian didn't see it coming. Usually, he kept himself sharp by reading a textbook the first day and then studying well ahead in it. In this case, the priest who presented the course had a booklet that he had not passed out until the day before he started teaching about sex and marriage. Even then, he ordered the students not to read the material until the day he was actually teaching that page.

This caused quite a reversal of the usual pattern for the class. For once, Mike--obedient as he was--did not read ahead but the rest of the class did. He was almost two years younger than most of his classmates. They had the big advantage for once. They had hormones working for and against them much longer than he had.

The priest who taught the course, Father Richard, was visibly uncomfortable. He had gotten the assignment by default. Others faculty members were more specialized in their subjects than he was in this. They were also more aggressive individuals and consequently found it easy to dump third year religion on him with its required treatment of the sacrament of marriage and the sixth and ninth commandments.

Although nervous and awkward, Mike steeled himself not to show it. He sought refuge in his adherence to the rule of remaining silent unless he was particularly certain of not being in error. As the course unfolded, he could not believe how often his basic knowledge proved to be defective. He had never experienced anything quite like it. He understood the basics of every other subject he had encountered, but not this one, even though his curiosity had led him on many attempts at understanding.

Father Richard had a simple way of teaching the course. He started each day by asking the class to open their booklets. He then requested a student in the front row to begin reading the text out loud. That individual worked his way through one and half pages before another was selected to continue. The professor thus was able to keep his face glued to his copy and did not have to look up at the seminarians.

One of the multiple difficulties of this approach was that the students had already read the material and found paying attention almost impossible. This was confounded by the fact that Father Richard was not in the least watching them and they felt free to do anything they pleased. This led to imaginative and sometimes humorous performances that ranged from throwing spitballs to passing around sketches of bees buzzing at each other. All in all, it was a pretty mild rebellion even for seminarians.

Mike paid attention with an intensity that contrasted sharply with that of the rest of his classmates. He was curious, partially aroused and, above all, determined at last to get it straight.

But, he was also confused.

Even though he had had the brief experience with the Old Spice-wearing Father Tom the year before, he had the words "homosexuality" and "pederasty" somehow confused with "fellatio" and "masturbation." He would think about one thing and then a word would pop into his head that was the wrong term. It was extraordinarily bizarre to him because it never happened in any other area of his life.

He had still not quite figured out a woman's anatomy even though on several occasions at the golf course he had been shown a picture of nude women with hair and nothing else between her legs. And, of course, there had been the matchbooks. These passing images provided him with mere fragments, insufficient to grasp the dynamics of the sexual act. Furthermore, his mind was not actively working on it.

The most confusing question for him centered on being sexually aroused. He knew that it was not a sin for a husband to have a physical erection when thinking of his wife or planning to have sex with her, but what about an unmarried man reading a novel with a scene in it that involved making love or intimacy? When does sin start and when would it become a mortal sin? If it was so important that an individual's eternal life depended on it, why was it not black and white? He asked that question in the confessional and never received a clear answer.

And then there was the matter of a woman being aroused. What was that all about? He had read several references to it, but in all the anatomical explanations in this booklet and elsewhere, he could get no understanding of how that could possibly work.

He felt everybody else, even his classmates, had the answers and the comprehension he sought. That was why they were doing all the messing around during this class. They knew it already. He was the only one who didn't. Somehow, it was grossly unfair.

And, yet, when the grades were read aloud, Michael Richard Jordan received a 100% in third-year religion and nobody else did. Such words as "masturbation," "fellatio" and "pederasty" were not on the test. Nor was there anything about that which he knew absolutely nothing, a woman's sexuality

Chapter 18

A person who explores unknown territories, climbs mountains, kayaks or participates in any other survival sport awaits a glow afterwards, one that ratifies the effort expended and the dangers undertaken.

So it is with surviving a prep school or college, but even more a seminary. The final goal, the one that is eminently rewarding, is graduation and ultimately ordination, but along the way there are also chest-expanding plateaus for those who persist. The senior year in high school was such a hiatus for Mike and his classmates. The fact that he had encountered a possible detour in the summer before reaching his senior year added to the sense of accomplishment in getting there.

That potential stumble on his pathway was, unbelievably, a girl. Her name was Millie Moran. She was two years older than he and was also going to be a high school senior. Millie and her family had moved into the parish only recently and therefore she had not gone to grade school with him.

How real was this moment of flirtation and infatuation? That was a difficult question, one that Mike could not begin to answer.

St. Mary's parish had a fund-raising carnival every summer and he followed a tradition established by his father of working as hard as he could to make it a success. This included selling raffle tickets after masses on Sundays at the Shrine of the Little Flower parish in Royal Oak, north of Detroit. His father and he used to do it. Now, this year, Millie's father did and Mike was asked to come along.

First prize in the parish raffle was $500 and tickets were 10 cents each, three for a quarter. The small crew, which included Millie, set up a card table at the entrance to the extraordinary, circular-shaped church, built by the famous radio priest of the 1930's, Father Charles E. Coughlin. The pastor had dedicated the edifice and the parish to the young 19th Century French nun, St. Thérèse of Lisieux, known throughout the Catholic world as "The Little Flower."

The church, stunningly designed in an *art moderne* style, was located on the northeast corner of Twelve Mile Road and Woodward Avenue. It could seat 2,500 people for Sunday mass and was paired with a bold 100-foot high bell tower of granite and marble, square in form and girded by four enormous crucifixes. The imposingly tall structure had a room at the top that had previously served as the radio broadcast center for Father Coughlin. Because of his overt political involvements and frequent anti-Semitic comments throughout the late 1930s and early 1940s, the pastor had been silenced in 1942 by the archbishop of Detroit. His acquiescence stunned his followers and surprised his critics. Because they had not experienced the powerful training a priest gets in learning to be obedient, they were confused that he had accepted both the decision and the limits the archbishop imposed on him.

The agitated reaction that the nation had felt in hearing the golden-tongued priest preach on the radio first in behalf of social justice and later against Roosevelt and the Jews still vibrated in the parish and in his sermons. While forbidden to speak on the radio, he could still do so as a pastor to his parishioners.

Mike was baffled by it all, by the extra collections each Sunday, by the altar being in the center of the round church and by a priest who harangued in such a dramatic voice about religion as well as political issues and personalities from the altar.

Father Coughlin had been discussed at the seminary. Father Bart did not think highly of him and said the terrible tragedy of the

number of Jews murdered in Germany made it especially necessary
for the church that the Royal Oak priest had been shut up by Detroit's
Archbishop Mooney.

"I used to hear him on the radio," the seminary disciplinarian
said. "Some of his ideas were all right, at least in the beginning, but
when he started on the Jews he was a disgrace to the church."

Unlike such critics, most of Father Coughlin's parishioners
were in awe of Father Coughlin. His sermons and the voice in
which he delivered them were so magnetic that the members of
the congregation sometimes looked as though they were ready to
do anything: cry, repent, give more money or do whatever else he
wanted them to. At first, the young seminarian was impressed with
the persona of this powerful preacher, but then he became afraid of
him without knowing exactly why even though he had once been
introduced to the priest and found him gracious.

Being who he was, Mike might easily have taken the occasion
to attend one or more extra masses while waiting for the parishioners
to come out and buy raffle tickets. He was reluctant to do so even
when an assistant said the mass. It was just as likely that Father
Coughlin might come out of the sacristy and give the sermon.

This left Mike with nothing to do while mass was going on
in the church. As a result, he found himself spending the time talking
to Mr. Moran and nodding to his daughter.

His initial curiosity was not in Millie as a girl but as a peer
of his living "in the world." He was aware that something had to be
missing in his comprehension of the simple fact that her life was the
normal one and his was not. He could not understand how this could
be since it was so clear that his choice of going to the seminary and
entering the religious life was a superior one. How could people not
choose it? At least those who were smart enough to be able to do
so? No girl could, of course. Nor could those who were not smart
enough or who were disabled. But, for anyone, it had to represent
a high, if unattainable, goal. That seemed to him a simple, logical
deduction.

It was the actual words of the Gospel that gave him a sense
of being called and so profoundly separated him from those in the
world.

139

St. Luke wrote:

And he said to another, "Follow me." But he said, "Let me first go and bury my father," But Jesus said to him, "Let the dead bury the dead, but do thou go and proclaim the kingdom of God. And another said, "I will follow thee, Lord; but first let me bid farewell to those at home." Jesus said to him, "No one, having put his hand to the plow and looking back, is fit for the kingdom of God."

These represented strong words to Mike, who took them literally and straight from the mouth of God. Those in the world did bury their dead and did more than bid farewell to their families. The young seminarian firmly believed that the underlying meaning focused on the differences between those who chose to seek perfection through union with God and the rest who preferred to accept less, including even the "Catholic faithful."

Did this also include Eddie Golf?

If Mike at 15 years of age did not quite understand what the body of a woman was all about, he even more had no grasp of the inner workings of a human being free from a near-total religious commitment.

For him, reality was the words of sacred scripture and other religious writings. Science and history were appendages to this revealed truth and important only in so far as they coincided and served God and the church.

Experience had little to do with reality for him. It was merely subjective and could be distorted by anyone's wants or needs. Truth was objective. Religion, an expression of God's will, was the central reality. He and the seminary authorities therefore deliberately limited what he might encounter.

For once, though, he was becoming personal with another human being, a girl, if not his own age, at least in his own grade. He was about to experience her.

He made the only decision he could, to treat her like another guy and as though there were not between them the huge gulf of sex and religious commitment. She would be to him "another caddy," a Catholic one, of course, who knew a little bit about who he was.

By giving her such leeway, he could talk to her in a slightly less-guarded manner.

The day and place it started was a warm, bright Sunday morning on the steps in front of the Shrine of the Little Flower.

Millie was outgoing, but did not find this boy very easy to talk with. Her first line showed a less than gracious side of her.

"You're a senior in high school?" she asked in a disbelieving tone of voice.

"Yes," he said, feeling himself challenged.

"I'm sorry," she apologized. "That was awkward of me. I know you are a senior and I even heard you had skipped a grade or two, but I was still surprised when I met you, I have to admit."

"It's a reaction I get," he replied in not an entirely gracious tone.

"Let's be friends," she said. "We're both seniors."

She could not have chosen a word that frightened him more than "friends." People, classmates or anyone else did not propose friendship to Mike. He was too confusing for them. They were either intimidated by his brilliance or put off by age and his lack of social skills. They could respect him or not, but friendship was out of the question.

"Friendship must mean something pretty casual to her to be proposed that way," he thought.

What he said was, "Sure."

Thereupon, neither of them had a word to add to their conversation. Mike felt he had spoken last and Millie did not know what to say next. Furthermore, she was not certain how much friendship she really did want to extend to someone with whom it was so difficult to talk. Besides, he was a kid and supposed to be a high school senior. That was confusing.

They stood facing one another, looked aside and went off to find someone to whom to sell raffle tickets.

The next Sunday they spoke even less.

She said, "Tell my father I am going to the bathroom and I'll be back." He said, "O.K."

"Is this what people mean by friendship?" he asked himself. "'Tell my father I'm going to the bathroom'? She was the one who had said, 'Let's be friends.'"

Complain to himself though he did, Mike was relieved at not having to make conversation with her.

Then an incident changed things for the two of them. He saw a wounded bird in the middle of Woodward Avenue. Instinctively, he raced onto the street, scooped it up and crossed just before several cars sped past. It was not so much a heroic deed as it was a resourceful one.

He was a little at a loss what next to do with the bird cradled in his hands.

Millie crossed Woodward to look in on the bird.

"What kind is it?" she asked.

"It's an Indigo bunting," he said. "It's a male. They are the only small birds that are entirely blue. Do you know anything we can do with him?"

"I do," she said. "There is this lady on the block behind us who takes in injured animals. How do you know what species it is?"

"I like to walk in the woods at the seminary," he said. "I've always made it a point to learn the names of the wildlife as well as the trees there. I saw a silver fox once."

"I think that's wonderful," she said, but she also seemed to mean 'I think you are O.K.'"

Mike felt a very unexpected pull toward her. He noted she was pretty. He liked her smile and he suddenly found it easy to talk with her. It was strange, because it was so sudden.

And so was the fate of the bird. One moment it looked all but dead and in the next it flew out of his hand.

Millie smiled at the little miracle and started talking to Mike, telling him about herself. She had planned to enroll next year in St. Mary's College at Notre Dame, Ind. She wanted to be a writer. When a high school sophomore, she had thought about becoming a nun and had even sent in application papers. The teenager never followed through with it even though the convent had accepted her.

She decided instead some day that she wanted to have children of her own.

She almost had one foot in his world, he thought. The gulf between them was suddenly much narrower than he could have ever imagined. What he liked best was that it was something about him, a personal thing that had impressed her. Millie liked his interest in animals and in nature.

Other things had been stirred up in him about her. These did not have words. This was the way it was with his memories of his father. It was amazingly simple what was happening, but these were not thoughts but something far more unfamiliar, feelings.

The pair became more relaxed with one another over the next week and went for walks together and even took a ride on the Ferris Wheel at the carnival. When they reached the top, his heart was pumping as though he had been running. When she smiled at him, it raced even faster. He stroked her hand and she did the same to his.

Mike looked down from the top of the Ferris Wheel, saw the crowd in front of the church and spotted a woman going in wearing a bandana. She looked like his mother, but he couldn't be certain. His body quivered and his mind grabbed the controls away from his feelings. He knew he could never again look Millie in the eye or smile at her.

After they returned to the ground, he said, "I think I saw my mother. I have to go find her."

And he then left his friend and never saw her again.

When he got home, his mother was there and had bought his favorite ice cream for him.

Mike never forgot Millie, but neither did he allow himself to bask in the feelings he had felt. He kept these behind a curtain deep inside himself. He chose not to crush them, but neither did he bring them out lest he re-ignite them. They were a threat to him and to the religious person who he was becoming. They represented a pleasure he had only begun to feel, but also promised incalculable pain if he let them loose while he traveled on his chosen path.

As he grew older, he would wonder whether his abruptness, his unilateral move to end what had started, hurt Millie. He hoped not, but he also feared that somehow she might have been relieved, realizing his age and aware of his deep confusion toward any girl, including herself.

He had these thoughts and knew there were no answers if he started questioning them. Millie joined a parade of people who had come and passed through his life. They included his father, Eddie Golf and now, her. They were not entirely gone. When he became lonely and felt sad, they were the individuals he conjured up.

Mike could not tell these things to anyone at the seminary, not even his spiritual director.

The seminary, when he returned there, was a haven. At home, he had feared his mother would bring up Millie and lecture him on the dangers of associating or riding on Ferris Wheels with girls,

His studies went smoothly and he spent time tutoring freshmen.

Mike also had been appointed head sacristan. It was a natural position that fit his personality and religiosity. He could also give it the extra time the job demanded and miss classes when necessary without his studies suffering. In four years he had never received a grade as low as the 95% he was given in geometry. Even that one he could have contested, but he did not.

The opportunity he received in being sacristan was that he was in charge of the mass wine. The first two months he resisted even sipping any of it but as the anniversary of his father's death approached in November, he began to feel sad and alone. His mother had never mentioned it in any of her letters and that omission added its own pressure.

He had a lot of special freedom and he began to realize this. If he did not show up for a class, he was presumed to be working in the sacristy or doing some independent studying.

Simply put, he started drinking.

Mike thought no one noticed anything about him. He was still a flashing star at report card time and when any other scholastic achievements were recognized. He was a senior and lived in an aura of permission-presumed behavior.

Then, he was told one day that Father Bart wanted to see him. Mike walked into the disciplinarian's office with the casual walk of a confidant senior. He did not leave with it.

"Michael," the priest said, using the name no one had called him in four years, "stop it."

"Stop it?" Mike stuttered.

"Yes, stop it," the priest said. "If you don't, you are out of here."

Neither spoke another word. Father stood up abruptly. Mike did likewise and they left the meeting.

The sky had fallen. He was 15 years old and thought he was at the top of the mountain but suddenly realized he stood on a precipice so frightening he could hardly imagine it.

He entered a proud senior. He exited a sniffling little boy.

His first impulse was to be angry with Father Bart, to protest but he was not certain what. He did not want to admit he had done anything wrong, but he knew he had to.

An hour later he returned to Father Bart's office.

He walked in bent and with a look of humility.

"I will," he said, bowed his head and left.

And he did. He never drank another drop throughout his senior year.

He was never forced to admit, to verbalize, that he had been drinking.

Years later, he wished he had. It might have helped. Maybe being kicked out might have, too.

Chapter 19

Harry Scheib, though 20 years older, took little note of his rider's youth. The kid had started working with him at the Acme Stainless Steel Works and was the son of his second cousin, the one killed in the war. That was it.

The subjects they talked about were the Detroit Tigers, work, their relatives and Harry's experiences in the South Pacific during the war. The boy, he decided, was kind of smart and a good listener. When you gave someone a ride back and forth to work, what more could you ask besides these things and that you were getting 25 cents a day for gas?

For Mike, spending such time with Harry Scheib could have been a door-opening experience had he let it be, but he found himself too directed, too much in his own world, to take a simple, firm grip on the doorknob.

Of his own single-mindedness, he had once overheard a professor say:

"Most people in this life get to the place where they're going, if they're lucky, with the energy of a coal-burning engine. That little Jordan kid has two of these new diesel engines and, if you said he had three, I think I would believe you. He's way out ahead of even himself there and, in the long haul, no one can keep up. It's scary."

The priest spoke not so much about his intelligence as his focus and energy. Mike, on his part, liked being compared to a diesel-run train, one with two or maybe three engines.

Harry, like most, was on his own short line railroad and there was no room for such an express train. The man could not state a single algebraic formula, split a theological hair or, for that matter, think of any reason to want to do so.

Still, the two did find subjects to talk about.

Harry said that, as a kid, he had once seen a baseball game in which both Ty Cobb and Babe Ruth had played. Whenever conversation in the rickety 1932 Buick hit a lull, Mike would ask the older man about that contest and urge him to recall fresh, new details.

Cobb, a Detroit Tigers legend, had long been the seminarian's all-time sports hero. The two shared a certain penchant for aggressiveness, but there all comparisons ended. Mike's character was based in his super ego; Cobb's, in his ego. Nevertheless, the boy studying to be a priest liked to fantasize becoming rather a tough, no-quarter-given baseball player and would repeatedly ask Harry the question, "So you saw Cobb go sliding into second base with his cleats high in the air?"

And Harry, savoring the second and the memory, responded, "Sure as I'm sitting here right now, he did it. It was 1927, the year the Yankees dominated everybody. He made the second baseman drop the ball. The Tigers won, even though Ruth hit one clear out of Navin Field."

Mike, who knew his baseball, was aware that Cobb in 1927 was playing for the Philadelphia Athletics. Consequently, the young traveling companion credited the narrator with neither accuracy nor believability, but it did not matter as he watched Harry's glow while conjuring up his account of what he said he had witnessed.

The pace of Mike's life, as they drove to and from the factory, slowed down a little. His anxiety-engendering purpose and ever-demanding intellect seemed, for once, to disengage. The very grime on his skin and clothes were akin to a costume hiding his inner identity. He was strangely comfortable in this environment that was far different from the one which he knew represented his certain future.

The two enjoyed each other's company and, as a result, the Buick often roared with their laughter and guffaws. They talked of many things, but avoided discussing Harry's hacking cough, the one that constantly interrupted his stories and seemed to grow worse when he laughed too hard. Mike suspected that while working daily in the plant with Harry he had been inhaling the same grit and grime himself.

One day, about a month after Mike started the job, his mother received a phone call from another relative saying that Harry would not be picking up her son. He was in the V. A. hospital for a lung operation, a very serious one.

Thereafter, Mike took two buses, spending 45 minutes a day longer traveling to work and getting back home. There was no laughter, no stories of a 20-year-old baseball game on the bus.

To get the job at Acme Stainless Steel, Mike had lied. He had said he was 18 years old, written it on the application form and then had signed his name. Other people in this world, even many in the seminary, might have been willing to accept that they needed to do this to get hired. For Mike, what he had done was soul wrenching.

He had intended not to lie, believing that his usually reliable shrewdness would somehow enable him to evade questions about his age, leave the spaces blank or write the number illegibly in them. This had not proved possible. Acting on impulse and under the pressure of the moment, he had called himself two years older than he was. Afterwards, he wanted to go back and tell them he had lied. But to do so would stop him from being able to put money in a bank account for his mother to take care of her after he entered the religious life in August.

His good intention, he knew, did not justify the lie and he would spend the full two months working at the factory under the cloud of a troubled conscience and who knows how long in purgatory.

At first, the job intimidated Mike, but he had no one to whom he could complain. All his life, the possibility of failing had been a problem for others, not for him. He had experienced a dose of it in trying to find work and now failure pursued him in meeting daily quotas that could not only keep him from earning but also seemed to raise a question whether or not he might be fired.

The factory was enormous, two blocks long and a half of one wide. High above, dull gray windows opened or closed utilizing a system of chains, pulleys and gears. Nothing in the plant, including the employees' washed-out dungarees, had any color, other than the black and gray of the grit and grime. Now, machines, pillars, walls, floor, overalls, shirts, bandanas, caps and the skin of the workers were the nitty gray from the polish dust emitted into the air once the machines began buzzing and screeching in the morning.

The area of the plant in which he worked was more crowded with machinery and stacks of supplies than with people. There were 16 machines in his immediate area, eight on each side of the aisle. Less than half of them, counting his, were manned.

His immediate boss was Jonesy, a lanky 35-year-old veteran of the war in Europe. The man proved patient with Mike throughout the first morning's briefing despite an obvious lack of Mike's experience with machinery, quotas or factory work.

According to the verbal explanation he received, his task was simple enough. He was to put a pot or pan on the round fist of a lead-weighted arm. This was then locked into place against a polishing wheel. As the buffer and product spun around against each other, he applied a stick of grit on the stainless steel being polished. After the item had been satisfactorily brightened, he disengaged the buffing wheel and swung into place a second arm with another pot on it. He next took off the finished, polished object while the next one was having its surface treated with in the same grime-emitting process.

The assignment was not only to polish pots and pans according to the best of one's ability, but also to do it at a speed and with a competency that met the company's demands. For his whole first day on the job Mike did not understand this. He had interruptions, awkward hesitations and took several bathroom or breathing breaks.

Jonesy came up to Mike after the final whistle. The new employee gave his foreman a smile. He did not get one back.

"Jordan, ya did about a third as many pots today as you will need to keep your job, much less to ever earn bonuses," his boss snarled. Earlier the man had called him "Mike."

The younger worker gulped as his boss continued, "Almost all of these should be done over, but I have picked out this stack what you will redo tomorrow morning. I never want this to happen again."

Mike said nothing. He just nodded and went home, eager to take a bath and scrub all the grit off and out of his skin. It was no easy task. As he bathed and brushed, the water grew dirtier but his skin did not seem to be getting much whiter. Later, he would realize that more than 30 minutes in the tub would be necessary should he want to be clean enough to go out to novena services on Tuesday evenings. He consistently chose not to go anywhere else on a weekday.

His production levels slowly improved as did the quality of his work but he kept reaching plateaus and it took sheer effort for him to reach a level at which he was earning small bonuses.

By then he realized that each new employee, unless he or she had experience in polishing pots and pans, would be subjected to Jonesy's friendly explanation of how to do the work followed that evening by his harsh criticisms. Few, except for a polisher who had worked elsewhere, ever reached the bonuses that had been assured them when they took their jobs.

By his third week, he had earned $8.50 in bonuses and grew angry with himself that it had not been more. Jonesy had become more friendly and came up to him one day during his lunch break.

"You ever think of going in the service, Mike?" he asked.

"Nah," he answered nonchalantly.

"I was," Jonesy said. "I was stationed in Germany for six months after the war."

"I speak a little German," Mike replied.

"How about this?" Jonesy asked. "A girl I was with over there asked me, 'Varum nicht ein *kondom*?'"

"Vas *ist* das, ein kondom?" Mike shot back.

"You don't know?" his boss asked. "It's a rubber." Jonesy laughed and reached into his wallet.

Mike was stunned. He thought the man might pull out a condom. Instead, it was a well-worn picture showing Jonesy with two young women. All three were completely naked.

"Here, this was taken when I was in Germany," the older man said with a smirk of pride.

Mike nodded. He could do nothing else. He was horrified and simultaneously incredibly titillated. If his curiosity were to ask a question or two nonchalantly, no one at the seminary or in his family would ever know. The answers could satisfy or might stir up something buried deep inside him.

Instead a voice within him spoke up and asked him, "But, what about this man's soul?"

His desire to know details was outweighed by his conviction that a righteous attitude on his part might only encourage this man in his already God-forsaken ways. As a person committed to God, he must avoid such temptation and work rather to help Jonesy find a way back to the true path.

Yet, he was torn. Here he was with a chance to be a missionary and, instead, it was all so awkward. Rather than feeling illuminated by a bright challenge of doing the work of the Gospels, he itched with a carnal curiosity that he knew could lead to sin, at least in thought.

He said nothing.

Jonesy, meanwhile, was onto another subject.

"I got good news for ya, kid," Mike heard him say. "I know ya only been around here for three weeks, but already you've done better than a lot of these other stiffs. Hey, ya listened to what I had to say that first day. So I put in for a raise for ya, 25 cents an hour. Ya don't gotta worry about making them bonuses."

Mike whistled gently as his mind quickly calculated the effects of the raise. It would mean an additional $10 a week, guaranteed. That was more than he had made with the bonuses.

"O.K." he said. "Great."

"But you gotta work on the line," Jonesy added. "It'll be new, a different system. You'll catch on to it."

"That's ten bucks more a week," Mike said.

"Yah, see me tomorrow morning when ya come in," the foreman said with a strange glance.

Mike had been warned at the seminary by his spiritual director that "Pride goeth before the fall," and he certainly was proud of his fast promotion at work. He was so very pleased with himself that he did not want to say anything to anyone, to share it even with his mother until he had the money in his hands. This was what he was, an inevitable force in life, a man destined to move mountains that rose up in his path.

He even wrote down the words, "Inevitable force - move mountains" on a piece of paper. He then tore the page into tiny pieces and threw them into two separate wastebaskets. He did not want them to be discovered the way his matchbooks had been.

The fall came the next day. The "line" meant an assembly line. He worked in a different part of the plant, where he had never been before. The work would no longer be polishing pots and pans, but rather chrome strips for the sides of cars. They came to him not as a stack of work delivered on a skid by a man with a forklift, but on a conveyor belt that passed his workstation.

He did not at first understand what all this meant because the conveyor had not yet started for the day. He had no sense of how fast it would bring new work to him. He looked to Jonesy, who gave him the same smile he had when he first started his job at the plant.

Mike worked there four more weeks. It was terrifying. The work was impossible, but somehow he had to do it. For eight hours a day, he was part of a mechanical process to polish automobile chrome slats at a speed set by a relentless, lurching chain that did not sweat or get tired as he did. He learned eventually to get up to speed to accommodate the work coming at him, but had to ignore all practical safety measures in order to do so.

Every day, and several times in the course of it, he reminded himself that this was not his future. Unlike the others around him, he would be leaving this place, and very soon. A desire to scream about his job grew day by day, but so did the sense of relief that he had one less day to put in at it.

"It is not my life," he told himself every time he rushed to take a piece off the belt before it passed him, but he was almost wrong. It came very close to being just that.

The plant had a contract to do chrome stripping for new car models, but suddenly that was over and he was back to doing pots and pans, brought to him, now, by the conveyor belt.

The motions had become so automatic he had to be careful not to get too absorbed in his daydreaming. One day he did.

As he swung the arm with its lead-filled form and the pot on it into the buffing wheel, he pushed it too hard. It went past the polisher and the second arm came around and followed the same course. This did as the first had and also spun around, picking up speed as they rotated. The two very heavy arms of the machine began spinning with a centrifugal force that threatened anything in their path.

Mike realized he had to pass within inches of the rotating arms to reach the switch to stop the machinery and while doing so go past the lurching conveyor belt. He had no guarantee from anyone, his boss or anyone else, that he would live through the effort to shut it down and stop the danger that was growing with every rotation of the armature.

"Act," something inside him said. It was a voice that had to be obeyed here and now, no matter how hesitant he might be.

He did so, slipping past the whirling pot, feeling it brush his overalls. And for a third time in his life, he had survived a threat to his life. It was akin to being cured as a baby and escaping from the trunk behind the candy store when he was five years old. If he had mentioned it to his mother, she would have spoken no word, not even "Oh, that must been frightening!" Her face, with the twinge of an intense smile, would have reminded him it was about his mission.

It was a Tuesday and, for once, it took determination for him to leave his house to go to church for the service.

On the Sunday afternoon afterwards, he took two buses to the VA hospital to visit someone who was not expected to survive, Harry Scheib.

His first reaction to the front corridor of the hospital was one of horror. It was filled with the walking wounded and maimed.

They were not the clean, neat brave, wounded soldiers pictured in those movies with the hero stopping off to be supportive toward his hospitalized comrade wounded in battle. What was sad were not the wounds or the missing limbs, but how much alone these former military men seemed to be. If two stood together anywhere, it was to share a cigarette rather than words.

He smiled toward the men as he went along toward Harry's room. They nodded.

Harry lay in his bed, pale and flat, but not coughing. He seemed to be nearly asleep, but he was not. As he saw Mike, his face lit up as it did when he spoke of the great baseball game he had seen as a kid.

"Hi, little Tiger," he said.

Mike was flattered by the instant nickname.

"Hi, big Tiger," he shot back. "You know what? Because of you I have to ride the bus and nobody'll talk to me about baseball."

"I knew I was good for something," Harry said in a voice that was weaker than Mike had imagined it would be.

"How you doing, Harry?" Mike asked, gently punching the older man in the upper arm.

"I wish I could say I feel better than I do," he answered. "They tell me I'm going to die."

Tears came to Mike's face.

"I been praying for you," Mike said.

"Well, I don't think it will help," the prone figure replied. "I don't believe in God."

The tears on the teenager's face increased in response to that statement and Mike felt his chest tighten.

"No, don't say that, Harry," he pleaded. "Don't."

"It's all right," the dying man said. "I'm all right with it. You know they say everyone in a foxhole believes in God, Well, that's where I lost my belief."

"Harry, no, please," Mike begged. "Salvation comes through belief in Our Savior."

"I'm sorry, little Tiger," Harry replied. "If I had known you would take it so bad, I wouldn't have said anything. Let's just leave it that I'm going to meet all the great legendary Detroit Tigers personally."

"Harry," Mike said, absorbing his tears, "I'm going to pray real hard for you. God will give you back your faith. He's testing you."

"Mike, it doesn't matter. It really doesn't. When you die, it's who you have been that counts. The manager can't step up and hit a home run for you. You don't win the pennant if you haven't earned it. Even God, if there was one, couldn't do that."

"Harry, it's not a baseball game," Mike replied, but he felt embarrassed at his chiding tone. He had come to cheer up a dying man, not to argue with him.

"Still," he thought to himself, "this is his chance, his last one, and so much is at stake, his immortal soul."

"Cheer me up," Harry said, almost reading his thoughts. "Don't preach. You don't want to become known as a preacher, do you, kid? That would be awful."

The older man chuckled and once again Mike heard the frightening, life-threatening cough mixed with the laughter.

Mike gulped at the rasping sound and at the words. In less than month he would be robed as a member of the Dominicans, known as the Order of Preachers. That is exactly what he wanted to be, a preacher. And this opportunity was precisely what he was looking for, a chance to save a soul. Why did it feel so different than he envisioned?

"St. Dominic would know what to say and how to save his soul," Mike thought.

For a moment, looking straight at his dying friend, the young seminarian had a doubt, a small one, about who he was, his vocation and his mission.

For a fleeting second, Mike felt that a hand laid on this man's bony arm was more important than a prayer. He touched him tentatively, swallowed hard and silently said the Our Father.

He then asked Harry to repeat once more the story of the game from his youth. Harry waved him off. He had spent all the energy he had.

The day Mike left for the novitiate he heard that Harry had died.

That same day, he also deposited in his mother's bank account $306.42; almost half of what he had earned working in the factory. The rest went for transportation to the novitiate and the clothes he would need there in addition to the religious habit, which the order would provide. Theoretically, he would never cost his mother another cent.

Together with what was still in the account from the benefits from her husband death, she would get along, he figured. He was going to be taking a vow of poverty and it meant he would not be able to support her.

Chapter 20

Before he left for the novitiate, Mike took a trip by himself to Belle Isle. When he told his mother of his plans, she pleaded to go along; but he refused to let her. It was the first time he could recall saying "No" to her since he was a child. How easy it proved to be when, for the span of his life, he had always considered it impossible.

There was a reason for his decision. He felt his father was calling him back to their favorite haunt. Although he mentally worked at ways to help make it something positive, the beckoning was not entirely a pleasant one. Underneath, there was pain.

To prepare for the day, he took down his dust-covered fishing pole from the attic, determined that, no matter what, he would catch something in his father's memory.

Mike would walk in the woods and name the trees and list their distinct characteristics aloud as though his father walked at his side.

To do these things, he would have to unbury his father from deep inside him. He had not forgotten Cpl. Richard Jordan, whose remains were somewhere in a forest bordering Belgium and Germany; but he had not intentionally called him up in his memory in more than three years. It was too painful for him to have tried.

Everything was about to change. Mike was going into the religious life. He would even be given a new name. Just as he had to ritualistically hug his mother before leaving home for the last time, so he needed to say goodbye to the man whom he had called, "Daddy."

His intentions were to recall every pleasant memory of his father that he could. He had for some time felt remote from his fear that his father's soul might have been lost.

It all was the other side of a mountain of pain, one he had not been able to scale since his father died—no, since he had seen off his father at the train station.

The night before, Mikey dug out from under his bed an unopened envelope with his name on it and stuffed it into his pants pocket.

The day was a Saturday late in July. It did not start well. The temperature had early started to soar into the high 90s, which meant Belle Isle would be packed, loud and raucous. So would the bus be that took him there.

He had no choice. It was the only day he had left, but he still hesitated to walk out the door and encounter what the coming hours had to offer.

The bus was full. He got up and gave his seat to a black woman and her little children. Several of her older children and other kids in the aisle shrieked and bumped up against him taking away the sense of reverie that he had worked so hard to create. He forced a smile and let his mind wander.

Finally, he got off several blocks short of Belle Island and chose to walk the final blocks. Even the sidewalk was a congested and unpleasant distraction.

He saw the children as nuisances and thought, "At least, I am not going to have any of them."

On the sidewalk, Mike found himself crowded up against a building as a large family passed. The structure contained a liquor store. Without thinking, he entered the store to catch his breath. With little more thought, he pulled a dollar out of his pocket to buy a small bottle of cheap wine. He put it in his hip pocket and let his mind deceive him that it was not there.

He crossed the bridge to the island, went directly to his father's favorite fishing spot. It was more crowded by far than it had ever been. He knew that, under these circumstances, no pleasant memories would be found. He would not be able to whisper his father's name as he pulled in a fish.

As he was leaving in a week for the novitiate, he would not be able to take his pole and fishing equipment with or ever again have any use for either. He gave them to a father with a large group of children who were using wooden poles with strings, hooks and corks at the spot where he and his father had fished.

The man thanked him with an appreciative nod and Mikey knew it was what his father would have wanted him to do.

Next, he headed for the woods, cutting across the open areas rather than following paths. He walked deep into them, ignoring old trees for which he had developed affection. He found one of his favorites, a magnificent elm, and sat down in its comforting shade, his back against its trunk.

Mikey let his mind rest as he listened for the almost imperceptible sound of the breeze that lightly moved the leaves. It was not, as his heart wanted it to be, his father's voice; which had been silenced in another forest, one far away.

He began reciting aloud the names of some trees, talking about their mid-summer stages and throwing in a few Latin words in an effort to stir his father's spirit.

His mind wandered back to the eighth grade and walking through these same woods on a beautiful June day. For his father's edification and benefit he had recited the beginning words of a poem by James Russell Lowell:

"Oh what is so beautiful as a day in June?

Then, if ever, come perfect days

And heaven tries earth if it be in tune."

Mikey had waited a second for a favorable comment from his father and instead had listened as his father hesitated and then recited the rest of the complete, rather lengthy poem.

Mike had been stunned when it happened. Now, the memory soothed him.

It was time to open his father's envelope. As he pulled it out of his pocket, he looked up in the branches and saw a morning dove staring down at him. He thought of it as his father.

Why had it been so hard for him to get at this envelope? he asked himself. He stopped for a moment. It was a horrible thing for him not to have opened it all these years. Now, he could scarcely remember why he had not. The pain and the anger were scarcely memories, much less realities,

"Sorry, Daddy," he apologized. "Deeply sorry."

The words broke the dam and the flood of tears came, flowing until the muscles of eyes and face hurt.

He felt sad for his father, who could not be here, who had died a violent death in a miserable, lonely place.

Mike regretted that he had not tried to know him better or shared more with the man who tried to reach out to him.

When it was in the course of his sadness that his sorrow turned away from his father and onto himself was not clear, but shift it did. Soon, he was feeling his own pain so sharply that he had to stand up. And with the hurt came regret and then the old, familiar anger at his father.

Trying to get his attention back to where it had been, he opened the envelope and started to read its long-ignored contents.

He did so with teeth clinched in an effort to stave off a headache he felt might take over his entire body. The contents his eyes perused did little to ameliorate the situation.

It was a poem; not a last thought, a shared memory or a goodbye.

It was a poem and that is all it was.

It was a poem and it was about roses.

His father's inheritance, his last will and testament was a poem and the subject was a rose.

How could his father have done this to him?

Still, out of a final filial obligation, he pushed on and read:

162

The Beauty of A Rose

We humans,
since voice
first uttered metaphor,
have attempted to pay homage
to a rose
and to share
its discovery and experience
with others of our species.
It is given
to each of us
to have done this,
to speak of its fragrance,

       its sensuous texture
       and its deep hues.

It surprises us
with its incomparable color,

    form,
    majesty,
    uniqueness
    and aroma.

We imitate the rose
in carvings,

    glass etchings,
    paintings,
    perfumes
    and paragraphs.

We use it to honor

    our graduates,
    our performers,
    our brides,
    our mothers
    and our dead.

163

We propagate,
crossbreed
and protect it,
planting gardens
and building trellises for it.
We grow,
buy
and sell them,
giving them away,
a dozen at a time,
with long stems
and short ones.
We know the prick of their barbs.
To our species,
a rose is synonymous
with fragile,
fragrant
and mysterious beauty.
Our praise for it,
however,
wilts even faster than the delicate
white,
yellow,
pink
or deep red petals.

      Only the words
      of Gertrude Stein
      survive
      because
      she avoided comparison, adjective, metaphor
      and verbiage
      other than reminding us
      a rose is a rose.
          Oh, yes!

It was a better poem than the other by his father, but it lacked the rhyme and traditional rhythm that he had been taught makes poetry, poetry. Ultimately it failed to make any contact with the bigger picture, which would have shown a rose to be the handiwork of God.

He squashed the notebook page containing the poem back in the envelope and walked to the nearest trash receptacle and laid it in there. He thought of tearing it up, but as angry as he was, he felt no need to insult his dead father. He laid it carefully to rest and walked away.

Mike returned to the tree, took the bottle out of his back pocket and drank deeply.

"My father, damn him!" he permitted himself to utter, but he immediately wished he had never said those words. He really wanted not to have said them. They were a sin.

Chapter 21

Michael Richard Jordan--soon to lose his name, his clothes and his hair--listened as the master of novices formally described to the small group of seminarians what was about to happen and why.

The year of novitiate and what life was like during it was a tightly-guarded secret kept inviolate even from those about to enter it.

The mystery was about to unfold with him in the middle of it.

"The novitiate," the stiff, gray-haired priest read from a mimeographed booklet, "represents the first 365 days in the life of an individual entering a religious community. In a time-honored tradition, it is intended to be a formative year, one in which connections with the secular world are severed and replaced with a new outlook, changed habits and a more complete commitment to God, the church and the order which you are joining."

The priest looked up from his reading and said to the 11 clerical and four brothers candidates in front of him, "Don't discuss with people, even those in the minor seminary and especially not your families, what the novitiate is like. They'll never understand."

"You are first going to be making a nine-day retreat," he continued. "The eight novices who are finishing their year will show

how we do things and answer your questions, although each of you should remember that silence, especially in the prescribed hours, will be a major part of your life here."

"The novitiate," the mimeographed booklet went on to explain, "is meant to shape the individual as surely as the hammer and anvil of a blacksmith forges a plow. The difference is that the object to be formed is a person rather than a piece of metal and the purpose is to make that human tool a servant in God's vineyard rather than an implement in a farmer's field."

He would not die separated from God as Harry had nor would the young seminarian succumb to what he had experienced toward Millie.

The novitiate, he had been told, would be a test. It would be a time when the Dominican order and its representatives would demand that he prove himself and his vocation. Indeed, some older members of the community believed him too smart, too young, too immature, too proud and too much of a goody-goody to be one of them. They would just as well that he went away. He was not the only aspirant about whom they had ever felt that wish. The others were gone.

"Obedience, rarely a weapon, is usually a shield," one spiritual director had tried to tell him. "In the modern world, young people entering business or military life learn that, to survive, you have to do as you are told."

For Mike, obeying was far more than the survival technique the priest had suggested. He perceived it as a direct connection with God, more reliable than prayer, although he was armed with that too. Obedience was a compass that would enable him not to avoid those major direction-seeking decisions that tended to confuse him.

What challenge obedience offered him! Call it a strategy, an art, a science. It was one he believed he might be able to learn better than anyone had in history.

"Give me regulations, even ones that are that are oppressive, and I will gladly obey the letter and the spirit of each one of them" he prayed. "Train me in the sacred 700-year-old Dominican rule of life and I will observe it inside out and live up to it as though it had been written for me. Say that something cannot be done and, with God's help, your obedient servant will do it."

"This prayer," he finished, "represents my mission, my calling."

The difference between himself and an automaton or robot, he felt reassured, was his brain, which was aware of what he was doing. The similarity was that both did what they were told to do. His assent would be there, but it would have been given even before the command was formulated. It would be his, but it would be buried deep within. His superiors could see the puppet. The ultimate control, the Grand Puppeteer, would be God. He alone would know that the young novice's will and power to choose was still there.

After the nine days of religious retreat had ended, Mike and his classmates submissively knelt before the provincial superior of the Dominicans to receive their religious habit. He was the last among them because the order established for entry into this life was based on age. Henceforth, seniority thus established would serve as the basis for everything. Since he was the last one in his class to be invested, he would have the least of it and always stand as the final person in line. This would always put him at the end of the list for each and every privilege and responsibility they might encounter.

"If our funerals were held together," he told another member of his class, "your casket would be sprayed with holy water before mine."

"Unless you had become a bishop," his classmate taunted.

"Little likelihood of that," Brother Brennan shot back while at the same time knowing that a degree in sacred theology could open just such a door.

At the ritual of investiture, as the ceremony was called, the provincial placed a Dominican habit over his head, shoulders and street clothes. In Latin, the religious superior then intoned the words, "Your name in the world was Michael. In religion it will be Brother Brennan."

It was the very name that Eddie Golf had for his one brief month. His departure had made it once again available.

Michael had requested it. Now, he accepted that for the next nine years, that he would be Brother Brennan. After that, God willing, he would become Father Brennan.

He felt an inner change along with the new name and the habit, which had been slipped over his shoulders. Barely suppressing a grin over having been given the name he sought, he was pleased by the pomp and ceremony and even more by having attained one of his most deeply-desired goals.

Others of his classmates had acquired the names of "Innocent," "Bonaventure" and "Odo." All things considered, the name of Brennan would do him just fine. No one else in the class, however, would have been more compliant than he if he had been given a name such as "Rupert" or "Englebert."

His mother was there and nothing satisfied him more than that. She no longer used hugs to show affection toward him. There was a new distance between them now, but the light in her eyes revealed how deeply she approved of his entering religious life.

Brother Brennan smiled as he spotted a man in the audience as preoccupied as he knew his father would have been during the two-hour mass and ceremony. Then he thought of him somehow being there and making a horribly inappropriate comment such as, "Mike, there is always a bed waiting for you at home should you ever change your mind."

He was distracted with the thought that he did not have brothers or sisters to leave behind. His mother's cousin, Sister Rosemary, had intended to come to the investiture and had received permission to make the trip, but became ill. She would die within the month. Other than his mother, she was the last surviving near relative Brother Brennan had. A cousin, slightly older than he, had been killed on Okinawa.

His visit with his mother after the ceremonies lasted less than an hour, as she had to catch the Greyhound bus back home. When she had left and the doors shut behind her, he would not see or talk with her for a year, possibly longer. Nor would he speak with any of his other past acquaintances, not even with the students in the minor seminary.

His world had pivoted on its axis.

Brother Brennan had been using his free time to complete his self-assigned task of memorizing the complete scriptures. As he had watched his mother walk out the parlor door, he recalled the words Jesus said:

"Amen I say to you, there is no one who has left house, or brothers, or sisters, or mother, or father, or children, or lands, for my sake and for the gospel's sake, who shall not receive now in the present time a hundred-fold as much, houses, and brothers, and sisters, and mothers, and children, and lands--along with persecutions, and in the age to come life everlasting. But many who are first now will be last, and many who will be last now will be first."

For what he was now doing, he would be rewarded many times over. Christ himself was saying that. The message was clear, it was certain.

And as he turned to go back into the cloister, his attention was focused on the new life, name and clothes, which he had this day adopted. He was starting anew. The faults, the awkwardness and even the sins of his past would be erased from his body and soul as had the grit and grime from the factory. God would forgive him the matchbook collection, his sexual curiosity, his pride, his interest in Millie, his doubts, his inability to convert Harry on his deathbed and the many, many times he had failed his mother.

He knew God would forgive him the times he had consumed the altar wine, even though he had never mentioned it in confession.

The *persona* known sequentially as Mikey, Michael and Mike existed no longer. It had been yanked up out of his being by the roots and had been dispensed with. Brother Brennan had been born, a new man, risen out of the ashes of the old, a fresh human being far more challenged to commit himself to God than his previous self had ever been.

He returned to his room, where he savored the few extra minutes in his schedule created by his mother having had to leave before visiting hours were officially over.

For the first few moments there, he stood motionless, looking down at the white wool garment or habit in which he was clothed. Fifty-four students had started the seminary with him four years earlier. Now, there were 11 and he was one of them. He continued to be among those selected by the seminary officials, by the order to which he now belonged and by God.

An adventure, as big as he could imagine, had begun. The challenge would be sweet.

"Oh yes," he said to himself quietly and with a wide smile that made him glad he was behind a closed door so no one could see or hear.

He picked up a book that would be like a bible to him. It was *The Dominicans* by Father John-Baptist Reeves, O.P. Those latter two letters were the same initials he now had after his name. He was proud that they stood for "Ordo Praedicatores," or in English, "Order of Friar Preachers" and that they told the church and the world that he was now a Dominican, albeit a fledgling one.

A copy of the small 88-page book, published in 1930, had been personally handed to each of the novice candidates by the prior or head of the monastery that housed the novitiate. With it, he gave them a welcoming speech that explained the structure and organization of their new monastic home.

"The prior," he said, "was elected by those members of this community who have professed their solemn vows.

"Such a way of choosing a religious superior was revolutionary when St. Dominic initiated it in the early 13th Century. He was living in a time when both theologians and civil authorities argued that democratic rule went against God's will for governing both the church and the state.

"The Dominican order is based on the rule of St. Augustine, which unlike that of the Benedictine order, does not bind its members to one monastery. Rather, it unites them in a shared life and houses by means of communal prayers, practices, exercises and love of God in order to carry out their mission 'to preach through word and example.'

"Your year of novitiate is geared to teach you contemplation of God and all things sacred, to mediate and to pray. We, your brother Dominicans, will make certain you are free to do that. You must do the rest."

Brother Brennan subsequently recalled these words of the prior verbatim not only because his mind committed things to its memory quickly and accurately but also because he thoroughly wanted to retain everything and anything said by his superiors as he had the catechism. It was fundamental to his concept of obedience.

Still, he found himself distracted by a sense of how much was new about him. He now wore the religious habit, he had this new name, he was living in a cloister, and his daily routine had irrevocably changed. Even God must be looking at him differently now.

He scanned through the small book on the Dominicans until he came to passages that said what his immediate future promised:

"The contemplative life was the vocation which St. Dominic first chose for himself...

"In the Catholic church the cloister is a traditional institution and a very venerable one. It has always stood for retirement from the world and contemplation.

"St. Dominic...remained a contemplative all his life. When in response to the needs of the world he came out of the cloister he was not taking a step backwards, or undoing anything already done. He was merely enlarging his cloister by making it as wide as the world, and increasing the community of contemplatives to which he belonged."

Brother Brennan, who occasionally daydreamed of becoming a second St. Thomas Aquinas, the most prominent of all Dominicans, Catholic philosophers and theologians, now thought he needed to model himself after St. Dominic, the order's founder.

In Father John-Baptist Reeves' book, he found a passage about St. Dominic to help him aspire to that goal:

Such glimpses as we have of his character during these early years reveal all those qualities which stamped themselves on his later work: a studious and well disciplined mind, an iron will tempered with sympathy for the misfortunes of others, a talent for leadership and government, a deep and virile piety.

Brother Brennan believed deeply and pervasively in reading the lives of the saints. They were a proof that perfection and great sanctity were attainable.

In later years, even as he learned that the writings about the saints were deeply and often intentionally untrue or at least distorted history, he clung to them. Without the stories, little anecdotes and high praise accorded to the canon or official list of the saints, perfection by living people was but a will-of-the-wisp. The church, in his time, would come to declare that many things written or orally passed down were made up, as was the very existence of some saints. These included such popular saints as St. Christopher, patron of travelers, and St. George, slayer of dragons. He had prayed to both of them.

But, on this day, the newly invested Dominican was committing himself to an ideal that he accepted without question or doubt. His God, his church, his religious order had created a mold. It behooved him to melt into it so as to attain the highest perfection to which a creature of God could ever aspire.

The novitiate would teach him the means to do this in ways that he did not expect. They would include a stifling silence, extraordinary long hours of prayer, an avalanche of minute criticism and even a measure of self-flogging. There would also be a smattering of sensory deprivation, a focus on self-denial and the deep impact from the self-confinement that the year of novitiate demanded.

All this was in the little book, which he read many times over, eventually knew by heart, and only eventually came to understand.

St. Dominic's 13th Century mission had been to counter the "Albigensian heresy," which argued that all matter derives from a principle that is evil. Therefore, it argued, the righteous life consists in the strenuous mortification of all natural appetites. The Albigensians condemned marriage and sex, called for rigorous physical self-discipline and practiced a strict poverty.

People willing to make such "holy" choices easily attracted admiration and often followers determined to earn redemption and salvation at any cost.

The Albigensian got into deep trouble not so much because of their heresy, but for their denial of the sacraments of the ecclesiastical hierarchy. They were all but eventually wiped out by a Pope Innocent III-approved crusade of bloodshed that would, by its effectiveness, establish the model for the Inquisition and its death-and-torture tactics in fighting heresy and opposition to the church.

But in Brennan's texts, it was the holiness of his order's founder that had blocked the spread of Albigensian doctrines.

Dominic was an extraordinary person. He imposed upon himself and his followers the burdens of poverty and chastity, taking them as voluntary vows. On top of these he added obedience, placing his order immediately under the pope.

If the Albigensians had created a respect and appeal with their rigor and self-denial, he showed nothing less in the treatment of himself.

As Father Reeves's book explained to its readers:

Though most solicitous that his brethren should have all the simple comforts their health required, he himself had no bed of his own. During his vigils he scourged himself cruelly, as though the daily discipline of rigorous fasts, long journeys on foot and much preaching were not enough to keep his flesh in training for the arduous service to which he had dedicated himself.

As the year progressed, Brother Brennan found abundant literature on the lives of saints who encouraged such rigorous means of seeking salvation as severe fasting and self-flagellation.

In the mornings, a part of choir prayer included reading "The Martyrology" in Latin. It recounted the lives of the church's martyrs, as its name implied, as well as short snippets about whichever saints shared that day as the date on which he or she had died. These accounts often stretched credulity beyond all bonds and lavished praise upon extreme acts of self-denial. About St. Patrick, on March 17, it said that as a baby he had fasted at his mother's breast on Wednesdays and Fridays.

He peripherally noted that the church had canonized far more men than women, a reality he embraced as reasonable. He acknowledged, nevertheless, there were several female saints such as the aesthetic St. Theresa of Avila and the meek St. Therése of Lisieux, "the Little Flower," who were both especially select servants of God.

In Brother Brennan's "cell," as in everyone else's room, a knotted rope whip hung, one which he was expected to use in self-flagellation while reciting in Latin the prayer of self-deprecation and atonement, the *"Misereri."*

A novice was expected to understand the common sense limits of these practices and of others such as the chapter of faults, in which one publicly acknowledged one's own faults and those of others members of the community. Excess in the pursuit of unattainable perfection, under these circumstances, naturally becomes inevitable.

How far does one push himself? What are the barriers in trying to follow the Gospels and to be perfect? For almost 2,000 years, Christianity had tried to answer this question. The Manichaeans, the Albigensians and the Jansenists each represented a major movement in Christianity, one that the church had ultimately decided had gone too far in its search for perfection. How then was a 16 or 17-year-old in one year supposed to come to the right balance for himself and at the same time not create lesions deep down in his psyche?

The whole year of the novitiate would be deeply troubling on this matter for the young novice. One incident would spell it out in dramatic fashion. It was Lent, the penitential weeks between Ash Wednesday and Easter. He had been a novice for more than a half year and had looked especially hard for self-discipline and denial appropriate to his search for self-immolation and perfection.

What he decided upon was a perfect adherence to the *magnum silentium*, the "great silence." It was the time in the priory between 8 p.m. and the end of communal mass the following morning. The rule called for the novices not to talk during these hours. It was not a sin to break the silence by speaking, but it was a fault and had to be publicly confessed in the chapter of faults.

Since no sin was involved, there was room for flexibility in dealing with the *magnum silentium*. One could talk with a good reason. Even then, not everyone kept it faithfully and, as time went by, the majority of novices felt that no dire reason was needed to ask a question or make a comment to another brother during those hours.

Brother Brennan rarely broke the *magnum silentium* and when he did, it was only for a valid and most pressing reason.

He decided to discipline himself during this Lent of his novitiate year by taking an oath not to speak during these hours, no matter what the provocation. He would accept the consequences without knowing what they might be even if an urgent need arose for him to talk or ask a question during the silence.

It was not long before his resolve was tested. He began to feel ill at supper and could feel his temperature rising during the short recreation period that followed the meal. The young novice said nothing. It was the flu. He would get over it.

Finally, he decided to mention it to the novice master, but then the bell rang and it was past 8 p.m. He went to his room and continued to feel sicker and weaker. His stomach started to hurt until it was as though his abdomen was going to explode. It was painful to the touch. His forehead began to feel very clammy and his body was as hot as he ever remembered it.

He had made his commitment not to talk and felt it included even his religious superior. He was very sick. He knew it was not the flu. His past readings of medical books told him it was either his appendix or his gall bladder.

He thought of possibly dying. He obsessed over it. If he did die as a result of this, he wondered whether or not it could be considered martyrdom. After all, it was clearly a matter of commitment and principle that would result in his death.

The pain was unlike anything he had ever felt or imagined. He thought of St. Sebastian, an early Roman martyr, who was burned to death on a spit. Legend says the saint told his executioners to turn him over as he was done enough on that side. The kind of excruciating pain that the young novice was enduring, he was certain, could not compare with that of that true saint. Furthermore, it was not St. Sebastian's first martyrdom for the faith. He had earlier been shot full of arrows but had miraculously survived.

Brother Brennan reached the end of morning mass without dying, however, and reported his affliction to the novice master. It turned out to be his gall bladder and he was in the hospital for two weeks. Fortunately, this was not long enough for one of the order's rules to take effect that would have required him to start his year of novitiate over had be been absent from the novitiate for a week longer.

Even though he was told he had come close to dying, he did not in fact regret what he had done. Still, Brennan sensed a strange uneasiness that what he had judged to be good and holy in intention had turned out to be confusing and frighteningly dangerous. He had headed in an unswerving, direct line but it had not gotten him where he had wanted to go.

This confused state that came out of the hospital with him continued for the five months until the novitiate ended. Questions continued to plague him. He never would have guessed what would happen, that a year which had started off in such bliss, would find himself relieved to see it over.

He watched the class behind him arrive at the novitiate with enthusiasm similar to his of a year before. Would it be the same for some of them, he wondered?

Or was he simply being tested on his way to his mission?

Brennan had not ever been as frightened before, at least not since he was a small child in wooden box underneath a stairway.

Now, he was. But he remained uncertain about what it was that he feared.

Chapter 22

Throughout the next four years, philosophy—scholastic philosophy—would serve as the core of Brother Brennan's college curriculum.

And, oh what an acid test his philosophical brilliance would provide him with during these years!

For him and his classmates, learning scholastic philosophy could lead to an inside understanding of God, truth and reality just as a car manufacturer's manual might provide all the basics required by an auto mechanic to master car repair. His studies also afforded him a glint of that special mission to which he had been called since early childhood.

Still, his life remained confined to the box of seminary life. About that, Brennan, for the moment, had no complaints.

The philosophy of the church inherited from the Middle Ages was a constricting and deadly-boring subject of study to most seminarians. To Brennan, it was exactly the opposite. He saw it as a force that had proofs and could help renew the world as it had done in the 13th Century. He saw potential; but others guffawed.

It would be the courage of his convictions that mattered and that would be what would be tested.

He and his fellow clerical students started their philosophical studies by memorizing terms and ideas, which had come from the works of the ancient Greek thinker, Aristotle.

To the young Dominican seminarian, the transition in concept and language from philosophy, which is about the world, to theology, which is about God, had been aptly achieved by the scholastics, principally St. Thomas Aquinas, the 13th Century Dominican and his followers, the Thomists.

For Brennan, the beginning of the world, the birth of Jesus, even Christ's death had happened in a long-ago, timeless era. The clock of real history had not started ticking until the 13th Century with the appearance on the scene of St. Dominic, St. Thomas Aquinas and scholasticism.

As some people are with sports, fishing or poetry; Brennan was enthralled with scholastic philosophy and theology. He stood before them in awe as an art student does before Michaelangelo's *Pieta* in Florence.

Brennan had read the history of the prior centuries and considered them merely a prelude to the great 13th Century. The flowering of scholasticism in those one hundred years, to his mind, opened the wisdom of the ancient thinkers to expound the truths of divine revelation and holy scripture. Thus, the intellect and its accomplishments finally assumed their rightful, honored place in Christianity helping to state and clarify God's truth.

This was about God's mind and about his own intellect.

Aristotle's view of man and of the world had come from the 4th Century BCE Athens, a very small city-state in ancient Greece. The latter had just gone through an unparalleled golden era that had produced some of the great minds of history and had provided the basis for the thinking underlying Western civilization.

Brennan's research showed him that the eras following Aristotle's death knew only a few of his works. The scholars of Alexandria, Rome, Constantinople and the Arab world thought of the eminent Greek philosopher as a reference point rather than the source of a universal, coherent philosophy. As many of his writings started to be translated in the 9th Century into the common language of Western scholarship, Latin, this began to change. These had come to Europe through Arab scholars in Spain.

Brennan knew the buds of scholasticism had still not yet been quite ready to blossom at the beginning of the 13th Century.

The ecclesiastical authorities who ran the prestigious University of Paris disdained the secular thinking of Aristotle and prohibited lectures on his natural philosophy and metaphysics. As usual, such censorship made the brighter scholars more interested.

Albert the Great, a Dominican professor at Paris, was St. Thomas Aquinas' mentor. He worked on an encyclopedic study of Aristotle. But, when attacked for doing this, Albert explained, "I expound Aristotle. I do not endorse him."

Brennan imagined the petals had begun to unfold and the flowering happened as Aquinas came into his own.

The pupil quickly went beyond his teacher in allowing himself to embrace the ancient Greek thinker's philosophical concepts. He boldly endorsed Aristotle's principles of matter and form, substance and accident, and body and soul.

St. Thomas, however, altered Aristotelian thinking by arguing that the individual human soul, seen by Aristotle as the form of the body, was separable from it (by death.) Through doing this, the Dominican theologian established a key philosophical basis for the theological position that the soul is immortal.

Aristotle's thinking, based on common sense and logic, attracted the philosophically-bent Dominican Brennan, as it had Thomas.

The ancient Greek believed in moderation and his views, for many philosophers today, tend to serve as ballast rather than a cutting prow on the boat of inquiry.

To Aquinas, Aristotle was the key to an intellectual underpinning for Christianity.

For the ancient Athenian philosopher, a person's ultimate importance was based on his citizenship in the city-state and on the potential it gave him to contribute thereby to culture and civilization. The 13th Century Dominican and his followers would adopt this model and substitute membership in the Mystical Body, the church with Christ as the head, for the citizenship in an Athenian-size city-state.

The strength of St. Thomas' theology was rooted in reason and logic. The weakness of his philosophy is that it was "the handmaiden of theology" and, to him, ultimately had no value in itself.

Brother Brennan could easily accept this submissive, servile role for philosophy. He followed St. Dominic, who proudly proclaimed that he never studied anything for its own sake. He acquired knowledge in order to defend the faith and refute its opponents, the heretical Albigensians.

The religion-centered thinking of the Middle Ages, like the art that flowed from it, was so dominant that many scholars subsequently reasoned that the modern era began only when scientists such as Copernicus, Galileo Galilei and Sir Isaac Newton embraced the idea of inquiry for its own sake.

In the depth of their hearts, Brother Brennan and his teachers still held to it.

His classroom philosophy courses were exclusively Thomistic and scholastic, with the texts in Latin, As Dominicans, his professors were required to take oaths that they would teach the philosophy and theology of Thomas Aquinas.

What Thomas had done fascinated Brennan. Was his mission to be another Thomas Aquinas? The young Dominican cleric, to avoid the pride that the Greeks called *hubris*, would not let his mind actually formulate the question, but it lurked in the back of his mind.

He acted as though it were. He read and poured over all the limited library copies of the works of Aristotle. He read a number in Latin and later switched to a few selected ones available to him in Greek when he learned that Thomas had gone to it for the accurate meaning of the original words.

Other aspects of Thomas' life also intrigued Brennan. The 13th Century saint was not only a scholar, but also a staunch one who brooked strong opposition in the Church for his pioneering work as well as from his wealthy family for his choice of vocation. His biographers say the latter once attempted to pry him loose from the church by locking him in a room with a nude prostitute. Subsequent biographies maintained that, after resisting her advances, Thomas was never again tempted in the matter of carnal desire.

Brennan was confused, however, about what further to learn from this story about St. Thomas, his intellectual and moral hero. The legend included the details of St. Thomas throwing a burning log at the woman. He thought of Millie, a person he could not get completely out of his mind. Though she remained at most an unreal and remote temptation to his own vow of chastity, he assured himself he would never throw anything at a woman trying to tempt him.

He loved Thomas' every thought and written word. No matter how much he read and admired Aristotle he could never feel passionately about him the way Thomas must have done.

Neither Aquinas nor Aristotle, however, could give Brennan the one thing he secretly sought, a completely new and totally logical proof for the existence of God.

He must have it. His brain was made for such an achievement. It would be the beginning of his mission if not the fulfillment.

The writings of scholastic philosophers argued that no one could prove the existence of God philosophically, although many had attempted it. Most of these, in one fashion or the other, argued from effects such as beauty or order in the universe to a first cause, i.e. a creator. The Christian philosophers, starting with St. Anselm of Canterbury in 1100 AD, attempted to establish by natural reasoning alone that God (the first cause) exists. Each thinker outdid the previous one by building a more elaborate and systemic argument, yet none of them ever quite accomplished the goal.

Seminarians, forced to study these proofs, found them difficult to understand but even harder to challenge. As did the early scholastic philosophers, they wanted to believe that one could prove through reason alone that God exists. Although still only a teenager, Brennan grasped both the reasoning and the flaws of their arguments.

Brennan played with creating an argument for the existence of God as he had tried in geometry to trisect a given angle. It was good exercise and kept his mind nimble, but the tree never bore the fruit he hoped to see ripen there.

Brennan was hesitant to acknowledge the limited perspective of the scholastic era. He was not ready to accept that a dialectic process rather than a simple creative act could be the fingerprint of an Ultimate Cause.

Most seminarians are, almost of necessity, impatient with studying scholastic philosophy. They rarely see the over-all picture that philosophical thinking presents but rather must deal with it piecemeal, taking such esoteric and often mind-numbing courses as "ontology," "epistemology," "logic," "natural ethics," and "rational psychology."

"Who cares about being, about essence, about reality, about existence, about proving everything the 13th Century thinkers believed?" Brother Julius, a classmate, asked Brennan rhetorically. "I mean, who cares?"

The questioner's brilliant young classmate had a ready answer, but he resisted the temptation to rebut the question and gave but a nod.

"Who cares?" Julius had repeated.

Brennan did. He systematically compiled information about scholastic philosophy the way a sports fan tries to add statistics about ballplayers or a game situation. He understood the intricate teachings of St. Thomas Aquinas and his followers called Thomists, the way a mathematician absorbs an algebraic formula.

For others, it was hard; for him, easy.

He loved the Latin language, in which his textbooks were written because it is so precise. The words no not change meaning. They meant, or at least seemed to mean, exactly what they had in the pre-Christian times of Julius Caesar or the Middle Ages of St. Thomas.

Not many other people cared that the language preserved the thoughts of the past or rather the expressions of them the way old photographs or newspapers in a box in the attic could. The young, earnest Brother Brennan did.

As a Catholic seminarian, a Dominican and a follower of St. Thomas Aquinas, Brother Brennan accepted that this subservient role for philosophy is something to be taken for granted. And, yet, it represented an enormous gulf between him and other young people studying philosophy in all but a handful of universities throughout the world.

Such students were reading historic philosophers including Adam Smith, Kant, Hegel, Descartes, Nietzche, Schopenauer and Sartre as well as the philosophies of humanism, stoicism, positivism, relativism, existentialism or Marxism. They were searching Eastern religions and Islam along with literature, art, theater, the movies, current events and dry scholarly treatises to find new roads to philosophic understanding.

Each of these budding young philosophers then challenged themselves to put the pieces together to form a quilt that showed the result of his or her search for the truth, or at least ways to understand it.

Not so Brother Brennan. Despite his intellectual brilliance, his basic responsibility in class and in examination was merely to repeat the answers given by Thomas and other Catholic philosophers. Why? Because they unerringly supported accepted church teaching. The object was to know them so well that one could refute the world and all its ills and errors. The other philosophers historically disapproved by the church were mentioned in his texts, but in condensed form and immediately critiqued to be wrong about whatever they had said. In his textbook, their names followed the Latin word "*contra*'" which in English means "against."

Brennan saw scholastic philosophy as a system that hung together as does a string of Christmas lights wired in series so that if one failed, all did. The theologian's job was to prove philosophically that no other philosophy worked because none could.

To him, each truth was part of the whole, from the principle of good and evil to the nature of the soul. He believed scholastic thinking could give final answers even to less basic questions including those that belong not to philosophy but rather to the positive or physical sciences. He read extensively in the subject area known as "rational psychology," which uses the deductive logic of syllogisms rather than inductive scientific inquiry to study human thinking.

He was aware that scholastic philosophy had tripped up on Copernicus and Galileo; but he, like his church, was not in the least apologetic about that.

Catholic thinkers adopted a fortified, defensive position against all modern philosophies and he found himself solidly fortified in the trenches with them. First and foremost of these positions was the belief universally held by the scholastics that *"Gratia supponit naturam,"* or "Grace is above nature."

Grace, as he saw it, represented the powers of God in action. Nature is merely God's creation, but is not God.

Brennan sought to prove "the truth" and the principles behind it rather than to search for wisdom, as do Eastern philosophies. The scholastics believe that what eastern and modern thinkers look to learn already exists in divine revelation. Meanwhile, other scholastics--principally Franciscan theologians such as St. Bonaventure and the English John Duns Scotus--developed somewhat different answers and positions in response to philosophical and theological questions.

The key to it all, Brennan accepted, was logic and the syllogism. The logic was that of the ancient Greeks and the syllogism, that of Aristotle. The latter's writings on logic advanced the concept by which one could prove things philosophically. First, he would establish the universal truth or fact and then show that a particular one was related in such a way as to be proven to be as true as the general one. His syllogism might proceed thus: All men are animals. He is a man. Therefore, he is an animal.

The syllogism was known before Aristotle. What he did was set up his universal statement (called the major) as direct principle that could be represented by a letter just as in algebra a known or unknown quantity can be noted by "a," "b," "c" or for that matter "x" and "y" or any other symbol. This allowed him to deduce his syllogism of the second and third figure from the first and was the beginning of strict deduction as a logical means of establishing proofs to achieve certainty and add knowledge.

For Brennan and the scholastics before him, syllogistic or deductive reasoning was a wonder of wonders for it extended the certainty of past-accepted truths to new conclusions. If all men are mortal and if you are a man, then you are mortal. To obtain this kind of knowledge, you do not have to die first. The syllogism proves the conclusion. On the other hand, the process fails completely in the area of physical science where inductive thinking and the scientific method supply answers that syllogistic reasoning cannot.

In many ways, except for the introduction of Christianity and the loss of the Greek-initiated democratic form of government, the world Aristotle studied had been altered little by the time Aquinas came upon the scene in the 13th Century. Well before the 20th Century, however, people had started using the scientific method and man's intellectual grasp of reality to change the body of human understanding dramatically. This had not necessarily happened within the confines of the priory in which Brother Brennan lived or the classrooms in which he studied.

The vast majority of the non-Catholic (and non-Islamic) students studying philosophy throughout the world would ignore, if not ridicule, the belief of Brother Brennan and other adherents of scholasticism who accepted philosophy as existing to serve theology.

The numbers were small indeed of those willing to accept two other premises which Brennan did: that Thomas Aquinas alone understood the truth behind the truth; and second, that those who disagree with him and the teachings of the church are out-and-out wrong.

Brennan was caught. His mind was too brilliant not to want to probe beyond the confines in which he found himself, but his commitments to the order, the church and obedience were absolute.

He was about to attempt a breakout.

Chapter 23

Brother Brennan's life seemed to be speaking. He was at last working on something other than getting more thoroughly educated. The young cleric was discovering a way to use his mind to reach out beyond the confines of the classroom, to please those above him in the order and to start to fulfill his mission for God.

He was 18 years old, at an age by which many great thinkers had made their most significant contributions and done their best work. This, he knew and it made him impatient for that which he felt was his destiny.

As he had attempted in high school to trisect an angle, an impossible task, so now he was again playing with the idea of a new proof for the existence of God. He had actually worked out several, only to find that another scholastic thinker--usually 600 to 800 years before--had already found his avenue and tried it.

Still, he plodded on. This was not something he would give up easily. The goal was too exalted, too lofty. The exercise was also too pleasant, too exciting. It gave him fresh opportunities to use logic, develop syllogistic thinking and work with the concepts of Aristotle.

He knew that that which he was looking for was not waiting along a straight line but was somewhere in front of him. Brother

Brennan moved ahead in a focused direction nevertheless. He worked as though that would be exactly where any discovery would be made, although he knew better.

His prayers were that God's grace would show him the way. He started to promise the Almighty that he would not sign his work, take no credit for it. Eventually, he backed off from agreeing to that promise.

He believed in God's grace, but he also trusted that serendipity might hand him an inspiration commensurate with his need.

"Pray as though everything depends on God and work as those it depends on you," someone had advised him. That was good enough for him.

The young cleric then got distracted from his task. He found an article in an encyclopedia about Einstein and his theory of relativity.

Brother Brennan was intrigued. He himself had an ability to jump beyond the facts in a situation, to understand relationships and to knit together an underlying theory to explain both the universal and the particular. That pattern is what he saw in much of Einstein's thinking. He perceived parallels between the reasoning of the German Jew and the ancient Greek, Aristotle. They each had a mind that produced marvels and earned his respect. Neither attained, however, the sublime thought that Thomas Aquinas represented, he felt. They did not have divine revelation as their guide.

To Brennan, there could be no valid comparison between the physical theory of relativity and the philosophical thought of Aristotle that had been used so aptly by the scholastic theologians. Ultimately, these truths alone counted.

Einstein's theory was empirical. It was not something that was deduced from immutable facts. The physicist's conclusions were, to Brennan, at best a temporary thing that someday could and probably would be superseded by clearer and better concepts to explain the relationship of space and time. Theology, as expounded by Thomas, has no such limitation.

Still, Einstein's thinking challenged the young seminarian and Brennan read and studied not only the theories but also the mathematical formulae used to prove them. Since he had never studied advanced mathematics or calculus in class, he had to work his way through them with his unique ability to fill in gaps.

Even though he grasped much of the theory, he failed to see any reason to make a connection between scholastic philosophy and relativity. The gulf between speculative, inductive reasoning and deduction was too great to fit into one field of study.

Then, one day, a sentence from Einstein leaped off the page at him.

"I want to know the thoughts of God," the great mathematician had written. "All the rest is detail."

"The thoughts of God!" The young cleric wanted to jump out of his skin. Aristotle had spoken of causes; Einstein was talking of the thoughts of God.

Albert Einstein, by using that expression, had perceived what Aristotle had not, what even Thomas had missed: a broader, new vehicle in which to travel from effect to cause, from creation to creator, in the mind's eye.

Within the category of "the thoughts of God," Brennan realized, one could fit everything: that Aristotle, scripture and the modern thinker might conceive. It was a term as inclusive as creation or cause.

Everything that was not God was his thought.

Everything from a rock to an idea was such. And if there were a thought, there had to be a thinker. THIS WAS THE PROOF. Establish the major and prove the minor and the conclusion was certain.

Define those terms. Make that connection and one has the proof that if the thought exists, then so does the thinker.

What Einstein had missed was that he could and did know the thinking of God. He himself was a thought. So was Brennan. Thomas Aquinas had been one and so had Aristotle. Everything, everybody, all were the thoughts of God.

This was not mere linguistics. It was reality that led to a new proof for the existence of God, a personal one.

Past arguments for God's existence went from effects to the first cause, from reality to a prime mover. You could reach an idea of a prime mover and a first cause without conceiving of it as a personal God. This is a jump beyond both logic and philosophy.

If, however, a philosopher could establish the premise that matter and form, essence and accident, theory and reality, are all thoughts, first and foremost, then one could argue to the existence of a God who is the thinker and therefore a personal God.

The young Dominican was deep into abstract thinking but wanted to develop a line of reasoning that the ordinary man like Harry Scheib could follow and articulate. He desperately wanted to become simple, clear and direct enough to become part of a grade school catechism.

Brennan would need to investigate the language, especially the word, "thought," just as Aristotle had used certain other key nouns in developing his philosophy.

The major premise for a syllogistic proof would be: "Everything the mind can know is a thought." Or perhaps it should be stated: "The only thing the mind can know is a thought." His proof (shortened form) for this: "Think about it."

The minor would be: "The mind potentially can know everything except God." His proof for this would arise from the definition of cognition or knowing.

The conclusion he wanted to reach would be: "Everything, except God, is a thought of God." He felt he could work from this conclusion to establish not a first cause, but a being who is to His creation as a thinker to his thoughts."

He had to work on all this. It was a door rather than an open and shut conclusion. It was a beginning. It headed in the direction he wanted to go.

There were several things he needed to develop. Part of this would come, he felt, from more thoroughly understanding Einstein's thinking processes and insights. The German physicist had reasoned to the theory of relativity long before it could be proved empirically. That kind of jump helped define the word, "thought," as did the thinking of Aristotle and Thomas. The words of scripture also did this. And here Brennan opened a forbidden door, if only a crack. He added in his mind, "So did, for that matter, the Koran and even the list of demands of a Martin Luther." He would never state it to anyone else. That was how close to heresy it came.

"Thought," however, had to be proved to be the all-embracing noun and it was in this context that he could safely include the Koran and Luther's theses. They were examples of it and nothing more.

Then, the young 18-year-old Dominican cleric had to tighten his syllogism to be an unchangeable piece of logic, one that screamed, "This is true. It is universally true."

Such a proof for the existence of a personal God had to be so persuasive that it would satisfy both Aristotle and the most skeptical Dominican philosopher alike.

He said nothing about his theory, but he worked at it. First, he did a broad perusal of the literature of philosophy and theology to see what other references he might find in them to the "thinking" of God. He was amazed that there seemed to be so little, and yet he was not.

The Gospel of St. John begins with references not to the thought of God but to the word.

"In the beginning was the word and the word was with God; and the word was God. He was in the beginning with God."

The Greek term for "the Word" in this context is *Logos*. It admits to broad interpretations and "the thought of God" certainly could fit as one of them.

What Brennan had conceived was consistent with this scriptural passage. Christ, to whom John was referring here, is "the Word." Everything that is not the word, however, is not God, but rather the creator's thought or thoughts as one might want to look at it.

Brennan's mind went to Aristotle and Einstein. It was not enough that each had insight and fresh thinking on various subjects, the two also had to do the hard work of presenting their ideas as truths or at least as theories and then attempt to prove them with the limited means available.

He later looked back on his early notes as comparable to the exam answers some of his classmates wrote on subjects of which they knew nothing. Even in a monastery, the word used—at least by some—was "bullshit."

This was something more than his attempts (now, clearly ridiculous) to trisect an angle. He sensed that he was indeed on to something. He had long experienced an intuitive feeling when he was on a road down which he would ultimately discover the answer or truth he was seeking. This process had become a piece in his remarkable brilliance. It was conceived in his deep intellectual confidence and born of his persistent adherence to rigorous logic.

He needed two items to proceed further: More of Aristotle's works on logic, preferably in the original Greek, and the complete works of Einstein. A word, a phrase, an insight from either of these sources might lock into place the reasoning and conclusion his mind had already grasped.

Brennan dallied, but finally took that next step. He asked the priest who headed the library for the two works, careful not to tell him the full truth of why he needed the volumes.

After a long silence, the priest-librarian said "Let me take it under advisement."

Those words panicked the young cleric. He knew exactly what they really meant. He was about to be visited by the priory's inquisition. He would now have to establish his reasons after having stated them.

The librarian had boasted that he was the most intellectually open-minded member of the community, but his hesitation and his words were full of foreboding.

Then it happened. He got the summons. It came directly from the prior and was presented in that request form, "Could you find some time to come to my office this afternoon. Say, about three o'clock?"

In a monastery, he knew, the harshest commands or orders come in the most polite, innocent language.

"Could you find some time to come to my office this afternoon. Say, about three o'clock?" he laughed to himself, but he was not amused. The prior was a very direct man. The more laid back his request, the harder the hammer would strike. Brennan tried prayer and various methods of steeling himself. Still, he entered the prior's office at precisely 3 p.m. holding his hands together so his trembling would not be apparent.

The prior was not smiling, a bad sign. Next to him sat the master of clerics and the venerable "master of theology," who served as head of studies for the province. It was clearly going to be worse than Brennan feared.

But why? What had he done?

"Brother Brennan," the prior said. "Knowledge of your brilliance and excellent scholarship preceded you here to our house of philosophy. And let me just say that you have lived up to the advanced billing. I speak for all in this room in saying this."

"Thank you, Father," Brother Brennan said in a squeaky voice that embarrassed him.

"But," the priest continued, "we feel we must ask you why you have asked Father Matthew for the books you have. Our tradition here is to study Aristotle through the great St. Thomas. Also, while we respect non-Christian writers such as Albert Einstein, we want our students to be acquainted with them only under the supervision of our faculty. So perhaps, you can help us to understand your independent interest in them?"

Brennan gasped. The prior could not have been more direct. He had clearly signaled displeasure. Under the concept of obedience, it was not for the young philosophy student to attempt to win over his superior but rather to appease him, to obey him.

To some other fledgling scholar, the prior's words might have represented a challenge, but they were not meant to. The religious superior was well aware that he had absolute power in a closed system and subtly made it clear he was exacting obedience in the form of intellectual acquiescence.

The whole structure of what could have amounted to an attempted proof for the existence of a personal God fell, not under the weight of reason or examination by scholars, but to the dictates of obedience.

He could not do something new, could not use the thinking of Aristotle or Einstein. Both were, in the words of his superior, "non-Christian" writers.

In the moment before he began to make his response, he felt emptied out. Just the day before he had heard a radio broadcast in which the U. S. Senator from Wisconsin went after a witness for his connections in his youth with people who were communists. While he sided with the Catholic senator, he felt that he was being more intimidating than reasoned. He suddenly realized that it was he, Brennan, who was sitting in the hot seat. He did not like it.

His throat began to constrict. His indoctrination and training took control to protect the only life and existence he knew.

"Father Prior," he said. "I want to thank you and the other two priests here today for the concerned words you have showered on me, but even more for the interest you have taken in me. I have been wrong and I have no excuse for it. A combination of vanity and pride on my part has led me to be curious about areas in which I should have known that only supervision by wiser, more experienced members of our order could keep me from going in a perilous direction. Fortunately, your intervention today has helped show me that I was in error. If you need a reason, please look to my youth and inexperience. I promise you this will help me grow and mature. Nothing like this will ever happen again."

The prior smiled lightly and nodded to his two priestly companions.

"Brother Brennan," he said. "You are young, but you speak well. I would encourage you not only to follow the course which you have just said that you intend to pursue, but also to pray about it. Pride goeth before the fall. I don't know if you were in attendance when I had the members of this community listen to the Senate hearing on communism. I daresay some of those who Senator McCarthy has exposed had started going astray by following the impulses of their youth."

"Thank you, Father," the young cleric replied.

As he left, he could hear one of the priests through the door say, "We must watch him."

For Brother Brennan, the peak he had seen ahead of him had become a pit. It would take two more years of philosophical studies to dig himself out of it. All he knew was that he had handled the matter the only way he understood.

Chapter 24

To reach ordination as a priest, it would take Brennan 13 years of study, including the novitiate. The last four would be a period in which at last he would be able to see light at the end of the tunnel. The anticipation grew month by month and even day by day as he flew past one milepost after another.

For the order and the seminary faculty, this represented the final period of education and testing to make certain the seminarians were learned and orthodox in theological matters and did not demonstrate heretical tendencies such as "modernism."

Brennan had looked forward to the study of sacred theology as a gourmet might an elaborate, delicate meal.

The morsels of religious certainty that he had found sweet in his grade school catechism were about to be replaced by a robust, heady dogma that represented God-given, church-ratified truths.

Like a theoretician who revels in mathematical certainty, the orthodox Catholic theologian glories in the absolute "proofs" he reaches by using scripture, "divine revelation" and logic.

None loved the "science" of theology and its rewards more than Brother Brennan O. P. He was "in" theology and took pleasure at the thought that it fit one of the definitions for theology in his

Webster's Dictionary: "A four-year course of specialized religious training in a Roman Catholic major seminary."

The definition of theology given in his textbook, *Brevior Synopsis Theologiae Dogmaticae* (*A Shorter Synopsis of Dogmatic Theology*) was:

The science, which by the work of reason and revelation, discourses on God and on creatures in so far as they refer to Him.

Brennan loved everything about Catholic theology. His dogma was his faith and his faith was his dogma. That his own order, the Dominicans, had contributed much to it was especially satisfying to him, but ultimately the core sweetness of it was the certainty it offered.

The young Dominican most certainly was not among those tainted with modernism. They questioned. They challenged. They boasted of having open minds. Not he. The price of their outlook was their loss of knowing that they could attain the absolute truth etched in the immutable doctrines of a church founded by God and protected by the power of the Holy Spirit.

If he had found satisfaction as a child in believing himself at the top of the mountain for being a white, American, Catholic male then this dogmatic certainty that he had was yet more satisfying. The reference point now was not a mere comparison of himself with the status of other human beings, but the proximity one could have to the mind of God.

The orthodox believer, no matter what his religion, derives a satisfaction that others cannot begin to imagine. It is a certainty that has created martyrs, inspired saints and justified wars.

Modern thinkers or "modernists," as Brennan's theology texts called them, look at dogma and doctrine with a relativism that enjoys none of the allure and sweetness of dogmatic truth and certainty.

Orthodoxy on its part flirts with a fatal flaw in that those who hold to it do not realize it can be so easily be attached to someone else's hook and line in the vast sea of daily living.

An inquiring mind could test that reality; but orthodoxy, by definition, does not permit a follower to have a broadly-focused one.

Some, such as philosopher-scientist Jacob Bronowski, argued that the mind that is stopped from questioning is the greatest fatal flaw a man or society can have because it inevitably leads to the kind of totalitarianism that killed his parents in a Nazi concentration camp.

The young Dominican could not see why the relativists could not grasp the distinction between the dogmatic thinking of Catholic theology and the doctrinaire ideas behind the false isms of the world. He did not need any means such as an inquiring mind to test God-given truth. Faith had already settled the question.

What kind of questions could be asked?

For example: Is theology "a science?"

Answer: In the broadest definition, yes. But it is not asked to meet the specific standards of natural or positive science, i.e. an open mind and the use of the scientific method.

Theology requires neither.

The scientific method demands "the principle and procedures for the systematic pursuit of knowledge that involve recognition and formulation of a problem, the collection of data through observation and experiment and the formulation and testing of hypotheses."

Scholastic theology does do not observe, collect data, experiment or form and test hypotheses.

Another question: Could reason and "divine revelation" be placed on the same level?

Answer: No. If a person believes in the Catholic teaching on scripture and divine revelation, then theological certainty ranks above any conclusions attained by reason alone. If one does not accept these premises as a source for doctrine, all purely logical conclusions are more certain than theological ones.

One other question: Is God a "He?"

Answer: The Judaic, Christian and Islamic scriptures refer in any number of ways to God as "Him," and the Western mind as a result finds it difficult to break loose from that metaphor. Certainly, the ancient Greek males who saw women basically as domestic and sexual slaves also thought that way.

These are not questions and answers Brother Brennan could have formulated when he began the study of theology in 1953. They could have resulted in him being expelled or not allowed to continue his studies in the same way the second classman was in the seminary for telling the joke about a girl's bathing suit.

The alternatives were not only unacceptable to Brennan, they were unthinkable. The dogmas of the Catholic church could not be challenged by any member of it without facing the charges of heresy or, worse, apostasy. The latter, called "the sin against the Holy Spirit," represents an abandonment or rejection of the tenets of one's faith.

He was well aware that a priest, charged with being a heretic or apostate, could be defrocked, stripped of his powers to perform as a member of the clergy. A theology student would simply be thrown out of the seminary or, if he were in solemn vows, expelled from the order.

Had Brennan been permitted himself a free, inquiring mind, it would have certainly led to either expulsion or a voluntary separation from his religious order. The seminarian, however, in reaching the stage of studying theology no longer could be of such a mindset. The theology textbook, lest there be any question, made it very clear to him that "The assent of a reverent faith must be most firm" and the dogmas and positions expounded in its texts "must be given true certitude."

This is the opposite of the open mind asked (although not always demanded) of the graduate student in most other areas of studies from science to literature. Absolute *a priori* adherence to accepted truth is expected of those studying for the clergy not only in the Catholic church but also in other orthodox faiths as well.

The word, "positions," says much. The dogmatic theology text in Brennan's hand held many such to be the doctrine of the church that was not.

As one author summarized, "The seminary manuals...helped to maintain the impression that the positions they advanced were perennial, immutable 'traditions' of the church. These authors furthermore interpreted the writings of the popes--and especially several papal encyclicals of a number of conservative holders of the papal throne--to be far more absolute and binding than they were intended to be."

Brennan would have been horrified to read this critique. The truth is that he would not have seen it for any book that might contain it would not have the bishop's *imprimatur* required for him to be permitted to read it.

Part of the church's problem (and Brennan's) was historical, but he was not allowed to read about that either. To the inquiring mind, the context of history is essential. It was not to Brennan. He believed dogma to be immutable and changes in society irrelevant.

But history does play its role.

In 1864, the papacy was in the process of losing the Papal States to the national revolution that created the unified state of Italy. The harassed Pope Pius IX had been changed in the process from a liberal to a frightened reactionary. He issued an encyclical letter titled, *Syllabus of Errors*. This letter, critical of the world and its views, took church doctrine and put it on the defensive in ways many others did not believe it had to be.

Subsequent popes, especially Pius X, who in his encyclical letters attacked "the evils of modernism", would reiterate this defensive position.

Thus, historical development from the 1860s through the 1950s helped create a climate in which Catholic church doctrine increasingly took on a posture of dogmatism. For Brother Brennan, receiving his initial training in dogmatic theology, the need to join the theologians who supported and endorsed this trend was unquestioned.

Pure and simple, this abuse of near-absolute power by the theologians who wrote the texts coincided with the views of the church's Office of the Propagation of the Faith. The latter, popularly known as the holy office, was the successor of the Inquisition.

For Brennan, there was only one direction open. To become a dogmatic theologian, he needed to begin focusing his attention and support on the growing body of defensive, anti-secular positions being touted as church dogma. If he had not taken that position, he would not be able to break into the field, could not earn membership and might get to first base. He wanted to become a theologian and his impulse to obey was far too strong to do anything but support the group that self-defined itself in the key term, "the majority of theologians," an amorphous group reputed in his textbooks to share infallibility with the pope.

Brother Brennan, in other words, seemed to have but one choice to partake of the power invested in those who assumed the mantle of being a Catholic theologian in the 20th Century. He would have to be willing not to abuse it from the start.

He relished the opportunities that orthodoxy afforded with diminished sense of the freedom he would be giving up. While a few areas of dogmatic theology allowed some innovative thought, they dealt mostly with obscure issues or semantics. Otherwise, if one of his professors had deviated in the classroom from the safe position of the "majority of theologians," it would have been his responsibility not only to reject the teaching, but also to report him to the authorities.

Most seminarians studying theology, and indeed some of the best ones, were not as boxed in by dogmatic theology as Brennan was. They spent 20 to 30 minutes each day studying a page of dogma and propositions about their faith. They stumbled through the relatively easy Latin when it came up with a new word or intricate concept. Otherwise, they memorized the material and then thought about it to a small degree. For the most part, it had little to do with their faith or way of life. Sometimes, they might raise a few honest questions or voice an occasional doubt; but when they saw Brother Brennan not challenge an idea, they found little reason for themselves to do so.

To his classmates, moral theology and canon law were more consequential, more important than was dogma. They fairly much knew church doctrine, having learned it in catechism. Dogmas separated religions.

To them, the Protestants were heretics, but so what? The days of war between religions and sects were over. All others seemed second-rate religions, one which did not have the traditions or discipline of Catholicism, but which made undeniable contributions on the American scene, if not elsewhere. The theologians in Rome, however, took their dogmatic errors most seriously. Let them be. They were not hurting anyone.

Outwardly, however, each of them paid full and total acknowledgement, respect, loyalty and obedience to every aspect of Holy Mother Church. Each day, they recited "the creed," an affirmation of religious belief that starts, "I Believe in God, the Father Almighty, the creator of heaven and earth,..." In it they stated that they accept as true all the dogmas of Catholicism.

Despite a lack of interest in the formulation of some of those doctrines and the debate over them, the seminarians were orthodox believers. They were also members of the religious order that provided the great houses of theological study in Rome and around the world with some of their most eminent scholars and teachers. Also, by tradition, the Dominicans traditionally provide the pope himself with his own "personal theologian."

Brennan did not share any ambivalence whatsoever on doctrine or on the conviction that Protestants and all other non-Catholic thinkers were heretics and were wrong. The dogmas of the church, to him, were the tectonic plates that were responsible for the future of the planet. If out of whack or sync, they could cause theological and moral continental shifts, earthquakes, volcanoes, tidal waves and serious havoc. Theology, to him, was the study of God, the highest function that the mind, the intellect, could perform.

This was the mindset of Brother Brennan Jordan, O.P. as he launched into the study that would turn into his profession.

The young theology student, however, sped through the textbook and could quote every passage in it from memory. He found dogmatic theology easier than any subject he had ever studied in his life. The text was not long; the Latin, easy; the surprises, very few and the formulations, exactly what he expected them to be.

The key to his study of theology would be the footnotes in the text. He needed to embrace them, go to their sources, read the original material and build a structure of his own. The book in front of him was but a compilation, a secondary source. Anything he learned from it had to be underpinned by primary sources. He would, in other words, do his doctoral work while his classmates were learning basic dogmatic theology.

This time Brennan would not be out on a limb as he had been by attempting to work with the writings of Aristotle and Einstein to establish a philosophical proof for the existence of God. He would be traveling a tried and true path, one that the majority of theologians were already on. He was not going outside the church to research but rather into the very cellars.

The young Dominican began to recognize in the dogmatic theological firmament names such as Hubry, Garrigou and Tiberghien. He came to realize on which papal encyclicals the dogmatic theologians relied. Repeatedly, the pope whom they went to was that of the turn-of-the-century pontiff who condemned modernism, allowed grade school students to receive communion at seven instead of 12 years of age and who eventually was canonized and became Saint Pius X.

Brother Brennan had started off wanting to be another St. Thomas Aquinas and had still not given this up.

In the meantime, as he focused and intensified his theological studies, he could not believe that his ordination was fast approaching. At the end of his first year of theological study, he had finally become old enough to take his solemn, final vows. His classmates had done so two years earlier, but he had to be 21 to commit himself forever to poverty, chastity and obedience and in his life as a Dominican.

Next, he found himself being admitted to the minor clerical "orders" of lector, tonsure, acolyte and exorcist. After his second year in theology, he was ordained a subdeacon and after his third; a deacon.

Ordination to the full priesthood would be in a year. He was intimidated by the idea, deeply so.

For 12 years, he had studied and prepared himself, but it had never been for something real. Now, it was 12 months; no, only 11; wait a minute, it was ten months. Was this possible?

Everyone--other theology students and even the faculty-- started treating him and his classmates differently.

He, Brother Brennan, would soon become Father Brennan. He would have the power to say mass, hear confessions and forgive sins, to be a part of the church's *magisterium*. He already was an exorcist and had the power to cast out evil spirits and, as a deacon, he technically could even perform marriages and give the last rites. It was as though he were maturing and transforming as a being, not just a human, but as part of a divine plan.

The final steps prior to his ordination were many, ranging from learning the rubrics of saying mass to being fitted for street clothes and a Roman collar. They also included one last year of courses in moral theology, devoted largely to sins against the sixth and ninth commandments; in other words, sex.

The classes were conducted in a classroom with both transoms tightly closed so the other, younger theology students would not overhear the professor list and elaborate on the various sexual peccadilloes the newly-ordained priests could expect to hear in the confessional and counseling sessions.

Brother Brennan listened and decided he would understand it all a lot better after he had become Father Brennan.

The Father Provincial held a special pre-ordination conference with each of the cleric deacons. He was the same priest who had served as rector of the minor seminary when Brennan was a student there. He opened the meetings with the words, "Well, it looks like you've made it. It's been a long 13 years, hasn't it?" He ended the session with the words, "As you've probably guessed, you will be heading for Rome. We are very proud of you, Brother Brennan. You are not only very smart, but you have an excellent attitude and focus. We both well remember that day when I came to your home and you were so clever in convincing me I should let you come to the seminary despite your youth. You were right."

The words brought a tear to Brennan's eyes, not because his superior was complimenting him but because he thought of his mother, who would attend his ordination and first mass, and of his father, who would not be there.

His seminary class had started off with 54 students in it. Nine would be ordained. Three of these had joined the rest along the way so that only six of the originals had made it through the gauntlet of 13 years.

Brennan was one of those six. His obedience and orthodoxy had seemingly paid off.

Chapter 25

The hustle and bustle before Brennan's ordination and first mass could best be compared with the commotion leading up to a wedding. The details seemed infinite and the event awesome in not only a beautiful, but also a frightening way. The two religious celebrations represented the culmination of seminary life as well as the irrevocable beginning of an unknowable new one. Just as the divorced person often looks back with at least a twinge of nostalgia about the day they were married to "him" or "her," so even the man who has abandoned the priesthood remembers the event with emotions that have not withered entirely.

The pace had sped up for the young deacon caught in the preparation. As a seminarian, he had rarely ever found himself responsible for events and doings that affected his confreres, his family as well as outsiders. This time, he had help from his superiors and professors, who go through this each year, and the liturgists who teach the rubrics for the ritual of ordination, the sacraments and the mass. But, while learning all this, he was communicating with his pastor about the first mass, with his mother about the invitation list and reception. And, at the same time, he was attempting to say some kind of good-bye to classmates with whom he had shared the last 13 years.

The answer to all questions seemed to be to speed up and cut corners. This approach quickly caught the about-to-be-ordained seminarian. He had spent his years in the seminary never running, except on those occasions when he participated in sports activities.

There were other, emotional preparations. The theology students had spent 13 years in a seminary, a word and concept that came from the Latin/French word for a seedbed. Now, they were about to be transported into a much more arbitrary and hostile environment, "the world."

Perhaps, the drama of this change could best be illustrated by their need for new language. Specifically, what should they call members of the other sex? In conversation, they realized what a major problem this represented. Up to this point, the seminarians had mostly used the term, "them." They could also use "she" or "her;" but the words, "women" and "girls," had been encrusted with the connotation of temptation and contact to be avoided. There was no sin in using the two words, but there was an underlying discomfort.

The new terms chosen to replace "them" had to avoid any hint at intimacy.

So, what to use?

"Members of the opposite sex" as a phrase showed a respectful distance, but was too formal and perhaps cold.

"Girls" could be used if the individuals in a group were much older or younger.

"Gals" was friendly if a little awkward. Selected use could be recommended at best.

"Ladies" was about the only acceptable term any of Brennan's classmates could come up with.

For once, the brilliant young Dominican did not engage in the conversation. He considered the whole discussion about as relevant as one about professional sports. He saw no great need to stop calling women, "them."

Still, life's pace—whether he was prepared for it or not-- would soon change. It would pick up, once he was "out." In some ways, just as in marriage, the event would represent deep, personal transition.

The seminary scheduled for the students a four-day retreat that helped slow everything down and assist in the transition. It was called a retreat. Admittedly, it was one interrupted by attending to pesky details, but the impulse of it was to allow the individual to be by himself and to reflect on the change in life and status that was taking place.

The retreat was a period of scheduled times of silence, meditation, prayer, reading and sermons geared to help an individual pay closer attention to his spiritual side. Dominicans were especially noted for being apt retreat masters both for other members of the clergy and laity. It was a chance for the friars to preach, a function, which members of the order believed to be at the heart of their vocations.

No role as a retreat master (save the one who serves in this capacity for the pope) was considered as crucial as that of giving these spiritual exercises to the class of young men about to be ordained. The man chosen for this occasion was always noted either for his ability to preach or his holiness, and hopefully for both.

Father Raphael was such a man. He was from a different province, but Brother Brennan had heard of him. The sentence used to describe him was "He preaches a mean sermon," but "mean" was meant in an entirely complimentary sense.

Brennan hit the retreat running. He had all but forgotten that there was going to be one. He was not alone. So had the majority of his eight classmates, all equally busy with the business of being ordained and preparing to say their first public masses.

The priest's first words were, "You will, within a week, be priests 'according to the order of Melchisedech.'" If there is any phrase an aspiring priest hears over the years of his seminary training, it is this one. It was part of the ritual, scripture classes, sermons, spiritual advice and even conversations. It attempted to connect the priesthoods of the Old and the New Testaments. These words represented history as well as the future and its promise. They struck a note of majesty and yet had become so familiar and were so often used that they tended to seem trite.

Coming from Father Raphael's mouth and taking into account the setting and the circumstances, the words proved a jolt rather than jargon to Brother Brennan and his classmates. This back and forth movement of old phrases in new settings happens often in a thorough training for something such as the priesthood. The process was full of repetition and the key lines were those most frequently repeated.

"If there is one virtue, a very necessary one, that I want to stress in this retreat, it is humility," Father Raphael continued. "It is the only way a human being can ever accept a role such as that of the priesthood."

Brother Brennan liked the retreat master already. The young, soon-to-be Dominican priest, who mistakenly confused his own willingness to obey with the virtue of humility, found himself giving a slight nod of agreement to the message of the priest. Such thought, however, ill prepared him for what the retreat master said next.

The man continued to sit informally in a chair rather than stand up while addressing the class of deacons. His hands clasped one another and gently moved over each other in a manner, which indicated the words he had started to speak would not be easy.

"Let us start, as we always must, in finding humility in those of us who preach in God's name," he began.

The seminarians squirmed.

"It is difficult," the priest continued, "to talk about being humble. I see your discomfort in being open about it. Uneasy sits the person who is public about it."

"Sure," Brennan mumbled under his breath, uncertain what this one-word response of his meant.

"You have probably heard things about me," the priest continued, "that I am a reasonably good preacher. Maybe, someone told you that I have a certain reputation for telling a humorous story. It would not be true humility for me to deny that."

His audience laughed in relief that something had been discounted from his offer to be humble.

"What you may not know, may not have heard, is that I am also an alcoholic," he said.

It would have been difficult for Brennan to imagine what he might possibly have said that could have been more startling. The young Dominican friars listening to the older Dominican had heard of his holiness rather than his drinking. They were aware that alcoholism was a problem for a number of members of their own province, but it was not spoken of publicly and never confirmed by the addicted person.

Brennan was disappointed, as perhaps others were. They were all preparing for the happiest and most important day of their lives and here this priest was introducing his own squalid personal problem into the preparations. It seemed neither fitting nor fair. If this assessment had validity, the retreat master was about to say something that would be worse.

"There are ten of us sitting together in this chapel," he continued. "Nine are here because you are completing your final preparation for the priesthood. I daresay two or three of us--however, you want to count--are or will be alcoholics. It afflicts doctors and members of the clergy disproportionately. And Catholic priests come up on the high end of the statistics."

The words startled Brennan and he would rather not hear them. Once upon a time, alcohol had been a problem for him, an all but unspoken one, but he had conquered it. Well, he had except for the two or three times he had drunken a little extra wine on the rare occasions it was served to the community. But the secret, sneaky part was gone. He drank wine openly and was not ashamed of it. The seminarians had not, on any regular basis, access to hard drinks.

He found himself distracted by these memories and realized his attention had diverted from the words of the priest.

"I once sat in a chapel such as this, waiting and praying during those last days before ordination," the retreat master continued. "I had no thoughts of becoming an alcoholic. I aspired as each of you does to becoming the worthiest priest on the face of the earth. I knew I could preach and that is our profession, we friar preachers. I knew it would be well."

Brennan did not know why his body wanted to squirm the way it did.

"I looked ahead and saw a placid lake," the preacher continued. "I saw myself sailing on it, propelled by the kind and caring hand of God."

The retreat master knew he had struck a chord. He saw the fear of self-recognition in several of the deacons in front of him. One of them was Brennan. The seminary had become confining, even trite and boring for him and all his classmates, he knew. Ordination would break the ties that bound them and the breezes that blew would be fresh and challenging. They had been preparing to carry out the will of God in the world, now they would be able to do it.

"Things didn't work out the way I thought they would," the priest added. "Let's just say that freedom is not always as easy as you might think. Personalities can be difficult to deal with. Ideals are not attained. Under these circumstances pressure grows and we find out our weaknesses and our flaws."

"He didn't prepare well enough in the seminary," Brennan said to himself in words that even he recognized as bordering on the uncharitable.

"I do not make excuses," the young friar heard Father Raphael continue. "I take responsibility before God and man. I am an alcoholic. Looking back on who I became, I must tell you that the most important day of my life was not the one on which I was ordained, but the one in which I joined Alcoholics Anonymous."

Brother Brennan was not only stunned, but also irate. His superiors had allowed a priest to address them who was all but heretical in what he had to say. You did not compare membership in the priesthood with that of a secular, even if sometimes helpful, organization.

"I want to read you the words of another priest on AA:

'Alcoholics Anonymous is natural; it is natural at the point where nature comes closest to the supernatural, naturally in humiliations and in consequent humility. There is something spiritual about an art museum or a symphony, and the Catholic church approves of our use of them. There is something spiritual about AA too, and Catholic participation in it almost invariably results in poor Catholics becoming better Catholics."

"I would add to that another line, 'It almost invariably results in poor priests becoming better priests.'"

Brother Brennan found the priest's message an intense distraction. Perhaps, he needed it, he felt, but as a point of reflection rather than as a message. He could possibly even learn something about humility from this man so willing to expose his flaws, he told himself. Still, his need was to focus on his ordination to the priesthood. He dared not let this happen without his full attention and devotion.

The retreat was over in what seemed like hours instead of days. Father Raphael lived up to his billing as an excellent preacher and a man who could tell a humorous story, but what Brennan would remember for years afterwards was the moments of silence during the times between the sermons. He had a need to use them as an opportunity to remind himself that his impending ordination was real. It had, he found, sneaked up on him even though he had known the date and place for 13 years. The white charger on which he had been riding all that time had started galloping at a pace he had not imagined possible. He had prepared and put things in place, and suddenly he was not ready.

The short time in which he could make his last reflective efforts, he found, were not filled with his final reality check but rather with a retreat master's exposure of his alcoholism. He had counted on one last opportunity to know and understand what was happening to him. Instead, he found himself imagining the priest dead drunk. And, what had gone wrong? How had Father Raphael himself not prepared in the seminary? And, if the same thing were happening to one of his classmates, how could he have seen it and warned him? And, which of them might fill the statistical probability of becoming alcoholics? Finally, he settled on Brother Richard, the slowest in his class at his studies, but he doubted it even about him.

And then it was the morning of ordination. It had actually arrived. It was June 22, 1957, the longest day of the year. He had awoken early. The sun had not risen, but it was already becoming light.

Ordination! This day on which he would be changed forever. On the day he would be buried, his casket would be lined up in the church with his head to the altar. For anyone else but a priest, it would be the opposite of that. His head and his hands would be anointed this day with oil that could be rinsed off, but the marks would be on his soul. He would be ordained a priest as had the twelve apostles, Peter and John, Matthew and the doubter, Thomas, and yes, even Judas Iscariot, the betrayer.

Brennan worried about himself, even though he knew no one else did. He was a member of a religious order organized in such as a way as to help individuals do repeated and extensive self-examinations, but he did not like to admit his flaws, except in a certain formulaic, impersonal way.

"I think too much," he liked to say of himself as though he were being critical. But the issue, he knew, was not how often he looked at his limitations, but rather how deeply.

He lay prostrate on the floor of in the sanctuary of the priory before the seated archbishop. Along with his classmates he was clothed in the white dress-like alb and rope cinctures that would be beneath his vestments, as he would say mass and administer the sacraments from this day forth.

As the about-to-be-ordained Brennan lay there silently, he thought not of the glory of the moment, but of his faults. He saw them as cracks rather than fissures, but he feared them more than sickness, death or any outside force. Nine years before, in the novitiate, he had set off in search of perfection. He had, to some extent, achieved this; but only in the image he projected, not in the substance of whom he was.

His nickname, usually used behind his back, but sometimes openly, was St. Brennan. Among his more naive fellow seminarians, some wondered whether there were not some substance to it as he indeed spent extraordinary time in chapel, was kind beyond belief and remained the strict, obedient cleric of his younger years. Others, with a certain degree of cynicism, suspected a certain amount of fraud, but could not produce evidence of it.

His mother alone had witnessed any indications of his inner impulses. She had seen and destroyed the matchbook collection. She had known of his interest in Millie. Though, "a woman wrapped in silence," to quote scripture, she had on rare occasions given him side glances that said she knew he was not all he presented himself to be.

Now, she was in the audience behind him, looking paler than he had remembered her. She had written him a letter he had opened after the end of his retreat. It had been full of several last religious exhortations, a promise that she would continue to say the rosary and make novenas for him and a strange request that he "pray for a special intention" at his ordination mass. He knew instinctively what it was, the only thing it could be. She was sick, truly sick, possibly dying. Brennan did not know where this interpretation of her request was coming from, but he was certain it was true.

The prostrate figure, who would rather have been bathing in the glory of these moments, began to obsess about his weaknesses, flaws and loneliness.

His mother was special to him, somebody who was there. His superiors were powerfully present in his life, but they were not real in the way she was. They could and would be replaced as his life got on. His classmates, just as he had begun to feel something toward them, were about to be scattered.

All of this left God, the person who was calling him to this life. But the Supreme Being came and went in his life like the wind. Sometimes, his presence was strong. Other times, it could not be felt.

God was at the top of the chain of command, his ultimate religious superior, He who was to be obeyed. He was above the prior, the bishop and the pope. His office was behind a closed door. Brennan worked hard to have feelings toward God, devoting himself to gratitude, humility, honesty and devotion.

But, in truth, Brennan knew little about real feelings. His relationship with the Holy Trinity, with Christ, with what St. Thomas called "the Beatific Vision," was more intellectual than personal.

Brennan was aghast. The ritual had continued and he was kneeling before the archbishop who was holding his hands over the young Dominican's head.

He was becoming a priest in this very moment.

A birth had taken place.

He was Father Brennan Jordan, Order of Friar Preachers.

Chapter 26

Whereas the anointing and laying on of hands by the archbishop transformed Brennan and chartered a new course for his future; his first mass, performed with as much pomp and ceremony as his small, parish church could provide, culminated his past. The ordination created Father Brennan. The Sunday morning celebration in front of family, friends and parishioners focused also on his mother and, to a lesser extent, his dead father.

Mrs. Jordan sat in the first row, as she would have were it instead the wedding of a son or daughter. She was in Father Brennan's mind and prayers, as was his father, whose body lay in Belgium.

Those who saw him on the altar surrounded by six other priests, including his aged, retired pastor, all saw a young boy, who looked more like a server at this mass rather than the celebrant of it.

Their comments were similar:

"He's so very young, don't you think?"

"He's just a kid."

"I didn't know they ordained them that young."

"I think he is the youngest priest I ever saw in my life. I mean, really the youngest…by far."

Inevitably, someone would add a comment such as:

"But I hear he's very, very smart."

"Hey, the Dominicans got a smart one."

His dogmatic theology professor, Father Eustace Farrell, O. P., gave the sermon and announced that Father Brennan, after taking some preliminary studies at Catholic University in Washington, D.C., would be going to Rome to get a doctorate in sacred theology.

"I have a vision of this newly-anointed priest's future," he said. "I see him, with the grace of God, standing strong against the winds of secularism and doctrinal error. We here today see a young man. We are startled by his age. But, let me assure one and all that those of us who have taught him, those of us who are his fellow Dominicans, know that he is not immature. He is not a reed shaken by the wind. This Father Brennan Jordan is a steadfast young man. Of that I can assure you."

"A steadfast man!" It was a phrase that others would pick up and use to describe him. He would eventually hear it as far away as Rome. It would be used sometimes in respect, but on other occasions in mild derision.

When he first heard it that day, Father Brennan liked it. He would grow to wish it had never been uttered.

After the sermon, the retired pastor walked to the communion rail and added a few words:

"We are very proud of our young Father Brennan," the elderly priest said. "I remember well when he came for my blessing. I immediately saw God's mark upon him."

His grade school principal, who had befriended him, had been transferred out of state. He had invited her for his first mass, but she could not find another member of her order to accompany her back to her old parish and therefore could not attend. Nuns were not allowed to travel by themselves.

She wrote him a letter that wished him well, promised her prayers and added, " I know just what the pastor will say. He'll take credit for you."

And she was right.

As the mass continued, the young priest, remembered Harry Scheib, his companion on the car rides to the factory. He wished that he were not dead and could have been at the mass. Harry would not have understood, especially the religious words and sentiments that flowed so freely this day.

The thought of the dead Harry brought Brennan front and center with the image of father. Connected, even now with that memory was something he never understood, an aspect that was comfortable. He wished his father were here so they could talk about it. During a retreat several years earlier he concluded that he and his father, in at least one way, had been headed in almost exactly opposite directions. He had committed himself to seeking God through obedience. His father always seemed to be put off by such an idea. It had been his father's mind, not his heart, which needed to be changed. He had believed too strongly in personal freedom as a virtue at the expense of truth and doctrine.

"I am the way, the truth and the life," Brennan quoted Christ as saying in an imagined lecture he had aimed at his deceased father. "Dad, maybe now you understand that."

Brennan then raised his hands toward the sky as if to speak to his father and, in a protesting tone, quoted the poet, Milton:

"License, they mean when they cry 'Liberty'..."

He knew his hand-raising gesture was more than a little bizarre. He could not recall a single instance in which his father had uttered the words, "freedom" or "liberty," but somehow the connection was there in an almost adversarial way between them and always would be.

It was his mother, far more than his father, on whom his thoughts focused at his first mass. He found it strange that while he was in the seminary he could go weeks without thinking of her and wait days before ever opening a letter from her. Still, as his ordination approached, she once again had become not only real, but also central in his thoughts.

Father Brennan had begun to think about her with true concern if not affection in ways he had not since he left home. He recalled how she had put his cold hands under her armpits to warm them when he was a little child, how she always insisted he have the last piece of meat or dessert left on the plate and how proud she was of him.

He recalled once overhearing her night prayers after she thought him asleep.

"Dear Almighty Father in Heaven, I ask you to take my little Mikey and to keep him holy and devoted to you," she had prayed. "And, for myself, if you would do it, I ask that you spare me long enough to live to see him say his first mass."

That prayer had been answered, although just barely. The next day upon arriving back in Detroit after his ordination, he learned she had had a breast removed two years before and he had never known about it. He asked Mrs. Bartman, who lived next door, about her. The neighbor was shocked that he did not know. She told him that his mother had once had cancer and now it had come back.

Father Brennan was stunned. No thought came. No tangible feelings arose in him. A tear, at least he thought it was, seemed to form in his eye.

The next day, as he began saying his first mass two months before his 25th birthday, he suddenly found himself feeling the emotions toward his mother that had been almost completely missing since his high school days.

He had lived the intervening years without a sense of any need to have feelings toward her. In going into the Dominicans and the monastery, he had literally renounced family and she had been it.

With his whole life, he was doing what she wanted him to do. That, whenever he had questioned it, had been enough. Somehow, it now seemed, the more he had renounced his family, that is, his mother; the more he had become her.

She was going to die. He was feeling some of the same ties and binds he had in seeing his father off at the train station. And it was sad, deeply, deeply so. But it was an emotion he could suffer from but not reach with a human response that might help either of them now.

Father Brennan stopped short of recriminating himself for what had not been there between them these recent years. He knew it was as much, if not more, her choice as his. At worst, they had cut each other off and, somehow, it had been necessary for the mission on which she had sent him. She did not want him to look back, even at her.

He was looking, if not back, at least straight at her for once.

The Saturday night before his first mass, they had sat alone back in the old furniture that crowded the small living room; he a priest; and, she his mother. Few words had passed as he thought of little but her now frail health.

She had reached into the folds of her lapped dress and pulled out an old letter for him to read. It had been written to her in 1929 when she was spending a short two months as a postulant in a convent. The dated missive was her own mother's, that of his grandmother, whom he had never known.

Mrs. Jordan now presented it to her son to demonstrate how deeply religious his grandmother had been and possibly to make herself look more reasonable by comparison. In handing the letter to him, his mother asked him to remember her own mother at his first mass.

He promised this almost incidentally as his eyes scanned his grandmother's letter. He grew more uncomfortable with each of her words, exhortations and sentiments, especially the last two lines, "And always remember that God has a special plan for you, a mission. You must give him back all the gifts you have ever received from him. I must go now or I will be late for the novena."

They were the words with which his mother had sent him on a special mission as a child.

Those words had always been his, spoken to him by God through his mother. His grandmother's letter, as he read it, struck at him as might a broadsword. His mother's urgent message to him had been an echo. He had always understood it, but now he was hearing it as someone else talking to him through her.

This was as loveless letter, with the signature being a simple "Mother," not even "Your mother."

The letter had detailed his grandmother's religious activities over the past week without a hint of affection here, not even at the end of it.

Then, in a thought that reflected a renewed coldness he suddenly felt in his relationship to the woman slouched in the chair across from him, he determined to make certain none of his letters to her would get saved after her death.

His grandmother, he suspected, had died from breast cancer; but no one ever used the term. He had never met her, but now, he was finding she still existed in his own mother, only a little less intense.

His mother was going to die and the message of the letter was that he would be carrying her in himself as she had his grandmother.

His mother had been God's agent in his own life, he had to remind himself, and it was she who knew and had said so clearly that he had a mission awaiting him that was indeed special and particular. This, if it were not an entirely happy consideration, was a deeply meaningful one, a vision that could keep him on his course and make him the steadfast person his former professor told the world he would be.

Such were the thoughts that beset him as he sat for the first time in the celebrant's chair while several parish announcements were made after the sermon. It was then that he looked out in the audience and saw a man, perhaps ten to 20 pounds heavier and 12 years older than when he had last encountered him. It was Eddie Golf, who had been the president of the senior class in the minor seminary, who had been kind to him, who had borne the name "Brennan" before he did and who had disappeared, not even responding to a letter sent to him.

"He's here," Brennan said to the little boy inside himself.

Eddie Golf, at the moment, was more important than anyone else in the world. For once in Brennan's life, someone had come back from among the lost, if not the dead.

After the mass was over, there was a picture taken of the young priest surrounded by the co-celebrants, his family, friends and as many of the parishioners who wanted to be in the photo.

Father Brennan kept trying to crane his neck in every direction to catch another sight of Eddie Golf. He was not successful. Even later, when the young priest scanned a crowd photo, the elusive figure was not in it.

The man he saw was Eddie, of that he was certain. It was not someone who merely looked like him. That was a look of recognition and a half smile for the newly ordained priest. But the clothes Eddie was wearing told him nothing. They were a light brown suit, a white shirt and a tie. That's all he knew and it said nothing.

The young priest tried to create an imaginary conversation with the former seminarian who had not stayed.

Brennan saw him married. No, he was not sure about that. A lawyer or a doctor, more than likely a lawyer. No, not that either. He was a will of the wisp and little more.

"Why did you leave?" Brennan asked the man whom he conjured up.

"I just left, that's all," the hypothetical Eddie answered.

"That's a very disappointing answer," Brennan retorted.

"Sorry, that's all I have to say."

"Eddie," Brennan said to the mirror in front of which he himself stood, "that's not good enough."

Eddie Golf had certainly not intended to do so, but he had put a big, disappointing question mark at the end of the most already haunting day of the Dominican friar's life.

To Father Brennan, as he looked back at the first day of his public ministry, Eddie stood out as the sole person with whom the young priest could honestly say he wanted to talk. What he had rather done was make small talk with more than a hundred people with whom conversation was painful.

With whom else might it have been real or easy?

The pastor was out of the question. His professor, whom he had personally chosen to deliver the sermon, was interesting; but he did not wish to speak with him. Each of his past acquaintances was a "no." Even his mother was one. He longed to give her a hug, but she pulled back and asked instead for his priestly blessing. The two exchanged very few words.

Most of all, he did not want to talk to his former teachers and fellow parishioners. Each and every one of them felt called upon to tell him, as though he did not know, how happy he had made his mother by going to the seminary and being ordained. And, if he heard the expression once, he listened to it over and over, "This has to be the happiest day of her life."

Several did ask if she were all right, although it was quite obvious that her health was not.

Each time as an individual spoke of her happiness over his being ordained, he smiled as though it were the first time he had heard it. Then, he nodded and gave the person his blessing.

Several of his teachers recalled his accomplishments under their tutelage, adding next that they always knew he would become a priest and make his mother proud.

Father Brennan thought about these things as he lay in bed at the rectory that night instead of in his mother's house. He had gone early to the room prepared for him, pleading that he still had a good part of his breviary to say. He had completed praying the final "hours" or sections of it as he paced back and forth in the small room. Now, he was lying in bed thinking, almost as though he were suddenly getting those moments to verify the reality that he had sought during his retreat days earlier.

It was over, all over. He was still vibrating from the hustle and bustle and pomp and ceremony, but he knew the reality was anti-climatic. It had gone flawlessly, but the substance seemed to be missing.

His life was changed, radically, but he could not get hold of the bigness of it. He could list details, but they added up to nothing solid. After 13 years of preparing to be here, he was not certain where he was.

In order not to be crazy, he had to know what had happened. Who he had become?

All he knew for certain was that his name had changed once more. He was no longer Little Mikey, Michael or Mike, as some of his old neighbors had wanted to address him. He was no more Brother Brennan, as he was still tempted to call himself. He was now Father Brennan and whatever that meant.

He would have to be even more attentive to those shoe prints he saw ahead of him into which he felt compelled to step as he obediently moved along the path life was affording him. He was free from the seminary and its rules, but not from his destiny, his mission.

"*Deus vult*," he told himself in Latin. "God wills it."

It said everything and in a language he had learned to think.

Chapter 27

The young priest was in transition and he was not ready for it. He had always carefully and thoughtfully readied himself for anything intellectual in his life. This was true whether the change represented studying new subjects, switching from philosophy to theology or writing a paper. Anything even remotely emotional or about every day living, he simply did not know how to prepare for or to meet.

This was the day after his first mass, the second of his two-week vacation. His scheduling for the morning, afternoon and evening at first seemed crowded. As he found himself closer to it, he realized it was not.

Father Brennan was not prepared for being responsible over his own time. During 13 years of seminary training, he had always followed schedules created for him by others. Most recently, as he readied himself for ordination, every moment of his time was programmed.

This day would begin with mass at 7:30 a.m. to be attended by his mother and several fellow members of the Ladies Altar Society. He would then take all of them out to breakfast at a local pancake house.

The next thing on his agenda would not be until late afternoon. He had promised to stop in the convent and share cake and cookies with the nuns. It had to be late because most of them were taking summer courses at the University of Detroit. They had invited several of the Dominican nuns who also took classes "to come meet the brilliant young Dominican priest about whom everyone was talking."

In the evening there would be a very different party, one at the rectory for priests of the areas. The refreshments would not be limited to cake and cookies.

The mass went according to schedule and expectation. He used his finest voice so all could hear the words, especially of consecration as he pronounced them distinctly. One of the servers for the mass was a diocesan seminarian studying philosophy. He looked older than Father Brennan did and a visitor in the sacristy came up to him and congratulated him on his ordination.

The breakfast included nine women, all more than 40 years of age. They peppered him with compliments and questions and made a fuss over his mother, who still wore her corsage from the day before.

He told them about St. Dominic and the Dominicans, making only a brief reference to the Albigensian heresy that had started it all. He spoke of priories and how they were organized. He explained about the vows of poverty, chastity and obedience and why he himself felt them necessary in his work for God. Then, he added information about his future life. How first he would study at Catholic University in Washington, D.C. and later in Rome.

Father Brennan looked at the women and at his mother and then spoke of her. He said how she had encouraged him and he told for the first time the story of him overhearing her night prayer that he would remain devoted to God and her request to be able to attend his first mass. He could see the story send chills through those at the table as the gossip had spread the word that she was dying.

He spoke of his father, telling the story of his death. Tears were visible in the eyes of several of the women, all of whom had relatives and close friends who had been sent overseas during the war.

"My mother could have reasonably asked me to leave the seminary and help support her," he said, "but she didn't. Why? Because that's who my mother is. She is, as the scripture says, 'a valiant woman.'"

She was touched by the story, he could tell, but still she waved off a hug from him and asked instead for his priestly blessing.

His mother, after breakfast, begged off from any further activities, by saying, "I'm feeling poorly. All the excitement has tired me. I need to rest up today."

That left Brennan on his own. He had no plans. No one wanted him.

He would, he finally decided, take a Woodward Avenue bus to downtown Detroit. He wished the streetcars of his childhood still ran there, but he settled for going to buy himself a Vernor's Ginger Ale with a cherry flavoring. They were sold, he knew, at the bottling plant on Woodward. He would hoist the drink in his father's honor, for it was he who had treated a little boy to one there on the day he left for service overseas.

What surprised the young priest was not the changes that had taken place in his native city since he was a child, but the ones in himself.

The world still saw him as young. He felt himself much older than he had ever been. Ordination had not changed his body or his face, but it had altered his mind and his self-perception.

The actual act of walking down the street amazed him. He had nowhere where he had to be, no one to whom to explain why he was going there. He had no assignment for this trip, no report to give.

His comparison for what he was feeling was an upwarping, the kind which followed the retreat of the glaciers that covered much of North America 10,000 years earlier and changed the landscape. As these masses of ice melted and receded, the ground that had been pressed down under their billions of tons, popped up much as a loaf of bread might in an oven.

He was now experiencing such a phenomenon. His life in the seminary had been lived under almost complete regimentation and detailed rules. He had to account for his time, his flaws and himself. At this moment he did not have to do that.

Father Brennan was wearing a new black suit and a white Roman collar. As he passed people on the street, he asked himself, what were they expecting of him? Did they wonder whether or not he had said his breviary yet? Was he on some kind of mission that was part of his ministry? If so, why was he not walking faster?

"What stupid questions I am projecting on these people, who could care less about me!" he exclaimed to himself. Brennan knew it was the after-effects of his day of glory.

He had the same experience riding on the bus. He was a priest. If there were a bad accident, he could minister to the others and, if they were Catholics, hear their confessions and give them the last rites. He had not yet received permission from the bishop to hear confessions, but in a matter of life and death, a priest can do so in an individual case without such a permit.

If any of his fellow passengers sat down next to him because they knew him to be a priest and had asked for spiritual advice or counseling, he would be called upon to give it.

Such was his role. He saw it clearly, but it had little to do with the other part of him. For that, he had no answers, not even many questions.

He arrived at the Vernor's Ginger Ale plant, purchased his drink, raised his glass to his father, choked a little and gulped it down.

Now, he was free, frightfully so.

To look at the buildings was boring. To go back to his mother's home or to the rectory would have been a retrenchment of the worst sort.

But, what to do? He wondered and continued on, passing a dime-a-dance hall that was not open. It made him curious, but he knew that in wearing a Roman collar he could not show his reaction in any way.

Several pawnshops received even less of his attention. Although he had received a camera for his ordination and he later wished he had checked them out to see if they might have a cheap light meter.

Then he saw it, a wonder of wonders, a used bookstore. He knew he could go in here even in his collar. And go in, he did.

Brennan at last was in among a collection of books where there had not been prior restraint. He realized that quickly when he saw a section of science fiction pulp magazines with covers that would have caused blushes on the faces of the artists who drew the matchbook covers in his childhood collection. The accentuation of the curves and the bareness of the women's bodies portrayed on them stunned him. He was too self-conscious, however, to stare for more than a second in that direction.

The Woodward Avenue store had nooks and crannies full of other books far more intellectually stimulating than the magazines promised to be.

Immediately, as he came in the store, he all but bumped into a section of "New arrivals." He gasped at the breath of the subject matter on the table before him. There were novels, self-help books, texts, religious tomes, train books, classics, workshop manuals, works in foreign languages, biographies and first editions.

It was a six-course meal for his mind and, until he saw it, he had not realized how hungry something inside him was. At the same time, he was constrained from even nibbling at it. It was an intellectual temptation, and he had committed himself not to sin with his brain, not to let his curiosity carry him into the area of license, not to get in trouble with his superiors.

But, he knew, if he were willing to throw the dice, here rather than in the 10-cents-a-dance hall is where he would sin, where he would cast the die.

He turned and started to walk out of the bookstore.

"Where are your religion and your philosophy sections?" he asked.

The bookstore employed grinned. He had seen the collared clergymen half glance at the pulps when he had entered the first time. An older man would have been far more nonchalant. This one was not only unusually young, but also obviously inexperienced.

In some ways, Brennan was doing something potentially even more sinful than if he had picked up the pulps and started reading them.

He handled a book in German by Martin Luther, a book on religion by a woman who was not even a nun and a volume by an apostate priest titled *The Errors of Rome*.

These were not as daring for him to handle, however, as the philosophy books he picked up and sorted through. He saw there works Sartre, Nietzche, Kirkegaard and Descartes, names that he had read only in his philosophy or theology texts with the Latin word *contra* before them.

The experience, as he started to peruse the volumes, became too intense.

He walked away and headed for another section, any other.

Brennan found himself in front of the authors' section, where the latest fiction was mixed in with that of the past

The young priest had taken up reading novels as a break from his philosophy courses. He was amazed at the range of them that the librarian had put on the shelves, especially since he himself had a copy of the religious novel, *Quo Vadis* taken away from him in the minor seminary. He was tempted to look for a copy now and to finish it. He saw some of the titles he had read, including *Rickshaw Boy*, a novel that had in it the most explicitly sexual passage he had ever encountered.

These novels, here and now, did not speak to him. He gravitated back to the philosophy section.

There he found a book published in the United States only two years earlier. As he started to read it, his early warning system came into play, but he continued any way.

The title was *Ethics*. It was written in Germany by Dietrich Bonhoeffer, a Protestant theologian. The dust jacket explained that the author had been hanged by the Nazis in April 1945 after two years in a concentration camp.

Bonhoeffer, Brennan concluded in glancing through the book, was attempting to create "a new Christian ethics." The author made the mistake of all Protestants, the young priest told himself, of trying to formulate ethical rules for life by conjuring up the name of Christ while ignoring the role of tradition, the church and the papacy. The latter alone, he believed, stood as "the rock" on which Christianity was founded.

Still, Father Brennan for the first time in his life was reading a book on theology that did not have an *imprimatur*, a statement on a book's title page that a specific bishop affirmed it was doctrinally correct, and could be read by the faithful. Somehow, he felt a little older, more grown up, when he skipped through Bonhoeffer's volume and did not feel any guilt.

He bought a copy of a book on the life of Cardinal Newman. It did have an *Imprimatur*. It was the first item he had purchased for himself since he had bought a suit nine years earlier.

Father Brennan arrived at the convent on time, only to be told the mother superior had been trying to reach him. She wanted to postpone the get-together because several nuns had exams the next day and had papers due. He was relieved.

He returned to his home, had a spaghetti supper with his mother, which he cooked, although not well. He left her next to her beloved radio as he went back to the rectory, more than a little anxious about what was about to happen there. The priests of the area were giving him what one of them called "a welcome to the club" party.

As he walked into the rectory recreation room the first thing he noticed was the table loaded with bottles of alcoholic beverages, a wide variety of them. Next he saw a buffet elaborately spread with snacks that included shrimp, chicken legs, roast beef, canapés, cheese, dips and any number of garnishes, slaws and salads. There were also some bowls of a brown substance that he took to be a pate.

He was flattered. The pastor was really putting on something special for him.

Soon, a variety of older men, only a few of them in Roman collars, began ringing the doorbell. He counted 26 priests before the evening ended, a total that completely surprised him.

"I am a Dominican," he said to one young priest. "I mean if I were a diocesan priest, I could understand this turnout. So why did they come?"

"The food and the booze," the young priest shot back cynically.

Most of the men had great appetites and the paunches to show for it. Any number of them spent the evening with drinks in their hands at all times; but, despite the priest's answer, those were not the only reasons some had come.

A Msgr. Albert Johnson—reserved, relatively young and notably dignified--shook his hand warmly and said he would like to talk to him the next day at the rectory.

"This is not the time or the place," the monsignor added.

After the arrival of the monsignor the tone of the gathering changed. It was evident that the man was highly respected and the other priests waited for his departure before bringing out their complaints. They started griping, principally about the chancellor and the priests at the chancery, whose dictates, they felt, were making their lives difficult.

"The men at the chancery don't get invited to these soirees," the same priest explained.

Several guests were especially vocal against the chancery for pushing integration and daring to mention "open housing."

An older Irish priest complained, "Two weeks ago there were three murders on the front page of the newspaper. All these were committed by Negroes. But, when the police decided to do something about it, all the bleeding hearts tried to stop them."

Father Ed, a young priest one who had been silent, rose to take him on.

"The police chief told the press his men were going to arrest 'any suspicious person in any suspicious place,'" the priest argued. "To the Negro community, that meant any of them anywhere. And, by the way, if you read the follow-up stories on the inside of the papers you would have seen one of those murders was done by a wife, who had blamed it on a tall black man. And in another one, a Negro was only allegedly suspected of having committed the crime."

Brennan was not pleased with the tension between the two men, but it subsided quickly.

Almost everyone there it seemed slapped his back at one time or other in the course of the evening. And many personally toasted him with a drink. It was difficult because, thinking of Father Raphael's warnings during his retreat, he had not intended to drink at all. But, it was evident that some of the priests wanted him to drink with them and would not take "No" for an answer. It was almost as though it were a test.

He took the drinks and only sipped at each or half drank them, but they were many and the total volume was far more than he had ever consumed before in his life.

His speech began to grow slurred, but he realized that with a focused effort he could adjust. Several times he laughed to cover for it, but it only accentuated his state.

Brennan turned down three proposed toasts in a row but the burly Irishman who had spoken against integration and Negroes absolutely insisted. The young priest responded to his "Bottoms up" with a similar comment and felt his knees give way and himself drop to the floor.

He was thankful the other priests acted as though they had not noticed and a few minutes later he excused himself, went to his bedroom and did not return.

When he arose the next morning, the bottles and every visible sign of the party were gone. Only the memory throbbed in his head. He wanted to take an aspirin and could have before saying mass without breaking his fast, as it was medicine rather than food. But he had been warned not to use them without food and that he could not do because one had to be fasting from midnight before taking communion at mass.

What surprised him was that, despite his headache and sick feeling, he could function.

"What a blessing!" he said.

"Why do people drink?" he asked himself, choosing not to answer, however.

Chapter 28

Reading his breviary by himself instead of in a priory choir stall was a relatively new experience for Father Brennan. He had done it on a few occasions, but never before over a week's time. And although he was doing it with a hangover, his attention remained focused.

As he knelt on the parish sacristy's *predieu* that faced the altar, he recited these daily Latin prayers that were his obligation as a religious and a priest. Composed of scriptural passages, psalms, hymns and other readings, they were divided into sections named after the ancient Roman hours of the day: matins, lauds, prime, tierce, sext, none, vespers and compline. As a Dominican he was required to chant these in choir each day or say them alone, if he couldn't.

For many hundreds of years these prayers had risen to the heavens in Latin. The daily breviary recitation comprised "The Divine Office" and, all together, took well more than an hour to recite, although some priests and monks could do so faster by themselves than in choir. In a church tradition for the most part gone, matins and lauds for centuries had been chanted in the middle of the night. Together, these two hours of the office generally composed the longest section of the daily divine office.

Brennan had been reciting the breviary every day since he had entered the novitiate nine years before. With just two or three exceptions, he had done so as a member of the choir rather than as individual. The priory itself was under the obligation that the office be chanted there in common.

The pace he now used in reciting from the breviary imitated that of a priory choir, one that took seriously its obligation as part of the church and the Dominican order to praise and appease God.

Any choral cadence was missing in his recitation, as were the musical tones of the Latin phrases recited out loud.

He felt as though he were a piece temporarily snapped off from the whole rather than as a person with actual independence.

When chanting the divine office in choir, he saw himself as a participating part of the official church at prayer. This private recitation of the breviary was as though he were just one person praying.

If, indeed, he were lacking in true friends, the sense of being a part of the whole compensated somewhat. This solitude in prayer, on the other hand, mirrored his awareness of being alone in life.

The sentiments also seemed different. In choir, the words of the psalms made more sense as he and his confreres recited passages from scripture, especially the psalms, that begged for divine help, lamented the success of the ungodly and cursed the enemies of God's chosen people.

He knew the psalms well, their context and their place in the historic struggle between the Kingdom of Israel and the ungodly. He accepted them. But today he was left somewhat confused as he privately recited:

He struck many nations and slew mighty kings: Sehon, king of the Amorrhites, and Og, king of Basan, and all the kings of Chanaan.

The confusion, however, was a minor distraction--one more change to which he could and would adjust, just as he was now doing with the headache left over from the drinking on the evening before.

Because of his lingering headache, Brennan set aside his breviary and his effort to finish the usually combined hours of prime, tierce, sext and none before he said Mass. He had much to do this day, so he planned to complete them while taking a leisurely walk in the afternoon through the woods of nearby Palmer Park.

After he finished saying mass, he would borrow a car from the rectory to drive his mother to the hospital for her cancer exam. They would then, if she were up to it, have lunch at a restaurant, and he could afterwards go for his walk. He would then have time to stop off at the convent for his meeting with the nuns and finally, in the evening, would have his scheduled meeting with Msgr. Albert Johnson.

His Mass, actually the fourth one he had said since the communal one at his ordination on Friday, just four days ago, still had the feeling of new power. For 20 years, he had watched in attention, curiosity and wonder as priests raised the round white host and recited the words of Christ, "*Hoc est corpus meum*" or "This is my body."

The word from the Latin for what happened as a result was "transubstantiation," which meant the change of something from one substance to another. The act, the center of Catholic doctrine, was one that few other Christian faiths accepted with the same intensity. It was also the center of his priesthood and his power as a priest.

A faculty member at the seminary had written a play in which Brennan had a minor part. In the drama, a priest in a concentration camp had obtained a piece of common bread and some illegal wine and had celebrated mass for several of his Catholic inmates. It was the climax of the play and showed the mass, as an act more important than individual lives.

As he recited Mass, Father Brennan thought or rather fantasized that he too would be willing to do it under the most dangerous of conditions and in defiance of any prohibition or threat with which the secular world might attack him personally.

The young priest had written out notes for what he intended to be his first Sunday sermon.

"Whenever we hear objections to Catholicism or to our faith," he wrote, "let our minds return to the Eucharistic offering or sacrifice as being fundamental to answering them. If any popes have sinned, if you believe the Inquisition went too far, if the church did not rise up strongly enough against the Nazis or the Communists, if individual missionaries have abused those to whom they were sent, if indulgences were misused...if some priest has become a womanizer or a drunk...let none of us be scandalized thereby. Such actions do not justify apostasy from the faith because, without it, there is no mass, no transubstantiation, no renewal of the sacrifice of the Last Supper and of the cross.

"The key for all and everything is the mass, an act of a priest in behalf of God for His people. Neither priest nor bishop has to be perfect to perform this act, to fulfill the exhortation of Christ, 'Do this in commemoration of me.'"

Upon this conviction, all that Father Brennan held to be true rested. This was the foundation, the basis of his faith and his belief system.

"True" was an important word. Only that which God knew, Brennan believed, was true. What man discovered in nature is a human hypothesis. What God revealed or what the human mind could deduce correctly from it, were truths. The Apostle's Creed succinctly told man what these doctrines or dogmas were. So did scripture as well as the catechism and Catholic teaching.

These beliefs, he told himself, were under attack from all of God's enemies: the apostates, the heretics, the relativists, the Protestants, the Jews, the secularists, the hedonists, the modernists, the Marxists, the communists and, yes, the devil himself.

None of them, he believed, had anything to offer as bold and as beautiful as the doctrine of bread and wine being changed into the body and blood of Christ. It helped mark Catholicism as the one, true church--something to be defended against attack and criticism, as one might do for the thorn-crowned, beaten body of the God-man himself.

Indeed, that body, he saw, in the language of the New Testament, to be "incarnate," as his theology book said, in the Mystical Body of Christ, a union of God with his church.

In the righteousness of his position, the fervent young priest felt defending God and church from attack was the prime purpose of his being.

To him, God was the Supreme Being manifested through the scripture and the person of Christ. Man's only tangible way of knowing the deity was through the dogmas of the Catholic church. As a theologian, Brennan's responsibility was to defend that doctrine against any possible question, doubt or challenge.

He felt called upon to protect the church not only in its noble aspects but also in its flaws. For, if people were scandalized by acts associated with it, they would separate themselves from Catholicism and ultimately deny the most basic of doctrines, the Eucharistic sacrifice which brought God's presence down to earth. He must, therefore, fight on the front lines against criticism of or opposition to Catholicism, just as his father had for America against the Nazis. He too must be prepared to die if necessary.

Each time as he said mass he renewed the "Sacrifice of the Last Supper" and the cross and his determination to be *defensor fidei*, a defender of the faith, to reach out and to protect his church and its beliefs.

Was not this, then, his mission? It felt great. It was indeed a knight's role in the world. It was good.

Yet, he did not receive the sense of completeness, of finality, from it that he imagined could and would ratify his pre-ordained mission.

He sighed. Everything was so right and, yet, something major was still missing.

Someday, he would find it.

His mass over, he stopped at the pastor's door to get the keys to a special car loaned to him through a member of the parish, a new Ford Fairlane convertible that was as handsome as he felt a car could be.

He would have liked to take the car for a spin, but instead drove his mother to Mount Carmel Hospital, a large, Catholic institution on the Northwest Side of the city. In delivering her there Father Brennan had a foreboding that he might never bring her home.

After an exam of Brennan's mother, the doctor, talked to him rather than to her:

"We'd like to keep your mother here," the physician said. "I don't like what I see."

This was it, the next-to-final verdict on her, he felt. The young priest did not ask questions, because the doctor spoke to him as though Brennan understood everything. He must therefore act as though he did. It was one professional to another, man to man. He accepted the words, the lack of elaboration and the verdict. It was, for his mother, God's decision.

"Thy will be done," her son prayed silently.

He called the convent and postponed his meeting with the nuns, but left standing the one with Msgr. Johnson.

His mother, not asking any questions about why or how long she was to be there, was ensconced in a ward. She soon fell asleep and he stayed with her for an hour and finally went for a walk.

As he strolled along Outer Drive, the street which the hospital faced, he thought about his mother and her impending death. He had no other immediate relatives, no real family. She was it. Soon, she would be gone, to be with God, to receive her final judgment or reward, whichever phrase one wanted to use.

Not only he, but also his other family, the Dominicans, would pray for her. He would notify the provincial, who would then request other members of the province to include her intention in their masses and their prayers.

She was a good woman, had remained faithful to God, he told himself, and certainly merited God's salvation.

Going to sleep, she had tried to smile despite her pain. He wondered about that. Was his faith not as strong, as direct as hers was?

Yet, recalling his thoughts at mass that morning about being a defender of the faith, he sensed his picture of himself more than a little ajar.

As he returned to his mother's room, a nun called him aside.

"Father," she said. "Your mother is very weak. If you have not yet administered the final rites, you might want to do it now. She is not necessarily going to die today, but it would not hurt to give her the last sacrament."

Father Brennan was stunned. He had not thought of this. He called the hospital chaplain and asked for his help. He had never done it before and had no desire to make a public or personal mistake at his mother's expense.

As he performed the rite known in the Catholic church as extreme unction, the final anointing, he started by thinking, not of his mother, but of his father. The latter, dying on the battlefield of the Hurtgen Forest, almost certainly did not receive this final sacrament. Yet, if either of his two parents might have needed the final ritual of the church, it would have been him.

Brennan could not think of a sin, other than an occasional uncharitable comment, that his mother might have committed. Even these, he thought, she would have faithfully reported in the confessional and had forgiven.

Touching her hands and her lips with the oils, he used prayers written hundreds of years before that asked God's forgiveness for any sins these body parts might have committed.

His mother remained unconscious throughout this ritual, occasionally moaning in pain.

He was thankful that, in performing the rite, he still could do something for the woman who had given birth to and raised him. He had never known what he could do for her personally. For the first time and but for a brief second, he thought perhaps she had asked too much in wanting him to go to the seminary and as she had said in her night prayers, "to remain devoted to God." She seemed to want nothing or at least little else. He had left her a few hundred dollars from working at the factory after his senior year of high school, but his mother had never complained about money.

After his ordination, she had wanted his priestly blessing even more than a filial hug. Such defined the frail woman lying on the bed in front of him.

In his response to her only want in life, he had gone extra steps and had, in effect, become her, except with a religious vocation, availing himself of the exclusively male prerogative of the Catholic priesthood that she could not have conceived for herself.

His achievement was the most a mother could ask and that a son could give, he decided. There were no siblings, so there would be no grandchildren. His actions, his deeds as a priest, would have to fill whatever void existed in her life and drove her forward.

He looked at his watch. If he hurried, he could be on time for his appointment with Msgr. Johnson. He could stay in touch with the hospital by leaving his number, calling in the evening and returning in the morning after saying mass.

Father Brennan once again gave her his priestly blessing and slipped out of the room.

Chapter 29

The city to which Father Brennan had returned has its own unique manifestation of the worldliness he had avoided by going to the seminary and taking his vows as a Dominican. It centered on the city's symbol of prestige: the automobile. There was no more Detroit way to tempt a young man to such than with a fresh-off-the-assembly-line, latest model car.

Thus, the young priest found himself driving a hot new model 1957 Ford Fairlane convertible with its folding top in the trunk. It was made available to him for the week by a parishioner, an executive for the Ford Motor Company. The latter was thereby able to demonstrate to his family and acquaintances the all-important connection in his life between his success and his religion.

Brennan, who had learned to drive while in the priory, had gotten little chance to do so. He relished doing it once he was ordained. The car, his religious instincts saw as the ungodly symbol of his hometown but he had a piece of male vanity that was willing to let himself be tempted by stepping on the gas on Northwestern Highway in Southfield to see what he could do. He did not get the chance. Other things were stealing from him the time in which he might have done it

For once, he was uncharacteristically five minutes late meeting someone: in this case, Msgr. Johnson. A Detroit squad car had stopped him, as the drivers of such do upon first noticing the latest model car. A ticket is not written, but the police officer gets a look-see and then is able to tell his friends of the encounter. Brennan's Roman collar and mention of having just given his mother Extreme Unction in the hospital further insured him a pass rather than a citation. The fact that he was detained, however, more than accounted for his actual tardiness.

The young priest arrived in the rectory parlor taking a deep breath to compensate for being mildly winded. Unlike during his encounter with the police, he offered an apology, but no excuse. He sensed the personality of the man before him would not brook one. If he had offended the right reverend monsignor, he would much rather accept his punishment than put himself in the position of demonstrating ineptitude.

The monsignor gave him a weak smile but a strong handshake. His rebuke was indirect as he stated simply that he was due someplace else shortly. His language, however, was direct as he told Father Brennan what he knew of him.

"The word I have received on you is that you are bright, very much so, and I think Father Eustace used the word, 'steadfast,'" he said. "Eustace and I studied together in Rome. He dropped in on me when he came here to give the sermon at your first mass."

"Father Eustace is very kind in his comments about me," Brennan responded. "You might say that is why I was glad he accepted my request that he give the sermon."

"You are modest, Father," the monsignor said. "That is good. I would like to share something with you. I have been notified that, unworthy though he be, the priest before you has been selected to be made a bishop, an auxiliary for the New York Archdiocese under his eminence, Francis Cardinal Spellman."

"My congratulations and prayers," the young priest said. He wondered, however, what this man's appointment as a bishop could possibly have to do with him and yet it apparently did.

"Thank you, Father," the monsignor replied. "You speak well. To get to the point, if I may. The church, as you know, faces troubled times. Earlier in this century the great pontiffs whom God gave us heroically attempted to protect Holy Mother Church from change and from the invading forces of modernism and secularism. We have every reason to believe that a new assault will be made, one that will come both from within and without."

The young Dominican was stunned at the words of the bishop-elect.

"I have heard rumors and even predictions," Brennan said, "but you would appear to have information that amounts to more even than you are saying."

"Yes, we have been fortunate to have His Holiness Pius XII sitting in the Chair of St. Peter for almost 20 years, but he is frail, and not well," the monsignor continued. "We fear, however, the next conclave and whom it might elect. We had hoped that the cardinals in their wisdom would select Cardinal Ottaviani in Pacelli's place. We believe he alone would withstand the forces of whimsical change in the Church, but now those who know such things no longer believe that it will happen for certain. Their expectations are of someone less forceful."

"Monsignor, you are telling me this for a reason?" Father Brennan inquired. It did indeed seem quite far-fetched to have this stranger making him privy to what was happening within the Vatican.

"Let me be blunt," the man responded. "We have little time. Many of the American bishops and theologians, it is feared in Rome, will be lined up on the wrong side in the battle to come. I have been asked to recruit among the young and the bright. You are going to Rome to study. When you get there, I want you make contact with Monsignor Luciano in the good Cardinal Ottaviani's office. You will use my name. I will give him yours."

Brennan took a deep breath. Adrenaline was pumping.

Just then a knock on the parlor door was followed quickly by the pastor walking in.

"Excuse me, Monsignor," the pastor said. "Father Brennan has a phone call. It is urgent. It is the hospital calling."

"I'm sorry, Monsignor, I will return in a moment," the young priest said.

The call was what he knew it would be just as he had understood his father had died by seeing a babushka in the seminary chapel 12 years before.

This time it was his mother. She had died 15 minutes earlier.

He returned to the parlor, where the pastor in the meantime was filling in the visitor on what had been going on in Father Brennan's personal life.

"She's dead," Father Brennan said. "I was able to give her the last rites this afternoon. My mother was a very good woman. She is with God."

Those were the thoughts and feelings he put into words. In truth, he felt distant from his own life, a sense of unreality that had had somehow always been with him, but now chilled the air around him even more so.

"I will remember her in my mass," Msgr. Johnson said.

"That's very kind of you, Monsignor," Father Brennan replied.

"We have said what I think needed to be said," the bishop-elect continued. "I have written out Msgr. Luciano's name and phone number. Here it is. I now ask one last thing of you, your priestly blessing."

He knelt before the young priest and accepted the benediction.

"And I ask yours," Brennan countered. And he too knelt and was blessed.

The prelate left and the pastor put his arm around the shoulders of the young priest.

"Father," he said. "This is a going to be a hard time for you and we will do everything we can for you. You have our prayers, as does your mother. We will, of course, help you work out funeral arrangements, including a solemn high mass here, perhaps Friday."

"Thank you, Father," the young Dominican replied. "I'm going to the hospital, if I may again impose on you by continuing to borrow the car. First, I want to stop in church."

"Of course, Father, and the car is yours," the pastor replied. "The owner won't need it until the end of the week."

Rather than kneeling down, Brennan sat in the front pew of the church. A creature of ritual, he always knelt, but not this time. He was caught in a vortex. His mother's death whirled around in his head along with what Msgr. Johnson had said. He and his thoughts were somewhere in this powerful whirlwind.

It was then that he realized that he had yet to say 35 to 45 minutes of his daily office.

He went to his room, picked up his breviary and returned to the chapel. He had started to think of his mother and whether or not she had known that she was dying. When, however, he picked up the book containing the Divine Office, his thoughts of her ended.

Brennan reflected on the words of the psalms and the picture of the stern God that the psalmist painted. He wondered whether or not Msgr. Johnson understood such a God better than he did. The prayers of the breviary, the official ones of the church, somehow daily ascended heavenward to appease that God and his disappointment with the actions of men.

He felt a comfortable familiarity in saying the office. It was a distraction from aspects of living that otherwise might now be overwhelming him.

The prayers he was reciting seemed much more in line with the urgent concern of the Bishop-elect Johnson than they did with the death of a simple and poor woman in Detroit, albeit the mother of a priest. The laments and curses of the psalmist seemed to support arming oneself for a battle against the dire dangers to the church of which the monsignor had spoken.

Still, his mother really had died. He felt confused, but unashamed that he was not crying. He was also glad, however, that he had this diversion of saying his office. It postponed that which would soon certainly have hit him hard no matter how well he might have prepared for it.

He continued reading the breviary. As he did so, intrusions came not from his mother's death but rather from his meeting with Msgr. Johnson. It had been so intense; the man, so direct. He spoke almost as though the church were facing Armageddon, the final battle. And, yet, what he said had a ring of truth to it.

And he realized, willy-nilly, that he would somehow be in the middle of everything of which the monsignor spoke. That was the meaning of the visit, of the effort to recruit him. The young scholar had not said "Yes." He had not been given a chance to do so. He was looking ahead, seeing his own future or at least a part of it. It was exciting, yet he was not certain he was ready for the battle part of it.

"God, give me strength," he prayed, but he was not certain what he needed to be strong for. It was for much, he did know that. It was for what would happen in the long run or even in the immediate future, feelings which he was struggling to keep out of his awareness.

When he had finished saying his office, Brennan still felt no relief or let up. He could not believe that so much in his life had become intermingled. The past and future, tragedy and opportunity, loss and gain: each sapped strength from one another. His mother had died and at the same time he had been afforded an opportunity to play a coveted role in defending his faith. The two events crashed into him at almost the exact same moment.

Brennan got in the car and headed for the hospital.

"Is fate playing games with me or is God giving me a test?" the newly-ordained priest asked himself.

He sincerely regretted that he could not concentrate on either his mother's death or his own future. When he started to think of one, the thought of the other intruded on it.

After he arrived at the hospital parking lot, he did not go directly to the administrator's office, as he had been asked to do, but rather to the chapel. He had not yet actually said a prayer for his mother and he wanted to do so.

He pulled out his rosary and started saying the prayers and fingering the beads. These were an unspoken bond between the two of them. His mother was most faithful to this devotion and said it several times every day. He was a member of the Dominicans, which fostered the rosary as a special part of their mission. He thought of this connection and was pleased. He would bury her with her rosary in her hands.

The idea of interning his mother, rosary in hand, forced him to begin thinking of her and of the other preparations.

Suddenly, as he knelt in the hospital chapel, a strange comment popped out of his mouth.

"Well, Pop," he said. "Now, you got her back."

He smiled at himself for having thought something so personal, so human.

With that, he rose and went to make the mandatory arrangements.

The inevitable visitation for his mother at a local funeral parlor was far more crowded than he had expected. The Detroit papers had picked up the story of a mother dying days after attending her son's first mass and the reception at the mortuary brought out friends and associates who went back many years, especially at the supermarket where she had worked.

She was laid out in her best dress, her fingers intertwined with the rosary beads.

The Friday morning solemn high mass was everything for which she could have hoped. Eleven priests and an auxiliary bishop filled the sanctuary. Brennan was the celebrant of the mass and his provincial came for the ceremony, acting as master of ceremonies.

"The mass was beautiful," everyone told him afterwards, "just as she would have wanted it."

Also just as she would have wanted it, he eventually cleaned up the house with the help of the parish handyman. Although he thought he might possibly find it somewhere in the building, his matchbook collection was not there. He did find almost $200 stashed away in a familiar rafter-hiding place. Brennan donated all his mother's possessions to the St. Vincent DePaul Society and kept only the photos. He was embarrassed at the thought of handling her corsets and underwear and asked the man to stuff them in a bag.

Brennan found all the letters he had ever mailed to her and was ashamed to see how worn they were from being reread and handled. He destroyed them. He did not open and look at them. Much of their content had been fabricated.

"I wrote what I wrote and that is that," he said to himself.

Only as he closed up the small rented house for the final time did he permit himself to consider the fact that he had not yet shed a tear for his mother.

And then in what he later considered a very unkind thought he told himself it was all his mother's fault.

"She never taught me to cry," he said. "I don't remember seeing her cry when Pop was killed. She may have, but she certainly never let me witness it."

He was aghast. Here, his mother was just freshly dead and he was criticizing her. That he could not shed a tear was one thing. He didn't have control over that, but he should not be critical of her memory.

Brennan wanted to go back downtown to the bookstore again. He had wished to visit with the nuns. He could do neither. Finally, he decided instead to go back for a long walk on Belle Isle, where he had spent time with his father. He took his breviary with him.

The Detroit River passing the shores of the island spoke of life and death to him, but he was not inundated with memories as he had expected to be. The trees seemed aloof, cold rather than friendly. He tried to make plans, but could not. He wanted to return to the priory where he had studied theology and which technically was still his residence. He could not, however, because he had loose ends to take care here. He stayed at the rectory. His mother's house was no longer his home, something of his past rather than his future. By staying in Detroit, he was caught, remaining temporarily suspended between his former life and what was to come.

Father Brennan had almost a week of his vacation left. He had no friends with whom to visit, no old acquaintances to look in on. During the day, he wandered about the city of Detroit, dropping in at churches upon which he happened and lit two vigil lights in each, one for his mother and another for his father.

Eventually, he did stop in at the bookstore; but was amazed to find how much he himself had changed since he had been there a week earlier. His mother's death had drained him of the energy of a newly-ordained, freshly-freed person and, for some reason, the message delivered to him by Msgr. Johnson had taken from him another avenue of escape. It had backed him off from any sense of freedom or right to explore philosophers outside the church. He once again saw that anything encouraging such curiosity was clearly the enemy of his focused life and inevitable mission.

If he were steadfast, his mother had proven more so. But, now that the real world and its conflicts lay ahead, she was gone from the field. Not, he thought, that she ever could have helped him any.

Chapter 30

As Brennan began to pack his things and take leave of the rectory, he discovered that someone had left a bottle of scotch in his room with a ribbon around it. It could have been any of several individuals responding in their way to his look of being lost and confused.

He would, he decided, have one drink and leave the bottle behind. He did just that. He took a gulp, kept it in mouth for a long second and then swallowed.

The young priest sat down and penned a thank you note to the pastor, one to the housekeeper and yet another to the handy man. In an envelope for the latter, he placed a $10 bill even though he had already paid him for helping to clean up his mother's house.

It was the first time he had felt relaxed since his mother's death and he attributed it to the alcohol. He was tempted to take the rest of the bottle back with him and he even screwed the top on tight so he might, but he realized that he must be firm about drinking and that meant following his earlier resolution about alcohol. He left the bottle in the room and went to drop off his letters.

Brennan then stopped in at the convent unannounced to apologize for not visiting with the nuns as scheduled. He had about

15 minutes now and those of the sisters as were available came to meet with him in the recreation room.

They were sympathetic and supportive toward him in the way only women could be. There was no teasing, backslapping, talking of sports or world news to distract him, no round of drinks. They did bring out cookies and several kinds of juice and reassured him his mother was a good woman and each nodded in assurance when the oldest stated that she certainly was with God and his Blessed Mother.

Several of the nuns revealed themselves to be much more genuine and softer than he expected they could be.

One, Sister Florence, who was staying at the convent for the summer while she attended the University of Detroit, said, "I don't know about you, but I didn't cry after my mother died. I was shocked and even somewhat disappointed in myself. I can cry. I had done so when my father passed away, but did not do so for my mother. I finally figured it out. It has something to do with the separation we made when I went into the novitiate. We turned away from our parents, but suddenly all our feelings about family are supposed to be front and center when they die."

Father Brennan looked, or, rather, stared at her.

"If she hasn't explained everything," he thought, "she has made a point."

Another nun, Sister Eustace, commented about Brennan's former grammar school principal not being able to make it to his first mass.

"Sister Grace got undercut," the nun said. "Her superior likes to be petty and made certain no one else was available to accompany her on the trip. Therefore she couldn't come."

A third nun gave him a warning.

"You're going to Rome," she said. "That place is more political than Washington, D.C. and all the state capitols put together. You're young and you're intelligent. They are going to fight over you there."

"I hardly think so," he said.

"I have a brother. He's a Benedictine," she said. "He was very bright and went to Rome. He practically came back in a basket without a degree. He's never really gotten over it."

"Well, to be honest that could happen to a person under those circumstances, but I'm not certain that's what I need to hear right now," he replied.

"I understand," she said. "I'm not pressing the point, but I will pray for you."

"We all will," the superior of the convent said. "We are very pleased that a boy from our grade school here has been ordained. You are the first, you know, although we now have two others in the seminary."

"Thank you, sister," Father Brennan said. "I must be leaving but I would like to give you my blessing before I go."

They all knelt and received his benediction.

He left, but stopped back at his room in the rectory where he reopened the bottle of scotch and took two ample swallows. He then let the pastor drive him to the train station.

The train ride was uneventful. He said his breviary, chatted about the Detroit Tigers with a passenger and stared out the window. It was not until the priory cloister door closed behind him that it hit him. He had lived "out there." More things had happened to him than he could have dreamed possible. He was pulled in directions he could not believe. With the death of his mother, he lost much, things he could not understand.

He had been ordained a priest. That is what should have been overwhelming him and dominating his thoughts and creating his feelings. It was not.

"They call it a 'vacation,'" he said to himself. "I could have done without it. My ship went from placid waters to a stormy ocean and I seem worse for the toll it has taken on me."

Several of his returning classmates and professors tried to console him over the loss of his mother but he was far too confused to come to terms with his feelings or even their comments about it.

Life at the priory had changed much more than he had expected. He and those of his classmates who had returned and were waiting to go to their first assignments now still associated with the seminary students, but they formally took their recreation with the older priests. Every morning, they went out on one of the chapel's side altars and said mass, except on Sundays, when they were sent to neighboring parishes to perform the ceremony.

He and the other newly-ordained priests no longer reported to the master of clerics, but rather were now directly under the prior himself.

These little things mixed with Brennan's experiences while at home served to disorient him. He could appreciate the advantage in such a situation of the Benedictine rule over the one which the Dominicans followed. St. Benedict's rule provided stability for the young men after they were ordained. They stayed, for the most part, in their monasteries and under the same abbots. He was facing instability and disorder that followed 13 years of strict routine. Several of his classmates assured him they had experienced the same thing, although he felt it was to a lesser degree than he was.

Some even used the same expression he did, "out there." Another called it "freedom," but not with any relish for what it represented. A third had "an older woman" come on to him, and he was anything but happy about it.

Brennan was surprised and somewhat reassured that each young priest had returned, to some extent or the other, troubled. He sensed that it was only the beginning. They lived in a monastery, but were expected to make excursions out into a world for which they were at best only partially prepared.

The seminary had been smaller than a village, an environment in which he had spent his time learning, one to which he had adjusted. Whatever the seminarians had developed inside themselves while there was meant to be transferable to the bigger, more chaotic world in which they would spend the rest of their lives. They had each experienced lessons attesting to the raw fact of life that it would not be quite as simple as they thought or been promised.

All they could hope to do was to go back into themselves and once more find out who they were and use that to help create a *persona* that could survive in the world.

Brennan found it interesting that so many called the world, "out there." It was as though the seminary and priory were not a part of the real world and he firmly believed that at a basic level they were not.

He had been surprised not just by the big things, but also the little ones. The newly-ordained priest had not expected to enjoy driving a spiffy new car in contrast to using the six-year-old one that the priory owned.

The young Dominican was amazed at how articulate the nuns had been. He had no contact with women for nine years and little before that. That had left him lost at sea in understanding or dealing even casually with "ladies."

Freedom was also confusing. He did not complain about being confronted with too many opportunities to make choices as several of his classmate had, but he had experienced the problem. Brennan had walked into the supermarket where his mother had worked and left immediately. If he had stayed, he would have been confronted with a limitless number of choices from the vending machines to the multitude of products and brands of groceries. Some of the sale signs seemed so helpful that he did not know how he could refuse to purchase exactly what they told him to. But, why someone might need three pies for $1.25, he did not know.

Not only must he return to this world, but also convert it to God and sensibility. That would be his job, his profession.

He had encountered a whole new music for young people and seen their new way of dancing, which was called "Rock and Roll." It had not even existed when he started in the seminary. At that point, they were singing such songs as "Don't Sit Under the Apple Tree" and "Mares Eat Oats and Does Eat Oats and Little Lambs Eat Ivy. A Kid'll Eat Ivy, Too. Wouldn't You?" That last one didn't make sense, but it was a lot better than the big new ones now, "You Ain't Nothing But a Hound Dog" and "Rock Around the Clock."

And what was all this in him about flirting with alcohol? He had beaten that temptation out of his life years ago. He didn't even like the taste of it all that much.

The seminary had not even begun to train or prepare him for his short excursion into the madness of "out there." Yes, he had returned a little less naive, but he also had been burned. And so had his classmates.

And then there were those loose ends. To start with there was Eddie Golf. Would they ever meet and why did he care so much? Why couldn't he break through and grieve for his mother? Was the package all too neat? Was whatever she might need in terms of prayers being taken care of? And, the bottle of scotch? Who left it and would Brennan have to start worrying about becoming an alcoholic?

Brennan concluded many of the matters were ruminating in his brain were there because he was reviewing the past instead of looking to the future.

He decided, and this was an extraordinary act of independence, to ask the master of studies for the province if he could switch early to the Dominican priory in Washington D.C. so he could prepare for his studies at the Catholic University.

As usual, such a request had to plod through the bureaucracy and, while he was told he could transfer there early, it was later than the date he had requested. He did get permission to go back to Detroit, however, and put all his mother's affairs to rest.

His return to his home parish found things much changed. It was as though he were not the same person. Father Brennan's attractiveness as the new kid at the altar had diminished. His own adrenaline was gone. He resisted visiting Msgr. Johnson and felt he would not be welcome if he had dropped in. He also hesitated to ask for the use of the parish car for the same reason. He met with the funeral director, made arrangements for a small grave marker, stopped at the social security office and asked a lawyer in the parish to handle some final details and send him a bill.

Brennan then prepared to return to his priory.

"You forgot this when you were here," the pastor told him, as he was about to leave. In his hand was the nearly-full bottle of scotch.

"Thank you," the young priest said and this time took the bottle and put it in his suitcase.

He had taken several additional swigs from the bottle when two days later he put it out on the liquor shelf at the priory.

Detroit was over. It was a place he now wanted to forget. He intended to go back there on the anniversary of his mother's death, visit her grave and say mass for her, but he had no reason to return.

He readied himself for Washington D.C. and a life with people, none of whom he had met or with whom he had ever spent time.

As he left the priory, he took the half-empty bottle of scotch down off the shelf and packed it in his suitcase without defending or verbalizing even to himself what he was doing.

Chapter 31

Father Brennan's post-graduate work at the Catholic University of America in Washington, D.C. proved contentious in a way he never would have expected. All the excitement--and that is what it was--centered on a class in dogma taught by an eminent theologian. His professor, a French Augustinian, sought to challenge the language used to express the most basic doctrines of the Catholic church. As a result, he and the young Dominican squared off, word by word and point by point, into elaborate debates that often brought other faculty members and students into the classroom to sit and listen.

This was something totally new for Brennan. He had not been challenged by his seminary professors, for they had gone by the book and that was what he knew. Any arguments that ever arose could and would be solved by appealing to the works of their fellow Dominican, Thomas Aquinas or his interpreters, the Thomists.

Father Rouge, or "The Red" as he was nicknamed, made it clear in his first class at Catholic University that he had not taken any vow to teach theology according to Thomas Aquinas, as Dominican professors had to do.

The theology professor was careful to state that he was not advocating that any dogma of the church could or should be rejected, but spoke rather of the importance of "understanding" them in the new light of modern language and semantics. According to traditionalist thinking such as Brennan's, this approach constantly risked the error of "modernism" in theology that Pope Pius X had condemned fifty years earlier.

Brennan knew the material of dogmatic theology, not only as expressed by Thomas Aquinas, but also by the full range of Thomists and other theologians of the 13th, 14th and 15th Centuries. He also could quote the writings of the Fathers of the Church and had committed to memory those encyclical letters of the various popes that had focused on the teaching of Christian doctrine.

With his knowledge of primary sources in Greek and Latin, he would often wait as Father Rouge expounded some new way of expressing Christian doctrine and would then pounce on it. At first, he surprised his professor and forced the latter to consider his objections. But as the French Augustinian began to anticipate the young Dominican's challenges, their debates became verbal fencing matches.

Brennan would parry at one of his professor's specific semantic efforts with an appeal to a passage from St. Anselm or St. Augustine or other worthy "father" or "doctor" of the church.

The professor would then counter with a statement such as "Yes, but in that letter Anselm was talking about something entirely different, whereas in a completely separate writing he said this..."

The two went at each other cite by cite and passage by passage, Father of the church versus Father of the church and Thomas Aquinas against Thomas Aquinas.

It was not the kind of hair-splitting theology that had bogged the church down near the end of the Middle Ages, but rather two informed men contending in behalf of different approaches to expounding church doctrine.

Father Rouge chose to veer off the exclusively scholastic and deductive approach to dogmatic theology. He wanted it to be understood by people other than those schooled in the reasoning of Aristotle or the thinking of the medieval scholastics. He sought to use language to force open musty, long-shuttered rooms of the church. Brennan, a fresh face among intransigent thinkers both because of his broad reading and enthusiasm, won away some of his classmates from the charismatic Father Rouge. Their classmate's stance was the easier one for these seminary graduates already held to his positions and language exclusively before they arrived at the Catholic University. Most of them had been chosen by diocesan officials to study dogma because they were strongly inclined to agree with the established order. Many, like Brennan, had taken a religious vow of obedience and felt that adhering to the dogmatic theology textbook was part of keeping it.

Father Rouge was on his way out at the university. There was little room for innovation and new ways of presenting tried and true doctrines. It was simply a question of whether he would go quietly or not. The administration was deeply pleased with what they were hearing second-hand of Brennan's performance. They felt the young American Dominican was humiliating the older French theologian, who heretofore had tied in knots anyone who had tried to challenge him.

Brennan thought the same way they did at first. He was surprised at how often his opponent let his guard down, but sometimes even that was a ploy. Father Rouge was good. He was extraordinarily well read and, without admitting it even to himself, his young Dominican student thought there was much to be said for the way he was trying to express doctrine.

Meanwhile, the young scholar, following the class outline, researched ahead into Augustine, Anselm, Origen, Justin Martyr, Bellarmine, Thomas Aquinas, Albert the Great and even the Franciscans, Bonaventure and John Duns Scotus in an attempt to pin down his professor and opponent.

In the debate, outsiders believed he was winning, because as the less prominent of the two, he was making a name for himself at his professor's expense.

Father Rouge understood this but his own goal was not to gain fame. He actually had enjoyed the relative anonymity of being a professor at the American Catholic University. He genuinely sought truth and the clarification of it. His very conservative young student, as he saw it, was contributing as much to that as he was as the two of them crossed swords and took on each other's ideas. His major problem up until now was that his ideas and expressions had not been tested. His arguments and proofs had not been subjected to the powerful challenges they needed to meet before being circulated further in the world of scholarship.

The French Augustinian's vision was to find new metaphors and phrases to describe the Mystical Body, the Incarnation, the Trinity, and the Eucharist and to do so in language to which such worldly thinkers as the existentialists and Marxists would pay attention. He sought a new epiphany of church doctrine, not simply a restatement of it in a language abandoned by secular scholars 500 years before.

You cannot hone a sword, even one made of the best steel, without a very good pumice stone and, by God, this young Dominican was offering him one of the best, he believed. He himself was indeed far better known than this young student was, but his positions were not. Brennan was defending arguments and doctrines in language that every theology student was forced to use, while he was attempting to create a new one. As he looked at it, his cause was the one which stood to win by their debate.

Brennan, looking only straight ahead, felt he was defending the faith. He lacked the broader vision Father Rouge had of what was happening.

Neither were aware how many in the school's administration and in the hierarchy were watching their battle. Almost to a man, they were backing the young Dominican and his traditional approach to stating church doctrine.

To test the young priest, Father Rouge did something extraordinary for him: He gave the class an exam. It was comprehensive and difficult. He allowed the students to write their answers at their leisure and at home.

He first scanned through the other papers, hoping he might perchance discover a bauble of unworked-through wisdom, an expression he might learn from, a point at which his students got struck trying to comprehend his ideas.

Then, he picked up Brennan's. He had phrased the questions to force the young Dominican not to present the traditional views of Catholic theology, but rather to require him to state what he had heard his professor saying. The young student could argue against Father Rouge's positions, but first he must find the best way to express them.

Brennan had heard, and had done this well. His language in presenting his professor's theses and expressions was like a Lincoln speech: simple, clear and direct. He then retreated to his own scholastic style and picked Father Rouge's teachings apart as though they were the writings of the Albigensian heretics or the proclamations of a Luther.

Sometimes, the young Dominican overstated his case. Occasionally, he relied too much on authority. He often lost himself in reaching back through history for a tenuous argument. And he did not use scripture often enough in establishing his positions. Other times, however, he was so right that Father Rouge found himself wondering whether or not to question or even abandon a position he had taken.

The professor decided to call his brilliant student in for a personal meeting. He did it not in his office as was traditional, but rather took him to a three star French restaurant, picking up the bill himself.

Brennan was confused. He could read and speak French enough to debate in it, but selecting courses at a French restaurant required words that were not in his vocabulary, so he let his host do the complete ordering.

He noticed that his professor was carting his briefcase with him and surmised that it contained his exam papers. The young Dominican had no idea how this dinner and meeting would go. He had been taking on the illustrious Father Rouge quite hard and consistently, so he was particularly surprised to be treated so well and specially as to be offered a meal at one of the best restaurants in the city.

The professor enjoyed the perplexity of his student and did nothing overtly to make it go away. The conversation was decidedly small talk, principally an effort to instruct the young Dominican in the fine points of ordering food and choosing an appropriate wine.

The student savored both the wine and food, as well as the conversation and company.

He began to form thoughts in the back of his mind that Father Rouge was doing all this to disarm him, to get him to abandon his positions and ultimately to recruit him. If that were it, his professor did not understand the depth of Brennan's convictions or self-image as a defender of the faith. In the meantime, he would let the French priest wine and dine him.

Just as the meal was over and Brennan was growing firm in his mistrust of his host, Father Rouge slowly pulled out his student's exam paper. He presented the second half of it to him with a grade on it: 85%. Brennan was stunned. He had never received so low a mark in his whole life.

"I assure you, Father Brennan," his professor said, "I was justified in every point which I have taken off your grade. Here, note that you quoted Origen, but you failed to cite his most cogent sentence on the subject. Here, you have Augustine making a point and do not mention that some scholars say the line was a later interpolation in his works."

Brennan was stunned. His professor was right. As he looked at his paper, he felt the 85% to be generous. He had underestimated Father Rouge's scholarship and overestimated his own.

The older priest watched as his student quickly looked through the rest of the handwritten notes.

The younger man nodded and finally said, "Father, have you really invited me to dine at the best restaurant I have ever eaten in to present me with the lowest grade on an exam that I have ever received?"

"Ah, my young student," he said. "I have played my little game with you. I have here the first half of your exam. It is better than your professor could have done so I have given it a grade of 115%. Therefore your mark is what you are probably used to getting, 100%."

"You have played with me," his student replied.

"Yes and no," Father Rouge answered. "I have used your exam to show you the parts and I have challenged you to do better even in those areas in which I disagree with you. In the first part, you have taken my thinking and expressions and improved on them.

The least I could do, as a result, is to challenge and help you in those areas in which you believe so firmly."

"You are something, Father Rouge," Brennan said raising his glass. "I toast you. But, and I'm sure you know this, you have only made me into a sharper opponent in that class of yours."

"Yes," his professor said, "that is my intention exactly."

And indeed in class the next day Brennan led off the discussion by challenging his teacher on one of the criticisms on his exam paper, pointing out that the discovery of an earlier text of St. Augustine had subsequently proved the line was not interpolation.

Father Rouge conceded the point but ended by saying with only the slightest of smiles, "I will not change your mark, however."

On the day after his final class, Brennan was called in by the assistant dean of the school and asked to aid in setting up a board of inquiry to examine the orthodoxy of Father Rouge's teaching. He would be asked, the administrator said, to supply all his class notes and copies of all his exams as evidence in the inquiry.

Brennan found himself caught in a powerful vice. He believed absolutely in the righteousness of acceding to the voice of God through the will of his superiors.

"Obedience," he automatically told himself whenever challenged by authority, "alone gives can give us certainty."

Such phrases belonged more in a textbook or as an answer on an exam than in a personal reflection, but the distinction always evaded him.

It was not a choice of subject matter, he felt, in which he could pick and choose. He knew that if he hesitated, the university could and simply would go to his prior and ask for his cooperation. Sooner or later, it would become a matter of obedience. So it was such already.

The young priest went home, pulled down his suitcase and took out of it the third-full bottle of scotch. He finished it off in less than half an hour and then put together his notes and exam papers, sealing them in an envelope and addressing to the assistant dean.

The next day he wrote an urgent letter to his provincial asking that he be allowed to go to Rome right after the semester. He saw no advantage in getting a supplemental degree at Catholic University.

"I truly have no more to learn here," he wrote.

That afternoon, he mailed both envelopes.

The provincial called him several days later and said he had already come to the same conclusion. Yes, Father Brennan could go to Rome and should make ready to do so.

Brennan was not available, as a result, to testify against Father Rouge, but nothing was more indicting at the inquiry than his class notes and exam as the French priest was found unfit to teach at the Catholic University of America.

Copies of the materials he had submitted were made for everyone on the inquiry board. One of its members, Brennan would later learn, released his notes and exam answers to a French ecumenical journal. Whether it was to support Father Rouge or cause him trouble was not clear. Brennan's name was mentioned, but only incidentally.

Chapter 32

Father Brennan Jordan O.P. was a Catholic, a Dominican and a priest. And, although he was also an American, the point on which his vision fixed was Rome, Italy. That focus had been with him since grade school. Stated in words from *The New Baltimore Catechism*, his thoughts and purpose drew him more specifically toward:

...the successor (to St. Peter), the bishop of Rome, the pope, who is the Vicar of Christ on earth...

For Brennan, reverence for God, expressed through obedience and loyalty to the Roman Catholic Church and its pontiff, represented a religious unified field theory. Like the sun in the solar system, this conceptualization hovered central in his mind and simplified his grasp of creation and his place in it.

Submission to the will of God and his representative on earth was how one found meaning and purpose, he believed. Scripture, church doctrine, liturgy and spirituality were the foundation stones of his life and told Brennan simply that God and His church are supreme and that man and the world prove but His unworthy creation.

The elementary school catechism had told him his purpose was "to know, love and serve God on earth and to be happy with Him in heaven." It also said the only way to do this was through "the one, holy, catholic, apostolic church," the congregation of the faithful "which Christ founded and of which the bishop of Rome, the pope, is the vicar and visible head."

When the young Dominican arrived in the Eternal City in 1958, the man who held the position of successor to St. Peter and Vicar of Christ was Pope Pius XII.

For Brennan, Pius XII seemed the ultimate role model. His image was so saintly that pictures of him looked as though they belonged on holy cards and in books of the lives of the saints.

Pius was aristocratic by birth, an ascetic with an emaciated, thin look. He was also a brilliant, articulate intellectual. As a child, he had been sick and fragile. He was isolated, as a result, from potential playmates. He had served in the papal diplomat corps, as the Vatican secretary of state and subsequently as a pope who expressed himself eloquently through words and ideas. Critics claimed that where pontiff came up short was not verbally, but in showing real emotions and sometimes in taking decisive actions.

In coming to Rome where Pius' image burned as a bright candle in his mind's eye, the young Dominican priest believed he was entering the realm, if not the reality, of paradise.

Thirty years earlier, as Vatican secretary of state, Eugenio Cardinal Pacelli had actually visited the United States. It was the 1920s and the occasion was the International Eucharistic Conference held in the newly-constructed Soldier Field in Chicago. Then, after the death of Pius XI in 1939, he was elected pope in the shortest conclave in more than 300 years. The Catholic press liked to refer to the pope as "the gifted and saintly" Pius XII.

In that position now for almost 20 years, he had held daily audiences with groups ranging from laborers and gardeners to nuclear scientists and astronomers and spoken to them about their "roles" in modern society. He talked to children, parents, teachers, nuns, tribesmen, Catholic Action groups, worker priests and Third World bishops, giving speeches and counsel that were carried daily in the Vatican newspaper, *L'Osservatore Romano*, and thereafter promulgated in different languages internationally.

At present, he was in his summer residence at Castel Gondolfo and had curtailed these audiences. There were rumors about his health, as there had been since he ascended to the office.

Pius XII, in the tradition of his predecessors, had authored important letters, called encyclicals, to the faithful and the world. Through them he had opened up modern biblical research. It was a field in which Catholics had feared to tread after the turn-of-the-century Pope Pius X had issued severe warnings about using new methods in scriptural study. The reigning pontiff had given a whole new impetus to the liturgy as a means of communal spirituality. To those who looked for a social message about the complex needs of society from the church, this was deeply encouraging.

His 1950 encyclical, *On the Human Race*, was more satisfying to those conservatives who condemned talk about "the social message of the Gospel" as incipient socialism and who were deeply suspicious of any give-and-take dialogue with the world, secularism or other religions

Even more pleasing to the traditionalist Dominican Brennan was the choice of leaders on whom Pius XII relied in the curia and the official bureaucracy of the church. These, led by Alfredo Cardinal Ottaviani, dampened each and every effort toward change within the church or a compromise with the world of modern ideas.

Pius XII was a captive to the church's bureaucracy, a self-acknowledged "prisoner in the Vatican." He had been born in 1876 to a family whose male members had long served as lawyers for the papacy. At the time of his birth and throughout his childhood, the Pacelli family still smarted from the loss by the pope in the 1860's of control over the Papal States, which included a large portion of north and central Italy.

Like his predecessors since that era, he had walled himself up in Rome in a long-sustained protest-turned tradition. The Vatican City, a tiny 0.15 square-mile state of its own, had been accorded independence and sovereignty in the Lateran Treaty and Concordat of 1929, signed by the pope and the government of Benito Mussolini.

It also encompassed some non-adjacent land including Castel Gandolfo, several miles away from the Vatican.

When it came to words and speeches, Pius XII had proved studied but forthright and brilliant, if not bold. However, in taking decisive action against the fascism of Mussolini in Italy, the nazism of Hitler in Germany and the communism of Josef Stalin in the Soviet Union, he agonized over what to do or how to do it. Time and again, his course was marked by inaction as he was fearful that retaliation would be taken against Catholics if he were seen as too forceful in what he said or did.

The young Dominican's filial and spiritual devotion to Pius XII was intense and unswerving. It was tied as though to the apron strings of his mother's beliefs and her aspirations for him rather than to any insight as to what his father had wanted for him.

Brennan could feel his breath slow down when he thought of the ethereal man who held the titles of bishop of Rome and pope. He had read and memorized Pius XII's encyclical letters and writings, especially the ones that supported the traditional doctrines of the church, even while trying to express them in intellectual, almost poetic, phrases.

As a theologian, Father Brennan consistently revered the past over the present or the future. Nevertheless, after reading a strangely positive and upbeat speech by Pius XII, he found himself doing a small but significant about face. In the document, the pontiff had poetically described the modern era as "the springtime of history" and said, in effect, that the best was yet to come.

His words presented a dramatic contrast with the vision entertained by those who believed Armageddon, the apocalyptic final battle before the end of the world to be just around the corner.

In Catholic church circles throughout the world in 1958, it was well known that "the Holy Father," as the pontiff was called, was personally holding onto the "third secret" that had been revealed by the Blessed Virgin to three children in Fatima, Portugal in 1917. This was generally believed to be the message that the world would soon come to a violent end.

And yet, somehow, Pope Pius XII had dared to call the 1950s "the springtime of history?" The phrase contained a dramatic, upbeat promise about the future that was inconsistent with the outlook of those who believed the end of the world was near and deservedly so.

In giving several sermons in Washington, D.C., Father Brennan quoted the pope's words about "the springtime of history."

He remained too prudent, however, to do so in talking to other theologians or to those who believed that the Soviet Union and godless communism would force the deity to cull out the true believers and then destroy what was left of the world.

Few of the more prominent theologians of the Catholic church preached or taught the end was for certain near, but they tended to look askance at anyone who did not view the present era and, even more, the future as being the most troubled and dire of times. Because the young newcomer wanted to belong to this group of church thinkers, he was careful to speak its language, especially in their presence.

The day on which Father Brennan actually arrived in Rome was bright and sunny, a warm one near the end of summer. The tensions of the city mingled with the heat and its hoaried traditions to create an excitement for the young cleric that was exciting if not joyous. The smell of garlic and other foods, of sweat and even of the river and the sewers, conspired to make him happy to have arrived. The Coliseum and other ancient ruins of Rome reflected gloriously in the sun and together with the distinct medieval architecture of the city's basilicas created an atmosphere of near euphoria.

Here, in the city founded according to legend by the twins, Romulus and Remus, and blessed by the presence of nineteen centuries of popes, martyrs and saints, the past could not be ignored. It lived, breathed and sang to Brennan.

The sounds of spoken Italian, the honking from discordant traffic and the screams of vendors seemed to share an environment of noise in which his own much beloved Gregorian chant could fit in a way it never did in his English-speaking homeland.

This city, he felt, called for something big from him and he was resolved to respond to that summons. He started his involvement with the city by checking into the Dominican priory where he would be staying and immediately changing into his religious habit.

To be able to walk proud and tall on the streets of Rome in the garb of Dominic, Thomas Aquinas and his fellow religious gave him a sense of having a special place in the city and its history. Here it was that his religious order had been founded and in this place it had always found a home.

As he entered the majestic St. Peter's Square in the heart of the Vatican City, several tourists looking distinctly American in their gaudy clothes, pointed at him as though he were a quaint part of the city's Catholic tradition. He indeed felt that they were right and that he was.

Others of the faithful, even the most Catholic of Catholics, did not see the Eternal City the same way he did. They might view it as the seat of their church and the home of the pope, but Brennan had once described it in a college history paper with a term he now repeated to himself: "God's second favorite city."

He conceded that Jerusalem would be the number one choice of the Divinity.

The argument he used for calling Rome the deity's "second favorite city" was that it had been the place "where, since the days of St. Peter, the Lord has most persistently manifested himself through the works and words of his church and his apostles' successors."

In attempting to present God's perspective of Rome, Brennan was willing to acknowledge the city's weaknesses and its excesses, even some on the part of the church, but he still proclaimed the city on the Tiber River, "sacred."

His arrival paralleled that of another young intellectual, who first visited the Eternal City in the late 1700's. That man, a young English scholar and gentleman, had likewise uniquely focused on Rome and also felt the city called upon him to respond to it by doing something big and important.

In his *Memoirs*, that man, Edward Gibbon, later wrote:

It was Rome on the fifteenth of October 1764, as I sat musing amidst the ruins of the Capitol while the barefoot friars were singing vespers in the Temple of Jupiter, that the idea of writing the decline and fall of the City first started in my mind.

The contrasts between the views of Gibbon, author of *The Decline and Fall of the Roman Empire,* and those Father Brennan Jordan O.P. were far sharper than were the similarities.

Simply put, on Gibbon's chart, Rome and the church centered here each had had their ups and downs, but the drama of good and bad had lessened as the centuries rolled past.

Living and writing in the 1700's at the time of the American and later the French revolution, Gibbon was principally a well-read, self-educated scholar. He had resided in Switzerland for a period of time. While a resident of that country in his youth, he had converted from Anglicanism to Catholicism and then back; but he subsequently became an irreligious skeptic, with his writings questioning Christianity itself.

Gibbon's seven-volume work, which covered the years from 180 A. D. to 1453 A.D., later proved to historians monumental and staggering.

The Decline and Fall has been called "probably the most majestic work of history ever written." Its genius was seen in the author's presenting the linked strains and threads of the ever-changing lives of people in a given place.

Passage after passage in Gibbon's *The Decline and Fall* demonstrated this as he did not hesitate to turn to metaphor as in the following one:

Private genius and public industry may be extirpated; but these hardy plants survive the tempest, and strike an everlasting root into the most unfavorable soil. The splendid days of Augustus and Trajan were eclipsed by a cloud of ignorance; and the Barbarians subverted the laws and palaces of Rome. But the scythe, the invention or emblem of Saturn, still continued annually to mow the harvests of Italy; and the human feasts of the Leastrygons have never been renewed on the coast of Campania.

While the work presented the history of Rome with unmatched brilliance, it also incurred the wrath of the church and, within ten years of its publication, it was put on the Catholic *Index Librorum Prohibitorum,* the *Index of Forbidden Books.*

Church theologians argued that Gibbons' chapters 15 and 16 seemed to question the right of Christianity even to exist, while others were pointed out to be unduly critical of the popes and their temporal government of Rome and the Papal States.

Gibbon's frequent use of irony and witticisms, even though aimed at pagan as well as Christian Rome, rankled church historians and theologians alike.

Brennan particularly did not like the historian's treatment of the Dominicans and St. Thomas Aquinas in particular.

But even the young cleric had to acknowledge having his breath taken away as he read with special permission the pages of Gibbon's *The Decline and Fall.*

Still, Brennan knew Rome and its history and could counter Gibbon as he had Father Rouge at Catholic U. He had his own sources, which included the voluminous *Annals* by Cardinal Baronius and the 1725 *Scienza Nuova* by Vico. Instead of being on the Index, these two works bore the cherished cherished ecclesiastical approval, the *Imprimatur* of a bishop.

Both authors represented not only excellent research and scholarship but also an unquestioned acceptance of Italy's Catholic past. The young Dominican found no problem with that. He was one of the few people on earth who had plowed his way through most of the large volumes of the *Annals* as well as Vico's history of medieval Italy. On his own, he had read in Latin at Catholic University the accounts of the Lateran and Vatican councils of the church and had practically memorized their findings to help bring himself up to date on church and Roman history.

He was acquiring the bricks and mortar for an intellectual structure that would be Rome-based and could somehow compete with the pagan and Christian edifices there as well as the work of Edward Gibbon.

The first earth-shaking fault appeared on a day shortly after his arrival in Rome. On Oct. 3, 1958, a major news story shot through the city and directly into his heart: Pope Pius XII, *Il Papa*, was seriously ill.

Chapter 33

Eight days later, as the cooler October weather took firm control of the Eternal City, Pope Pius XII was dead. He had died at Castel Gondolfo, no longer capable of giving the world a last audience, unable to express a final deathbed sentiment.

Bumbling morticians, trying a new form of embalming on his frail, thin body, attempted thereby to help with his immortality, but botched it and did not do well even by the mortuarial measures of Italy's back streets.

The funeral procession chanted the traditional phrase used upon the death of a pope: "*Sic Transit Gloria Mundi*"--"Thus passes the glory of the world."

Rome and the rest of world turned its head forward and looked to the selection of his successor.

Father Brennan Jordan O. P., in the priory cell that was now his home, wept, sobbing loud enough to be heard by those passing by it.

The young priest ached out of embarrassment, not because he was weeping, but because he had not cried for his own mother a year and a half earlier.

Somehow, this death seemed more momentous in a God-centered universe.

In the death of Pius XII, Brennan foresaw his own, as he had understood in the pope's loneliness, that which he himself felt.

In the works of the deceased pontiff, in his intellectual style, in his strong, religious convictions, and in his firm ties with the past, he recognized himself.

In coming to Rome, the youthful cleric had sought a beginning. In Pius XII's death, he sensed rather an end. And he was not at all certain what that included.

Somehow, he no longer felt as young as he had the day before. The change had to do with the man whose life had slipped away and with the fear he himself had started to feel.

Brennan's own life had been comfortably headed in one direction. Now, it was different, less definite, far more complicated and uncertain.

When in grade school Mikey Jordan had prayed for the pope, the man whose name he mentioned was Pius XII. All through his seminary studies and after his investiture as a Dominican, his highest superior was that same man. As he said his first mass and at every one after it, he had fervently asked God to bless the pontiff, the one who was now dead.

When Brother and later Father Brennan had incipient doubts about who he was and what he was becoming, he had often called up his admiration for the pope and pulled out Pius' writings and reread them.

An intellectual, Brennan realized, at least mentally, that not every answer to a theological question was as simple as the catechism and dogma textbook portrayed it to be. As a religious person, he often found it a long, almost impossible leap from church doctrine to personal sanctity.

The personality, the intellectuality, the apparent goodness of the pontiff helped smother with an avalanche of assuredness any frightening little concern Brennan had about his faith.

The Roman Catholic church uses the Latin word, *pontifex*, for the pope. The English word is "pontiff." In translation, however, the student of religion is separated from the basic idea of the name, "bridgemaker." *Pons* means "a bridge" and *facere*, "to make." In effect, it places the person with that title in the position of a negotiator or liaison between man and God or God and man, if one would.

The young Dominican had a realistic sense of how uniquely brilliant he was, but he had always felt that Pius XII was smarter, a lot more so than he. Certainly, the pope with the name, Pius, was far holier than he could ever aspire to be.

Despite the tremendous and obvious importance of Pius XII, the newspapers, the radio and the people on the street seemed to be forgetting the man and his life and were getting on with their own. At the same time, Father Brennan was immobilized and could not stop obsessing about him.

Was Father Brennan the only person in Rome who did not care who the next pontiff would be? His man, his "Holy Father," was dead. The life of His Holiness had been snuffed out as though he were just a common person.

Brennan was in mourning and the fact that there would now be another pope was in no way consoling.

The best, the noblest and the holiest human he could imagine was dead and he, Brennan Jordan, had not even been given the opportunity to hear or see him in person. Attending his funeral would not help. It would remind him that he had been cheated in never viewing him in life.

Brennan could not believe how unplugged, how disconsolate, he felt. He said mass in the mornings and went to choir but not to meals. He could not think of going to class.

The prior called on him in his room and they spoke of Pius and of Brennan's great regard for him, but the American friar did not open up about his sadness and depression, nor did his superior inquire.

"If you need anything, let me know," the prior offered, without intruding further. He realized that in a closed society such as the order the death of a father figure, even a religious one, could hit a young man hard.

Father Brennan took off his religious habit and with black pants and a sport shirt on went for a walk up and down the streets of Rome, the euphoria and ecstasy of his first days in the city completely drained from him. A close scrutiny of his attire could have told people he was a member of the clergy, but he cared not whether or not passersby so identified him.

He was a different person, completely distracted by his own thoughts. He was almost run down several times by the reckless drivers of the Italian capitol city. It did not matter to him and once, when he was actually knocked to the ground, he simply waved everyone off.

Rome is built on seven hills, but he little noticed whether his steps were taking him up or down sidewalks or streets.

He thought, but his thinking was blocked. He felt, but his feelings were stifled.

Pius XII was dead. That was all he knew. He could not make it go away.

Brennan did not eat. He was not hungry.

It was as though he were in the army and the general--a Hannibal, a Caesar, a Napoleon or a Robert E. Lee--had been killed. Not only was leadership now missing, but also purpose seemed gone with it.

He found himself on the *Ponte Garibaldi* crossing the Tiber River. As he stared at the water, he noticed how slow the current was moving. It seemed this day to have no message of life for him.

Brennan walked toward the center of the old city, ignoring as best he might the ever-present motor scooters that roared past and that contributed to a cacophony of noise and a tangible cloud of pollution. He was momentarily distracted by recalling that in the First Century BCE, Julius Caesar had ordered these streets not be used by any wagon during the daytime. Oh, how needed such a decree was this day as the vibrations of the speeding traffic shook the city's monuments and jarred the young Dominican's fragile spirit!

Instead of turning right off the *Corso Vittorio Emanuele II* toward the pompous white statue of Victor Emanuel, he veered onto the *Via del Corso*, the main street in the central city.

His journey took him in a direction out of the city on the route that had in ancient times brought people into it. Known in the days of the Roman Empire as the *Via Flaminia*, it served as one of the major roads that led into the heart of Rome from the Adriatic Sea and the powerful eastern half of the empire.

To Brennan it was just another crowded street of basilicas, palaces and monuments.

He no longer viewed *Corso Vittorio Emanuele II* as a tourist, but as a burdened captive, eyes cast down rather than up.

His pace eventually led him to the city's ancient gate, the *Porta del Popolo*, which was used as a ceremonial entranceway. Along with the adjacent *Piazza del Popolo*, it had served as a stage for grand entries to Rome.

Brennan's stumbling, almost stuporous walk represented more an actor making a forlorn exit than a grand entrance, a soldier who had experienced defeat rather than a victory.

The Roman stage on which he once had been certain he would star had become a noisy, clamorous and lonely place, a large platform on which he had again become a small figure, abandoned by his confidence and even his hope.

He was walking and then suddenly he wasn't. He had collapsed, fallen to the ground as a result of the tiredness and hunger his consciousness had denied and ignored.

A man and woman, speaking Italian, lifted him to his feet and led him to a small restaurant-cafe nearby. The hostess offered him wine. He sipped it and then swallowed the complete contents of the glass.

Brennan felt a little more aware of who he was and where he was, but he said nothing, holding his head in his hands.

The couple and the hostess hovered around him. Realizing he was a member of the clergy, the Italian woman addressed him as "Father" and asked him several times what was wrong.

In the most confused statement of his life, he answered in Italian, "My mother is dead."

"You mother died?" the woman queried.

"Why did you say that?" Brennan asked.

"Because that is what you just said," she replied.

"I said that?" he questioned.

The couple shrugged their shoulders and left.

Brennan sat quiet for several more moments and ordered a bottle of wine. He drank it and started on a second. He began to feel some relief in the form of forgetfulness of that which had been plaguing him.

"How many days have passed?" he wondered, but not long enough to think the question through.

"Did I say my mother had died?" he questioned himself, but probed for no answer and no reason for asking.

He spoke to the hostess one time in Italian and the next in English.

She insisted he eat some bread and tried to get him to order some pasta, but he waved her off and returned to his wine.

His mother was dead. He knew that now and he started to cry.

He paid for the two bottles, took the second one with him and continued his walk.

Now, it was his mother and her death that was on his mind.

He stopped in the doorway of a house and sat down. He tried restoring his ability to go on by taking deep breaths, but it was what he heard over the radio that brought him back to reality.

"*Habemus Papam,*" the radio blared in Latin, rather than Italian. It was the traditional announcement that the conclave of cardinals, meeting in secret, had sent a white puff of smoke up the chimney to announce they had been successful in electing a new pope.

It was too early to know whom they had chosen.

Brennan had repeatedly told himself and others he did not care who it would be, but suddenly he did. He felt only a remote curiosity, but he now wanted to know.

Placing the empty bottle in a garbage box behind a restaurant, he slowly and deliberately found his way back to his priory.

The friars there were excited, talking and speculating among themselves about who the new pontiff would be. Brennan, without smiling or saying anything, nodded and repaired to his cell. He would sleep and when he awoke, he would learn.

Father Brennan woke to the bell for *magnum silentium*, too late to talk to anyone to discover which cardinal had been chosen pope and with too sharp of a headache to care much.

He went to the chapel and sat in a choir stall and tried to think or possibly to pray.

The thing with Pius XII was over. The man was dead. He could no longer recall all the reasons he had so fixated on the death of the pope. He was not one to give up control over himself, but it had been wrenched from him nevertheless. The pope had died. He felt a loss, let down; but it was something he would get over.

His mother was dead and he now felt the sadness he had not at the time of her death, but it was not he who was dead. Life would go on.

Then strange words started to beat in his head as though they were some kind of mantra. They were the last lines of his father's poem about roses:

"Only the words
of Gertrude Stein
survive
because
she avoided comparison, adjective, metaphor
and verbiage
other than reminding us
a rose is a rose.
Oh, yes!"

Until now, he had never been able to recall any part of the poem. Now, the final lines crashed through his mind. He wanted to write, to make a copy of the whole poem that he had abandoned in a Belle Isle garbage can.

The rest was not there for him to recall and even the final lines began to fade.

He recognized it had come at him from the deepest part of his memory as a distraction from the fact that he had gotten drunk.

Had that act of drunkeness been a sin? Of course, it was. It was a weakness. He was supposed to be in control of himself. Why? Because God demanded it of him. Once you let that go, you could lie, cheat, steal, commit adultery or kill someone. And why not? If someone wanted to do something wrong and had surrendered control of himself, then he would do it.

It was the giving up of control that was wrong. That was the sin. He had done it and, as a result, at this very moment he was not in the state of grace. If he died, he would go to hell. The logic was inescapable.

It was not until he reasoned all of this through that he began to feel guilt. This emotion, if one could call it that, was not only painful, but also horrible and miserable in itself. It was disabling and discouraging. It tempted him to act and to do so with a frightening measure of panic.

The longer Brennan sat, the more he thought until he felt inundated by waves of strange, upsetting new sensations.

In all his life, he had never had an experience anything like this. Where did the ball of thread start? Was it with the pope's death, his mother's? Was this all about sin, guilt or something else?

Getting drunk was a sin. Definitely. He was not in a state of grace as a result, but at the same time he knew it had helped him, had pulled him out of a hopeless situation.

Why did he not have answers? Brennan Jordan was, he acknowledged, an extraordinarily intelligent human being. He was a religious, a person seeking perfection and therefore seeking control over his animal nature. As a seminarian, he had studied moral theology and understood it well enough to earn perfect grades on his exams. The questions in the books were the very ones he was asking himself now. They involved the issues of free will, sin, drunkenness, guilt and punishment for one's transgressions. Yet, he knew nothing and understood less.

Worse, he did not feel capable of answering these questions when they pertained to himself. Yes, he could come up with the right answers, the ones in the book, but then they would slip away and he would find himself asking yet a different question. Nothing stood still for him.

Brennan, the theologian and the conservative, suddenly feared there was another side to him, one that believed, out of convenience, in situational ethics or relativistic morality.

He had committed a sin and he was going to be eternally damned if he didn't get it forgiven. No, he had not committed a sin and, no, he wasn't going to hell. It all depended...

Yet, if there were any greater error than accepting the belief that all moral questions are relative, he did not know what it was.

He told himself he immediately had to answer the question whether or not he had committed a mortal sin. If he could not do that, everything else in his life would fall apart. He could not teach. He could not counsel. He could hear confessions. And most of all, being a Dominican, he could not carry out his primary mission of preaching.

Father Brennan slipped to his knees and prayed for guidance. Nothing happened. He pulled out his breviary and said the hours that he had missed by walking the streets and fretting about he could no longer remember what.

He finished his office and pulled up the rosary that dangled from the rope around his waist.

Methodically he repeated the Hail Marys and the Our Fathers of the rosary. The peace of the possible began to descend on him. The questioning started to fade away.

He was not happy with what had happened and neither must God be.

Brennan determined to find another priest and confess his transgression through him.

And then he would also find out who the new pope was.

Chapter 34

The moment he heard the results of the conclave, Brennan concluded it would mean a near-tragedy for the church, comparable to the one in the late 13th Century when the cardinals had elected a hermit, Celestine V, the pope. He was incapable of grasping, however, what it would mean for him.

To him, the ideal pope would be a vigorous young man with the intellect of a Thomas Aquinas or Pius XII. The new pontiff would be outstanding in protecting the vast body of doctrine and moral teaching of the church, clarifying the truth and attacking error. With a brilliance that Catholicism desperately needed in a hostile world, Brennan felt, the new pontiff would integrate doctrine and morals, liturgy and spirituality, tradition and scripture.

The models would be Dominic confronting the Albigensian heretics, the compilation of another *Summa Theologica* of Thomas Aquinas and the continuing lectures by a new Pius XII to the clergy, laity and the rest of the world.

One man in the church could do this, Brennan had decided. He was the powerful and brilliant leading member of the Roman Curia, Alfredo Cardinal Ottaviani. And, if the opposition to his forceful conservatism were too strong, there were two other acceptable candidates: Giuseppe Cardinal Siri, the archbishop of Genoa, or

Milan's Archbishop Giovanni Montini, even though the latter had not yet been made a cardinal. A case could even be made for New York's Francis Cardinal Spellman.

It was not any of these whom the cardinals had chosen. They elected instead an elderly man, Angelo Cardinal Roncalli, archbishop and patriarch of Venice. He was almost 77 years old and it was obvious to even the most casual observer that he was at best a "provisional, caretaker pope." At most, his reign would provide a chance for a younger, more forceful man to come to the fore, in all probability, someone like Archbishop Montini.

A complete disaster, in Brennan's mind, would have been the selection of the ultra-liberal Dutch Bernard Cardinal Alfrink of Utrecht, Holland or one of several other European cardinals. As it was, the curia and the holy office had to be vigilant constantly that ideas from these countries be held in check.

One of the worst examples was their encouragement by their bishops of the so-called Priest-Worker Movement. Brennan, and almost every other conservative in the church, believed they had in promoting this mingled the church and the world in a most inappropriate way. The young clergy in France were allowed to go to work in factories and offices in the belief that they could spread the gospel there.

Brennan had worked in a factory. He had not converted anyone there. The world would not be leavened by such foolishness; but rather the holiness and spirituality of the church and clergy would be compromised.

The major intellectual battle that would have to be fought and won in the coming years, he had said in class, evolved around the writing of Father Pierre Teilhard de Chardin. The man, a scientist and theologian, had an enormous underground following among Catholics and some outside the church. The holy office had found it necessary to place de Chardin's writing under a serious *monitum* or warning as he openly espoused evolution, which contradicted the account of creation described in the *Book of Genesis*.

This issue had to be clarified and such teaching that openly challenged scripture, Brennan was convinced, needed to be squelched not only for itself but also as an example to others tempted to question the basic beliefs of the Catholic church.

It was obvious to Brennan that Cardinal Roncalli was not a pope who would be up to such challenges. His inadequacy for the job was attested, according to rumor, by no less an authority than the newly-elected pope himself. It was being told that, after it had become obvious he would be the compromise candidate, he had spent the last night of the conclave weeping. This was not the sign of a strong leader.

Father Brennan, who knew his church history, was horrified when he heard the name the new pope had chosen, John XXIII.

"John" was a terrible name for a pope, so bad that a cardinal earlier in the century who was a viable candidate for the papacy had made a bad joke about calling himself, if elected, John XXIII.

The last time that the name "John" had been selected was 500 years before when Baldassarre Cossa of Naples, who had been selected in opposition to the legitimately elected Gregory XII, chose it.

Cardinal Roncalli's reasons for selecting such an historically inappropriate name were hardly satisfying to those who argued that he should have more respect for history. "John" or, in Italian, "Giovanni," had been his father's name and St. John was the patron of the humble parish in which he had been baptized.

While his choice of a name did not augur well, some other facts known about him seem to do so. Even though he was not brilliant like Pius, the new pope had been a believer, like Brennan, in obedience and was recognized as a true conformist. He was also respected for his piety, but his holiness was clearly the personal, individual kind. It was not one "based on the social message of the Gospels," as the liberals liked to describe theirs.

Cardinal Roncalli was a man who turned inward to find God, not outward to reach others, it was said.

Still, the strongest feeling for Brennan was disappointment. John XXIII would probably reign as pope for only two or three years, but they would be the ones in which the Dominican scholar would be in Rome getting his doctorate. He, as a result, would find himself not on the side of those steering Catholicism, as he would have been under Pius, but rather as a part of the church's brake system under John.

"How can I identify with a man who has chosen the name, John?" he wondered, shaking his head in answer to his own question.

Although he had not gone to Pius XII's funeral, he would attend John XXIII's enthronement. It would be an excitement he would not want to miss. He was too much a part of the church and its penchant for ceremony to consider missing one that had not been witnessed in Rome for almost 20 years.

When the day of the ceremony came, he was in St. Peter's Square early, realizing he could not get in the church itself. That was largely reserved for the hierarchy, the diplomats, government officials, Roncalli's large Venetian following, religious insiders and others who enjoyed the benefits of Vatican protocol. It was enough for him to see the pope carried by on his chair in formal procession as well as to hear the ceremony and the pontiff's speech broadcast live to the crowd.

The pomp and the ceremony were staggering to Brennan. His wait on that November day, he felt, was well worth it. He was a part of what was happening, of Rome, of history and of the church.

That church, he had believed since his catechism days, bears four marks: It is one, holy, catholic and apostolic. Today, he would have awarded it a fifth one: majestic. More than 1900 years of liturgical and ceremonial tradition were behind the pomp of this occasion.

The vestments, the tiara or papal crown, the chair, the large feathered fans, the incense, the chant, the music, the people assembled from around the world, the unifying language of Latin: none of these escaped Brennan's attention and enjoyment.

Each and every one of them said to him that here and now a man is being raised up to a special place among men and in history.

What was most fascinating to the American Dominican standing clad in his religious habit was this man himself. Brennan was close enough to make out the face and physical features of the new pope. What he saw was a peasant in a pope's vestments with a broad, flat-faced man, who looked like he would be more comfortable in the fields or in retirement with grandchildren and great-grandchildren at his knees than on the throne of Peter.

He thought of the turn-of-the-century Pius X, who had also come from the poorer classes and who had also risen to be patriarch of Venice before becoming pope. Both seemed to him simple Italian parish priests. Pius X had become a pontiff, one now canonized, who had struck hard and directly at modern trends in the church and the world. Perhaps, John XXIII might be motivated to do the same and, if he did, he would more than adequately fill the needs of the church even though he was merely a short-term, provisional pope.

The pontiff's speech was reassuring to Brennan.

"What matters," the pope said, "is not so much what we do as the manner in which we do it."

These words signaled to the audience that John XXIII had no intention of becoming an activist pope, the biggest fear that Brennan and other traditionalist theologians had.

The pope continued in words that were especially encouraging to the American Dominican: "Especially close to our heart is the task of shepherd of the whole flock. All the other human qualities--knowledge, perception, diplomatic tact, organizing ability--can serve as embellishments and completions of pontifical rule, but they can be no substitute for it."

While Brennan liked what he heard, he had never lost the fear of change that had invaded him with the death of Pius XII. And, for him, it was not enough to be frightened and hold back his whole-hearted endorsement of any impact Pope John XXIII might have, he needed to act, do something, make a contribution. He must, as his mother told him when he was but four years old, give back to God the gifts that had been bestowed on him.

He had made his peace with God. He had ducked into a parish church in the city and confessed his sin of drunkenness anonymously and in Italian to an unknown priest in the confessional there. It was not easy. He had mumbled the words. He was sure the priest had heard them. He knew for certain that God had.

Brennan was aware of what he had to do in order to move toward his mission, the goal that was offered to him. He must make contact with Msgr. Luciano, assistant to Alfredo Cardinal Ottaviani.

This was especially relevant since his eminence was now rumored to be in line to be elevated to the prefecture or head position of the powerful Congregation of the Holy Office.

He had considered renewing his contact with Msgr. Albert Johnson, who had met with him right after his ordination. He was now Bishop Johnson, an auxiliary to New York' Cardinal Spellman, and in town with the latter for the papal coronation. He did not do so because he was embarrassed he had not yet presented himself to Msgr. Luciano, as Bishop Johnson had urged.

This, he did that evening. He phoned and was given an appointment for the next day. He had taken a deep breath before making the call, keeping his eyes closed during the first part of the conversation. It helped that the monsignor had known who he was. The man on the other end of the line had attempted to be informal, proposing that they speak in English, but Brennan declined the offer.

The next day, the right reverend received him hospitably and with a friendly smile that contrasted with his austere appearance. The fabric of the Msgr. Luciano's clothes said it all to Brennan. He was in his late 30's, but his dress was of a neat, shiny black material that looked as though it came from a bolt manufactured long before the war. His glasses were the same, small pinched style that Pius XII had worn and his round clerical hat was one only a traditionalist Italian cleric would don without being embarrassed.

The man was quick and well informed. Yes, he had received a note from Bishop Johnson. Yes, he knew about Father Brennan Jordan, O.P. There was little about the life of the young Dominican Msgr. Luciano did not seem to know.

Brennan was stunned. He would be surprised if the man before him did not know his grades, the papers he had written and even his reaction to the death of Pius XII.

"We believe we can find a place for you here, Father," the monsignor said.

The Dominican did not know what he meant, but neither did he worry about it other than to say, "I would, of course, first have to seek permission for any formal arrangements from my religious superiors."

"Yes," the monsignor responded, "but let me assure you that we would be in contact with them first. They generally prefer it that way."

Brennan whistled lightly to himself. He was not, as he had thought in coming here, making contact. He was joining up. And, he suspected, he was going to be put through officers' training school.

He thought for a second it still might be prudent to signal his provincial back in the United States as to what was happening, but he was not certain exactly what was the proper protocol.

Brennan later realized better how it worked. Cardinal Ottaviani would say something or pen a note to the prefect of the Congregation of Religious, who would inform the minister general of the Dominican order, who in turn would speak to Father Brennan's provincial. One Dominican already on the holy office staff was also a bishop. He might be the facilitator. Whatever would be requested, would be acceded to. It would be a matter of holy obedience and each cleric down the line would accede with total and willing obeisance.

Meanwhile, the theology student would return to his education, where his professors understood clearly that his silence in class hid a quickness they would find formidable if they ever challenged him, which they chose not to do.

Brennan met with his prior and was surprised to find in him a man with whom he could talk, if not one in whom he could totally confide. The older Dominican was laid back in a way his father had been. He seemed non-judgmental, yet aware of what was going on. He too was well-informed on Brennan's background and potential. For all this, and for a certain air of honesty he perceived in the American friar, the prior had respect.

Less than a month passed before things started to happen. The city was ripe with the rumor first that Cardinal Ottaviani would be appointed prefect of the Congregation of the Holy Office. Then, Brennan heard that the new pope was being pressured to appoint someone less conservative and controversial to the post. Finally, there was official confirmation that, indeed, the cardinal would get the job after all.

The day after the news became formal, Brennan received a note from Msgr. Luciano inviting him to supper the following Friday with his eminence Alfred Cardinal Ottaviani.

Brennan was stunned. He was 26 years old, ordained a year-and-a-half, a student in theology, a still wet-behind-the-ears Dominican and an American. Yet, he had been invited to have dinner with the man about whom all of Rome and the Church was now talking, the second most powerful man in all Catholicism; and, if the pope faltered or proved weak, possibly the leader.

In a reaction that was purely American, he expressed himself in one word, "Wow!"

Chapter 35

"Ottaviani, that reactionary," Father Edgar Hunt, a fellow Dominican from the United States, challenged. "You are actually going to meet with him?"

Brennan now painfully regretted he had told his confrere about his proposed supper with the cardinal. Mentioning it, he had to acknowledge to himself that it had, indeed, been a bit of a boast on his part.

"I really had to say something to someone," he told himself. "Otherwise, the dinner invitation would not have seemed real. Still, in doing it, especially to Edgar, I made a mistake."

The fellow priest who had made the utterance obviously did not share Brennan's opinion of or respect for Ottaviani, even though the cardinal was about to ascend from being pro-secretary of the Congregation of the Holy Office to the top position there. Brennan had felt he could confide in Father Edgar. His confrere's comments certainly had made it clear that he should not have.

What could Brennan do now to repair or pass over any potential damage? He smiled and shrugged his shoulders.

"Well, we'll see what comes of it," he said, trying to be somewhat enigmatic.

Father Edgar shook his head, and in a voice filled with irony, added, "Say hello to the good cardinal from an American fan."

For Brennan, there had been one small advantage in hearing the blunt word "'reactionary." He needed to remember that not all the world shared his own opinion of Cardinal Ottaviani. He was aware that his eminence's reputation in certain corners would have fared better if he had what they called in the United States, "better public relations." He was quite certain the cardinal did not care.

The rules of the priory where he was residing allowed a friar to have his habit dry-cleaned once every two months but washed as often as needed. This was the time, Brennan figured, for the former. He wanted to look better than his best.

"Is there anything, a document or a book perhaps, I might take along with me?" he asked himself. Even though his habit was sparkling clean, he needed more security than he felt he had. He could think of nothing.

This would not be a simple chitchat session. He could expect to be under microscope, examined, tested for his brilliance, but above all for his orthodoxy. He would be grilled, could pass and still be allowed to stand tentatively among or on the fringe of the eminent cardinal's coterie. That was a reasonable probability or else he never would have received the invitation. A second possibility was that he would be found unacceptable, would fall short, but then would be patronizingly shooed away. The third was that he might displease the man altogether, would reveal something that would get him in trouble or give a wrong answer. As a result, he could spend the rest of his days as a theologian under a cloud from the Congregation of the Holy Office.

These were real considerations, each intimidating in its own way. Still, it was he who had knocked on Msgr. Luciano's door and there was now no turning back.

Brennan needed some device to back himself up, to ensure his confidence. He felt he must find a means to guarantee lest he be betrayed by his awkwardness or nervousness. What was required was some guaranteed way to underline his own basic, conservative thinking on the church and dogma. Otherwise it was entirely possible a different strain of thinking, an unacceptable willingness to test and experiment, could sneak out through an unguarded portal.

Then, he thought of a solution. To anyone else, it would have been too simplistic. But Brennan's technique was always to simplify matters to the point where grasping and remembering them proved utterly easy. It was the way his genius worked.

So, he did it. He went to chapel and there sat and reviewed in his head the complete *The New Baltimore Catechism* of his childhood. As he recalled each question and answer--and he remembered every single word--he used it to remind himself to stay basic. There were more than a few phrases and sentences awkwardly stated in the catechism. The question was always repeated in the answer, for example, but there was nothing heretical, not a word of theological experiment or exploration.

Here was how it would help him: Any answer he gave to the cardinal about doctrine or a church matter, he would first test in his mind against his now refreshed memory of catechetical answers.

Yes, it was indeed simplistic, but in the interview he was about to face, he would get better grades for being right and orthodox, than for being brilliant and sophisticated. Too much was at stake. It was all right if he were judged as less intelligent than he was, but not as less conservative.

He had almost completed his mental review of the questions and answers when his memory drudged up a final section listed as the "Appendix." Each question in the first part of the book bore a number from one to 499. The appendiced 16 were noted with Roman numerals.

It was in this supplement to the catechism that he found or rather recalled several key answers that seemed able to make his lengthy mental review of *The New Baltimore Catechism* worthwhile.

The theological issue of the day, the one he knew to be central, as almost certainly Cardinal Ottaviani agreed, was a question that profoundly divides Catholics and almost all Non-Catholic Christians.

Protestants and many orthodox sects saw *The Bible* as the sole source of divine revelation. The Catholic church maintains, however, that God's truth has been revealed through two sources: scripture and tradition. Other denominations cannot and do not accept as doctrine such beliefs as the Immaculate Conception, the infallibility of the pope and the assumption of Mary, for these cannot be found in the gospels or other books of the New Testament.

Catholic teaching says these beliefs have been revealed through tradition, both written and oral. This constitutes a deep split within Christianity. Even within the Church, several schools of thought contended in the late 1950's over how to express whatever inherent relationship exists between such revelation and scripture.

To the theologians as well as to the preachers and priests, it was a trench as wide and deep as the Grand Canyon. Even to the outsiders, it was a noticeable crack between the two lines of Christian faiths. The Protestants hold to the Bible as the only way in which God had revealed His truth to mankind. Catholics said He had also done so through certain traditions handed down by the Church.

Catholic scholars termed this "the question of the sources of Revelation." It was, especially at this time, not only a Protestant-Catholic issue but also a conservative-liberal one. Inside the church, it remained a challenge as to how to answer it. Inside the church, the debate, scripture vs. tradition, was over whether to state the Catholic position in the hard-line terms that angered the Protestants and other non-Catholic Christians or to try to find some language to make the differences less strident.

The formulation of the terms of this question would most certainly be a litmus test with which Cardinal Ottaviani would want to use on any recruit such as the young Dominican.

In his memory culled from the appendix to *The New Baltimore Catechism* Brennan found guidance in how to pass the test. The relevant material, which he had been mulling over as he sat in chapel, came from the catechism's appendix. It was:

Question: Are all the truths revealed for us by God found in the Bible?

Answer: Not all truths revealed for us by God are found in the Bible; some are found in divine tradition.

Question: What is meant by divine tradition?

Answer: By divine tradition is meant the revealed truths taught by Christ and His apostles, which were given to the church only by word of mouth and not through *The Bible*, though they were put in writing by the fathers of the church.

Question: Must divine tradition be believed as firmly as *The Bible*?

Answer: Divine tradition must be believed as firmly as *The Bible* because it also contains the word of God.

Question: How can we know the true meaning of the doctrines contained in *The Bible* and divine tradition?

Answer: We can know the true meaning of the doctrines contained in *The Bible* and divine tradition from the Catholic church, which has been authorized by Jesus Christ to explain His doctrines, and which is preserved from error by the special assistance of the Holy Ghost.

Brennan did not know exactly how these elemental questions and answers would help him in a face-to-face meeting with his eminence, but he knew they could and would.

The dinner offered in the cardinal's Vatican apartment was simple, almost sparse. The food, the cardinal and the objects in the surrounding room were all distinctly Roman. His host offered to speak in English, but Brennan answered in flawless Italian and the conversation proceeded in that language.

His eminence, as the young priest addressed him, sat very straight in his chair, a slight, wry smile on his face. The cardinal across the table from him, Brennan quickly discovered, could be witty, caring and friendly. At the same time, he displayed an inner reserve that commanded both complete compliance and a formal respect. This quality warned the visitor that whatever it is that this man chose to hold back could be prove extraordinarily intimidating.

The cardinal wore his humble roots the way a short man does his size. Both his appearance and manners said he was not to the aristocracy born. His background had obviously helped propel him onward and upward in life, drove him to excel and never ever allowed him to bow to anyone. He was a man who held his head erect. His posture was stiff, not out of physical but rather from social discomfort.

The contrast between his impression of the cardinal and Brennan's image of the late pope was startling. The appearance and mannerisms of the man before him, though very proper, marked him as coming from one of the city's multitude of unmoneyed, untitled families. By contrast, Pius XII and everything about him had been upper class, aristocratic.

"The poor you will always have with you" had been a true statement in Rome from its beginning. With a population of almost 2.5 million in the late 1950's, it seemed especially true. The country was still economically rusted from the tragedies of Mussolini and World War II

Brennan knew that Alfredo Ottaviani, with almost a dozen siblings, came from one of the city's many deeply impoverished families.

The rank of cardinal is an extraordinary honor and the prefecture of the Congregation of the Holy Office represents almost terrifying power. Neither, however, is it a title nor does it bear the marks of privilege in that it could be passed down through one's family along with genes that alone admit one to membership in societal circles in the city. Cardinals, archbishops and prefects of sacred congregations are only occasional guests there.

If Ottaviani had worn the papal tiara rather than the cardinal's hat, he would still not be of the "us" who made up the aristocracy as Pius XII had.

Rome was the capital of Italy, a democratic state, but it was also loaded with a plethora of aristocrats. Its "black nobility" came from families with papal titles and forms a society within a society. In addition, there is the "white nobility," which received their right to claim membership among the nobility from the king of Italy. Individuals from both groups pride themselves in being *Romano di Roma*, a Roman Roman.

Nothing about the cardinal indicated he was a member of either group. The club to which he had long belonged was that of seminary professors. Of this fact, he intentionally and deliberately reminded his Dominican guest.

Brennan later described Cardinal Ottaviani as a scholar, a man who was intellectually keen and who often used wit to make his point. The young Dominican, having been raised poor himself, spoke not about the cardinal's lack of aristocratic status, even though he was aware that the cardinal must have been sensitive on the point.

Two additional facts Father Brennan learned about his prominent host surprised him. In addition to his work for the holy office, he operated a school and a summer camp for poor boys in Rome. Secondly, although he was a priest and a cardinal, Ottaviani had never been raised to the level of or consecrated as a bishop. This was unusual and later would be "rectified."

Cardinal Ottaviani was perhaps the most observant person the American Dominican had ever encountered. The cardinal constantly picked up details, many of them irrelevant, and did so thoroughly and quickly. It was an apt quality, if perhaps a dangerous one, in the man who headed the holy office, the doctrinal policing force of the church.

Brennan would later hear the cardinal explain his view of that office in an Italian radio address:

My personal position is that of a man who has, from the nature of his office, the duty to keep the deposit of faith intact and who, at the same time, must leave full freedom to the progress which is necessary to better clarify, understand and expose Catholic teaching.

Let us never forget that not all that is new is good and true merely because it is new. There are some opinions in theology today which are, if not false, at least debatable. In this situation, it is a completely positive action to defend the basic data of holy scripture and of tradition, to avoid permitting some truths of the faith to be obscured, under the pretext of progress and adaptation.

It would only be in retrospect that the cardinal's speech would remind Brennan of two other magnetic voices he had heard. The first was in his childhood and in person. The second was while he was in the seminary and over the radio. The other two men were: the "radio priest of the 1930's," Father Charles Coughlin, and the grand inquisitor of the U. S. Senate, Senator Joseph McCarthy of Wisconsin.

In all three cases the voices projected a focused mind, unquestioned righteousness and a dominating sense of authority.

Fresh out of the seminary, Brennan fully understood the power of a theology professor over his students and doctrinal orthodoxy. Such authority seemed absolute, it was formidable and it could bring an abrupt and complete end to a seminarian's aspiration to be a priest. As a young student, the Dominican friar had been extraordinarily orthodox and yet had felt intimidated at the hands of his own professors. Cardinal Ottaviani seemed to believe he played just such a role in the lives of every member of the clergy and faithful anywhere in the world and at all times.

Strangely, Brennan was strongly attracted to that power in this man that he had feared. He too felt it "a positive action to defend the basic data of scripture and tradition" and to do so, if necessary, by stringent and sometimes retaliatory means.

This man, Brennan felt, had the possibility of replacing his so-recently deceased hero, Pius XII. And while the young Dominican had never viewed the late pontiff, here he was sharing a meal with his trusted advisor, his eminence Cardinal Alfredo Ottaviani. He experienced an eerie transference of veneration.

Cardinal Ottaviani had done most of the talking and all of the questioning as the meal progressed and they retired with glasses of port from the table to hardback chairs at the end of the room. Much of the conversation had been about Brennan's classes and professors, many of whom the cardinal knew personally. He then inquired about the Catholic University of America and several professors and administrators whom he knew there. He was obviously well informed about events that had taken place there. Brennan half expected him to make a passing reference to the controversy over Father Rouge but he did not do so.

The discussion flowed easily, even though Brennan was always aware of the differences of their positions and power. While friendly and capable of a good laugh, the cardinal made no effort to disavow his would-be protégé of the awareness that their roles were teacher-student, powerful man-subject and interviewer and potential employee. As it progressed, the younger man was aware that the older one was acquiring details and personal nuances that could somehow prove important to him.

Suddenly, the transition was made. It was exam time. Brennan indeed had correctly guessed the subject matter for the test.

"Scripture and tradition as sources of revelation, how do you see that question, Father?" the cardinal asked, settling back in his chair.

"Your eminence," Brennan replied, "that issue was settled for me in the second grade."

"Oh, and how was that?" the older priest queried.

"Our catechetical book in the United States was titled *The New Baltimore Catechism*, as I am certain you know," the Dominican replied. "It took on the question of the sources of divine revelation in its appendix. If I may quote that to you, I would like to do so. Would that be all right?"

"Yes, do so," the cardinal instructed.

Brennan promptly repeated all four questions and answers on the subject, just as he had reviewed them in the priory chapel the day before.

Cardinal Ottaviani raised his eyebrows and nodded.

Brennan then personally ratified the catechetical text, commenting, "I learned that then and I have had no reason to question it since then. Nor do I ever expect to."

"And in your own words?" Cardinal Ottaviani challenged.

"It is obvious in the catechetical source that there were two sources of divine revelation. Both represent the word of God, that each must be believed as firmly as the other and that it is the Catholic church that has been authorized by Christ and inspired by the Holy Ghost to explain them."

Cardinal Ottaviani was taken aback by the answer and was not used to having such concise, compressed responses to his entrapping probes. Any other answer, he could and would have challenged with further questions.

"I know that your Eminence believes that the presentation of Church doctrine should be kept simple if at all possible," Brennan added. "I am a member of the Order of Friar Preachers. God wants his servants to preach His word to all men and, to do this, it must needs be phrased in terms they can understand."

The cardinal hesitated a moment and then said, "I applaud you, Father. You have done well."

As Brennan was leaving, his host pledged, "I will have Msgr. Luciano get in touch with you."

After he had exited the cardinal's residence, Brennan found himself skipping down the ancient pavement.

He had indeed impressed the formidable man whose supper he had shared and was enthusiastically celebrating that fact. Brennan remained completely unaware that a seminary professor in France was inserting a copy of a recent Father Rouge article in an envelope and was addressing it to the Congregation of the Holy Office in Rome. The man had underlined several items in the article, including the footnoted reference to Father Brennan Jordan, O.P.

Chapter 36

In an attempt to portray the stage on which Brennan found himself in Rome in the late 1950's, the author offers the following reflections into what was then happening there. It is not as personal as some of the other material in these notes but represents, as they do, an effort to help clarify rather than to give a full explanation or even actual accounting of what took place.

Within the Catholic church, it was the announcement of the century or rather perhaps of the millennium.

In early February, 1959, a little over two months into his reign as pope, John XXIII announced to 20 surprised cardinals assembled to commemorate the 1,900th anniversary of the Epistle to the Romans that he intended to convene an ecumenical council to meet probably in 1961.

The cardinals, to a man, were silent. It was not the reaction the pontiff had expected. He was stunned.

He later stated his disappointment: "Humanly, we could have expected the cardinals, after hearing our allocution, might have crowded around to express approval and good wishes."

The pope had misread his audience.

Subsequently, they individually began to explain their silence.

Simply put, the concept was bigger than they could comprehend. Some felt it a good idea, but argued that it would take ten or twenty years to prepare for it. More simply believed it just would not work. Yet, others seemingly did not want it to succeed.

Catholicism had stumbled in dealing with the modern concept of freedom since it had been birthed during the Age of the Enlightenment. The church had, from its early days, pledged salvation. A new, secular thinking that gained hold beginning in the 17th and 18th centuries promised instead happiness on earth and claimed it was attainable by following the road to personal freedom.

What powerful adversaries those two ideas are, and how different!

Brennan had followed the logical core thought of orthodox religion: obedience, the voluntary surrendering of freedom. The world, on the other hand, listened to the sentiment of the American patriot, Patrick Henry, "Give me liberty or give me death."

It was a shimmering reflection of these contrasting ideas that separated Pope John XXIII and the 20 cardinals who heard his proposal to hold an ecumenical council to renew the Catholic church and to work toward Christian unity.

Both agreed on the ultimate goal, but saw different roads.

John XXIII, believing the highly centralized Catholic church put too much power and responsibility in the hands of the pontiff, wanted to shed some of it. The church's administrators, most of them Italian, were aware that the papacy had been stripped of civil authority a hundred years earlier by enemies willing to take away other forms of papal power. The results appeared to be a collective persecution complex that wanted to deal with fear the same way it did with responsibility and authority, by pushing them upward to the pope.

The new pope was horrified. He knew that responsibility went with authority. He also noted in his speech to the cardinals the enormous problems and confusion in the world. If, as the supreme pontiff, he could not adequately deal with the major issues of the world, how could the church?

In calling a world council of the Church, he was simply saying he was willing to share the authority with its bishops, and thereby lessen papal responsibility.

Some of the cardinals around him saw what he wanted to do and did not like it. First of all, he was already sharing his authority with them through the administration of the Church. Secondly, there were dangerous movements within the Church itself, ones polluted with the ideas of moral freedom and rationalism. These, they felt, would spread like the flu or any other contagious disease if a council were called of bishops from all over the globe, not to mention observers from Protestant and orthodox Christian sects.

A turbulent time was ending, one marked by two world wars. Each of these had created extraordinary periods of isolation in the world. Many peoples, as a result of them, stopped communicating. This had halted the proliferation of the ideas of freedom and its diffusion into the realm of the church.

But, starting in 1945, this had begun to change. Among Europeans, some American, and a few Third World Catholic thinkers, new ideas were perking, ones that questioned authority and called for freedom.

Wherever they came to life, these notions challenged authority.

Several worldwide secret movements within the Catholic church vigorously fought such change and ideas. The "Pian Society" collected the writings and works of Catholics in every field and forwarded them to the holy office. Likewise, many pietistic and devotional organizations in the church ranging from the "half-secret" society, *Opus Dei* to various ladies' sodalities, by their nature, helped church administrators drop anchor against any meaningful alteration of the *status quo*.

In the battle against change, creeping relativism, dogmatic dilutions, modernism, secularism and even the dangers of atheistic communism, a self-determined leader had arisen. He saw all these as devil-inspired, Enlightenment-begotten manifestations of evil. He was the man with whom Brennan had just broken bread.

Cardinal Ottaviani saw change as the problem, not the solution. He perceived grave dangers lurking in the actualization of such an ecumenical council as the pope had proposed. Viewing it as a military strategist might, he worked to defeat the enemy "in detail." He used his position with the holy office, his alliance with other church administrators, especially several powerful cardinals, his friendship with the pope and his control of the powerful internal mechanisms of the church to recommit himself to the battle he had long been waging.

Pope John XXIII, on the other hand, was painfully aware of his own limitations. He once told a Protestant visitor that while he might be infallible in matters of faith and morals, that did not mean he was a brilliant theologian. On obscure theological questions, he simply deferred to the experts around him.

John XXIII opened the windows of the stolid Church with seemingly little idea of what might fly in or out of them.

One of the experts to whom he turned at the beginning was the man who headed the Congregation of the Holy Office. Brennan might be concerned about the cardinal's lack of public relations ability, but the truth was that Ottaviani was extraordinary good at it, especially in his dealings with the pope. He shrewdly approached the pontiff not about the issues that divided, but rather about the questions that called for expertise and scholarship.

If Brennan was impressed with his eminence, the pontiff seemed even more so. Not only did John XXIII appoint Cardinal Ottaviani to the prefecture of the Congregation of the Holy Office, but he also raised him to an honorary bishopric and, even more important, he named him to head the most important of all the pre-conciliar planning commissions, the Doctrinal Commission on Faith and Morals.

The whole effort, many observers felt, would depend on the work of the Cardinal Ottaviani-led commission. An ecumenical council does not bring together blocks and caucuses, much less liberal or conservative parties, but rather polyglot individuals, few of whom knew each other. Each of the ten pre-counciliar commissions would work out a *schema* that laid out an agenda and terms, which the council's assembly would use to consider questions and vote on issues.

These commissions were expected to determine what the disorganized council could eventually decide and do. Lack of organization on the part of those invited would make such a projected result a certainty.

The council would be held, it was determined, in the actual Basilica of St. Peter in the Vatican. About 3,000 delegates from around the world would be invited to attend, with approximately 2,500 of these council "fathers." These individuals had votes, all of which would be recorded electronically.

The opening ceremonies were set for June 1962.

Cardinal Ottaviani would have much preferred the ten or twenty years that some cardinals had seen as necessary to organize such an affair. He had much to do. Heading the Doctrinal Commission on Faith and Morals called for him to create a detailed proposal called a *schema* and to sell it to an unwieldy commission. He would also play an important and sometimes heavy-handed role in the ultra-secret work of the key Central Preparatory Commission.

These took center stage, but the ubiquitous cardinal also appeared off stage in the two years preceding the council. He created and waged battles, which he hoped would send clear messages to those coming to Rome for the main event. Some of these, he won. He convinced the pope to remove the name of a man to whom he objected from the list of those to be appointed cardinal. He managed to get condemned, without any opposition from the pontiff, a book by Father Lombardi that criticized both the Roman Curia and the Index. The author was actually one whom Pius XII had often quoted.

Many of these fights were battles to stifle what his opponents saw as the kind of rising voices of diversity and intellectual investigation that should have preceded the council. The holy office would have none of this and indicated that it felt that what was called for was a tightening rather than a loosening of restrictions.

It was into this environment, this maelstrom that Father Brennan stepped. Msgr. Luciano had, indeed, called. He explained "the offer," if it were even that much. The Dominican theology student was invited to come and join the monsignor as an aide.

He was offered neither a position nor even a stipend "for the time being." He would continue his studies and work unofficially under the aegis of Cardinal Ottaviani and the holy office, but probably more on matters of the impending council than on any doctrinal policing of the church.

Brennan had unspoken questions about all this. It was obvious that he would have responsibility with no authority, recognition or compensation. Having taken a vow of poverty, the latter did not concern him directly, but it also indicated his value or worth in the eyes of his new bosses.

He was given a desk, but it was isolated from the other staff members. Somehow, it seemed as the cardinal and monsignor wanted to isolate him, use him, all the while regarding him as a non-person.

The seriousness of his task, of his responsibilities, however, was made eminently clear from the first day. It was then that Msgr. Luciano took him into a small chapel in the buildings that housed the holy office and encouraged him to stay there and pray until he returned. He then came back an hour and a half later with several Latin statements for him to sign. They were all ponderous documents.

The first was the standard church oath against modernism. It had to be taken by every bishop-elect and potential theology professor throughout the world. Brennan knew its words and had long realized that he would have to take it in order to teach dogma. He believed in it. He signed it.

The second was a similar one that bound him to absolute secrecy in all matters pertaining to the planning of the upcoming council. He signed it.

The third, longer and more detailed, did the same in regard to the holy office. Nothing that the holy office ever did or even considered could ever, under any circumstance, be revealed. Its rules and regulations guarding and maintaining secrecy were far harsher and more demanding than those of either the KGB or the CIA were. Simply, they made it clear that any violation would lead to excommunication and condemnation ultimately to hell.

The Congregation of the Holy Office had not only rules, but also weapons that were formidable. In the process of defending doctrine and the expression of it, Cardinal Ottaviani's staff was police, prosecutor and judge. The rights of the accused were non-existent and the trials of suspected violators were never open to the interested parties or any members of the public.

"The holy office has changed since it was the Inquisition," someone once explained. "It no longer burns anyone at the stake."

With Cardinal Ottaviani's blessing, Bishop Romoli, a Dominican who served eight years in the holy office, gave the Divine Word News Service a defense of the sacred congregation and its policies and procedures. One has to distinguish, he said, between the condemnation procedures it uses for people and published materials.

He said:

If one member of the Church accuses another of a crime for which the holy office is the competent tribunal, then the accused is always given a full hearing and has every opportunity of defending himself. He receives the assistance of a lawyer and may himself present the lawyer of his choice to the tribunal.

Such court procedures, although he has used the word "crime," do not include a jury of peers, an independent judge, an appeal procedure or an open trial. Yet Bishop Romoli added without thought of contradiction that "The precautions taken to safeguard the accused in such a case are so extensive and elaborate as to appear at times excessive."

The bishop pointed out, however, that the condemnation of publications was altogether a different matter and the holy office does not feel called upon to contact the writer at all.

He gave the reason:

Where the orthodoxy of Catholic doctrine does not appear clear, or where orthodoxy is put in doubt, the holy office does not always listen to the interested party before pronouncing its verdict.

"Once the uncertain or false doctrines have already been published, what purpose would such interrogation serve?" he asked rhetorically.

Brennan would have much preferred to fight error by using a scholastic syllogism than by helping the holy office issue, as called for, a warning called a *monitum*, a condemnation or an excommunication.

He continued to wonder what exactly he was getting himself into and it did not take long for him to find out.

The young Dominican, while he had always pushed himself beyond belief, had never suffered a time or energy shortage because of the demands put upon him. He could keep up with any constraints or requests made of him. He was the runner who would finish the race before the rest of the competitors were halfway done. People underestimated, not overestimated him and his ability to get tasks done.

Msgr. Luciano changed that. Brennan had his classwork to do every day and classes to attend. In the meantime, the monsignor had him working on two major projects. The first was to prepare a documented, footnoted paper on "The Two Sources of Divine Revelation."

"No sweat," he said to himself, using a favorite American expression.

"Don't stop when you think you are done," Msgr. Luciano warned.

The second, a simultaneous effort, was to research the history and organization of all the major Catholic theological schools, especially the ones in Rome and Jerusalem.

"I want it to come out with the Lateran University looking good, if not in fact, then in potential," the droll monsignor said in a matter-of-fact voice.

"And the Dominicans are not even being compensated for this," Brennan mumbled to himself.

No explanation was given him of why or how his pieces fit in the over-all puzzle.

He could not have imagined that his research, with some amendments, would land in the hands of the delegates to the Vatican Council at the opening session.

These council fathers would respect its accuracy, clarity and the extent of the research behind it, but they would never find out who had worked on it prior to its coming through the theological commission that Cardinal Ottaviani headed.

The paper, transformed into a commission-authored *schema*, fit Ottaviani's needs perfectly and stated exactly what he wanted it to say. That was Brennan's mission and responsibility. He thought of no other and he accomplished it.

The council fathers, on the other hand, would individually and collectively find the *schema* difficult. The very idea of separating tradition and the Bible by expressing them as the "Two Sources of Divine Revelation" would be offensive to the non-Catholic observers and prove objectionable to many of the bishops who sought a way to bridge rather than emphasize the differences between Catholicism and the rest of Christianity. It would create anger, isolate Cardinal Ottaviani and eventually result in a key vote against it. The majority of the delegates (but not the required two-thirds) would indicate they had problems with the terminology presented to them by the Doctrinal Commission on Faith and Morals, led by the prefect of the holy office.

Brennan's second paper would suffer an equally disappointing fate for the cardinal and his supporters. It would be the written basis of an abortive effort to preempt all major Catholic houses of theology. The effort, led by the Congregation of Universities and Seminaries and by the holy office, sought to take control of and centralize the teaching of doctrine, morals and scripture in the major theology schools in Rome and Jerusalem. Uniquely heavy-handed, even for an effort by Cardinal Ottaviani, it would have established the weakest and least scholarly of all such schools, the Lateran University, as supreme among them. This would have represented a gross insult to the other houses of theology, which established their reputations over hundreds and hundreds of years.

An Italian bishop incidentally showed an article about the plan to Pope John XXIII. In a rare outburst, the pontiff exploded and deliberately humiliated the cardinal (not Ottaviani) whose name was signed to it.

Brennan, as he worked on these two projects, was plagued by a general uneasiness of the kind he had encountered as a novice, when he sought but could not find perfection.

He was especially unhappy and lonely as he realized there was no one with whom he could discuss it. The oaths he had taken weighed heavy on him even though he had not the least inclination to violate them.

Time, for once, was a problem. He found himself hurrying and cutting corners as never before.

He did not eat with his confreres at the priory, but took his meals at his desk or at a little restaurant between the Vatican and his residence.

Brennan found he was consuming a bottle of wine with almost every meal.

As always, it made him forget. It also helped build an increasing tolerance level for alcohol.

Chapter 37

Do not shed a tear for Father Brennan Jordan O. P. He had gotten a chance to dance the dance. And, as they say in gambling and in the theater, "He'd had a good run."

As the person he saw himself to be--a Catholic, American, white, male--Mikey Jordan had climbed a mountain on which others were not even allowed to tread.

He had gone to the seminary; received a free, prep school education; survived a powerful weeding-out process and earned all the scholastic honors to which anyone could aspire. He had become a Dominican, a member of a religious community in which intellectual capacity and accomplishment was uniquely revered.

The young people with whom he had attended grade school and who had gone into the auto factories of Detroit as machine operators and served in the Korean War as cannon fodder, had seen him return home uniquely honored as a Catholic priest and called "the brightest of the brightest."

His mother, who had planned his life from early childhood, had been a witness as he was ordained and said his first mass, putting her as close to the Catholic priesthood as any woman could aspire.

The United States could not hold his brilliance and potential and he reached a ledge that had once seemed a speck in a faraway sky, Rome.

There, he had risen above the clouds and been harnessed to the most wily old climber on the mountain.

The harness was not secure, however, and the young climber slipped and slid far back down the slope.

The hard thing for him was not the bone-cracking fall, but the fact that he could still feel the rarefied air in his lungs.

Father Jordan had handed Msgr. Luciano the two completed research assignments. He had first read them through with the determination of a doctoral candidate getting one last look at a thesis on which future his career and future would depend. The brilliant young scholar found no error, no typo, no misplaced reference, and not even a question. He had completed his task and done so with thoroughness far beyond human expectation.

In doing so, he had become a part of history, even more than he knew.

So, why did he still have doubts?

That kind of uneasiness, he told himself, was what always drove him, why he had often received grades of 100% instead of a 96%, a 97% or even a 99%. Father Rouge at the Catholic University had taught him a valued lesson, that he could make errors and that he could do something about it.

The French Augustinian priest and former professor would have seriously objected to the material in both papers as well as the oaths he had to take to be able to write them, but he would not have been able to fault his work on them.

"Are you certain you are finished, Father?" Msgr. Luciano asked.

Brennan suspected that the man liked to call him "Father" just as a reminder that his own title was "monsignor."

"Yes, Monsignor, *finis*," Brennan replied.

The older man simply nodded, but withheld the small smile and nod he had bestowed at the end of each of their earlier encounters.

"What comes next?" Brennan queried, but immediately felt foolish for asking.

"We'll see," the monsignor replied.

Afterward, muttering to himself as he wended his way to his favorite local restaurant, Brennan complained, "No supportive comments, no 'Thank you, Father,' no 'I'm sure this will be a fine statement.'"

The Dominican quickly dismissed the need for such self-pity by dwelling on the fact that his scholarship had just flown to new heights. He had no need, he told himself, for any patronizing approval by the monsignor. He determined to confine his luncheon libation to a mere two glasses of wine rather than his usual bottle and he was as proud of that as he was on the two papers he had completed. It told him all would be well and he still had control of his life.

"What does the future hold?" he mused.

The council would have positions open, he believed, especially one titled "theologian-expert." Could he dare hope for that, even though he did not yet have his doctorate and was still in his mid-twenties? He did, he had to admit, have the best entree possible, a personal connection with the chairman of the Doctrinal Commission on Faith and Morals.

His name was not on the papers he had researched, but his eminence Alfredo Cardinal Ottaviani knew who had written them, the man who had personally told him after he had answered a question, "I applaud you, Father. You have done well."

It was the best grade Brennan had ever received as a student because it came from the ultimate dogmatic theologian and teacher.

"And," Brennan told himself with unabashed pride, "I am not yet to the top of the mountain."

With that thought fresh in his mind, he waved off the restaurant owner who offered once more to refill his wineglass.

The joy, the pleasure, that he felt was itself sipped and imbibed, a compensation for all that the world had to offer and that he refused: sex and marriage, money and possessions, but above all freedom and the kind of happiness it could promise. He had chosen God and austerity above these and over the easy, self-directed life.

Kenan Heise

He had, Brennan believed, chosen well. He had stood for the past and the past had been good. He had married tradition, Catholicism and the priesthood.

He had returned to his priory and participated with pleasure in the communal recitation of vespers and compline. As he did so, he thought of Edward Gibbon hearing monks in the city chanting the same prayer and coming to a realization that he also wanted to do something momentous.

Father Brennan smiled and reassured himself that he had already done something big with more to come.

In his excitement, he had difficulty getting to sleep that night, but when he did, he slept well.

The next day at noon, he left his class and returned to his isolated desk at the holy office. A large brown envelope lay on top of the green ink blotter that covered the wooden surface. It was addressed "Father Brennan Jordan, O.P." He fumbled in getting it open because it had been sealed with the wax stamp he had come to recognize through his research as that of the holy office.

The one-page, typed cover document inside read:

Father Brennan Jordan O. P.,

Your work is not satisfactory.
You are dismissed.
Do not return to this office or attempt to contact any representative of it.
You are reminded of your signed, sacred oaths.

It was not signed.

An article from a theological journal was attached. It was in French. The subject matter was Father Rouge and his views on a new language for Christian doctrine. Underlined in a footnote was the name, Father Brennan Jordan, O.P. It said that he had written the quoted portion as part of an exam while Father Rouge's student at the Catholic University of America. It added that pupil so well represented Professor Rouge's views that he had received a grade of 115% for it.

The material, Brennan knew, had been disseminated not by his former teacher but rather by someone connected with the investigation of the French theologian. He also knew that throughout the world members of the Pian Society and others regularly reported suspect materials to the holy office.

The name of the person who had sent the article to the holy office was blotted out.

He had been endplayed, as they say in bridge.

The cardinal had seen this. In such matters, the holy office did not speak to an author. To do so would have been against policy. The cardinal and the monsignor had given it the interpretation and spin that he was in Father's Rouge's camp and had been rewarded by him with an abnormally high grade. Believing this to be true, the pair had chosen to continue to suck him dry of his expertise and then cast him aside.

He was not someone they could or wanted to trust. This was clear.

The European university term, he knew, is a "licentiate," basically a license to teach an academic subject such as Catholic theology. He must not be allowed to receive one. He must be erased from the blackboards, never be permitted to teach Catholic theology or speak as a church theologian. The Sacred Congregation of the Holy Office, indeed, well knew how to achieve this and had quickly set the machinery in motion.

His superiors, he would find, had been notified and so had the rector at the university.

His name was entered in the ledgers of the holy office, books that were never open in any way to the public. There it would remain, nevertheless, readily available to those making crucial background checks needed to endorse a candidate for a doctorate or a chair in theology at any house of theology or Catholic university.

In effect, the listing banned him even from writing. His articles would be rejected by each or every conservative theological journal and he would be refused forever even the possibility of a *nihil obstat* on whatever book he might write.

One belongs or does not. Brennan had. He no longer did. In Catholic theology, there was no freelancing. His career was over. He had nowhere to go in the only direction in life he had ever wanted to head.

Brennan was stunned at how clear everything suddenly was to him. He had been hit by a semi-trailer in the middle of the road. There was no confusion, no daze. The sunlight still shone very brightly.

It was over.

He would never be allowed to teach in a Catholic seminary or university. He would not be told why. Explanations in such matter were never given. He knew the rules, he had agreed with them and now they would work against him.

There would be change in the church. He knew that. But it would not be deep enough to save him unless the Sacred Congregation of the Holy Office itself were abolished and that would not happen.

In the Church there was an immune system. Sometimes reasonable and sometimes abused, as in this case, it protected the organism from invasion from the outside. The holy office and its array of powers were but one manifestation of it. The coming council would be another. The pope in his benevolent paternalism was yet another.

It might have helped if he had seen all or any of this ahead of time, but he hadn't. Pride that he had never begun to realize he possessed had stopped him.

Father Brennan had not received a mere setback. He was a resilient person. Now, this was far more devastating. He could not go to confession and say, "Father, I have sinned." Nor could he go to the holy office and say, "Cardinal, I have been misunderstood."

Every moment he had spent at the desk over which he now bent had helped him to understand how the holy office and its apparatus and secrecy worked. There was neither a charge he could rebut nor a paper trail he could bend backwards to save himself. He could not plead prejudice or unfairness. There was no one to listen.

Where was God? He had done what his mother, the catechism, his seminary training and, yes, his conscience had told him to do. He had been obedient. Martyrdom, he could accept. But this? He had been shot with his own arrows. And the church had no category for suicide-martyrdom.

What had happened was not that he was dead, but that he had become a non-person in the only arena in which he wanted to fight and to win. The signs had been there when he had joined up. Msgr. Luciano had studied him not as a protégé, but as a spider might a fly. He knew that now.

An attendant appeared and, without saying a word, pointed the way out of the building. Without thinking, Brennan put the brown envelope under his arm as he started to leave what had been his desk. The silent figure hovering over him motioned for him to put it down and leave.

Brennan, silently but with an angry face, protested any such accommodation to the institution that was pillaring him.

The man, stronger and larger than the Dominican friar, flexed his body in an aggressive manner and, as Brennan reacted to the intimidation, the attendant physically grabbed the envelope from him.

Stripped of the dignity of even retaining his walking papers, Brennan left the building with a deep sense of fear and horror.

This could have happened to him earlier in life. He knew that. If he had fallen into the trap in grade school of watching his female classmate undress, if the rector at the seminary had expelled him for his drinking or if his novice master had arbitrarily blackbeaned him, he would have encountered similar ruin. If he had tripped any of the thousand times in his prior life when he had made certain he did not, it could have come to pass.

The depth of his current problem was marked by the fact that in each of those cases he had worked and planned and not tripped. He had given up his home, his drinking (several times), Millie, his proof for the existence of God and as much of his ego as he could afford.

Brennan had whipped himself, denied himself, followed the holy road of poverty, chastity and especially obedience. He had prayed and had thought he had at least a loose guarantee of heaven.

He had been dedicated, suffered humiliation and tried to be humble.

Even now, not all was lost. He must pray about this, seek guidance as he had before when confronted by difficulties and tragedy.

And pray, he would, all night if necessary. With his heart, his breviary and his rosary.

But, first, he would return to the restaurant and have that glass of wine he had waved off in his exuberant view of the future.

As he ordered it and asked the owner to leave the bottle, he looked down the mountain and saw nothing, absolutely nothing, that could impede his continued fall.

Chapter 38

Aftermath

After returning from Rome, I stagnated and became a project waiting to be taken on, a challenge looking, as it were, for someone willing to climb the mountain, swim the channel or slay the dragon.

To those who saw a priestly gem to be reset, it was simple. I was an alcoholic, one who could, under their aegis and through their concern, be cured.

I did not see it that way. I saw facts and understood some ideas, but not that I had been bitten by the apple. I knew I had lost something very basic, meaning and purpose. But, at a personal level, I had questions that could not be answered, a conundrum that could not be solved.

The drinking was a symptom. I did not begin to comprehend this. Neither did they.

Following are some scrambled thoughts, more in retrospect than reflective of what I was thinking or feeling at any one given time.

***

A parallel could be made with the Vatican Council in Rome. There, an historic effort had been launched to revitalize the Catholic church, which seemed to many hesitant, if not faltering in its mission to save the world. During the years 1962 through 1965, some 2,500 Catholic prelates took their seats each day in the chapel of the Vatican's Basilica of St. Peter. They voted on proposals to renew the structure and language of the church, bring some unity to Christianity and make effort to help bring the world back from a case of raging secularism.

In scope, an attempt to rescue a Dominican priest in a priory in a midwestern city, a man who had obviously strayed off course, was in no way comparable. A try, nonetheless, people argued, needed to be made, for *The Gospel of Matthew* reads:

What do you think? If a man have a hundred sheep, and one of them stray, will he not leave the ninety-nine in the mountains and go in search of the one that has strayed? And if he happened to find it, amen I say to you, he rejoices over it more than over the ninety-nine that did not go astray. Even so, it is not the will of your Father in heaven that a single one of these little ones should perish.

The image of the Good Shepherd in Christianity is a central one. Pope John XXIII had used it as the theme for his reign as pope and called upon the delegates to the council to make it the focus of their work in renewing the church.

The clergy, while in the seminary, had been indoctrinated with the shepherd metaphor. The word, "pastor," comes from the Latin *pascere*, to feed, and shares the meanings of 1) a leader of a parish and 2) a tenderer of a flock.

Catholicism, as a personal and a social religion, says its members not only have responsibility for their own behavior, salvation or damnation, but also are at least partially accountable for working to save others. This could be done, school children were told, by prayer, example, missionary work, teaching, preaching and simply helping others.

Such a religion, in attracting people who want to save others, readily produced would-be rescuers who range from the caring and the loving to the righteous and the zealous. One might have become a monk in a monastery who held to a vow of silence or a nurse on a battlefield who cared for its wounded and maimed. The individual could be a child in a catechetical class or the pope on the throne of Peter. Each of these could pile up credits in heaven for joining in the godly work of helping to redeem others.

It was apparent inside and outside of the Dominican community that Brennan was much in need of redemption. People were confused at first as to why he had returned from Rome. It had been rumored that, as the brilliant theologian that he was, he would play some kind of role in the Vatican Council. Instead, he had returned prematurely and without even a doctorate in sacred theology.

The word quickly went out that he was a broken man, an alcoholic. He would talk to people, but the flash in his eyes and the quickness of his tongue were gone. He was a man who had been some place, but who was not going anywhere.

Brennan was "stationed," or in other words, lived at the priory that served as the motherhouse for the Dominican province. It was there that members of the religious community with "problems" wound up. This was where such individuals could be watched. Here, Father Tom, who had attempted to molest Brennan as a seminarian, had resided until his death three years back.

The returned priest did not say mass, but he attended it daily and chanted faithfully the daily office as part of the priory choir. At first, it seemed to others that he did not have any specific assignment. Certainly, he did not go out to nearby parishes and say masses on Sundays, hear confessions or preach. He did, however, work on several projects. He was helping to write a history of the province, translating a book on vocations from French into English and inventorying the property of the province, especially the goods and collections in the attic left after friars who had accumulated them died.

In addition to these tasks, Brennan took on the work of a religious brother. This was awkward, as the division of labor between priests and brothers was quite distinct and represented traditions going back to the days of St. Dominic. Nevertheless, as a result of his persistence, he cleaned rooms, swept floors, cooked meals and did the laundry. In the kitchen he proved adequate at best, but his genius came to the fore in caring for the province's automobiles. He was becoming a respected mechanic, able to diagnose and resolve the most complex and the greasiest of mechanical problems.

And then he would get drunk. He would disappear from the priory, not coming back until he was sober, although rumors of his drinking binges would filter back. It was well known that when he drank it was to the point of sickness, of oblivion, of being an embarrassment to anyone who happened upon him in that state.

Each time renewed the call for his redemption. When he was sober and had been for a while, he blended into the walls of the priory. He did his multiple jobs extraordinarily well and his confreres genuinely were glad to have him available. The awkwardness was for those who had known him as a prodigy and a genius. In the past, they had come to take great pride in Father Brennan. He had been seen as their ace pitcher, their home run hitter, the pride of the province.

At first, after he had become something else, they offered excuses.

"He's had a breakdown," they said to those people to whom they had bragged about him earlier.

"There's a problem there," they reluctantly admitted.

"He's become an alcoholic," they began to tell people in a "We knew it all along" tone of voice. Sometimes, they added, "That's what happens to prodigies, you know."

Many did not remain that passive. They set out to save, to cure and to redeem.

The first and foremost was the provincial and his council. Endless hours were taken up in discussing "Father Brennan's problem." Consultations were made with psychologists, priests who had experience with alcoholism, medical doctors and each other. Some progress was made. Tasks and assignments such as writing a history of the seminary were found to keep him busy and use his talents. Much consideration was given to encourage him to consider teaching subjects at the seminary ranging from algebra to philosophy.

Asked about becoming a teacher, he simply shook his head. Eventually, the provincial board came to realize that the classroom would not be a good place for a person so fractured, so broken. Students would come to like and admire the brilliant Dominican scholar and then be bitterly disappointed when he faltered. He knew it instinctively. His superiors came to realize it.

Only in the previous few years, had the Church come to believe that psychiatric counseling might be helpful for priests with problems. As recently as the mid-1950's, Rome had put out prohibitions that psychological profiles and studies of individuals should not be used in selecting candidates for the priesthood. In the top-heavy administration of the Catholic church, this carried the added message that one should be wary in letting the psychological understanding of the human side of man encroach on the spirituality of the priesthood. Many priests and church officials, feeling that spiritual advice should be used to cure most human aberrations, welcomed the idea of limiting psychological counseling, especially for religious and most especially, for themselves.

By the mid-1960's, there had been breakthroughs in intention but not in fact. There were no studies and little research material for counselors to use in treating priests and religious. Did one start with their sexual frustrations? Hardly. Did the psychologist need to be a Catholic in good standing? That was a good question. Was leaving the answer? Who knew? Overall, a man giving up the priesthood or the religious life relieved religious authorities of having to deal with a host of problems.

The provincial, despite some disagreement on the part of his advisors, sent Father Brennan to see a psychiatrist, albeit a Catholic one. The man came to understand many things about his client. He realized the problem had much to do with his mother and there was something there about his father. He grasped the fact that his being a prodigy had created many long-smoldering difficulties. He listened to Brennan talk of Rome, but he hit a blank wall about exactly what had happened there. The priest was bound in obedience by the secrecy imposed on him by the holy office, as if God Himself had collected the papers on which his signature was attached.

"I have taken oaths," the patient stated. "I will keep them."

The psychiatrist could see the parts. He understood the stress of commitment to a life-defining purpose and the strain of drinking that had threaded through their parallel ways through Brennan's life. It was not he, the therapist understood, but rather his Dominican patient who alone could untwine them and that individual had no will to do so.

Brennan believed there would be no resolution of anything and each time quit the sessions before the psychiatrist gave up on him.

The provincial did not retreat in his effort. He sent Brennan to a priest-psychologist who specialized in working with other members of the clergy with such dysfunctional problems. The counseling effort, however, went for naught. The priest found his brilliant patient had erected a fortress. Sometimes his efforts managed to get into it, but in the next session, the counselor found himself again on the outside.

The provincial had one last trick, if one can call it that, up his sleeve. It was prayer. Father Brennan became his most important spiritual project. Wherever he went, whichever priory he visited, he never failed to ask the Dominicans there to pray for a "special intention." He did not tell anyone that it was Father Brennan.

Individual Dominicans also took shots at saving Brennan. He saw it coming when they started trying to get close to him. He did not shoo away or discourage them. Often, they would chat about a variety of subjects and then bring out an article from some Catholic magazine or journal about priests and alcoholism, journalistic pieces full of "With the grace of God I did it" stories. Or else, lacking an appropriate publication, they would tell of friends or relatives who had overcome a drinking problem. Sometimes, it was themselves.

Despite their efforts, he remained uncured, unsaved.

Several women, who came to know of him, also sought and wanted to rescue Father Brennan. Some felt their maternal instincts had the power to save. Others believed their wiles could. Each hit Brennan's wall and quit, frustrated and sometimes angry.

Next to come calling were former alcoholics, although none called themselves "former."

"I have not had a drink in 17 years and three months," one explained, "but I know I am still an alcoholic."

Most were members of Alcoholics Anonymous but some were not. Those who had been helped either left behind for Brennan or offered to give him AA materials and books.

Brennan had long ago read these and absorbed the points they made and the stories they told, tales of failure and then, tentative but usually dramatic success. Still, he saw one big difference between AA members and him. They had wanted to stop. He did not.

He felt his drinking willful. It was, therefore, a sin, a serious one. He simply did not want to cease. Brennan did not choose to drink every time he thought of it or had an opportunity. But when he started he knew what was going to happen.

If he had been willing to give up his religion and what faith he had left, his drinking possibly would stop. Brennan could not tell people that. He could not say it to himself.

The belief system he had developed, beginning when he was four years old did not fit with something inside him. There was a contradiction, one which he had run into while in Rome and was the basis of his confrontation with the holy office. It had to do with obedience and freedom. In his heart, and even in his mind, he could not find room for both of these concepts. Other people had problems with them. He knew that. They eventually compromised. He could not.

Many burned-at-the-stake heretics renounced the Catholic faith in order to affirm they had the right to choose what to believe. The martyrs canonized by the church as saints chose obedience over any such freedom. Their biographers tell us little of their consciences struggling with any contradictions which they might have found in Christianity or in submitting to its leaders. They were intelligent. They had to have seen contradictions arising within the church from the holy office, the Index of Prohibited Books, the misuse of indulgences, and the abuses of power by the popes and the cardinals. Still, was there ever a saint on record who simply stood up on any of these issues, who protested or who rebelled?

The reformers of the church were many: Sts. Gregory, Benedict, Bernard, Francis, the Dominican Pius V, the Jesuit Robert Bellarmine and even a few women, especially St. Teresa of Avila.

Not one of them took on the leaders of the church or their power. St. Robert Bellarmine, for example, was made a cardinal in 1599. He was a consultor to the holy office and played a major role in helping it to condemn Copernicus' theory that the earth revolved around the sun as "false and erroneous." It had to be, because it contradicted scripture, which had spoken of the sun "standing still" in the sky.

In his world, many simple, direct people as well as great scholars stand outside of the church over the question of freedom and obedience. One might say it is because an individual priest would not give them forgiveness in the confessional. Another might add it was a consequence having committed the "sin" of practicing birth control. A third might list the cause as a pope who decreed that women cannot have real power in the church because that is shared only by the apostles and their successors, all of whom must forever be male.

These, in themselves, were not the issues that troubled Brennan. They were the problems of mothers and fathers or of women, groups to which he neither belonged nor with which he identified.

Their conflicts were his only in so far as they dealt with obedience. He had believed strongly in church authority, had fervently adhered to it and then had unexpectedly encountered an insurmountable impasse. It was akin to his experience in the novitiate when he sought perfection, but was confused about its limits. He had come to question whether such existed in the absolute even as a possibility.

The issue, underlying everything else, was no longer perfection. It was the unswerving commitment he had made to surrender his will to that of his religious superior.

Should a church, a congregation, a religion, he started to wonder, have any power other than the moral authority of goodness and of serving as a way to come closer to God? Yet, to exist, orthodoxy, whether it be Christian, Moslem or Judaic, requires much more. Ultimately, it demands blind obedience to follow rules and regulations even when they sometimes do not make sense. In the name of righteousness, can such requirements violate the rights of the intellect to pursue the truth and compromise a person's soul to follow his or her conscience?

Brennan knew the answers to these questions were not simple, but he began to feel doors opening that had been latched shut. He had believed in total submission to the church's authority and power that left no room for him to have doubts. Even experiencing the unhampered power of the holy office over him personally failed to create them.

The battle between obedience and freedom could leave many an individual seriously wounded. As a soldier committed to one side, he should not be surprised to find himself a casualty on the battlefield even if the shots had rung out from behind rather than from in front of him.

For Brennan, any questioning of this was as disturbing as cleaning out his room when he moved from one priory to another, only more so. He steadfastly stuck to his early formulations and positions on the righteousness of formal authority. They offered the security of not offending those around him, from his mother to his religious order. They had provided the assurance of his being on his road to heaven. And they were marked with the pride of being his moral conclusions, even though they were borrowed.

His catechetical instructions, his dogmatic theology and his seminary training all taught him about the authority of the Church. The ultimate power in Catholicism, he had long accepted, does not lie in the hands of the members, but rather in those of the pope, who sits on the throne of St. Peter, and the bishops, as successors to the apostles.

The logical conclusion of this, in Church teaching, is that the Holy Spirit, the Third Person of the Trinity, does not and can not operate unchecked through the people. Otherwise, it would be possible and good for them to share power in the structure of Catholicism as they do in democratic forms of government and other institutions.

Kenan Heise

This is the viewpoint of many mainline Protestant denominations. He could not accept it as being superior to the hierarchical structure of Catholicism.

But, if these views were the sum total of Brennan's beliefs, it would be a simple matter for him to leave the Church and personally seek salvation outside of it or through some other religion. Over the years, it was a road well traveled.

Not Brennan. He still believed in the four marks of the Church, that Catholicism was one, holy, catholic and apostolic; and that no other religion was.

Inwardly, he was more and more choosing to give the church his full reverence, but not his full obedience. That was creating in him a profound conflict, one that built up an itch that would eventually need to be scratched. He could not resolve the issue either in his heart or in his brain, but neither could he make it go away.

When the torment it brought to him became too painful, he drank to the point of oblivion. He forgot about the conflict and that gave him release and he could face life again.

He would have gladly considered leaving Catholicism; but, as did Peter in the Gospels, he asked, "Where else is there to go, Lord?"

All he had to do was compromise. But he couldn't. He wanted to be as free as a heretic is and as certain as an orthodox believer, If not, on which side should he compromise?

Time and again in the confessional he had encountered tortured souls who saw themselves on the road to hell but unable to give up the teachings that told them that or the behavior that guaranteed it.

Why could he not give up one or the other?

He did not know the answer to that question.

"Thank God for alcohol," he assured himself. "Without it, only the pain."

Chapter 39

Brennan remained lost.

More than 20 years passed and what had happened in Rome grew blurred.

After Brennan had returned to the United States, his memory played tricks on him as a result of continued encounters with alcohol. During that time, versions of past events sometimes seemed fudged. He embroidered on portions of what he told himself about Msgr. Luciano and his eminence Alfredo Cardinal Ottaviani, but only in his mind.

He had become a drunk, an erratic, but persistent binge drinker. What research he had done as well as much of the language in his background papers had been used in the *schema* presented by the cardinal to the Doctrinal Commission on Faith and Morals to the Vatican Council.

The account contained in the preceding pages, as best he could tell now that time had played its games, was what actually happened. There were other versions of it in his head, ones he once had wanted to believe were true. They were crazy stories full of details with sharpened edges, more black and white than real.

Had there been a personal and direct confrontation afterwards with the cardinal?

No. His imagination almost certainly concocted any seeming memory he had of having had such a meeting.

"What if there had been a confrontation?"

"That might have helped explain the drinking," he concluded. "Yes, indeed, it would have."

Every so often over the years he would refine his latest version and then start adding details; mainly, reconfirming ones from the past, imagined or real.

Drinking, he had once read, often performs this kind mutation with an individual's memory.

Before writing the preceding pages, he never spoke of his days in Rome. Still, a full-blown version, one complete with embellishments, existed in his mind as he eluded those who wanted to work to help him. It was the wall, or at least part of it. The psychiatrists and counselors saw a structure there, realized something suspect was behind it and were aware that somehow it had been constructed with a mixture of truth and fabrication.

He felt uniquely clever about his elaborate recollections, especially that he had never told them to anyone. No matter how he deluded himself, he knew this. In having a bigger-than-reality story that no one else shared or could test, he had created a deception aimed at anyone trying to get close to help him.

Over those two decades, the lines between self-delusion and verifiable reality lost much of their significance for him.

Mostly, he aimed his distortions at God, or rather at his own deity-centered system of belief.

Brennan, afraid to take on any religious superior, certainly was not willing to take on the ultimate one, his Creator.

His imagination gave him what his reason could not, justification.

To live a deception one has to continue to deceive.

The person who had fabricated incidents, he came to realize, can get angry over a slight or an injustice that never really occurred, One starts to think, "It could have happened" followed by "Maybe, it did." These openings become enough. Years go by and one feels angry over the possibility that it could have.

People would say that a person is sick, mentally i
thinking this way. Of course, they are right. But, these indivi
do it too. They also imagine that things had happened in their past
and have somehow become pieces of reality.

When drunks are confronted at the bottom of their souls with
the pathetic weakness that is there, devices such as this--which are
normal or small aberrations for others--become every day props.

Since Brennan came back from Rome, a long time had
passed. He never once said mass during those years. He was not
worthy. Nor in the confessional did he ever ask God's forgiveness
for his drinking. At first, it was because he knew he could not say the
words "I won't do it again."

Brennan occasionally heard Ottaviani's name. In late 1969,
the cardinal had co-signed a letter to Pope Paul VI supporting a
document called *A Short Critical Study of the New Order of Mass.*
It attacked the Vatican Council-inspired changes in the mass, calling
them "a striking departure from the Catholic theology of the mass as
it was formulated in Session 22 of the Council of Trent."

The study itself came to be known as *The Ottaviani
Intervention.*

The cardinal died in 1979. Afterwards, staunch conservatives
in the church continued to venerate him, but the Catholic mainstream
had long before cast him aside as his work at the holy office and his
rigid defense of doctrine had become out of sync with the changes
brought about by Vatican II.

In a moment of reality, after hearing of the cardinal's death,
Brennan felt sorry for him. Both the cardinal and he were victims
of the same trap, one that rapidly changing times had sprung on
them. Committed to the past, they were confused by the present and
stunned by the future. The two churchmen were like secretaries who
could not or would not learn to use new equipment, clerical workers
who resisted it and could not get up to speed, salesmen tied to old
techniques and executives who did not understand the ever-changing
environment of the business world.

"No," he said to himself. "Erase that. Cardinal Ottaviani,
Father Brennan and many others were like the medieval church
calligraphers, who had the job of hand-copying the scriptures and

early writings of Christianity. To them, it was a sacred task, but then printing came along. Such individuals once had possession of the Divine Word itself. Occasionally, when they felt it necessary they added a piece of punctuation or changed a phrase in the firm belief that such ought to have been said or possibly had been.

What they placed into the texts became known as "interpolations."

A calligrapher had put such an addition into the late First Century AD *Antiquities of the Jews* by the early Jewish historian, Josephus. The interpolation was a made-up reference to a Jesus of Galilee and his teachings. For centuries, it was accepted as part of the text until scholarship proved it was not the same style of writing. If it had been valid, the reference would have been the only First Century, non-Scripture mention of Christ.

A scribe in the Third Century before Christ had earlier made an even more significant alteration in translating the Torah or Old Testament into Greek. He had changed the phrase "a young woman shall bear a son" to "a virgin shall bear a son," a twist that was not discovered until scholarship using the Dead Sea Scroll showed that the word, "virgin," had been an interpolation. The Gospel writers, working from the Septuagint, probably knew only the "virgin" interpolation.

Cardinal Ottaviani did not change words, but he sometimes managed to put narrow, literal interpretations on passages from scripture as he did during the Vatican Council when he resurrected a quote from *The Book of Genesis*, "Be fruitful and multiply." He used the exhortation to challenge those who believe in birth control, seemingly even the "rhythm method" that Pius XII had already approved.

In 1958, any ultimate ascendancy of his eminence or of the young Dominican newly residing in Rome died along with Pope Pius XII just as the fate of monk-calligraphers had in the 1450's with the invention of movable type printing by Johannes Gutenberg.

Oh, but see how clever Brennan can be! He has switched the reader off himself and onto his eminence again. He has created another excuse by showing himself as an outdated person. Many can identify with that. He knows that.

The death of Pius XII had brought the young Brennan into contact with a consciousness of the conflict that arose out of his pending obsolescence. This was the initial wall into which he ran. It helped trigger his breakdown and alcoholism and eventually was a root of new problems, excuses and self-deception.

While the voice inferred this be written with as much painful honesty as possible, exposing the truth remains difficult for a person so long buried under self-delusion.

How the years had gotten to be the mid-1980's and how Brennan had aged into his early fifties, he did not know. He had long before this taped over the mirror in his cell and shaved daily from memory rather than face his own reflection. He dared not see the change.

But change there was in the form of slow, inexorable deterioration.

Others around him came and went. The older friars at the priory died. Many of the younger ones left, some going back into the world and taking their confusion and problems with them.

Brennan was an ordained priest, a precious commodity in short supply as the 1980's moved in. One more person decided that it was worth a try to resurrect Father Brennan Jordan, O.P.

The new provincial, Father Edward Keegan, devised a plan that was assertive, but subtle. He started attempting to make use of Brennan's intellect and knowledge, incidentally asking him technical questions about doctrine and about church history.

He then formed a small, three-person study group. It included himself, the prior of the house and Brennan. Following an outline, they discussed the church and the changes in it in recent years. None of the trio, especially not the priest who was the object of the provincial's efforts, had any particular responsibilities to prepare for or follow up on the discussions.

The group seemed to work well. Brennan, after a while, even showed animation no one had seen in him for some years. He moved from remaining silent to speaking occasionally. Some of his extraordinary intellectual acumen flashed before his companions.

Then, one day, he disappeared, went off on a binge. When he returned to the group, nothing was said. It was obvious that the other two had met without him and had continued on, following the study outline without missing a beat or note.

Brennan was reassured by this. It indicated he was not responsible for the other two. He knew it was a test, but at least it was not a game in which the object was over-simplistic.

He amazed himself. Brennan entered a room he had not been in since returning from Rome, the library. He began to read again, his favorite subject, doctrine. He said nothing of this to the other two in the study group, but they knew.

"Father, you might want to try doing a little writing, just for yourself," the provincial suggested.

The wording as well as the content of the suggestion was significant.

No one called him Father Brennan anymore. Of course, he was always formally referred to as a priest, but since he performed in the role of a brother, it had become simply "Brennan." This made it especially easy for the other brothers who were expected to address all the other priests as "Father." No one could quite remember how or when he had lost that title among his confreres, but the provincial in his comment was signaling that it was time for it to come back.

Writing itself was also an issue. Brennan had finished neither the history of the seminary nor the translation of the book on vocations. Both projects withered on the vine of his efforts and signaled that no one should make any similar requests of him in the future. None had.

Finally, there was no command by his superior of "holy obedience" connected to the suggestion.

"You might want to try" was the phrase used.

Could Brennan live with that? He didn't know. It had been so long. Would people start expecting things of him?

He would see.

Finally, he decided he would read up on the subject on which he wanted to write and would sit down with a typewriter next Monday morning. He said nothing about his plan to anyone.

The days passed. On Monday, he was not to be found in the priory. He was gone, had left to drink, to get drunk.

He returned and surprised even himself by showing up for the next study group meeting. Again, the two others had met without him, had moved on through the outline which they were following.

Brennan did not write in the way the provincial had suggested, but he did start keeping personal notes.

Father Edward tried another suggestion. He invited his confrere to go along on one of his famous walks through the city.

Brennan did so, remembering Rome. It was passive enough for him, but he realized his superior had something he wanted to say.

"You might want to try going to an AA meeting," the provincial suggested.

Brennan agreed to look into the idea, feeling he was not thereby committing himself to anything.

He went to a meeting, not as a result of planning to do so, but simply on an impulse one night when he knew there would be one.

It was exactly what he expected it to be from having read the literature. One man, obviously a clergyman from a Protestant denomination, said: "Alcoholism, I have found not to be a sin of the flesh. Any sin, I believe, is one of pride and of not seeking help. When I tell God I have sinned, that is what I mean."

Brennan did not relate to the minister or to anyone else in the group. He did not believe there was a person in the world with whom he could talk or share anything meaningful. They were not separated from themselves by vows as he was. They could never understand this about him. The people in AA seemed to have had each other.

He had no one, not even himself.

Chapter 40

Brennan was aware that the provincial had received the report on him. He also knew it was not a good one, not at all.

The Franciscans friars who operated the Arizona retreat where alcoholic priests and religious attempted to rehabilitate themselves had found the bottle of gin in the tank of the toilet in his room. Also in the report was a mention of his tardy arrival, late by a day, and of the subsequent warning of expulsion from the program.

It was not the first time the Franciscans had found a sequestered bottle in a "retreatant's" room. Their unwritten policy was that those who came to them might, in certain circumstances, get a second chance; but never a third. Brennan had been officially notified that a letter had been sent to his religious superiors. He knew it bode him ill and would have consequences.

"Kind of a dumb idea," Brother Solanus, a member of the Franciscan staff, had chided him. "That's the first spot anyone in this place checks when we become suspicious."

The brother seemed to have a concern above and beyond any rules, written or otherwise. He was himself an alcoholic on the mend.

Brennan shrugged his shoulders.

Matters in his life had been moving toward a climax. He knew this. It was as though he were deep in a dream—a heavy, slow-moving and nightmarish concoction of somebody else's brain.

People finding themselves in their fated traps might sometimes prove to be an Odysseus, Captain Ahab or Alice in Wonderland; but more often they are ordinary persons caught in one of the turbulent rapids of life.

Almost every religion in the world, he reasoned had some concept of a determined outcome for human beings and of a stage on which God or the gods were the leading performers. Historically, the analysts, playwrights and religious writers have called it fate, destiny, the hand of God or the will of Allah. In such tragedies, man, as an individual, plays the pre-set role of a hapless actor caught in a course of events beyond his or her control.

The Catholic version of this scenario answers questions of determinism with words about responsibility, of a belief in the will of God mitigated by the idea of individual free will. Underlying this philosophical-theological duality lies the conviction that a human being, once he or she reaches "the age of reason," basically determines his or her own fate. Such is underpinning of the concept of free will. Opposing this is the commonly-held notion that we but play out a design mapped out by the Almighty.

The early restless years of Brennan's alcoholism saw him get little sleep at night as he began to question his own meaning and purpose. He found himself cast adrift from the clear heaven-directed wisdom of St. Thomas Aquinas, the font of all answers. For want of any, he floated about unanchored.

He began to recognize, for the first time, deep contradictions and he was disturbed.

Who had the strings, he or God?

He knew ahead of time, but the actual pull of alcoholism was something different than his catechism and moral textbooks had ever described.

He was a priest and a religious. Those were roles in which he had performed in certain pre-set ways. Now, as an alcoholic, his *persona* on the stage of life had changed. He was a drunk.

Did God want this for him?

What a question! But it encompassed every aspect of fate, determinism and free will.

He pondered it as an intellectual, philosopher and theologian.

As a drunk and a person with an addiction, he thought about it every day and sometimes, it seemed, constantly.

Was his drunkenness God's will? Was there a devil and was it he who was in control Somehow? Was it fate or was this drinking his responsibility and his alone?

Deep down, Brennan, more than any Alcoholics Anonymous member wanted to take complete blame. He did not want to share it with God, the devil, his mother, Cardinal Ottaviani, the priest who had abused him in the seminary or anyone else. The thought that someone had gotten that far inside him was nothing less than humiliating.

He wanted to, but...

If he ever tried to think too seriously about that issue, he knew what would happen. He would get drunk.

Still...

His life, to him, was all staged in God's theater. Even as a child at his mother's side, he had believed that. Her role was temporary director, telling him what to do and what to think and then explaining that it was what the producer, God, wanted.

She informed him of his mission and he knew that he was to find it as a special, chosen actor on God's stage.

The whole performance of one's life was programmed with a beginning, middle and end as well as in two acts, the second of which was sequential to the first and a jumping off place from it.

The applause that counted could come only from the hands of God. Not hearing it, he did not know.

The inevitable would happen, but rarely in the way he might predict. God was mysterious, capricious and caring, in ways no one could fully understand.

Brennan's script, the one he was following, had switched in Rome from the epic to the tragic.

The bottle in the toilet tank; yes, he had put it there. That stupid act now did not matter. It was a trigger leading to an inevitable climax. In his own story he was no longer required to be heroic, a person bigger than life, one who could stand on the stage and affect the story's outcome.

Fair enough, he believed. Brennan still saw his bit role on the stage as valid. At least he was doing something somehow right in showing up, in being there. That's what actors do. No more and no less.

The proof of all this had come with his father's death. How dramatic it had been when he went off to war and died on a battlefield. What a script God had to write for that to occur! It involved millions of people and all of the earth.

Brennan tried to accept full responsibility, but inevitably slipped into fatalism.

Now, he was in a retreat house in Arizona and a significant event, either his exodus from the Dominicans or some other further slide into oblivion, was about to happen. There was no cast of millions. Maybe a half dozen to a dozen people who would know of it, and few of these would much care, if at all.

At this retreat house, having been forced to leave it, he would remain a statistic. Over the years, seven other Dominicans had undertaken this program, he had been told. Two of these had successfully quit drinking and returned to their daily lives as members of their religious order. Brennan would make it six out of eight who did not.

"Whatever!" he shrugged. The consequences of his failure were inevitable, but was it predetermined? The dramatic device was a bottle discovered in the tank at the back of a toilet. It was simple, clean-cut, direct. The fact left no "What if?" questions, no room for half-completed excuses, and no opportunity for almost-valid explanations.

The strings would be pulled, the hand of fate played, the will of God acted out.

If it were not so, he would have guilt and he did not.

The provincial appeared that afternoon. He arrived from the airport by taxi. Brennan noticed him out the window and saw him motion to the driver to wait. This would be short and to the point. That was guaranteed.

Father Edward's air contrasted with the fact that a taxi was waiting in front. He came in the room and sat down as though he had all the time in the world.

Brennan awaited his religious superior's first word and knew it would tell everything. If it were "Father," then he would get another chance. If it were rather his first name, the one which the order had given him, there would be a probing discussion, followed by a decision about his future. The most ominous message he might receive would be one that started with the word, "you." That would mean that the provincial had arrived to deliver a message, a decision that would cut Brennan off from the Dominicans.

On the one hand, neither priests nor religious are routinely expelled for alcoholism. He knew many are helped in their efforts to hide their drinking from the faithful and are often transferred to less responsible, unobtrusive positions. They are encouraged to seek help and often treated sympathetically.

On the other hand, the process of defrocking a priest or expelling a member from a religious community was set down in canon law and affords certain rights of due process. It was used only in the more blatant, resistant cases that involve public drunkenness.

Between those two alternatives lay vast opportunities for dealing with all manner of remiss behavior on the part of members of religious orders and the clergy.

As with a member of any corporate structure, a religious could be pressured out. The message could be given that he or she was not wanted. The bishop or religious superior could set a tone indicating to others that the individual had become a non-person. One's daily life could be made to feel uncomfortable, with the future looking worse. It would become unpleasant to stay in a diocese, company or community if it were clear one was not wanted.

The person in charge inevitably would express compassion and support, while at the same time undermining the individual's sense of belonging. Of course, it would be most clear as to where the fault lay and therefore whose decision it really was to leave.

Father Edward had another card up his sleeve. He knew Brennan and his extraordinary sense of obedience. A hint to him would be a command. The provincial knew that the man before him would never utter the word, "but."

All these possibilities confronted Brennan the second his provincial opened his mouth.

The man whose fate hung in the balance stared at the other priest's lips. They seemed to hesitate to part and speak their message.

Finally, the words came out.

"You, shall we say, 'screwed up,'" Father Edward charged. "You blew a very important opportunity to deal with your problem."

Brennan continued looking at his religious superior's mouth. He remembered having done so several months earlier as they had sat in the study group.

"You must have wanted to be caught," the provincial continued.

"Ooh!" Brennan thought to himself, "Three sentences beginning with the word, 'you.' He has not come here to be compassionate, to negotiate a third chance."

"Father Provincial," Brennan said. "I think you want to cut to the quick. I know you have a taxi waiting outside."

"Yes, I do," he acknowledged. "I was told it was hard to get one here and I have to fly on to Los Angeles to give a talk there."

Brennan was no longer amazed at how glib and quick on his feet this man was. He had resided with him at the motherhouse for some years. He sensed at the time of Father Edward's election that the priest as his religious superior could and probably would threaten his own unique existence in the order. The provincial went too much by the book to allow the lifestyle, the "sin," of an alcoholic friar to go unchallenged.

Now that the long-expected confrontation was upon them, Brennan saw that all the nervousness was on the provincial's part. He himself remained calm while the man delivering the message sat working his hands in and out of each other as though he were cleansing them prior to consecrating the host at mass.

"Your actions have not pleased the definitors or myself," the religious superior said. "I have prayed, and I am sure the others have, that you might find yourself here. We are disappointed, as are the Franciscans who run the retreat house."

There followed a silence that was stunning and painful. Or, perhaps, Brennan only imagined its depth.

He was distracted by it and for a moment unaware of the words with which it was being broken.

"I would hope," the provincial was saying, "that at this point you might be willing to seek laicization. It might be best for all."

The world was not round. It was square and had edges off which one could fall and Brennan had just come upon one of them. He was frightened, afraid of being expelled, shunned by the only family and friends he knew, and yet also he knew he must sail on and drift out of their sight and beyond their lives. His Dominican brothers were as much a way of life for him as they were individuals.

The provincial, forgetting his earlier resolve, turned around and looked out the window toward the taxi.

"I do not make this recommendation lightly," he said, with his back to Brennan. "I have prayed over it and consulted with others. I have feared that we are part of your drinking. I owe it to God and to you to call it what it is, 'a sin.' You know what St. Paul wrote in his letter to the Corinthians: 'Neither fornicators, nor idolaters, nor adulterers...nor drunkards...will possess the kingdom of heaven.'"

"The Apostle Paul is back in all his righteousness," Brennan wanted to say, but he knew he had no real answer.

"Hmmm," he said out loud.

"My thought, my prayer," the provincial said, "is that by leaving you might give yourself a wake-up call before it is too late."

And, then something unexpected happened. Brennan stood up. And, for the first time, he questioned a religious superior. It was though he had taken off the yoke of obedience and become a person.

"Let me challenge your scriptural interpretation a moment, Father Provincial," Brennan said. "I think somehow a lot of drunkards are going to possess the kingdom of heaven and some of them are going to be at the front of the line. I don't, however, necessarily believe that of myself."

The provincial turned and looked Brennan straight in the eye.

"I can only quote from St. Paul," he said, "'Flee immorality... Your members are the temple of the Holy Spirit.' I truly believe God will give you the strength to do so if you ask his help."

Brennan fully grasped what was being suggested by laicization. It would mean giving up being a priest and a Dominican and returning to the state of a lay person. The Franciscans, in kicking him out of their retreat for drunks, had set in motion this request by his provincial that he also leave the priesthood and the order as well.

It was a suggestion, a request, if you will. Many might consider responding with a "No" or a "Let me think about that." Brennan could not. He slipped back into the yoke, still bound by the will of his superior, no matter how gently or harshly it was expressed. He knew no alternative to following the course of obedience, the third of the solemn vows he had taken when he was 21 years old.

He could match the provincial in quoting St. Paul:

Let everyone be subject to the higher authorities for there exists no authority except from God, and those who exist have been appointed by God. Therefore, he who resists the authority resists the ordinance of God; and they that resist bring on themselves condemnation.

Just because he was already headed for hell for his drinking, an addict such as Brennan rarely feels himself free to commit other sins. Just the opposite. The obligation to love God, to honor and obey Him, was not totally gone from Brennan's heart and his soul. It was part of his nature. He could not voluntarily give it up. Nor did he condemn the Divine Being for condemning him. Such was the script. That was the way it was.

An additional reason propelled him in the only direction in which he could now head out the door, his concern for the provincial as a human being and for the Dominicans. His presence among them was awkward, if not scandalous. To push back would amount to afflicting pain on them.

He looked down as he spoke, but his voice was firm.

"I will apply for the necessary dispensations," he said. "I will leave. It would be best."

The provincial thought to say something kind to the priest in front of him, a man in obvious pain. He held back. He knew it would be hypocritical.

"Give me your blessing, please, Father Provincial," Brennan asked.

And then he knelt to receive it.

The provincial did not ask for Brennan's

Chapter 41

The Dominicans, he felt, had been more than generous. They offered to give him $4,000 to help get himself established, with more available if and when necessary. They also pledged to pay premiums on a medical insurance policy.

He accepted instead $500 and told them he would pay that back. He firmly declined the hospital medical insurance.

Technically, his separation from the order was to include a probation period. But, for him, there could be no going back. If he were somehow cured of his alcoholism or were willing to try, he could again be embraced with open arms by the Order of Friar Preachers. Even under those circumstances, however, he could not, would not ever look back or return.

His farewell consisted of visiting two elderly brothers and a priest in the infirmary. The latter had taught him in the seminary, but they had never been close. Still, he had always felt a bond with the sick and the elderly, and it was especially true now. He did not say he was leaving. No one in the priory knew except the provincial and the prior.

The most difficult possession he had to give up was his religious habit. Brennan was acutely aware of the meaning of taking it off for the last time. He had worn it in recent years only for church services and on the anniversary of his investiture, but it had not lessened in importance to him.

As he walked out of church after mass on the day of his departure, he took his habit off slowly and laid it out neatly on his bed.

What had been placed over his shoulders four decades before as the emblem of a new life, as a badge of God's election, he now removed.

He bent and kissed the religious habit that had proclaimed him a member of the Order of Preachers. It was the same gesture he had performed the morning after being invested as a Dominican. This time it was not a salute, but a good-bye.

A note he left on the bulletin board on the way out said, "Please pray for me. Your brother, Brennan."

It was the last time he used "Brennan" as his name. In leaving, he took back "Michael."

It was strange to call himself that name again after 40 years as Brennan, but he needed to do it in order to convince himself that the break with his religious community was real. He was heading out into the world, a place he was not certain he had ever lived in before. Somehow, the name "Michael" might work better.

Despite urgings by his prior, he had made no preparations whatsoever for himself once he left. He had not made a room reservation anywhere, applied for a job or established any contacts "on the outside."

He was not unmindful of the Gospel admonition:

"Take neither staff...."

The prior, concerned for him, pleaded with Brennan to stay until he could make better arrangements, ones on which he might build his new life. The exiting Dominican nodded in respect but ignored the suggestion. The provincial, personally affronted about his stark manner of leaving, departed town for the day so as not to have to be associated in any way with the situation.

Michael Richard Jordan walked out the door, having left his key to the priory behind him and in his pocket had no new one to any other room or door. Without a job, he lacked a means of support as well as a career or a profession with which to define and support himself.

What seemed most different to him was the lack of having anyone whom to obey. He still felt bound by the vows he had taken of poverty, chastity and obedience even though the Papal dispensation for which he had applied had relieved him of them. He had made solemn, personal oaths to God, and that was that. Yet, the most important one, the obligation to obey his superiors, had become confusing rather than comforting.

He would no longer have their commands or even their suggestions as to what he should do. He would have to presume what was wanted of him and that would be an illusion at best.

How does one obey when there is no one to tell you what to do? How can the tail of a kite fly when it has been cut loose?

Still, he did not feel sorry for himself. He was acutely sensitive to a comparison he might make, one with someone his age coming out of jail instead of a monastery. He had the advantage, little baggage and no prejudiced judgments against him. Such a person as he had few of the disadvantages and none of the disdain and resentment that await ex-convicts.

What people might think did not concern him. The only person whose opinion he would have to fear, the one who would increasingly try to put him down and would do so was himself.

During both his waking hours and his dreams, he was flooded with thoughts and reminiscences of his father.

He was certain his father's voice told him to smell the roses and share his story. Before leaving, he had sat down and wrote for ten days, recounting his life as best he could.

It was a reflective period and brought with it painful memories and torrents of insight. Perhaps what he discovered foremost was that his father still lived in him as a powerful, kindly and caring force.

Oh, how he needed that man with his love and sense of freedom, his caring and unselfishness!

As he physically walked out the door of the priory, he heard himself mumble a prayer, "Lord, I am not worthy." He said it, but connected the words with neither his drinking nor his being asked to leave.

"Say but the word," his mind added, continuing the prayer he had repeated often during his years as a Dominican, "and my soul shall be healed."

"What does it mean?" he wondered.

There was in his life no catechism, no *Rules of the Order of Preachers* and no religious superior to point the way.

There was now only that which his father had written about and which he had considered a wrong answer: personal responsibility?

Here and now, he did not know even which direction he would turn once he closed the priory door on his way out.

It was as though there were a stage with a backdrop curtain and he would be coming out from behind it.

To his right, as he departed, was a street of nondescript bars. In the past, it had been where he often stopped for his first drink.

To his left, several blocks down, was a florist shop. He now remembered a newspaper article that had said the woman who owned it was struggling to breed the lost aromas of the past back into roses, even the inexpensive ones.

"Perhaps," he said aloud, "these two hands can help."

It was there at the florist shop that he would meet Virginia Golf, Eddie's widow.

About the Author

Kenan Heise--a playwright, poet and award-winning author--was a journalist with the Chicago Tribune for 34 years. For 11 years, he had been a Franciscan seminarian, seven of which he was a member of that religious order. His Aunt Ella Stories (Academy Chicago, 1985) won the Vicki Matson Award from the Friends of Literature and his book of poetry, Our Dinosaurs are Dying (Chicago Historical Bookworks, 1994), was praised by Pulitzer Prize-winning poet Gwendolyn Brooks as, "Big, cleverly conversational, appealing, indeed contemporary and easy to read."

Printed in the United States
22083LVS00002B/82-171

9 781418 419257